In Our Midst

Martha Johnson

Martha Johnson
May 2013

This is a work of fiction. Names, characters, places, and incidents either are the product of the author's imagination or are used fictitiously. Any resemblance to actual persons, living or dead, events, or locales is entirely coincidental.

DEDICATION

To Elaine Mumford

ACKNOWLEDGMENTS

It is now time for me to separate from the world of Stanton, Indiana, and turn it over to you, the reader.

I have carried Stanton with me for a long time and over much distance: on the commuter bus to Washington DC, on business trips all over the country, and from the study couch to the dining room table and back. It has been a wonderful place to visit when the rest of life's landscape has been parched.

The inspiration for this story came from Gundel, Nancy, and Will, giants of faith and courage, who ask tart questions and laugh through it all.

The audacity to write a novel, having written mostly business memos, was encouraged by my dear, steady, big-picture, all-things-are-possible husband, Steve.

The source code for this book is from the expansive theology of grace that I received from my father, Ted.

The characters of this story emerged from my faulty constructs, enriched by the children, teachers, colleagues, friends, family, clergy, choir directors, and neighbors around me. First novels are autobiography, they say, but it will take dozens more to capture the tremendous lift that my own community has given me.

The meter and metaphor in my writing are genetic code from my mother, Lovina.

The emotion of the story comes from my own experience as a mother to Anna and Lucas.

The sharp pencils and what-year-are-we-in-comments were supplied by Carolyn, Jan, and Tina. The invaluable, father-son, technical team of Ted and Sean wrested the manuscript from me and arrayed it on the web.

The tenacity to finish this project pales next to the work ethic of my siblings, Julia, Kelley, and Ted.

The shortfalls and imperfections of *In Our Midst* are all mine.

Martha Johnson
Annapolis, Maryland
October, 2012

CHAPTER 1

The dog's low growl vibrated through the blankets. Victor stirred, and in an instant, the warm weight that had been curled against him turned into a pulsating mass with a wet tongue washing his ear and cheek.

"Jumpy, stop it," he said as he rolled to face the dog straight on, defending himself with his arm. With a sharp bark, the dog jumped off the bed and ran to the closed bedroom door. A groan from the second twin bed brought him racing back to bark at Kyle, who was invisible except for an arm hanging nearly to the floor.

"Hush, boy," Victor said. "You want to go out?"

With a whoosh, Kyle's arm powered back a mess of blankets, and he rolled on his back chanting to the ceiling, "Jumpy, Bumpy, Lumpy, Grumpy wants to go out."

Victor looked over at him and laughed. Typical Kyle, he thought. Did he dream in weird words, too?

Kyle swung his legs over the edge of his bed and stared down at Jumpy, who was in a frenzy of barking. "Why can't I have a plain old alarm clock?" he asked the dog.

Victor watched Kyle stretch and amble to the door. As he disappeared with the dog down the hall, the room grew silent. Victor bunched the pillow better under his head and lay still. He could hear Kyle's mom downstairs, "Sleepy head! Serves you boys right for staying up to watch videos."

Victor loved spending the night here. Kyle, the twins, and the dog made it livelier and fuller, not like his quiet home where he was an only child. When he was at Kyle's, he wasn't the center of attention. They didn't ask about every detail of his life. The Jordans treated him like family and made him do the dishes like everyone else.

With unnecessarily loud stomping and door banging, Kyle returned to the bedroom and threw himself back on his bed. "You go first in the shower."

"No, you!"

"No, you!" He bounded up, pulled Victor's pillow out from under his head and started whacking him with it. Victor started kicking back, trying to shove him away.

The two boys scuffled playfully. Victor was taller, but Kyle was a strong and flexible gymnast and soon pinned Victor down. The beds creaked as Victor thrashed back.

"You won't be ready for church if you don't take your shower," Kyle mimicked a parental voice.

Suddenly, with a quick calculation, Victor went limp, and Kyle sprawled on top of him. Victor savored Kyle's weight on him, along with its spasms of laughing and panting. He knew it would only last an instant, but he stored it away in his mind and carried it with him, as Kyle pulled him to his feet and pushed him out the door.

*** *** ***

Across the southern Indiana town of Stanton, the windows of a compact blue bungalow glared back at the early sun. Inside the house, all was quiet. Bridget Wallace floated on the edge of her dream, but finally the constricting sleeping bag was too annoying to ignore. She forced herself awake enough to arch her back in order to find the zipper pull. With jerks she freed herself and then sprawled happily back on the bed. Packing boxes filled the room, forming a rough cityscape against the freshly painted bedroom walls. Fluorescent tags glowed against the dull cardboard. Stretching out her arm, Bridget flipped over the nearest tag to read the contents. Shoes, boots, mittens. Nope. That wouldn't help right now.

Maybe Mom found the towels, she thought, as she rolled off the bare mattress and headed for her very own bathroom. She loved their new house after living in a Chicago apartment. She wasn't sure she loved anything else about their move to Stanton, but having her own bathroom was totally awesome.

"Bridget! Good morning, honey! You up?" her mother called. "We've got about an hour and a half before church."

"Church! Why didn't you tell me? We haven't found our towels, and you want to go to *church*?"

"I know," June said, now standing at the door with her second cup of coffee. "But when you're new in a town, you've got to jump in with both feet. If we don't go today, you'll be off at Grandma and Grandpa's for the month, and it will all be delayed until July. Here's a beach towel. It'll work."

2

Her daughter grimaced at her. "I guess my other choice is to stay home and unpack boxes."

"Bingo," her mom agreed. "I thought we'd stop for donuts on the way. Maybe that will convince Lexie to come along." Bridget wasn't sure her younger sister would agree.

She started again for the bathroom. Church! She would have to wash her hair. The mirror in the bathroom reinforced the point. Her one great feature, long brown-black hair, was tangled and gross. She rubbed her eyes and turned on the faucets full force.

June heard the shower start and tapped on Lexie's door. What a wonderful thing for the girls to have their own rooms now. "Lexie!" she called.

"My full name is Alexandra! Start practicing." Alexandra had decided to try on a new identity along with her new life in Stanton. Why couldn't she use her full name? Her mom needed to pay attention.

"Sorry, Alexandra! I keep forgetting. But it's time to get up. We're going to get donuts for breakfast on our way to church."

"*Church!* Je-e-e-sus, Mom. Do I have to?"

"I will assume that language is from some R-rated movie script you are writing."

Alexandra grandly did not respond.

"I agree, you don't have to go to church," June continued, "but I would like you to. I want to get to know our new town right away. The donuts are a bribe."

Alexandra groaned long and loudly. "But I don't know where my clothes are," she grumped. "I sure hope we find sheets and blankets today. I'm all tangled up."

"Your suitcases are at the foot of your bed. We'll come straight home from church and get sorted. Besides, you don't want to completely unpack, because you'll be off to Grandma and Grandpa's."

June was all efficiency. The two weeks had been too short to pack up the apartment and move before starting her new job, but to her it was a luxurious stretch of time. And she would soon have a month with the girls gone, during which she could run down all the details of driver's licenses and water bills. It hadn't been very long since she had been in the grip of the extended nightmare - Sam in Hospice care, his death, and the girls' struggle to comprehend what was happening. The pace of work at the *Tribune* had not let up all spring. No day had been long enough, no night restful, and no morning had presented promise such as this one.

Ruffling her stylishly cropped hair, she moved toward the master bedroom to find her own clothes. She could pull out any outfit, and it would be like new here. Thank the Lord for this fresh start! It was a blessing that it was working out so far. Now her job was to keep moving, keep hugging the girls, and keep working at it. These impulses had helped her get out of the city, with its expense and cramped living. As a southern Indiana native, she had hoped that a move back to the area would be right for her and the girls. Getting to church would be another foot forward.

*** *** ***

About the same time, George Morrow was downtown tugging at the heavy front door of the First Presbyterian Church. The massive brass ring set in the center of the panel gave him no leverage. He tugged again. His elbow groaned while the door rasped, but held fast.

The Sunday morning service didn't start for over an hour. George paused, sourly regarding the door and mentally cursing his spreading arthritis. Shifting his stance, he mockingly looked upward as if in prayer. His gaze slid up the soaring carillon tower, and he felt the startle of visually rocketing to the sky. The quickly moving clouds tricked the eye. Perhaps the tower was moving, and the sky was stationary. George stood still, teasing the sensation to last. Too soon, a flock of starlings swooped by the tower, killing the illusion, and securing the tower back on its foundations.

"Nothing is what it seems," he said to himself for the millionth time in his life. "But this door is real." He grabbed the knob in hand-over-hand fashion. The door slowly swung open.

George stepped inside and headed for the large coatroom. A beige raincoat drooped from the closet rod, which was sheltered by a high deep shelf. A shovel stood in one corner, and George claimed the two folding chairs leaning against the low windowsill.

They flopped open with clangs as he put them side-by-side in the sun. Collecting the box of bulletins to be used at the service, he settled on one chair and started folding. Three at a time. Using a credit card, he creased them sharply. As he completed a handful, he looked up, monitoring the sidewalk to the church.

The pile of folded bulletins was about to topple when the first car pulled into the parking lot. Porter and Mavis Hofmeister were on schedule - which is to say they were early. As choir director, Mavis never allowed herself to get frazzled by being late. It was frazzling enough getting music out of her singers.

"George beat us here," said Mavis, waving to him as she got out of the car. "He's got his red on," she added, referring to George's jolting red plaid jacket. Today was Pentecost Sunday, the celebration of the birth of the church when the Holy Spirit in the form of flames roared through an assembly of believers. Parishioners often wore red for the service. Porter's red Christmas tie was also getting an airing.

Mavis had done her part. Her red cookies had red sprinkles for good measure. She always baked for her choir, hoping they would smile more readily and, therefore, stay on pitch. "I used a full bottle of red food coloring," she said as she opened the trunk. "Pentecost isn't supposed to be pink."

Pulling at her purse strap, she loaded Porter, the packhorse, with baskets and a huge tin of cookies. Gathering the linens, she closed the trunk. Porter lugged along beside her as they crossed the street. He couldn't remember a time when he had just strolled into church with his hands in his pockets.

George was storing the folded bulletins. "Bring me a cookie, too," he said in greeting. Porter grimaced and steered his load carefully toward the kitchen. There he turned on lights, unlocked cabinets, and made a pot of coffee. It was a weekly routine.

"Got any left for me to do?" he asked, as he delivered George his cookie and coffee.

"All done. Only one insert today, about the committees getting in gear for the Wood Carving Festival."

The two men enjoyed their coffee together in silence. The cookie was dyed shortbread: sweet, dry, and perfect for dunking. George wondered how Porter had avoided getting fat with a wife who was always baking.

Porter brushed red sprinkles off his tie. "Can't be getting this dirty. I only wear it twice a year," he grinned. When his coffee was gone, he methodically shredded his cup. The sound of tearing competed with the chirping birds and scampering squirrels in the unfolding morning.

"I'm thinking about getting married again," Porter suddenly announced.

George stared at him. "What in the name of…? I had no idea you and Mavis were splitting up. You still come to church together."

"Huh?" Porter was momentarily mystified. "Oh, no! I mean re-married to the wife. Mavis. Not someone else. Like having a second wedding, a church service and all."

They looked at each other and chuckled. "You had me there for a minute," said George. "Why are you planning to do all that? You should spend the money on a cruise."

"Well, I haven't decided. Been thinking about it, though. It would mean a lot to her." He sifted the pieces of his cup through his fingers. "I have this idea that I could re-propose to her. You know, do it better the second time. I was pretty green the first time around."

"Then have at it," George said supportively. He could sympathize, although he sure wouldn't discuss that with Porter who over their years as ushers had thrown out various, acidic, anti-gay comments.

When George and his partner, Duke, had fallen in love, there had been no guidebook. Duke had been an admissions officer at Purdue University, and they had joked about submitting applications to each other. Was one of them supposed to kneel? Instead, the two men had stood in front of the fireplace and formally asked each other the same question. "Will you accept my love and live your life with me?" The improvisation in front of the white bricks had worked just fine.

As for anniversaries, neither George nor Duke had dreams of a public renewal of vows. The world had come some distance during their 29 years together, but he was certain that Stanton wasn't ready for a gay couple owning to vows – much less renewing them. Maybe in the next millennium! But, hey, that shouldn't stop them from planning a cruise, say, for their 30th. How could he be sure no one from Stanton would be on board? George turned over the thought in his mind. They could make it work.

Musing about their particular worlds, the two men quietly let the time pass.

Killing time at church involves skill. All churchgoers grow proficient at it, withstanding a windy preacher or waiting for a mom to finish her chat. Hanging around is a major part of a church usher's job, and Porter and George were masters in the guild.

Soon, people began to arrive. In the sanctuary, individual staccato voices pierced the air, and in due order, like an orchestra warming up, the huge room swelled with life and sound.

People were swamping the doorway. "Hello there, buddy." George shook hands with every child. "I'm glad you brought your mom and dad to church," he said seriously. The children nodded back seriously.

"And I am delighted to see you, too," warbled an elderly woman to George. "It's wonderful to see everyone in red, and I love that plaid jacket." Her own red ensemble, including hat and red stockings, was a standout. "You know what I say," she confided to him in a loud whisper, "when you're too old for sex you can still have color." George grinned broadly back at her. She was such a pistol.

June Wallace, along with Bridget and Alexandra, was coming up the sidewalk. The girls exchanged glances at the sight of the woman's red outfit. That was something they expected to see on the streets in Chicago, not here. Bridget felt a sudden bubble of curiosity about Stanton. Porter greeted the new family and gestured vaguely that they were welcome to sit anywhere.

The red-robed choir crowded through the doors. In beat with the trumpet pipes from the organ, the choir started down the aisle. Porter and George closed the vestibule doors and retired to their folding chairs. Happy to be helpful but able to enjoy the sunshine, they settled into their respective vantage and views.

CHAPTER 2

A sedan almost two-wheeled it into the parking lot and slammed into a space. Porter and George watched the Beck family hustle out of the car and across the street. Loretta's prematurely white hair gleamed in its tight French bun. Spencer automatically checked the knot of his tie and buttoned his suit jacket as they came up the walk. " 'Morning," Spencer said in a strained voice. Porter pointed them towards the staircase to the balcony. Victor trailed behind, not sure why being ten minutes late was such a crime. He could have ridden to church with Kyle's family, but his parents had insisted upon picking him up. His mom probably wanted to be sure he was dressed the way she wanted. As it was, she had handed him a comb in the car.

The family's footsteps on the uncarpeted stairs were loud. Loretta winced and slowed to a tiptoe. Spencer guided her into a pew. His persistently correct manners were one of his hallmarks, and she leaned into the slight steering touch on her lower back. Tracking the service, he reached for a hymnal, and they smiled at each other. It was a favorite tune, and they enjoyed blending their voices together.

As soon as the music ended, Victor slumped into his seat. From there he had an aerial view of the congregation as it also sat down. The rustling and stirring was like a huge bird gently shaking her feathers and pulling her wings into place. She settled on her nest with fluttery shivers. Hundreds of quivering red feathers.

Spencer noticed the flashes of red below. "Pentecost," he thought. "Of course." He greatly appreciated the church calendar. The older he got, the stranger time became. He couldn't pace things properly anymore. But, if he were losing his grip, he could depend on the church to mark the days.

When he explained this to Loretta, she was dismissive. "Oh, you men! If someone asks if you are hungry, you'll check your watch."

But it wasn't about *telling* time. It was about the *passing* of time. The church regularly reminded him to take stock, rejoice, mourn, and confess. Pentecost was the annual nod to the founding of the community itself. Good.

Victor could have cared less about Pentecost. His parents were way too much into church. It never ended. His deep brown eyes maintained a blank expression. In contrast, the pink across his cheeks hinted at his annoyance.

Sitting in the balcony wasn't bad, though. He rarely came up there, and it was cool to watch everyone below. He could see Kyle sitting with his twin sisters and parents down front.

Continuing to peer over the rail, Victor noticed a new girl sitting with her mother and, apparently, a younger sister. A new person in church was *something* interesting.

Idly, he wondered what her face looked like. Her dark hair was held in a bun with sticks. Maybe they were chopsticks. But a haze of frizz blocked her profile. He imagined a camera on a boom, swinging out and away from him up in the balcony, sweeping slowly down in a large circle, and then panning towards her face.

Victor imagined much of the world through the eye of a camera. How could he crop a shot or find a balance of shadow and light? In movies, a long slow camera approach set up a scene. When the face of the actor finally filled the screen, Victor liked the feeling that he already knew him. It was better to meet people that way, first getting a 360-degree scan.

This girl, despite the spilling of curls, seemed calm. She was a freeze frame, unlike her sister who was squirming and whispering to her mom. Victor guessed the problem. She didn't want to go up front with the little kids for the Children's Sermon. She looked too old for that. He wondered what grade she was in, and then what grade the older girl was in. Was she in high school or finishing middle school? He hadn't seen her in any classes. Where was her dad? Did he go to another church? Some families did that.

A roll of laughter rose from below, as Rev. McDaniel turned on a fan with red streamers taped to it. The Jordan twins held out their hands and giggled as the streamers tickled them. "The Pentecostal wind didn't put out the flames. It blew and spread them. And they were like tongues of fire, licking at the people."

People at church laughed at anything, Victor thought. Grownups often adopted goofy, jovial behavior, and things that were flat-out-not-funny got chuckles. "Bet your nickname is 'Beanpole'!" Ha ha ha.

Down in the main sanctuary, Bridget checked the chopsticks holding back her hair and smiled as the congregation laughed. People here seemed nice. This church was more comfortable than their Chicago church. It was cute that they did all this stuff on Pentecost, like a kid's birthday party. The lady sitting in front of her had a big red hat on, and the tags on her blouse were hanging out. She must have dressed fast, too. Bridget felt slapped together. She had tied up her wet hair in a knot, but as it dried it was frizzing on the sides.

Meanwhile, Alexandra was busy writing her name in the Greeter Pad that she had found in the hymn rack. "Alexandra Wallace, and call me ALEXANDRA. No nicknames." She checked three items:

✓ **First Time Visitor**
✓ **Interested in Membership**
✓ **Would Appreciate a Pastoral Visit.**

She wanted people to know she was a grownup, whether her mom did or did not! She was way too old to be part of the Children's Sermon.

Rev. Cord McDaniel mounted the two steps to the pulpit. His black robe was heavy with its tight smocking at the shoulders and velvet striped sleeves. He felt weighed down. For the next 20 minutes he was expected to deliver a sermon with brilliantly crafted sentences, carefully calibrated emotion, and a sense of sacred challenges.

Whom was he kidding? People didn't sit still that long. The cultural metabolism could barely digest sermons these days. Cord's flock would judge him on a boredom meter, and then judge themselves righteous for sitting through it.

His *flock*. Cord wished the image was better understood. Flocks of sheep wandered throughout the Bible. The great David herded them. The shepherds watched over them at night. Docile and stupid, sheep would follow each other off a cliff--or sit passively in pews.

Cord wanted it to be different. Why couldn't his congregation be a flock of birds, operating with glorious connecting radar, full of a spirit that guided them in unison through swoops, dives, and long migrations? He dreamed of sparking a flock like that - not to be a workhorse, bread-and-butter minister. Could he ever shed the routine and be a wild man--a prophet--speaking of amazing things?

He flexed his shoulders and peered at his sermon notes. He needed larger type to read without his glasses. He was getting old, too. He sighed internally. Better just to get on with it.

"Were they drunk?" Cord launched into his sermon. "Wind and fire have roared through the house, but no one was burned." He paced his words. "It does sound as if the storyteller had been sipping a bit too much."

A brush of chuckles confirmed that some were listening.

In the balcony, Victor lost interest immediately. So what if the church had started with a party of drunks? Why did everything have to be so dramatic? Was Rev. McDaniel trying to be a shock jock?

That was like stupid kids' stuff. Kids were always saying something extreme to get attention. They talked about shaving their heads over the summer or getting drunk with an older brother. You couldn't believe half of what they said.

Victor's world was full of private thoughts. And they needed to stay private. It would be crazy to say too much. He knew he shouldn't have the thoughts he had. They were weird and bad. And he sure couldn't risk telling them to anyone or having them find out! What he wanted was *not* to stand out or be noticed. Better to be ignored.

His dad recrossed his legs. Victor shifted, too. At least they were in the balcony. No one would see him sticking his legs into the aisle. He'd learned a long time ago to shut down at church and go inside himself. It was like pulling a baseball cap over his eyes.

Yesterday hadn't been bad. He and his dad had checked out the camera store and had bought a better light meter. Victor had plans to photograph ordinary things in odd ways, in different light. He wanted to be more precise about shadows and maybe use unusual angles.

He also wanted pictures of himself to check what the rest of the world saw. He could photograph himself every day… and watch his hair grow. Naw, that was as lame as putting your face on the copier.

Downstairs, fidgety Alexandra Wallace was also making plans. She wanted people to know that she was grown-up for her age. Leaning against her mom, she practiced her new phone number in her head and thought about making business cards. She could use them when she met new people. If she made a card, her mom might copy it at work. She almost asked her out loud but caught herself just in time.

June felt the shift of her daughter's head and heard the little intake of breath. What was Alexandra cooking up now? June loved the warmth of her nine-year-old leaning against her. She shifted her arm around Alexandra and smiled. It was an added bonus to hear this minister. His sermon was both intelligent and a little irreverent. Imagine a church with a sense of humor!

People shifted and coughed as the Confirmation Class moved to the chancel steps. The teenagers each had a red carnation. Bridget looked the group over carefully, checking the girls' clothes and wondering if the cute boys were also nice. She figured these kids were high school freshmen, a year older than she was.

Victor watched as each kid was introduced and received the blessing. They had to *kneel!* He was signed up for Confirmation Class in the fall. As if he had a choice. But he hadn't thought about it much. *Kneeling!* He was glad he had a year before he had to deal with that.

He was more than glad a few minutes later, when the service concluded. Not waiting for his parents, Victor dashed down the balcony stairs in anticipation of a chocolate donut at coffee hour. There was no dignity in the scramble. With luck, he could beat the little kids swarming out of their Sunday School classes.

In Fellowship Hall, the youth group was gathering along the food table. "Coffee!" the girls shrieked at Victor. "I hate coffee. How can you drink that stuff?"

Victor used lots of sugar and cream. He thought drinking coffee made him seem older. "They're exaggermorating," said Kyle. "I've seen them drink coffee, too."

"Well, it's better than that warm apple cider." Victor nodded in the direction of the little kids' table.

"And coffee has caffeine, except now that church is over, you don't need chemicals to stay awake."

"Hey! I think there's a new family here with kids like about our age," said Victor. "I saw them from the balcony."

"I didn't see anybody." Tiffany Cantor smiled at him. She raked her fingers through her streaked hair and tossed her head. They had known each other their entire lives, and he found her annoying.

"Yeah, well, whatever," Victor sipped his coffee. They all looked around the room.

People were flowing in. The tables had red tablecloths and centerpieces with masses of red and orange. One of the youth advisors came through the double fire doors. He had the new girl with him and made a straight line for them. "Hi, guys," he called on his way. "This is Bridget Wallace. She moved here this week from Chicago."

He introduced each of them. "Tiffany Cantor. Victor Beck. And Kyle Jordan here speaks in tongues." He said it as if it were the funniest joke on the planet.

"That's correctaculus," said Kyle.

Bridget smiled a half smile, wondering what he was all about. She noticed the dark haired boy - was it Victor? – grinning, but the girls were visibly rolling their eyes.

"And you have a sister, right?" The advisor kept rowing the boat.

"Yeah. I have one sister, over there. Alexandra." Bridget spoke with an inflection of sisterly protection. She wanted Alexandra to be accepted in spite of her totally irritating personality.

"I've got two sisters, one older and one younger," commented Tiffany. Bridget could tell she was trying to be friendly. "But the older one has enlisted in the military so she's not around to drive me places, and I have to do all the babysitting now."

Enlisted, thought Bridget. Does she mean in the marines or something?

"Around here you have to drive to get anywhere. It's, like, an hour to get to Indianapolis to shop."

"Yeah, girls think the only thing to do in the world is to go shopping," one boy said.

"Yeah? We saw Victor shopping yesterday," retorted Tiffany. Victor was surprised. "Sure. I saw you and your dad at the camera store at the mall," she explained.

Victor stayed quiet. He hated being watched.

"Have you started at school? I don't think I've seen you there." Tiffany prided herself on keeping track of everyone.

"We already finished the year in Chicago."

"Lucky you! We've got another week. Why, what is *wrong* with you?" Two younger kids were contorting their faces and holding hands over their mouths. "This is my little sister," she said, indicating one of them.

"It's the fireba-a-w-ls," they said with tears in their eyes. They pointed to the basket of cinnamon balls, another Pentecostal ritual. Everyone laughed. Bridget turned to see Alexandra reaching for a handful.

"I think my sister is going to have the same problem," Bridget said to Tiffany.

Victor's mom signaled that they were leaving. "Gotta go," he murmured and slipped away from the group.

"Bye, Victor," said Tiffany.

"See ya around," said Kyle.

Victor lifted his chin instead of smiling, "Yeah." He tossed his coffee cup into the trash and grabbed at the candy basket as he left. Out on the sidewalk he trailed after his parents and thought about Tiffany. Snoopy girl!

"I met June Wallace," his mom was saying when he caught up with them. "She's on the staff down at the *Gazette*. She used to work at *The Chicago Tribune*."

"The new family? Yeah, they just moved here from Chicago," said Victor.

"Oh. How did you know?" His mom was looking directly at him.

"Well, you just said *The Chicago Tribune*, and they were introducing the new girl." He nodded towards the church. "Her name is Bridget, I think."

His mother studied the flush in his cheeks. Could he be excited about the new girl?

It was a double cinnamon, for sure. "Wow!" he exclaimed. "This fireball is super hot."

CHAPTER 3

Kyle Jordan had finished the quiz. Looking up, he saw the English teacher check her watch. "Two-minute warning," she said. Kids groaned. How could they be having quizzes so near the end of the year?

Vocabulary words came easily to Kyle. He figured it was because he just liked them. He didn't know why exactly, but his teacher had said that English was one of the most *robust* languages in the world, offering multiple ways to say things. That was a great word, *robust.* What if it were "nobust" or "lobust" or "sobust," and what about the bust part? Was it bust-as-in-boobs or bust-as-in-break-something?

The bell rang. "Okay, everyone, put down your pencils. Leave the papers on my desk as you go out."

The kids poured out of the classroom, into the ocean of noise and motion of the hallway. Kyle fought past a bevy of girls twirling locker combinations and shrieking with laughter. He caught up with Victor. "Easy quiz."

Victor shrugged, "I hope it's the last one."

"Listen, Victor, I've got to ask you something." He shifted his backpack to his other shoulder.

"Yeah?"

"For the gymnastic camp this summer over at IU, I want to be sure that they put me in the right group. I should be upper-intermediate - like high school level - but they've scheduled me for the wrong week. Coach Sanderson is calling over them, but just to be sure, could you take some pictures of me on the bars? I could send them, too. You know, to show them what I can do?" He was desperate to get into the right session.

Victor thought about it. "You flip around on those bars, don't you? That would be fast motion. Like, shouldn't you use a video camera?"

"Well, maybe. But some pictures of working on the horse and the

13

beams would show my strength, too. I was just trying to think of ways to convince them…" he trailed off. "Maybe it's a dumb idea."

"When's practice?"

"Right after ninth period. You can catch the late bus home after that." Kyle looked eager.

"Well, I brought my camera today. It's in my locker. So, I suppose so." Victor thought the idea was unnecessary for the gymnastics camp, but he would enjoy taking pictures of Kyle bending his body around and showing his muscles.

"You mean it?"

"Sure. It'd be okay."

"Awesome!" Kyle gave him a thumbs-up as he turned into his history classroom.

*** *** ***

Tiffany saw Bridget standing in front of the principal's office, peering at a sheet of paper. "I thought you were through with school?"

"My mom decided it wouldn't hurt for me to sit in on some classes to get a feel for the place and maybe meet some people. At least that's how she says it." Bridget was a little shy about the idea, but also curious about the school.

"Does it matter what classes you attend?"

"Not really, I guess. They gave me a list to choose from and gave me a note to show the teacher to explain what I was doing."

"You could come to my classes," suggested Tiffany.

"Do you mind?"

"No. I'm happy to show you around. It'll make things more fun. Come on, or we'll be late." She chattered down the hallway, enjoying the tour guide role.

Before each class she introduced Bridget to the teacher. Her self-important bustling was friendly and quite practical. By the end of the day the girls had discovered a lot in common, not the least of which was that neither had a father in the house. Tiffany's parents were divorced. "I actually don't know my dad. He sends a card at Christmas, and that's about it."

Bridget was horrified. "For real? That must make you sad."

"Since I never knew him, it's okay. It's harder for my older sister. She remembers when he lived with us. My mom says it's all for the better."

Bridget had never met anyone so matter-of-fact. What a cool friend to have already. She was beginning to be sorry that she would be visiting her grandparents for the next month.

By the time her mother got home from work, she was bursting to tell her all about it. June listened as she changed out of her work clothes, and then the two sat on the bed together. Alexandra leaned on the doorframe. Bridget couldn't stop talking. "And she's got a summer job at some diner in town. We'll have to go over there and have milkshakes some day and leave her a tip. That would be so fun!"

"Then let's do it."

"Maybe I could have a pineapple milkshake or a tomato milkshake. Do you think they would make me something like that?" Alexandra asked the room in general. "I think a tomato milkshake would go really good with pizza or a hamburger, better than something sweet."

"You can give it a try, honey. I don't know if they will," June said, chuckling.

Alexandra and Bridget looked at each other significantly. Getting their mom laughing was a shared goal. It was sure getting easier.

*** *** ***

Loretta Beck stood in front of her refrigerator staring at the calendar. There was nothing marked for Victor after school. So, where was her son? The last bus had passed their corner a half an hour before. He hadn't been on it.

She ticked through her memory bank. He stayed late at school on Tuesdays for Yearbook Club, and summer soccer didn't start until next week. What could be keeping him the last week of school? Maybe he had stayed late to decorate for the eighth grade dance and graduation on Friday.

She knew that was a bit of hopeful thinking on her part. Victor was tall for his age, and his complexion always had a charming flush, as if he had been out jogging in nippy air. But, he was still a boy, really, not even fourteen yet. And his passions were for very noisy team sports and photography. Not girls or dances.

Picking up the black cat at her ankles, she studied the row of Victor's school pictures arrayed above the calendar on the freezer door. She enjoyed the reverie of remembering Victor's earlier years. He had always been a somewhat moody boy. Now he alternated between the tumultuous chaos of soccer and his intensely solitary photography projects. He liked to follow sports, and his room was filled with pictures of famous athletes. But, he could also isolate himself for an entire Saturday wandering around snapping pictures, and then endlessly cropping, sorting, and mounting. Spencer had created a little darkroom in the corner of the basement, and they had worked out the chemicals, the washes, the clothesline, and pins. They had found a used lightboard at a yard sale and added that to their dark den to study negatives. Both had been bursting with delight this Mother's Day in presenting her a small book with pictures of Toodles.

She smiled as the cat purred in her arms. "Yes, he was an adorable boy, wasn't he, Toodles?" She lifted him up to her shoulder and buried her face in the fur. "But that's slipping away. What will we do with him all grown up?"

His childhood had gone so fast. Sports had started early. Spencer had taught Victor about sports scores before the child could read. Spencer and his numbers! The first team sport was T-Ball, which Victor didn't like. Soccer proved more exciting to him, and he had stuck with it. He loved to run. Dutifully, Loretta attended matches, but watching her son colliding with other boys had not been something she enjoyed. She never felt comfortable as the other parents shouted from the sidelines. She didn't know what to shout, and she wasn't the shouting type.

Turning, she surveyed the kitchen and then wandered into the hallway. The pictures on the wall were Victor's. She encouraged him to frame and hang them. But she found the photos stark and severe. The subjects were metal forms, cars, and work tools. She had a good eye, and what struck her was the two-dimensional, reductionist quality of his work. There were few shadows--nothing that softened the setting or the subject. He was too young to be so severe, but she thought he showed not a little talent.

She wondered for the hundredth time what went on inside her son. He had some friends and got good grades, but he didn't talk much. He didn't want to go to church, and that particularly concerned her. Church was a discipline and connection that would support a person all his life. Sighing to herself, she stared harder at the pictures. There was some code here that she couldn't decipher.

Talking about this to Spencer was useless. He wouldn't have noticed if the pictures were in color or black-and-white. Whenever she started to fret about Victor, he put on his soothing voice. She wasn't mollified and instead turned her thoughts into prayers. "Help him through life. He's at a precarious age. Open him up to your spirit." Stooping, she let the cat out of her arms.

*** *** ***

Victor arrived home simultaneously with Spencer. Loretta heard their voices and the door slam as she was putting away the laundry upstairs.

"Where've you been, dear?" she called.

Spencer looked up the flight of stairs and said, "At work. Where did you think I was all day?"

"No, I meant Victor. I didn't know he had any after-school activities." She started down the stairs carrying a stack of kitchen towels.

"Hi, Mom. I stayed late to help Kyle."

"Oh? Is he okay?"

"Yeah. He wanted me to take some pictures of him doing gymnastics stuff, for a camp application." He pulled two rolls of film from his pocket. "I want to get them developed tonight. I might bike over to that one-hour photo place downtown. It's not too late."

"We could work on them downstairs, if you like," offered Spencer.

Victor hesitated. He wasn't sure he wanted to be talking about Kyle's poses with his dad. "I've got some studying for the final test in algebra and don't think I should take the time."

"Fine with me. Your choice."

Loretta disappeared into the kitchen. Too bad. It would be nice to see him working on pictures of friends instead of wrenches and hammers. But, of course, he should study.

Spencer pulled off his tie and folded it carefully. "In that case, I should mow the yard this evening." He and Victor alternated doing this chore. He rather liked getting outside and running the mower in diagonal patterns across the lawn. "Is dinner soon, or do I have time to do that first?"

"I'll hold it off and give you both time for your projects."

"Great." Spencer gave his wife a squeeze across her shoulders as she bent over a wide drawer of precisely squared linens.

*** *** ***

The next morning, Victor passed the photos to Kyle in English class. He was disappointed with most of them, but Kyle was delighted. He held them under the desk and flipped through them out of sight. "Thanks! What do I owe you?" he whispered.

"Couple dollars."

"Later. I don't have any money with me right now."

Victor nodded and turned his gaze, though not his full attention, to the front of the room. The project had been fun, different. He had been able to stare all he wanted to at Kyle's muscles by simply looking through the lens at them. Kyle was pretty strong. He had held himself in handstands on the horse and balanced on the bars. It would have been better to use a video camera, because most of what Kyle did involved flips and turns. But, the pictures showed his balance and control. Kyle's body was pretty awesome.

Victor thought about his own efforts at lifting weights. He was trying to look less spindly on top. His legs weren't bad from running in soccer and would get better playing in the summer league. But his shoulders were puny and narrow. It would be good to work out hard this summer. He should put himself on a routine every day. And get a tan. It would be different being in high school next year, and he wanted to get past looking like a kid.

CHAPTER 4

It has been said that when farmers first plowed Indiana soil, it was like zipping open the earth. The black soil had built up over eons of decay and only opened in a protest of sound.

Every summer the sounds return. The peonies groan on their stems. The early beans sag over their chicken wire frames as if twanging old couch springs. And the strawberries are like slurpy kisses.

Along with much of Indiana, the good people of Stanton celebrate summer with a festival. Theirs is the Wood Carving Festival, and it showcases the town's craftsmanship. For fundraisers, the Disciples hawk pulled pork, and the Rotary Club dominates in fried chicken.

First Pres has long claimed the franchise on shortcakes – both strawberry and peach. Long tables are set up outside on the lawn, and the line forms first at *Plates and Cakes,* which is run by the women, and then moves to *Fruits and Toppings* with its crew of men. Spencer Beck always takes part, tying on his chef's apron with a dancing lobster on the front.

To avoid all that, Victor took refuge at the booth where the church trustees were selling tickets. They welcomed him warmly. "Hey there, Victor, how's school going?" Since it was July, and summer vacation was well underway, the conversation staggered, even as it opened. Eventually the men settled on the subject of baseball, and together they discussed the Pete Rose story.

"Do you think he'll go to prison?" Victor wasn't sure. How could someone so famous do something wrong like gambling on his sport and not expect to get caught? He didn't understand how people could live dangerously like that.

As he listened to the discussion, Victor counted the change in the box. When that was exhausted, he said that he might take some pictures for the church newsletter.

Nodding his approval, the cashier tore off four tickets for his next sale. "Yes, sir, and it's all you can eat." The tourists looked overfed already as they lugged themselves away. The parents wore remarkably cheesy flat hats, with a fringe of balls like a Mexican hat. The teenage boy, though, was all muscle, with a couple of earrings and an Indiana Jones hat over golden-tipped hair. Victor gazed after him, noticing the back of the sleeveless t-shirt and his molded shoulders. He wanted to trace the tattoo that fit neatly between two muscle surges. Wow.

Instead, he fingered his camera, wondering if he would look stupid taking their picture. The parents and their kooky hats would be just the thing for the newsletter, and maybe Indiana Jones would say something to him. He peered through the lens and aimlessly surveyed the entire corner.

Suddenly the new girl, Bridget, appeared in the lens. He put the camera down quickly as her mom said, "Hi, we're new here and figure we should try the strawberries and the peaches."

The younger sister was wearing a huge summer hat that looked like a tray loaded with paper flowers. What was with all the hats today?

"And this is Victor Beck," he heard one of the men introduce him.

June responded, "Glad to meet you, Victor. I'm June Wallace, and this is Bridget and Alexandra."

"We met at coffee hour, that first Sunday we were here," said Bridget easily.

"Oh, good. Familiar faces already," said June. "So, Victor, do you recommend the strawberries or the peaches?"

Victor didn't know what to say particularly. "They're both good."

"Great! Then let's go chow down," June said with gusto.

"Mom, don't say that! It's like from a cowboy movie," groaned Alexandra.

"Okay, sorry," said June, corrected but undaunted. She started for *Plates and Cakes.*

"Bye," said Bridget, and she followed her sister and mother.

Raising his camera again, Victor peered around and said, "I think I'll catch some pictures of those tourists with the hats." The men amiably waved him off.

Victor found the tourists seated side-by-side at the long picnic tables, gorging on their shortcakes. "Hi," he said framing a shot. "I'm taking pictures for our newsletter. Where are you from?" He hoped he sounded confident in front of Indiana Jones.

At *Fruits and Toppings,* George Morrow's bad elbow was taking a rest. The whine of the food processors filled the air as they whipped the cream. The power cords snaked in bleached vines off the tables. Spying Alexandra's platter of a hat, George started to vamp with his own sun hat, but immediately winced as his elbow protested.

She recognized him and giggled.

"Tootsie," he said, "you belong on Broadway."

Bridget scooted in front of her sister, impatient to load up on whipped cream. She spied the boy who made up the funny words sitting at a table. Hesitating in a minute of shyness, she wondered what to do. She couldn't remember his name, but Victor was standing next to him checking his camera, and there were other kids at the table. Don't be a mouse, she said to herself.

"So, is that a good camera?" she asked as she put her food down.

Victor was startled.

"They were talking about you being at the camera shop that Sunday, remember?" she added.

"Oh, well, sort of, I guess."

"Victor here is a camera fanatic," said Kyle, balancing far back on his folding chair with his arms out wide. "We're so proud of the boy!" He began to lose his balance, grabbed Victor's leg and hauled himself upright.

"You have to ignore Kyle," Victor laughed as he took a seat.

Bridget quickly noted Kyle's name. Yes, Kyle! And Victor. "My dad was a photographer," Bridget said. "He used to develop pictures in his darkroom, which should have been my bedroom. So I always had to share with my sister."

"He's a photographer? Like a professional?"

"Yeah, well, he was. He worked on a newspaper. He got cancer and died in January. That's why we moved here, so my mom could have a new job and we could have a saner life. Is it sane here?"

Kyle grinned, "We are absolutely *insane*." He was glad to deflect her story about her dad by saying something silly.

Bridget grinned back and dug into her shortcake.

Victor idly watched as Kyle dismantled his shortcake. He had rimmed his bowl with whole strawberries and was dipping them in the whipped cream, biting and sucking them off their stems. Victor reached over and dipped his finger in the whipped cream. "Hey, get your own shortcake!" grumbled Kyle.

"Naw," said Victor. "I've had a big peach shortcake. I just wanted to see what yours was like." He watched Kyle's mouth close around the strawberry and his lips purse, as he twisted out the leafy stem.

"Do you guys know if the summer trip is still on? Are you going?" Kyle asked between strawberries.

"Why wouldn't it be on?" asked Victor.

"Well, with Mr. Sykes so sick and – like – maybe dying, I wasn't sure." Kyle looked at Bridget and explained, "He's one of the youth group advisors."

"Where do you go?" asked Bridget. She was grateful that her mom was steering Alexandra to the next table over.

"Oh, we go to Kentucky and stay in a country church and fix up places.

Mostly we paint. It's not bad, especially when we paint each other." Kyle elaborately mimicked painting Victor's arm and cheeks.

Victor felt himself blush and quickly turned to Bridget and rolled his eyes. "It's something we do every year. You should come. We never have enough workers."

"Okay. I'll think about it," Bridget smiled, already knowing she would sign up for sure.

Mayor Brent Sykes was working his way down the aisle between the tables, shaking hands and slapping shoulders. He noticed Alexandra. "Quite a hat there, young lady. May I introduce myself? I am Brent Sykes, Mayor of this fair city, and I'm pleased to make your acquaintance." He kissed her hand with a flourish and turned to June. Alexandra was uncertain if she was pleased or grossed out.

June laughed, and Brent noticed the long sweep of her bare arm as they shook hands and he learned her name.

"Hi, kids," he said, turning to their table.

"Hi, Mr. Sykes," the boys chorused.

"How's your dad?" Kyle asked.

"Not so good. But thanks for sending him that small card." He was kidding. The card from the church youth group had been the size of a quilt.

The boys smiled, glad Mr. Sykes could make jokes, even lame ones. Their parents had told them that the elder Mr. Sykes was dying.

The mayor was always kidding around. Maybe that's what politicians did, because his dad always teased them, too. The mayor's dad had also been Stanton's mayor years earlier before they were born, and he had been a youth advisor for generations of kids at church. He had always been a favorite, in no small part because of his other badge. He was a mortician. This gave their youth group an advantage over the Lutherans, who had a boring junior minister as youth advisor, and the Methodists, who had a couple of moms.

As Brent moved on, the boys explained this to Bridget, and the three gazed after him. "He's an undertaker, too, like his dad. I guess it's a family business. It's called Sykes Mortuary. He took us on a tour once."

"I hope I don't grow up to be just like my dad," said Kyle. "But that won't happen. I don't want to be a teacher." Bridget's smile had disappeared, and he suddenly realized she had said something about her dad dying. Stupid. Sometimes he needed to shut himself up.

Down at the end of the row of tables, Brent finished his greetings and felt a tap on his shoulder. "Mr. Mayor!" Rev. McDaniel exclaimed. They both extended their hands with the speed of gunslingers and shook. It was a running gag whose job required more handshaking. "Working the crowd, I see."

"Calluses all over my hands," returned Brent.

"Yes, it's a good crowd this year." Cord's hand waved aimlessly towards the tables while his voice pulled back with concern. "I had quite a visit with your father yesterday."

"Thank you for visiting him so often. It means a great deal."

"It's one of the most important things I do," replied Cord. "He's been a faithful member all his life."

The Sykes family extended back generations with the church and the community. An ancestor had established the funeral home so that it could post "Faithful Service Since 1890" on its sign. Guy had assumed the helm in the 1950's, and now it was Brent's business. When Brent had put his hat in the mayor's race, people knew the name and liked the combination of his young energy and deep roots.

Guy's advanced cancer was the talk of the town. The news was tough, given he was only in his early 60's. And, it had to be tough on Brent, handling it alone. He was single, and there was no other family. The people of Stanton had long sensed that father and son treated Stanton as their extended family, filling a gap.

Cord was now paying Guy daily pastoral calls at the hospital. He had been sincere, though impulsive, in saying his visit the day before had been a standout. He was glad that Brent had not been curious about the details.

Guy had been alone, lying quietly in his private room, its windowsill overflowing with flowers and planters. Cards overlapped each other on the bulletin board. The huge card from the youth group was taped to the back of the bathroom door.

Greeting Guy, Cord had settled into a chair by the bed. He allowed the time to stretch out a bit. Guy's decline had been rapid, and Cord tried to be alert to any signs of change.

Guy picked at the sheets with fingers so thin now that the joints looked bulbous. He had been a strong, lithe man, happy to toss kids around and wrestle with them. Now there were tubes and tapes everywhere – jabbed into his arms, positioned under his nose. His skin was mottled and fit tightly over his skull. His collapsing face spoke of pain.

"I didn't want any drugs today. They make me stupid," Guy said, speaking slowly, as if to check that each word came out right. "I was looking forward to your visit, Reverend. I need to tell you something."

"Yes, of course, Guy. What's on your mind?"

Guy's intensity was unmistakable, seemingly fueled by the tubes and needles. His voice was a little high. His fingers, which Cord had squeezed in greeting, had offered a hot, shaky clutch.

"I am leaving something hanging. It's a secret that I've held a long time. I've never been able to tell it to anyone," Guy said with a catch, "to be a man and say it outright."

Cord filled the pause steadily and honestly. "I appreciate any trust you put in me, and I will hold whatever you say in confidence."

"Thank you, pastor. I've been haunted by this since I was a kid."

"Guy, we all have regrets. A life can serve up many. God welcomes each of us as we struggle to live in His grace."

"Yes." Guy took a heavy breath, and his eyes skipped anxiously, seeking something beyond Cord's face.

Over the course of his career, Cord had sat with many people nearing death. He knew better than to urge or rush.

Guy's fingers scratching on the sheet sounded more and more like clawing. He pulled up a knee and created a sharp pitch to the blanket. A magazine slid to the edge of the bed and slapped onto the floor. Machines purred. Heels clicked in the hallway.

"I hurt Grace and Wash Evanston," Guy said quietly.

The scratching stopped, and the knee dropped out of sight.

"You know they had a son, Vaughn. My age. He was my best friend. We grew up together, played ball together, went to school together, the whole nine yards. And I was with him…" he slowed as his voice began to break, "…when he died."

He carefully swiveled his face toward Cord, trying to find the right angle to focus. Cord nodded his head, maintaining, rather than interrupting the available silence. Grace Evanston was an elderly widow in the church. He knew that her only son had died a long time ago.

"I was young, and we were celebrating Vaughn's return home from Korea. This was 38 or 40 years ago. I hadn't been drafted. I had some medical problems. I was married by then, and Brent was on the way." He drew a breath.

"It was a step-away night for me. Usually, I had responsibilities. I was a young man with business and family responsibilities. But it was like old times. We went out to the lake. We were drinking. We were drinking rough stuff."

Guy's demeanor shifted from explanation to memory. "We got into a tussle, and then it turned into a fight." The tears flooded Guy's eyes. "In the midst of it I… I knocked him hard… We had traded some punches already. He had gotten me in the stomach, and I was doubled over and swung back from that angle. I think I hit him in the neck, and he fell off the pier. But then he never came up. He drowned."

Guy paused and pulled his knee back up, creating a small suction on the sheets. The air in the room was becoming a distorted pressure vacuum. He took a long breath, sucking hard and exhaling, as if it was the very last breath in the room.

"I was so angry at him. He had been a soldier and was coming home to all sorts of attention. I must have been jealous. But it all went too far. It all went way too far. It was my fault."

23

Guy continued, "I can hardly say it, but I had been egging him on. I was trying to get under his skin. He was like a brother to me, but it got ugly. Bad ugly. I am so sorry! I've been sorry all my life."

Cord sat very still. Guy had broken down into sobs. Cord waited. Guy roughly pushed away the oxygen at his nose and put a fist to his mouth. He bit down on his knuckles, tearing at himself.

Cord leaned over and gently put both of his hands on Guy's forearm. He could feel the tension in the muscle. He squeezed lightly, as if massaging the rigid tendons. He said nothing, only giving Guy the soft signal that he was staying with him.

Slowly the tightness loosened. The sobs lessened. The fist came away from his face. Cord offered him a small towel. Guy wiped his eyes and scrubbed at his cheeks until there were hot pink circles in the wrinkles of gray.

After a time Cord said deliberately, "Your story has been a burden to you." It was a hideous and regretful situation. And it was much too late to unpack more of it. Guy was on his deathbed.

"I was never able to tell anybody." Guy was clearly exhausted. "I wanted to come clean." His voice was scratchy, and each word was an effort.

Pacing himself and searching for a neutral statement, Cord said gently back to him, "Losing a friend." He let that settle into the room. "I have heard you, Guy. Your story is spoken."

He paused again, giving Guy any time he needed to say more. Eventually, he stood up slowly and laid his hand on Guy's head. "I am going to give you a blessing, Guy. This blessing is to call down on you the grace of our Lord. You have opened your heart. Let us speak in prayer."

Guy moaned quietly and scraped the sheets with his fingernails.

"Gracious Lord, you hear of our misdeeds, and you carry the burdens of our sorrows in your heart." Cord deeply appreciated the act of praying aloud. It was music, sometimes, to push the sounds slowly over his vocal cords and out of his throat into the air. Each word grew bigger that way, as he spoke them up and forward and out. It was part of his tradecraft. Often the old-fashioned and overwrought language was mismatched to a setting, but it relieved people of fear and hysteria.

"Be with your faithful servant, Guy Sykes, with the assurance that will bring peace to his troubled mind and comfort to him in these weary hours." Cord watched as the words smoothed the air. "Give your forgiveness and your blessing to him, and to all those whom he loves and remembers, and hear us as together we say the prayer which we have been taught." The clawing fingers had relaxed. The chafing was becoming a rubbing, and Guy's head was settling back into the pillow.

"Our Father, who art in heaven..." Together they turned over the words and phrases of the Lord's Prayer.

"I'm going to stay here awhile," Cord said. "If it's all right with you, I'll use my bells."

He fished his chanting bells out of his pocket. These came in handy at a time like this. "When I ring them, we can be still and listen to them for as long as the chime lasts."

He held the silken connecting cord and swung the brass bells in a mutual strike. The shared note was surprisingly low and lingered long in the shiny, hard-surfaced room. Guy had closed his eyes and was listening hard. Cord struck them together again, and he could see Guy's face slowly loosen.

Cord kept his vigil as Guy's breathing lengthened and deepened into sleep. He watched the man's chest faintly rise and fall. He sat staring hard at those last bits of life. He absorbed again the confession and considered its ramifications. Was there value in the truth? For Guy? For others? Was there justice to serve? Had Guy served a sentence of guilt already? Had the goodness of his life paid the debt? Was he forgiven? Finally, quietly, Cord left the room.

In the snacks alcove, he pulled a can from the soda machine and gulped the sweet cold liquid. Ministry was a privilege, he reminded himself. Few are called to be at the spike points of people's lives. Few have access to the deep fears, longings, and truth of others. Few are in the position to make decisions to push things to the side, to wrestle with real instances of integrity, and to let things be buried.

So, what was wrong with him? He admitted to himself that despite Guy's riveting story, he couldn't engage in it. It was dramatic and tragic. Guy was so troubled by it. But, the whole episode was long ago, far away. It felt like yellowed parchment or old newsreels. It was during the Korean War, for heaven's sake. That's when he had barely been playing in a sandbox with his sisters.

His immediate response to Guy had been pastoral. His routine and ritual were ways to soothe and find healing. They neutralized the terrors, bringing them close in. When everything was out of control, he produced shared words, and their meaning stabilized people. "Forgive us our debts…. deliver us from evil." He measured out those words for people under all sorts of duress.

But they didn't soothe his personal terror. Where was *his* voice? Where were *his* words? Why was he always taking care of things, using healing mantras, and catching the world as it started downward? He longed to be throwing his sight upwards, pursuing visions, and witnessing to the powerful and mighty pulsations of the world.

He walked out to the parking lot. The sun was pounding down, and the inside of the car was an oven. Mechanically, he buckled the seat belt and turned the key in the ignition. Everything was too formulaic--all rote and gimmicky bells. What kind of ministry was that? If he wanted to be a prophetic voice, where was his own soul?

Did he have compassion fatigue? The journals were full of pastoral counselors warning about its signs. But he could hardly complain of burdensome emotional demands. He didn't have an AIDS ministry or a mission in the third world. He was running dry in solid, prosperous, heartland America.

He used to feel heartened when he redirected a person from despair to calm. He had mastered that script. But the capable feeling that he enjoyed when he was younger now felt hollow. *Feel-good ministry.* That's all it was. The words were chalk in his mouth.

The car rolled heavily on the hot street. He needed to check the suspension. In addition, the air conditioning wasn't cutting it. His soda had grown stale. Just like my ministry, he thought.

And soon Guy would die, and Cord would preside over the funeral. He could see it now. The Sykes Mortuary always did a beautiful job, but would he only be going through the paces?

Guy deserved more. He had probably prepared hundreds of dead bodies for funerals in the course of his life. Maybe thousands.

Cord halted himself for a minute with the image of thousands of bodies on slabs. Guy certainly knew about death. Or did he? He knew about the aftermath of death. Morticians see the dead all the time, but do they see the dying? Nope. That's where ministers stepped in. The clergy were the ones who worked the fine line between the body quick and the body dead. Get a grip, Cord said to himself. A ministry is inherently special, full of unique moments where a person can make a mark.

So why didn't he feel the pulse and vibrancy of that?

Automatically, he shoveled a forkful in his mouth; the sweetness of the whipped cream and strawberries jammed his thoughts and brought him back to reality. Oh, yes! The Wood Carving Festival! Here he was doing more of God's Really Important Work, hawking food in the hot sun. He swallowed hard and swabbed the syrup with another chunk of cake. He couldn't even stay on his diet.

Brent had taken his leave and was heading for the parking lot, waving over his shoulder to someone. He presented his usual picture of awkward humor and public earnestness even in this hard time. Cord watched him go and swallowed again.

Well, if Brent could carry on, so must he.

Cord looked across the tables. Spencer in his lobster apron was calling to Victor, who was clearly dragging his heels as he talked with Kyle and the new girl. Hmmm, he needed to get to know this new family. The husband had died of cancer, he had heard. It would be good if he could get them to join the church. He put down his plate and waded into the crowd.

CHAPTER 5

"Will you look at that!" Porter Hofmeister's voice was heard down the counter at Nell's Diner. The place was thinning out from the midmorning coffee crowd, but most of the counter seats were still taken.

Tiffany's job in the mornings was to help Nell cover the counter and some of the booths. The coffee in her pot sloshed as she swung around to see what Porter was saying.

"That AIDS kid!" Porter slapped at the paper. "They're planning on passing some law named after him."

"You mean Ryan White?" she asked. Everyone in Indiana knew the story. He'd had to fight in the courts to go to school in Kokomo after he had been diagnosed with AIDS. His family had eventually moved to Cicero, and he went to school there.

"Yeah," Porter muttered. "Goddamned homos who started that disease. It's a crime that they've spread it to kids."

Tiffany was uncertain what to say. She had just been bantering with Mr. Hofmeister about always having a pastry along with his coffee. Mrs. Hofmeister was such a good baker, why would he come down to the diner?

"I'm sorry to be taking the Lord's name in vain, Tiffany." Porter seemed to catch himself. "There's no excuse for that. Don't go telling Mavis."

Tiffany's smile recovered some of their earlier conspiracy.

Duke looked up from his own over-indulgent piece of pie and coffee. He was a couple of counter stools away. Porter's words and sentiment were clear enough. There was no covering it over. AIDS had merged in people's minds with homosexuals and had turbocharged the homophobia already in the culture. Stanton, he ruminated, was more closeted than West Lafayette, and he had to admit that he missed the relative openness of a university town. He took another bite of the famous Nell's Diner rhubarb pie, but it had lost some of its delicious comfort-food appeal. Steady, boy, he said to himself.

Duke didn't know the man who had spoken, but he had gathered from the earlier banter that the young waitress knew him from their church. He wondered if it was George's congregation. Duke had happily abandoned his religious life when he was a young man. To him, it was another institution that was insensitive and constitutionally blind about him as a gay man. But, his partner George was faithful to his church. From what George said, Pastor McDaniel was smart and liberal. This testy guy with the newspaper surely wouldn't put up with that kind of preaching. It must be a different congregation.

Tiffany had left the counter and was taking orders from a couple at a table. The man on the other side of Porter leaned over and said genially, "Ya heard the one about why AIDS is a miracle disease?"

Porter shook his head. "No, not sure that I have."

"Well, it's a miracle disease because it turns a fruit into a vegetable." The man gave a snort.

Porter chuckled. "Good one."

Good Christ, Duke half prayed, feeling the scorch in the air.

The double glass doors swung open, and Brent Sykes strode in. He slowed down to greet people at the counter. Porter shook his hand and pointed at the paper. "You're right," said Brent. "I've heard that Congress is considering legislation to fight the disease."

"Why should they spend money to find a cure? Good, honest tax money. My money! They should fight it at the source and stop these people from their..." Porter glanced at Tiffany who was setting out silverware for her customers, "...activities." The mayor offered a useful audience for his opinions.

Suddenly Porter caught himself. "I'm sorry, Brent. You don't need to hear this right now. How is your father?"

Duke couldn't help listening and marveled at the skill with which the new mayor managed the conversation. He clearly could sound deeply sincere while listening to and deflecting cranky constituents. Who would have imagined that a mortician would make a good politician? But, of course, the profession demanded a certain measure of unflappability. George had told him that Brent's father had also been mayor, some years ago. So he'd learned it at the knee.

Brent extracted himself from the conversation with Porter, smiled at Tiffany, and joined two women in the corner booth.

"Mayor Brent," one greeted him with silky superiority, her gold doorknocker earrings pulling at her earlobes rather dangerously. "Thank you for your time today. It's most generous of you."

"Of course, my pleasure." He shook hands with the second woman who had also trowelled on pancake makeup. They clearly wanted something. He wondered if they expected him to lift their hands and touch his lips to their knuckles? "You must know how much we appreciate the hard work of the Arts Commission."

"We are enormously gratified that the relationship between the Commission and the Mayor's Office is continuing to be cordial. We know that is due to your far-sighted leadership."

Yes, they clearly wanted something. Brent nodded and smiled. The women continued, eager to impress on him their concerns about the signage at the Wood Carving Festival. The city was trying hard to bill itself as an artisan community. But the signage didn't promote Stanton properly. It was temporary. It looked sloppy. It was amateurish. Brent would understand. He surely knew about ambiance, setting, and staging from his own work. Details are very important. He could appreciate how the town's *image* could be improved.

And, they had a solution.

Brent grinned up at Tiffany who had come to his rescue. Yes, he would like coffee. No, regular and black--a straight shot to his heart.

Wouldn't it be great if the Festival's signs were made in decorative woods, carved by artisans? There could be a competition to select an artisan. The Commission could sponsor the competition, lay out the guidelines, and choose the judges.

Brent couldn't agree fast enough (no skin off his teeth). "But, of course." Great idea. Initiative. Taste. Proper governance. He added only one thought, to indicate that the Mayor's Office wasn't without inspiration of its own. "How about building on Wash Evanston's legacy? Perhaps we could name the competition after him, or see if Grace Evanston has any thoughts. Shall I approach her and then hand it all back to you?"

In his heyday, Washington Evanston had created wonderful signs for downtown businesses. Most were still in use, adding a unique flavor to the historic main street of shops. "That would be marvelous. Yes, of course."

With all sides in a win position, Brent wound things down. He deliberately looked at his watch. "I have to be off."

The three slid out of the booth, and he bowed them out the door.

Duke looked up from his magazine to watch the women leave. Brent nodded his way as he also left. They had a passing acquaintance, literally, from jogging past each other most early mornings. Duke wasn't sure that Brent knew him otherwise. He doubted strongly that Brent associated him with George. The couple worked hard to keep their private life out of view from anybody other than very close and trusted friends.

He was curious about the mayor, however. Brent was successful, good-looking by a lot, athletic, and had an awkward sense of humor that made him hometown charming. Was he gay? Duke and George had wondered aloud about this. Their gay friends dismissed the speculation. Their gaydar wasn't going off. He was just single and keeping his love life very quiet.

But, think about it, they argued. If you were gay and really wanted to be in politics, being seriously closeted was the only option, especially if it were a quasi-inherited position. If Brent was in line behind his father, he had a couple of extra pressures for keeping it under wraps here in Stanton. Yeah, sure, maybe two or three political people were out about their sexual orientation in San Francisco or Massachusetts, but it wasn't easy sledding for them at all. It was only ten or so years since the Harvey Milk tragedy.

He let the thought go. He didn't usually dwell on thoughts about the gay community. But, Mr. Homophobe-with-the-newspaper and Mr. Homophobe-jokester had stirred them up. Duke had that familiar pang of anxiety about being recognized or noticed. Rationally, he told himself, it was the gift of being gay that it wasn't visibly evident to anyone. Nevertheless, when the men had been bantering, he had sat very still.

And that was part of the reason he was still sitting on the stool. It was high time to be moving along. It was his week to buy groceries. He tossed some change on the counter for Tiffany as he got up to leave.

*** *** ***

Brent pulled up to the curb and waved to Grace Evanston, who was sitting on her porch.

"Why, Brent Sykes," she called, reaching for her cane.

"Don't get up, Grace. I'll come to you." He hustled through the gate and up the walk. The porch swing and the porch railings were handcrafted with beautiful carvings. Wash Evanston had been an imaginative and prolific woodworker. Grace, his widow of ten years, had a lap rug over her knees and a soft peach-colored sweater over her shoulders.

She beamed at him. "How are you, Mr. Mayor?" Her son, Vaughn, had been Brent's father's best friend. When she had lost Vaughn back in the 1950's, she couldn't help transferring some motherly affection to Guy, and then grandmotherly affection and pride to Brent. "How is your father doing?"

Brent answered the familiar question, knowing her concern for his dying father was genuine and longstanding. "We're losing him, Grace. And in some ways I wish it would go more quickly, because it is a terrible disease."

Grace was hardly disturbed by his candor or the situation. The wheels of life kept turning and, to her way of thinking, it was the charity and clarity of one's life that mattered. Guy had both. He had cared for bereaved families, teenagers, and his city. That took a heart and no shadows. Death was death. Adolescence was adolescence. People were people. His passing would be a loss.

"Of course you feel ambivalent about him dying. Mercy! And from my

30

perspective he's so young." She looked directly into Brent's eyes. "As usual, I'm still here while everyone else bites the dust."

Brent heard both the irony in her voice, as well as a lilt.

"But, is this why you came? To talk about Guy?"

"Not really. I'm on my way to the hospital. I visit him a couple of times a day, but he doesn't want me hanging around. He tells me to get back to work, as if that's a surprise. So, I'm here on business, on city business. It's a good excuse to drop by."

Grace studied him as he spoke. She had watched him grow up directly alongside his father, without his mother who had died so early. He was almost Guy's double, his spitting image. They had the same height, hair, and occupations. Their differences were mostly stylistic. Otherwise, they were carbon copies.

What would happen when Guy did pass? She could imagine some forks in the road. Brent would be the last man standing. He would have a legacy, but also a new freedom. She laughed at herself for meddling. Better to think about some other family succession, like the British royals and Prince Charles's never-to-be transition.

"Well, I'm glad you came by today. If you had dropped by next week, you would have missed me. In fact, when you are visiting your father, you can come visit me, too. I am going to have that knee replacement surgery on Monday."

"You are? You must be in some pain to go to that length. But, I've heard it is miracle surgery," Brent responded. "They say it is worth the effort. Of course I will visit. You can count on it."

"Good. I will be ever so grateful. And now, what is the business that brings you for a visit?"

Brent took a seat. "Brace yourself. It's an idea the Arts Commission is hatching." He launched into the story with good humor.

Grace listened, nodded, and quickly agreed. "Of course!" Wash would be thrilled at the recognition, and the project was delightful. She was tickled that Wash's basement hobby and artistic sensibility were turning into a bit of a legacy. Who could have anticipated that? She gently rocked for a moment longer in silence, enjoying the gentle companionship.

"I'd best be going," said Brent, standing up. "Time to see how Dad is doing." He gave Grace a kiss on the cheek. "Good luck going under the knife!"

She waved him off and gaily gave a little push with her foot to set her swing in motion.

He latched the gate and returned to his car. Her sunny mood and sweetness stayed with him until he saw the package on the back seat. Yes, he needed to stop by the post office. He sighed to himself and made a U-turn in order to head back towards Main Street.

Sharon had phoned him over the weekend. Was it only three months since she had given up on him, as she said, and called it quits? It felt like yesterday. The calm and logic of her announcement or *pronouncement* had bruised him. He was ready to admit that now, but he still wanted to argue with her in his head.

It had been strange to hear her voice, natural and practical over the phone. She asked about his dad. She had been gracious about that. And she was calling him to remind him again to mail the cookbook and sweater back to her. Had she left anything else? She was still missing those new running shoes. Where could they have gone?

For his part, the call had been guarded. She was the one who had said, "Not enough," and he didn't want to go over it again or hear that repeated. She had a measuring cup that she wanted filled with--Success? Security? Children? Devotion? Romance? He honestly didn't know what, anymore. The whole thing was a calculation, and he didn't add up to the right answer, whatever that was.

Yes, he was gun-shy. Who wouldn't be? He thought he was offering his heart, but she only saw an incomplete commitment. She said he hadn't been able to step up.

It was the children thing, when you boiled it down. He had met all of the rest of her demands, but he couldn't get his mind around children. That was the long and the short of it.

"You don't really mean it," she had shot back dozens of times.

But he did. He didn't want the responsibility. How was he to keep up on all of the other demands on him? There was his business, the house, his elected office, the community, his church, and a public image to maintain. He was always on call. He listened to constituents; his evenings were booked; people died at all hours. If she had a biological stopwatch, he had a 24/7 alarm clock. They had fought, at first bitterly, and then regretfully.

He reviewed the phone call in his mind. Yes, she had been remarkably matter-of-fact. The thought struck him that she had already found another man. Well, let him try jumping the high bar. Good luck, buddy.

He pulled up at the post office and carried the packages into the counter. The clerk greeted him, figured out the postage, and accepted his money. As she tossed the stamped box into a cart, he winced. There wasn't anything breakable in it, but he didn't want it to arrive bashed in. He didn't want her to associate him with anything bruised.

Oh, give it up, he told himself. Hang it up for now. You've got Dad to worry about.

Seeing Guy in the hospital was always horrible. The drugs made him woozy and incoherent. His skin had a burned look. He tried to be cheerful and show the old spirit, but the treatments were grueling. No two ways about it, cancer was hell.

Brent started the car and turned down the street towards the hospital. He noticed the stop sign on 15th Street had twisted over. It looked like a mini-tornado had hit. Had there been an accident that he had missed?

See, he said to himself. There's not room for much more right now. Stick to business and taking care of Dad. He jotted a note to himself on the notepad that he kept attached to the dash

Arriving at the hospital, the nurses' station was quiet. Brent tapped on his dad's door. "It's me," he announced as he entered.

Guy was lying quietly and turned his head slightly to smile.

"Grace Evanston sends her love," Brent continued. "I stopped by her house to talk with her about an Arts Commission idea."

Guy's smile faded. "She's a good woman."

"Yes, she is. Going strong. She's coming in for knee surgery next week. But she's as cheerful as ever. You would never know she was in any pain, and that's remarkable given her age."

"She's a very good woman."

"Yes, Dad. She's a star."

"Will you promise me that you will take care of her?" It was an enigmatic question, and Guy's eyes were glazed. Brent wondered if he was confusing Grace with someone else. The drugs must be muddling things more than ever. He pulled up a chair, took his dad's hand, and squeezed it.

CHAPTER 6

With great discipline the church officers left the fragrance of summer and stepped inside the church for the evening meeting. Dressed in shorts and sandals, they further demonstrated their stoicism by not mentioning the chill of the folding chairs on their bare legs. The retirees were ready with files and notepads. Others had bolted their dinners after work. "It's fast food, but I can't eat it that fast," one said, nibbling a slice of pizza she had grabbed at her son's baseball game.

As usual, Porter Hofmeister produced a tin of cookies. "You'll never get voted out if Mavis keeps this up." The comment was made at every meeting.

Cord called them to order, and a sense of generalized grace coalesced as he shared the news that Guy Sykes was in a coma. Everyone nodded.

The Peach and Strawberry Shortcakes had broken records at this year's festival. "Worth the effort, for sure!" The budget update raised some pulses, but that energy dissipated in the tedium of committee reports.

A mission newsletter requested support for a youth suicide hotline. Loretta Beck was appalled. "I can't imagine how children get into such trouble." The others knew better than to engage her anxieties.

"We're planning to launch our 175th anniversary celebration on Hymn Sing Sunday," Cord announced. "We'll sing music representing the historical periods of the church's life." Cord paused. "And I have one issue to flag."

The clerk looked up from his notes, one very bushy eyebrow raised.

"The carillonneur will play various historic hymns, and *Onward, Christian Soldiers* is bound to raise some hackles."

"Oh, for heaven's sake!" Complaints about hymns were an annoying staple of church life.

"*Onward, Christian Soldiers* was removed from the hymn book years ago.

As you might know, people objected to its forward-into-battle language. It is bombastic, at best."

"That's politically correct horse hockey!!" Porter found this sort of thing totally ridiculous.

"No," protested another. "It's a terrible hymn. I agree completely."

"It's like singing a Stephen Foster song about happy slaves."

"But that was the idiom of the day."

Cord interrupted. "I'm actually not here to debate the hymn. We've settled that debate already." He moved his Bible onto his stack of papers. "The point I want to make is that an anniversary year gives us a chance to look at our history, and we shouldn't turn it over to nostalgia." His voice deepened. "I plan to preach this year outside of the strict lectionary schedule. I'll be talking about our faith, our history, and the real lessons underneath that. I wanted to give you notice about that."

The mood of the room turned responsible. People nodded. "You could explore the history of our congregation, too. We know the folklore, but not the real stories."

Another spoke up. "My ancestors were German, like many in town. My grandfather spoke only German. I wonder about what life was like for them, especially during the wars."

Porter nodded. He liked genealogy.

Loretta was holding her hands together with the index fingers brushing her lips. "It's nice to share stories, but I come to church to worship and not to hear Indiana history. We don't have enough prayer and praise to God in our lives as it is."

"We are first and foremost a community of worship," Cord responded. "You can be reassured, Loretta, that searching our history will bring us to a deeper capacity for worship."

Others interrupted. Yes, it was a year to take a fresh look at where they had come from.

"But this should be more than a scrapbook history lesson. We can't pretend we were saints."

"Yep. That's for sure."

Easy to say, thought Cord, as he closed the meeting. But faith communities were notoriously locked into tradition. Nevertheless, he wanted to shake things up. This was a little step, but perhaps it could become a big stride.

He knew there were ministers who would simply open a Bible, point to a verse, and start preaching. The thought both terrified and inspired him. How could he break out of the mold? Arguing with himself, he closed the meeting and methodically returned his papers to his office and locked up the building.

His wife drove up. He got in the car and kissed her.

She smiled. "What was that for?"

"Oh, I don't know. Good meeting, I guess."

"Was Loretta Beck there?"

"Yes. Why?"

"The usual. I bumped into her at the supermarket, and she stood right there in the cereal aisle and told me about how Victor is in some mortal danger because he is a little hard to reach emotionally, he puts up a protest about coming to church…" She was ticking things off on her fingers. "And, there was something about his photography and how she sees it as troubling. She didn't say all that exactly, but she has always hovered over him too much for my taste."

"She makes me think about 13th century women who joined convents and prayed all day."

"Maybe." She laughed. "But she's not really like a nun. She just doesn't roll very much with life. She's high-strung. It's more about how her piety can get in the way of good sense. I told her Victor is a great kid."

"Spencer will keep them in balance. He's a sensible dad. Victor will be fine. They'll figure it out."

"I suppose so. People do choose their parents, you know. You get the parents you were meant to get."

He smiled at her, indulging her New Age ideas. She had an unconventional side, and he loved her for it. "I don't know about the parent bit," he said with a tease and a need to change the subject, "but I know that I chose my wife with great deliberation and forethought."

"Hmmm. Forethought? You told me before it was the *foreplay*!" She laughed in her utterly cheerful way.

Cord rolled down the car window and smiled as the summer night air poured in, and they drove off.

CHAPTER 7

It was a choice between the tile floor and a pew in the sanctuary of the country church. One looked really hard, and the other was awfully narrow. "Boys on one side, girls on the other," called the youth advisor. "Get your sleeping bags unrolled and stuff sorted out. Treat the place gently. And don't you *dare* leave any gum anywhere!"

The kids had ridden for six hours in big vans and were dazed and lethargic. "Come on! Come on! I'll start the charcoal, and you'll need to be ready to work on dinner."

"Charcoal-ee-oo-lee," said Kyle to Victor.

Bridget started to unpack her duffle bag. Alongside her, Tiffany was reciting items as she tossed them over on her side of the pew. "Cards, Bible, sunscreen, bug spray, flashlight, ibuprofen, nail polish... If you need anything that I've got, just let me know."

"Thanks," said Bridget. "I didn't bring a Bible. Was I supposed to?"

"Don't worry. Looks like there are plenty right here." Tiffany pointed to the racks on the back of the pew filled with hymnals and Bibles. "That's one thing this church does have a lot of."

They were in rural Kentucky for a week of work, and their accommodations were simple. Tiffany had explained to Bridget on the trip down that there was no shower, just a hose that they would rig up with a little fence of towels and tarps for privacy. The bathrooms were effectively outhouses. "It's like camping, and you get pretty grubby. But everyone does, so it's okay. If everyone is smelly, no one notices."

Bridget had worked at a soup kitchen in Chicago but had never been inside a poor country church like this. "It's even smaller than I expected," she said, as she looked around the room and counted ten pews on each side."

"Yeah, and it means we're really close to the boys all the time." Tiffany waved in the direction of Kyle and Victor and grinned.

Tiffany loved to tease and flirt with boys. Bridget had been amazed at first, but as they became fast friends, she realized that Tiffany had the biggest heart she had ever known in a person. She was warm and open to everyone, and that made being her special friend even more special.

As for the boys, Bridget was partial to Victor. She wasn't sure she had a crush on him exactly. His dark hair and the high color in his cheeks made him look intense and serious, and a little older. He was clearly nice, and maybe a little shy, although anyone seemed quiet and reserved next to Kyle. She liked Kyle, too, but more as a fun guy to have around. He never stopped with the jokes and teasing. It was like having a brother.

A horn blew, and they were summoned to help with dinner. Immediately after eating their dessert of brownies, the counselors held a meeting, gave assignments, and told everyone to get some sleep tonight. "You'll need it." The kids ignored the advice and stayed up late playing cards. When they finally turned in, no one slept well on either the pews or the floor. It was a tired and grouchy start for the week.

The next day, their first job was to clear the brush around a lady's house before reinforcing the porch and building a ramp. They had to dig places for extra foundations under the porch and then pour cement. *Pour cement!* The wheelbarrow was incredibly heavy. And it was hot. Really hot.

Sleeping the second night was easy. Bridget had barely noticed how hard the floor was.

Rev. McDaniel joined them midweek and had spent time after dinner blowing up an air mattress. When he sat on it and shifted his weight, the mattress squeaked loudly. Kyle had exchanged grins with Bridget. They were sitting cross-legged on their sleeping bags, and Rev. McDaniel had been trying to start a serious conversation – he called it a rap session, like he was someone rapping on the door. Rap rap. Squeak squeak!

In answer to his questions, kids described their work on a second house where you could see the ground between some of the floorboards. They had worked on the yard, mowing and raking, and repaired a fence so that the elderly man's vegetable garden was safe from animals. "People here have hard lives," Rev. McDaniel said. "You have to have great respect that they find energy to put into their church."

What can you say to that, thought Victor. It looks like they need their church so they can team up and help each other. That's what church was all about for some people. Not that his own family needed help like that. He wished his parents actually needed the church more like that, rather than in his mom's emotional, religi-oso way.

Bridget had chimed into the discussion. When she lived in Chicago and her dad was sick, the church had helped a lot. The minister had come often to visit, but he didn't pray or do any of that kind of sticky stuff. Instead, he talked with them about their homework and helped her mom with some paperwork. Other deacons had helped with grocery shopping and picking up medicines.

"So," she said, "the church helped us, and I should help others."

"That's admirable, Bridget," Rev. McDaniel said. "What do the rest of you think? Does Bridget owe anyone anything?"

"She doesn't owe me anything," said one kid. "I mean we just met her this week. We never met her dad."

Some of the boys agreed and pointed, instead, to another kid. "But Zach owes us because he took the *whole bag* of chips."

McDaniel was undeterred. "Well, think about it. Does she owe something to the church?"

Bridget defended herself. "It's not like that. I don't think I owe anyone. But if someone does something for you, it's only fair to give back."

"I don't think you owe anything, either," Victor chimed in. "That's not how church works." He hadn't meant to say anything, but he didn't think Bridget needed to justify herself. "I mean, you are sort of expected to pitch in, but if you don't, it's not as if they'll throw you out."

"No? You don't think you could get thrown out?" Tiffany's tone had a tease in it.

"Me? Well, yeah," interrupted Kyle. "If I murdered someone, I suppose. Or if I tortured animals, or gassed little kids, or stole from old people, or went AWOL, or was a fag, or burned down houses, or something extremely, very evillissimo like that."

"Well, we're supposed to be forgiving." Another kid sounded superior.

"Yeah, but those are pretty bad things," responded Kyle.

"Hold it, everyone," said Rev. McDaniel. "That's quite a list, Kyle."

"Shall I list some more?"

"No!" responded the minister, laughing. "That's quite enough. But God wants us to forgive even horrible things. Stretch your mind to understand that if you admit your failings, there is room for God to forgive you."

Victor didn't move a muscle. He couldn't believe Kyle had said the fag word. Had there been something that had made Kyle think of that? Of course, Kyle came up with crazy stuff all the time that didn't seem connected to anything. But why had he said the fag word? Nobody had reacted. Did they all think that fags were really bad? Like baby killers?

"Yeah," joked Tiffany to Kyle. "*Stretch... your... mind!*"

Bridget laughed. That was a good phrase to describe Kyle. His mind ran all over the place. She liked these kids. They knew each other so well they could tease each other like that.

The conversation shifted as some older kids took it over. Eventually it limped to a close, and with Tiffany's engineering, the four moved to a corner of the room and spent the evening playing cards.

The next day, they were assigned together as a crew to return to the first house and finish varnishing the ramp they had built. Victor brought his camera and took pictures. Kyle and Tiffany were sanding, as Bridget touched up a section the sixth graders had slopped up a lot. She stepped back to be sure she hadn't missed spots. "It looks different when it is wet. You can't tell for sure until it's dried that it's done right."

The door opened, and the woman of the house came out slowly in her wheelchair. It took her a couple tries to get over her threshold to the porch. Kyle and Tiffany looked at each other, and both rose to their feet. "Can we help you?" they said.

The woman looked at them sharply. "No, I'm just fine," she sparked at them. They looked at each other again, and then quietly returned to sanding. Victor stepped back a bit to take her picture.

"What ya doin' there, young man?"

Victor lowered his camera, not sure if she were curious or reprimanding him. "I was taking pictures so we could remember the project better."

"You should ask me first if you are photographing my home."

Victor lowered his camera and then put it in his backpack. He picked up a paintbrush. He didn't know what to think, and the four of them quietly worked until the woman wheeled back into the house. Bridget looked at Victor and said softly, "It's hard to be nice when you're sick."

Victor thought about that. He was pretty sure Bridget hadn't said that to make him feel better. It was a statement of fact. She was probably smart about such things because of her dad. It made her seem more mature and interesting. Not all flirty and silly like Tiffany.

The rest of the week was filled with more hard work and fewer card games before they collapsed on their bedrolls. Victor and Bridget didn't talk much – Tiffany and Kyle supplied the whirl of jokes and chatter. But Victor realized he liked being around Bridget. He felt calm and relaxed with her. Everything felt more normal.

In the van ride on the way home he glanced at her napping next to Tiffany, who was reading magazines. Bridget was pretty, he thought. Her black hair was dramatic.

His mind suddenly took a loop. Maybe he could like her! Like her, as in a boy-girl thing. The thought was a surprise and confused him. The whole subject of relationships made him crazy. He was always having crushes on boys, if that's what you called them. He liked their looks, and they were funny. Girls never cracked jokes. They just giggled and talked endlessly about nail polish and clothes. Boys were different and cool. He loved their wide shoulders, arms, legs, and their strength.

His secret bothered him nonstop. It haunted his thinking. Would someone see into his mind and his feelings? Things that were so real for him must be obvious to others. But it would be awful if anyone found out.

And, he sensed it would be dangerous. He tried not to think about that very often.

But maybe he wasn't weird. Here was Bridget, and there was something different about her. Victor felt a wave of something. Relief. Maybe he could be interested in her – in that kind of way.

Girls had always put him off. They were cute, sure, but in a little bunny way. Being around a girl was like going to church. You had to pretend it was nice and special, when actually it was mostly silly and boring. But, hey, Bridget was different. She was actually nice, not pretend nice. She was pretty. He was glad he had a moment to think about this.

Maybe it was a stupid kid thing to have crushes on other boys. Maybe it was what his father always said: "Your mother was the best thing that happened to me." Maybe it just hadn't happened to him until now. If he could hang out with Bridget, he could fit in and not be bad and weird. It would keep his parents off his back. It would make him normal. The whole idea made him feel super good inside. God, it would be great! He grinned to himself.

"What are you smiling about?" Tiffany was poking him.

"Nothing," he said to her with a shrug. But to himself he was saying, maybe everything.

CHAPTER 8

Grace Evanston had arrived at the care facility in an ambulance from the hospital. The knee surgery had gone well, but she couldn't manage at home alone for some time.

The pain medication allowed her good sleep after those first bad days. The chirpy nurses and aides kept her nerves from failing as she slowly learned to stand and walk again. Other than therapy sessions, her days were mostly quiet. She read, prayed, and received a few visitors. Her needlework was always at hand. The Presbyterian Women had sent her a deep purple African violet. She admired the determination of its center stalk as it extended its leaves in a circle skirt and never allowed them to touch the soil.

She was wheeled to meals in the dining room. Her morning routine soon added a stop by the large bay window in the foyer, where she read the early paper. Today, as she sat reading, she could sense a muggy summer day building outside. The gauze curtains provided only a thin veil of protection from the early blazing sun.

Grace soon closed the newspaper. The flimsy paper refused precision folding, but she took care to shake out the wrinkles and square it up as much as possible.

"So, Guy Sykes is dead," she said to herself, as she smoothed the creases. He was only 61. She had not counted the years for some time but, yes, that's how old her son Vaughn would be if he had lived.

Yes, if he had lived. She gently lifted that idea from the folds of her mind. Time had drained her memories until they became dried pressed flowers, rather than the earlier thorny and succulent ones.

Vaughn had drowned nearly forty years ago. On the night he was celebrating his homecoming from Korea with Guy, he had fallen off the pier at the lake and never surfaced. He was a young soldier, home from his tour of duty. But just after he had taken the dog tags off his chest, it had

42

been swamped by local lake water. Now Guy, too, was gone. Grace was left holding the memory of both of them. She felt as old as the biblical Sarah.

Guy and Vaughn were so young back then – both just boys, and foolish boys at that. They were much too confident and sure of themselves, with their bronzed bodies and solid muscles. Vaughn had survived war, and surely nothing could touch him now. But, to her ever after sorrow, something had, and it was their rotgut whiskey.

The accident happened on a summer night with a full moon. Guy told them he turned off the car beams because they could easily see their way out to the pier with the bright sky. The lake, however, was particularly dark.

The boys had come from a party to sit on the pier, each with a bottle of whiskey. Guy might have passed out for a bit and had been slow to realize that Vaughn had disappeared. She remembered his throttled anger at himself as he told the story. "I thought he was crazy to go find bushes so he could take a leak. It was dark. He didn't have to find a private place like that." It had taken a while for Guy to miss him, and then to think that maybe Vaughn hadn't gone in search of bushes, but had, instead, fallen off the pier. But he hadn't been able to see anything in the water. Under the sparkling reflection, it had been black and blacker. They must have been terribly drunk.

Vaughn's death was the blackest time in Grace's life. Her entire body, her heart, and her soul felt shrouded. She was bereft. That single word summed it up in the rip of the second syllable. *Bereft!* She whispered it in her prayers as she moaned to God.

Vaughn's funeral was at the peak of the summer heat, like today. Back then, with no air conditioning, she remembered struggling to breathe. Visitors at the house after the services hugged her with clammy arms. She couldn't face the dinner plates loaded with ham, beans, slaw, and runny Jell-O fruit salads. Everything tasted like glue. She sat on the couch sweating into the cushions.

Over and over, she groped her way down the hall to her bedroom and stripped off her clothes. She bathed, powdered herself, and dressed all over again. But none of that effort rewound the day. It was heavy hot, and she had just buried her son.

In the evening, when everyone had finally gone, the dark heat wrapped her in more claustrophobic hugs. Her skirt hung heavy and long, as if trying to reach the ground and trail its hem along in the dirt. Her son was in the ground. No moving air lifted the dust.

Her sweat oozed and leaked out of her and stuck to her skin. Her mind did the same, oozing memories. Vaughn was their only child. Once she had unrolled the cuffs of his jeans and found his stash of bubblegum. She remembered holding his squirming body in a towel after a bath. He always hated onions. The memories came without invitation. Some were new memories, if that could be possible. She felt herself going mad.

Would a drive help? Her fingers were wrinkled from bath water. The car was in the garage. Wash had walked to the shop to see if they had closed it up properly. Grace guessed he had walked off to look at the sky so she couldn't see him crying. Perhaps he would see the new star there that was Vaughn. Is that where a spirit goes? She could almost believe it. She had to believe something.

She rolled down all the windows before backing down the driveway. Maybe the breeze would sandblast the sweat from her skin. She drove fast, but the hot wind was worse and made her gasp for air. She decided to drive to the lake.

The memories continued as she drove. Vaughn had been a contained child, always a private little person. He had pulled away from her early. For years he had left the house at dawn to deliver his papers. He had spent his evenings with the mimeograph machine at school putting out the high school paper. At first his journalism had been a light interest. Then it became serious. The paper had won an award, and Vaughn took to cigarettes early – along, probably, with liquor – imitating the big city reporters in movies.

Sons, she lectured herself, pushed their mothers away. She had read that in a magazine somewhere and didn't want to be a clinging mother. Nevertheless, the distance between them seemed wrong to her. She was suspicious. Did ink really run in his veins, or was there something else? Had something happened? Had he closed down behind some hurt? Her heart was never sure. She couldn't frame the questions clearly, and her prayers for him felt selfish and confused.

She moved her foot from the gas pedal to the brake, turned off the blacktop, and steered down the dirt road to the deserted lake. No one was lounging on the pier or snuggling under the hypnosis of the car radio. For a hot summer night, that was odd. No one was there, just as Vaughn was no longer there. How had this happened?

The lake amplified sounds from miles away. She heard rustles and splashes. Noises skimmed across the water and collided around her. Distance disappeared. Vaughn's last living moments had been in this spot, a collection point for nature's music. Five nights ago, he had been right here alive. God's world had been traveling across the water to him.

She listened and then stepped out of her sandals to walk down the pier. A wood splinter stabbed her first step. She winced, and then her face collapsed. What had she done that required such a punishment? Why kill her son? She would have bartered anything. Please, God, I would walk the earth barefoot to have him back. Her eyes blurred with tears, and she hugged the empty heat in her arms.

The lake remained calm. Its flat surface waited, while the crying tore her throat. Each deep crumpled wail depleted her, and it was only reflex that forced her lungs to suck in the hot, dark air. Patiently, the lake reflected the galaxy of stars above, while her body bowed over, heaved back up for air, and bowed again in a terrible curtsey to grief.

It took a long time, but slowly she had worn down. Imperceptibly, her body quieted itself as she ran out of tears. In the lengthening moments of stillness her swollen eyes began to take in the placid water. She knelt and dipped water to splash on her face. As the ripples calmed, the surface had glazed over. The brightness of the stars blurred together. When Vaughn had fallen here, it had been into a sheet of light, not into the dark. She stared at the water and its sheen. God was talking to her. She could see the light on the water that had received Vaughn. He was with God.

She stayed on the pier for a long time. She talked to God. To the water. To the stars. To her son. "Go with the light, Vaughn. He will take care of you." By the end, when she returned to her sandals and the car, her grief was still great, but her despair had lessened.

Afterwards, Wash refused to appreciate her story, and, in fact, he could not listen to it. The irony of Vaughn's death was an agony to him. How could they lose their only child, not in war, but in the safety of his hometown? It was a bone-deep ache. There was no salvation by starlight at a lake. What mythology was Gracie cooking up? Wash woodenly went about his duties, and Grace gave him the only thing she had--space and time. There was nothing else she could do.

The summer continued its heat wave, threatening drought. The days were bright hot and silent, the nights dark hot and noisy, with blowing fans and banging window shades. Finally, one night, Grace slept hard for the first time. It had been a deep dreamless sleep, a dark freedom that left her heavy and limp. Eventually, something penetrated it, dragging her up to consciousness. She was confused. Wash wasn't in bed and, oddly, their bedroom door was closed. Disoriented, she got up and fumbled to the door. From the top of the stairs she could see a light from below, and she held the handrail and started down. Her sheer summer nightgown inflated like a cloud around her from the fanned air below. Was she heavy or light? Asleep or awake? She was in two places at once.

The door at the bottom of the stairs was blocked open. Their house was an old one, dating back to the 19th century. It had once been a small boarding house and was built in either spasms of quirkiness or the need to accommodate additional single men. Rooms had been added at slightly different levels so there were odd sets of steps between rooms and doors at every turn. The living room was all doors: the stair door, front door, closet, the hallway to the kitchen, the side porch, as well as one on each side of the fireplace into the dining room.

The dining room lights were on. "Honey, it's so terribly late," she said automatically, as she both plodded and sailed in. Wash sat at the table on one of the hard-backed dining room chairs. He was as straight and rigid as a prisoner being interrogated. His eyelids swollen from crying, so swollen she knew he could hardly see. Vaughn's letters from Korea formed a pile on the table.

"I had to read them again," he said. His voice was stunned.

Wash had a gift of sight. It was not exactly second sight, but he saw things that Grace never noticed. He had an eye for color and detail, he made their decorating decisions, and he bought her beautiful scarves. He also stared at things--at sunsets, and at the interlocking branches of a tree. Grace had long ago given it a name: sight-cramp. He would get stuck looking at something, caught in the lines or shapes or colors. He was doing it now with Vaughn's letters. He had locked up reading them.

His business was a sign shop that was adequately successful and provided stimulation for his keen eye. But it wasn't enough. Grace knew his patterns: while some people cried over music, Wash could emotionally lock on the strokes of ink on paper or the flickers of the fireplace. It didn't happen often, but it was real when it did.

He needed a jolt, so she returned through the living room and down the hall to the kitchen. She made them each a very strong mug of tea with honey. Reaching for the brandy was out of the question. Liquor had become a devil to this family.

Urging Wash up from his chair, she guided him to the living room couch. Taking a place next to him, she sipped her tea. It burned her mouth, and the honey barely masked the gritty taste. She watched Wash. His stiff expression loosened as he braved the tea. She sipped more herself and waited.

The mantelpiece shone in the low light. Wash had made it, carving, polishing, and buffing it. Inlaid wood undulated along the grain--yellow and brown flames, and bits of sparks. Grace suddenly wanted to feel the smoothness of the wood, not just look at it. How had she missed such ranges in textures all her life: the airiness of the breeze on the stair, the rough tea, the glossy wood? She marveled at the variation. Her mind wandered further.

Wash took a deep breath. He could frame words, but his voice sounded like gravel. "Gracie, he was a responsible young soldier, doing his job. He didn't complain, and he sounded very matter-of-fact. You can see it on the page. The lines are straight, and his script is even. He spaced everything properly on the page. You know how his handwriting is--I mean was--so small. You can tell he had a lot of discipline."

He sipped some more tea. "He was paying his dues, and he understood that he had to do that. I can't believe he missed the payback. He missed so much!" Wash's voice shook. "His life hadn't started yet in so many ways.

46

He never had a love, never had a child, and he hadn't made his own home yet."

Grace listened. Their grief was too new to be second nature yet. When she woke in the morning, there was an instant when she didn't remember that Vaughn had died. Every morning started with the shock. Wash's voice held that shock in it.

Grace could only find awkward things to say. When would she collect herself? Each time she talked about Vaughn, she still made sentences from scratch.

Which is why she blundered out, "No, that's not quite right."

Wash hadn't expected a response. He looked at her.

I'm drifting out of control, she thought. Is this what happens? Everything goes out of control. You intend to be kind and gentle, and suddenly you are clawing at the air.

"I've learned something about Vaughn that I didn't know before." She took a deep breath. "Listen to me, dear. Last week I was going through his room. It's an odd feeling. There are two generations of him in there. There's his boyhood single bed, and right next to it was his soldier's duffle bag." Her voice caught.

"Gracie, you can leave that for a while, can't you?"

"No, it gives me something to do. I wasn't trying to clean the room or go through his things. But we got that letter from J.J. asking us to return his letters, the ones he wrote to Vaughn. You remember the Korean buddy who came to the funeral? So I went looking for the letters. That's all."

She was a little breathless, and she sipped her tea. She had to say it.

"Wash, honey, I found the letters. And I sent them to J.J. But before I did that, I learned something about Vaughn."

Wash looked at her puzzled, but not worried. Now it was his turn to wait.

"I found the letters, and I wasn't planning to read them. I was curious, you know, to learn everything I can, since he's gone for good." Her voice quivered. "But it seemed important to respect him and his privacy, and to honor the fact that he was a grown man. So I was going to package them up straightaway and send them along." It was ridiculous that she felt so guilty.

"You see, the drawer, the top one of his bureau, is sticky, so when I pulled it out, I jerked it. That shook up the stack of letters in it. The letters spread out in the drawer like Pick-Up Sticks." She knew she was going on and on.

"One letter was loose and open, and I picked it up as I was gathering them together." She set down her cup and gestured with her hands as if she were lightly waving together puffs of air.

It had been open right there on the top of the little mayhem of envelopes. The words had been available for her to read. She had held it up and read the words before she had thought about it, before she had connected them together into sentences.

Dear Indiana Man,

How crazy is this? I am going home, and if I were normal, I would be thinking about my mom's apple pie and a hot shower. But we know about normal, don't we - and I miss you like hell. How long will we have to count until your orders come and you can roll out, too? It's now 27 hours since we said goodbye, and I can still feel the aching and the touch of your skin, and your warm wet mouth surrounded by that gritty rough beard...

She had surprised herself with her own gasp. The walls around her started to move. She groped for the side of the bed and sat down quickly. Time stopped for minutes, as she watched her world change.

Then she shuddered out a sob, or was it a half laugh of shock? Her son, her beloved child-man, was taking a new shape. The odd hidden spaces, the private man, were now in absolutely pure white light. It wasn't two people – the boy and the soldier – haunting this bedroom. There were two men--the one everyone knew, and the one that had been hidden.

She had read a few more lines of the letter. Oh, sweet Jesus!

This meant that Vaughn was a man who liked men. She thought they called someone like that a homosexual person. Was that the right word for it? Maybe it was one of those Greek words, a person's name. She knew there were common words for men like that, words like *fag* or *pervert*. But she couldn't equate those words with her son.

She had started to shake, her legs quivering as if they were receiving electric shocks. It couldn't be true. She didn't want it to be true. It was too hard, too hard to understand, and much too hard to absorb. No, it wasn't possible! How could this be about Vaughn? Vaughn Evanston. Her Vaughn. It had to be some other person. There was some mistake. Her Vaughn was the wriggly boy, the birthday boy, the helping-his-father-clean-the-garage boy, the growing boy, the graduating boy, her boy. Her *boy.*

The physical shaking had subsided slowly, but her internal conversation extended into incoherent ranting. She covered her ears, bent over. Her stomach hurt. She stood up and started moving for the door, and then another door, and then another one. She wandered the house for hours, looking out windows. She wondered about God, and Vaughn, and love, and life, and her family, as the floor changed from carpet to tile to floorboard to throw rug to linoleum, and refused to give her sure footing.

Somehow she had stumbled through the day, but she could not remember it later. When Wash came home for dinner, she set out a plate of food for him. And then she did something she had never done before: she took to her bed for a stomach problem, a woman's problem, or perhaps the flu. She had been vague but must have looked ghastly, because Wash had stayed away, telling her to sleep. Instead, she had tossed and turned and stared at the ceiling, while tears turned the pillow into a mash of dampness.

The next morning she had woken up feeling sour, cross, and deeply shaken. How much did a person have to bear? He had died, and now he was dying to her again.

The clarity and horror of the thought pulled her upright. Her vision went black for a split second, and she held her head and waited. *No!* She would not lose him twice. She would not.

Her vision had cleared, and she got up, carefully. She held her hand out to the wall for balance. Slowly she walked to her dresser and stood for a moment, looking in the mirror. She picked up her brush and started to brush her hair. Her scalp had reacted, feeling the scraping of the bristles. Her arm and shoulder extended and stretched purposefully, as she gripped the handle and tugged at the snarls.

Pulling and straightening, she had taken a deep breath and had begun to reach out to her son. I didn't know, Vaughn. I don't understand, but I love you so very much.

Her throat had caught, and she had taken another breath.

It had never entered her mind that he was... different in this way. She took another breath, deliberately, looking in the mirror.

Why would it? she asked herself. Vaughn had been very masculine with his broad shoulders, cigarettes, and the rough talk of news reporters. And he was a soldier, for heaven's sake.

Yes, there was that sense of distance he kept from her, and he had always had a way of insisting on his privacy, even as a child in the bath or as a young boy getting dressed. Perhaps that hadn't always been modesty, but something else about holding to himself.

The girlfriends? She stopped to think about that more carefully. There had been prom dates. All boys had something of an obligatory approach to prom. He had been cooperative, not deeply engaged. The Sadie Hawkins dances also stood out to her. They had been such nice girls but, of course, they had invited him each time. In hindsight, he had done little to instigate anything. She had assumed he was a late bloomer.

Wash had clearly left the house for work. She dressed and made breakfast. Later that day she took a deep breath and went back into his bedroom. She sat on the bed, closed the drawer with the letters, and stared hard at his bureau. Its heaviness gave her a point of grounding. Blankly, she stared at his razor and kit and a small pile of loose change. Next to them she noticed an odd thing--a colorful talisman of feathers tied together with bright string. Was it something he had made in Vacation Bible School years ago? She stared at it. She hadn't seen it before. It didn't seem possible that this beautiful bit of feathers and string had been here all this time, and that she hadn't seen it. Well, she had missed seeing many things, that was for sure.

She picked up the colorful bundle, twirled it in her fingers, and watched the feathers spin. Her son had received love letters from a man. She sat twirling the feathers for a very long time.

It had taken the rest of the week before she could exhibit a steady imitation of her former self. But that was for show. Inwardly, she continued to wander the streets of a foreign city. Every street corner was a decision, and every block presented new signs, doors, and windows. She was astonished about so much. How blind she had been! She had carried on life in one city with her Vaughn, and yet, he had lived in another. It must have been a very different life. What was that world like for him? She wondered endlessly.

She clung to the bits she knew. J.J., to begin with. He seemed to be a pleasant, nice boy, respectful and well-mannered. She looked deep into her heart and realized she was grateful that Vaughn had been in love. J.J. had been unobtrusive at the funeral. He had come all the way from Chicago. She had assumed soldiers developed intense loyalty; his presence to mourn Vaughn had seemed appropriate at the time. The two of them, he explained, hadn't worked together, but had been good friends almost from the first days of his posting to Korea. She hadn't known the depth of his feelings. Of course she hadn't. She had easily accepted that explanation. The extent of her obliviousness was amazing to her.

Again and again, she returned to her mirror. Would people see that she was changing? Did she look different? Her whole world had changed twice in just a month. Surely, it must show.

She examined the lines around her wide set eyes, the few gray hairs in her brown hair. She was still the same person, a middle-aged housewife with a husband, but also with a dead homosexual son. What a thing to say! But it was the truth.

And, it *explained* everything. It explained Vaughn. Her puzzle over the distance between her son and herself was solved. She wondered if he had stared at himself this way in this mirror. She loved him more than ever.

And her loss was doubly bitter. She had lost a son before she had known him. The hurt went in twice as deep. Perhaps she would never have known him. He wouldn't have told her. That wasn't something people talked about, and most probably considered it quite sinful. But she couldn't find it in her to label her son sinful. He was exactly who God made him to be. And in her silly blindness she would have looked everywhere but right in his eyes and into God's handiwork. It was only in his death that he was brought fully to life for her.

And now, sitting next to Wash on the couch, she believed that Wash should know, too. Or perhaps she hadn't fully made that decision, but her words kept coming anyway. "He did love someone. The letters in his room were love letters," she said quietly. "I didn't read them beyond the first page that was lying open. But they are love letters – from J.J."

Wash looked at her with a completely blank stare. "From J.J? Why would he send his love letters to Vaughn?"

"Because they were love letters that J.J. wrote to Vaughn. They were love letters – from J.J. to Vaughn. They loved each other. They were letters written on those blue overseas aerograms, and he wrote from Chicago to Vaughn while Vaughn was still in Korea." Maybe Wash would understand if he could picture them in his mind. "They are written in black pen."

Wash's eyes started to lock, as if he was trying to hold the frame of a picture, and it kept melting or vaporizing. His back was bolt straight again. His mug started to jitter. "No, Gracie. That's not possible. How could that be? This J.J. might have written them, but Vaughn wasn't like that."

"No, Wash," she had needed to say. "He wouldn't have kept them so carefully if that were so. They wouldn't have had affectionate nicknames for each other. They talked about loving each other in the letters."

"What kind of nicknames? No, I don't want to know." Wash put down his mug. The tea surged up the sides but didn't splash over.

"Oh, Wash," she continued. "It makes sense. You know how he was so private. Remember, he didn't want to go to the prom. We said he was shy, but he wasn't shy. The truth was, he didn't have a taste for women. Or maybe he did, but he had more taste for something else." She was saying much too much.

Wash shivered. He put a quieting hand on her knee and held it there for a long moment. Then he slowly rose and stiffly walked over to the dining room table. Like a curator, he stacked the letters Vaughn had written home and put them back into the shoebox for storage. Tucking the box under his arm, he started for the stairs. "I love you, Gracie. I love you very very much." He held out his hand to her. "Let's go to bed now." It was a quiet invitation. Doors were closing and opening. She clasped his hand and followed quietly and gently. That was the first and last they ever spoke of it.

The following Saturday morning he was up before dawn. She found him in the basement, working at his hobby stand. His business was in a small building off 15th Street, but he also made decorative signs at home as a hobby. He embellished numbers for their house and beautiful nameplates for her garden. The church session periodically asked him to make memorial plaques. Each was exquisite with touches of metal, carefully carved wood, and glints of varnish.

He was working on a new one. He had stenciled letters on a board. "What are you doing?" she had asked automatically, as if to ask about the weather. But she could tell immediately what he was doing.

"I'm making a plaque for Vaughn."

That was enough. She knew he would carve and carve, and then sand, shellac, glue, and paint. He was fully occupied.

She kissed him lightly on the top of his head. "I'll not bother you, then." She took a few steps towards the stairs and then looked back. "Except, do you want some coffee?" She could feel his craving to work undisturbed, to use his hands, and to create.

"No, Gracie. I'm fine."

She left him in the basement. He worked all that day and more. She heard the saw, smelled the varnish.

Finally, one evening he brought his finished project to the dinner table. It was beautiful. The wood was silky, so smooth it could have been suspended nectar. *My son, my son.* The words melted into the edging of curves and twists.

The plaque occupied the place at the table that was Vaughn's.

"It's the most beautiful thing you have ever made."

"I'm going to hang it at the church, Gracie," was his only response. She didn't ask questions. He left that evening and was gone for about two hours. When he returned, he took a long shower and went to bed.

She never spotted the plaque in the church. She often wondered where it was but never asked. She imagined the plaque tucked under a pew, acting like a silent prayer from her husband directly to his God. Or perhaps it was behind a pipe, feeling and responding to the resonance of the great organ. Wash went to his grave without telling her where it was.

Their life had gone on. Grace continued to mourn in her own ways. She longed for her son, to have him growing further in maturity, doing good work, and opening up the world for them. She regretted the lack of grandchildren, but had to catch herself on that thought. There would have been no grandchildren even if he had not died.

Vaughn's birthdays were markers of their sadness. It also marked the ways they mourned differently. Wash reminisced about Vaughn the baby, the boy, and the teenager, the person who had lived with them.

Grace was left to remember the rest of him, the part that hadn't lived with them, that had gone to Korea, and had seen some of the world. She, too, grieved the loss of the baby, boy, and teenager, but she also grieved the loss of the man, the soldier, the faithful and special companion, the man who had begun to make his own way.

Grace had shared her grief in a small way with one other person--J.J. Having sent him the love letters, she had his address. She started by sending a Christmas card, just a greeting and holiday wishes. He sent her a card in response, and the pattern repeated annually. Wash hadn't noticed them in the pile of correspondence at Christmas, and she had not pointed it out. Occasionally J.J. added a sentence or two at the bottom. Two or three times he included an entire mimeographed Christmas letter, full of news. These letters gave her a glimpse of his story--his maturing, his medical studies, and work. She saved all those cards and notes. They were precious to her, representing the one other person who had fully known her only son.

He must be in his early sixties now, the same age as Vaughn and Guy. Grace patted the paper on the arm of her wheelchair. She hoped he was healthy. She had lost Wash and Vaughn, her only family. Now, with Guy's death, another piece was gone. She was glad she had kept in touch with J.J. She would write him a longer note this year. She pictured the box of his cards, which she kept on the shelf in the spare bedroom. She wished she were at home and able to pull them out and reread them all. She sighed.

An aide appeared at her side. Yes, she had been sitting too long in the borrowed alcove. Her knee would seize up if she didn't move. She gripped the arms of the chair and leaned forward, knowing that she had to move through the pain in her bones in order to relieve it. "Good work," the aide said approvingly. "The more you can walk, the faster you'll heal."

Once she was standing, Grace took a deep breath and started down the hall to her room.

CHAPTER 9

Sitting deep in the leather couch in Brent Sykes' living room, Cord McDaniel was not sure he was exactly comfortable. It was all quite formal and a little masculine. The brass shone, and the rugs were deep. The orderly woven fleur-de-lis marched into the seams of the couch pillows. It was a muted and muffled environment which reminded him of a mortuary without the pastels. The crystal tumbler with iced tea was very heavy. Cord had banged it against his front teeth on the first try.

The two men were working out Guy's funeral arrangements. Brent was on familiar territory. It was to be a closed coffin affair.

"I don't know why I assumed that," said Cord.

"You assumed correctly. Dad was clear about it to me often enough. He didn't want his own funeral to be an advertisement for the business."

"But he did want a funeral, not a memorial service?"

"Oh, yes. Just a closed coffin."

The doorbell interrupted them. When Brent answered it, Mavis Hofmeister rolled in, breathless. Cord hoisted himself up from the couch. Mavis had cooked up a storm, and she bustled down the hallway towards the kitchen with her load. Both men put down their glasses, the universal signal that they were willing to help but didn't have a clue what to do. They trailed along behind.

Mavis explained the extra jars of sauces and then re-claimed the insulated carry-alls that had cushioned the casseroles. "No," she waved off an implicit invitation. "I can't stay." She addressed Cord, "Reverend, let me know the music choices when you have them nailed. Just call the house, and leave a message if I'm not there. I'm sure Guy had some favorites."

She gave Brent a hug as generous as her casseroles, grasped his arms, and leaned back to look directly at him. "Your father loved you a great deal."

And she was out the door.

Brent peeked under some of the foil and then said with resignation, "Looks like broccoli." It was the one thing he hated.

"Ah," said Cord. "And I thought politicians could eat anything. Ministers sure have to."

They exchanged ritual grimaces and returned to their seats.

"Tell me a bit," said Cord, "about Guy's earlier years. It helps me frame my comments in the eulogy. I know he took over the business when he was fairly young."

"Yes, he started working right out of high school. And he married Mom. They were very young. She might have been 17. I'll have to think about the dates. I came along pretty fast after that.

"But Dad never seemed to have other ambitions to travel or do something else. He assumed they would have a big family, and then he could hand the business down to his sons. I think he got into politics to fill the time when Mom died. I don't think he ever looked at another woman. I think his loneliness was also a motivation behind his work with the church kids. They were filling a place in his life."

"You've carried some extra responsibility, then," commented Cord. "Being an only child, I mean. Filling some big shoes."

"I guess so. I was all he had. I was young when she died, so he had to raise me single-handedly. He was all I had, too. I left only to go to college. After that, I moved back home and lived with him until I was 30. I think about that sometimes. Why didn't I get this place sooner?"

For a second, Cord saw Brent sitting in his chair as if he were just a kid, his hair carefully combed, his tie tight, his suspenders taut, and his expression puzzled.

"Dad believed that I should follow in his footsteps. I never wanted to disappoint him. And the business was a solid one. So I didn't have a good reason to object."

Brent continued, describing his father's time as mayor. Cord watched him carefully. After years of knowing Guy, the hospital bedside confession had come as a surprise. It had added a new dimension. He was trying to fold it in with his impressions and knowledge of the father and son. No, he didn't think Brent had a clue that his father was carrying a lifelong woe. But something was in the air.

"…I bought into his enthusiasm. He expected me to do that, and it wasn't hard. When I ran for office, he was absolutely ecstatic. He was all over town talking about His Boy Brent."

Cord noted the language. Why not His *Son* Brent? He could imagine that Guy had been something of a larger-than-life father.

Brent had paused for a moment with his memories. "He was delighted to campaign. He loved it. You can mention that in your eulogy. He couldn't get enough of barbeque and community picnics."

"Maybe I will," responded Cord with the appropriate chuckle.

Brent was on a roll. "Yes, he was the guy for everyone, the guy who cared, the good guy. I thought his name said it all: Guy!"

Cord raised an eyebrow as if to start a question, but Brent continued without noticing.

"He banked a lot on his reputation as a mortician. It was more than a family business or a profession – more like a calling." He pretended to tip a hat to Cord. "You know the drill: you have to be available all the time. No telling when a call will come in. No long vacations. Steady Eddie. Ready with the right word at the right moment. Always there."

Brent rubbed his thighs, as if ironing out the crease in his pants. "He was grounded in the idea that you had to be there for everyone. Not just at a funeral, but in their lives, too. It wasn't a business thing, although I suppose it helped.

"He talked about integrity. I imagine he talked about it with the church kids, too. He had a code. Everything was about trust--you could lose it in a split second, and it would take years to rebuild. He took the long view. He particularly insisted that to be a good mortician, the most important thing was to be meticulous and proper. It closed the loop of trust."

Cord was discomfited by people's talk about integrity and honesty. "Let me be perfectly honest," was a tag line that always set him wondering whether the person was otherwise dishonest. Guy had led an upright life in his son's eyes. But was the harping on integrity about values, or about values eroded? He thought again about the bedside conversation.

Setting that aside, Cord trusted the bereavement process; he knew that Brent was at the beginning of reworking his world to fit losing his father. You can't sleep fast, he thought, and, you can't mourn fast. Whatever was and would go on for Brent as he buried his father would be deeply individual and personal.

For now, Brent was concluding his thoughts, so Cord pulled out of his brief reverie. "Guy led quite a life. He and I worked closely together on any number of funerals and, of course, with regard to the kids. I saw his care and perfectionism up close."

"Thanks. I think about everything he did, and it seems to me that the church kids meant the most to him."

"And I have plenty of stories about them for the eulogy." Cord knew many tales, some that had become oft told church lore.

"He always put them up first. There were camping trips, mission trips, weekly meetings, and tours of the mortuary, don't forget. He was with those kids through all kinds of things, and then he tracked them when they graduated and went on to college or a job." Brent waved a hand towards a bookshelf of crystal and art books. "He must have two dozen albums in his living room, plus all the scrapbooks stuffed with wedding invitations and baby announcements. Everything about them was special. And I expect that many of them will be at the funeral, saying their goodbyes. He touched many people."

"Listen, Brent," Cord suddenly had to say. "If I have one wish right now, it is that you will find – or use – the funeral to say goodbye to your father in your own way. You know funerals, and you know the details, and you know the protocols. It's going to be a big event. There will be many people there. But, make it work for you. It's about you saying goodbye to your father."

Brent raised a hand in acknowledgment, but also a signal of assurance. "Thanks. I know it will all be done well. That would have pleased Dad. And that's right by me, too."

That's not entirely what I was saying, thought Cord. "Listen to Mavis," Cord stood as he prepared to leave. "Guy loved you very much."

Brent stood at the picture window fingering the change in his pocket as he watched Cord drive off. Pastors were a peculiar item. They had all sorts of prerogative to cross the line between public and personal. They could intrude on matters that were meant to be kept under wraps. You were supposed to peel things back with them.

Brent liked Cord. He thought he was a good pastor. He was a sincere guy doing his job, and he didn't do things in a formulaic way. But Brent had done this funeral thing before, hundreds of times. How many families had he worked with at precisely this juncture, planning a funeral for someone they had lost? He'd been the one asking the questions. What were the deceased's activities? What was he like? What were her wishes?

He knew the answers. He knew his father. He had watched him, followed him, and imitated him. He would do just as his father would have wanted. The funeral would be exquisitely executed. People would be able to say good-bye properly. It would all be fine.

Brent shifted his feet and leaned forward until his forehead pressed on the windowpane. It was cool and hard.

*** *** ***

Kyle, Victor, and Tiffany had agreed to wait for each other on the church steps. Only Kyle had been to a funeral before, and he led the way in, accepting a bulletin from the usher and waving them into a pew. The room was filling up as the organ played quietly. People were sitting very still. No one was talking or even whispering, and the boys looked at each other uncertainly. I guess all we do is sit, thought Victor.

The coffin down front was swamped with flowers. You could hardly tell what it was made of, although the bit he could see reminded Victor of his father's car: silver finish.

It was hard to imagine that Mr. Sykes was inside that coffin. He was probably dressed in a suit. Was there all that white satin material around him? Did he have shoes on? They couldn't quite picture it.

The door on the lectern side opened. Rev. McDaniel entered with Mr. Sykes and ushered him into the first pew. He was alone. Tiffany looked stricken and mouthed to the boys, "No family?"

The pipe organ urged everyone to stand for the hymn. The room was now packed, and the singing was full. Both boys mumbled the words, but Tiffany had a clear voice and loved to sing. She poured her heart out for Mr. Sykes. *"Now the day is over."*

At one point, Rev. McDaniel looked directly at them during his homily. "He loved you young people, and he would want you to grab life and live it fully. Grow and flourish. Take care of each other, and you will honor and remember him well."

Brent shifted in the pew. Cord was right. Guy did want the kids to grow and flourish. He wanted me to grow and flourish, too. And I have. "Dad, I have," he argued internally. "I've done what you wanted me to do."

Why was he arguing? He never argued with his father. Why would he be arguing with him at his funeral?

After Cord finished speaking, he stage-managed a stream of earnest speakers to the lectern. Each spoke from the heart, remembering Guy's generous soul. He had been a mountain of a man, a true Christian, an uncle to all... the personification of service to his community... a steady beacon of good. Returning to their seats, each speaker patted Brent on the shoulder or offered him perfumed whispers.

Brent tried to breathe. The fragrance of the flowers clogged the air.

His father had been a valued member of the community. He knew that. Everyone appreciated that. They all had a connection to him, and this was what funerals were about: people had to say their good-byes.

But there were so many of them, so many people saying the same thing.

He wanted to be alone. He didn't want them here. He didn't want to hear stories about his father--endless stories.

Mavis stepped down from the lectern and paused to hug him. He had to stop himself from flinching. What was wrong with him? She was simply being kind. He shifted in his seat, crossing and recrossing his legs, wishing for all the world that he could stretch or run. His body felt completely stiff.

Finally, Cord brought the service to a close. "Guy Sykes, we, your friends and family, remember your spirit, and with our hearts and love we commend you to God."

Solemnly, the congregation rose to sing the final hymn. Cord remained standing over the coffin, singing as if a cantor. He nodded for Brent to follow the coffin as it was taken down the aisle. The coffin's silver sheen sparkled as it passed from the dark, cool foyer into the sunlight. The carillon tolled.

Victor, Kyle, and Tiffany had slipped out of the church ahead of the congregation. They stood on the sidewalk and watched quietly as Mr. Sykes accompanied the casket to the curb. The pallbearers loaded it smoothly and closed the massive curtained doors of the hearse.

Brent felt the crowd pressing out of the door. Turning, he saw the three kids. "Would you stand with me?" he asked suddenly. He wanted a buffer.

"Sure," said Kyle automatically. "What do we do?"

"Just shake hands, and tell them about being in Dad's youth group."

They lined up next to him. Brent moved people along, saying, "Tell the kids, too. They are going to miss him."

Cord waited by the hearse. Eventually they would drive to the cemetery for the burial. But, for now, he could almost imagine it was Guy, not Brent, greeting people and flanked by Victor, Tiffany, and Kyle. Oh, my, he said to himself. He is his father's son.

He remembered the flash image of the taut suspenders. Yes, his father's dutiful son.

CHAPTER 10

The school year was underway. Posters papered every corner of wall space in the high school administration offices. Victor studied them as he waited to meet with the counselor. College banners were everywhere. A bright *Uncle-Sam-Wants-You* recruiting poster covered one office door. Posted on the health board were two large warnings about AIDS. Victor tried not to appear to be reading them, but he gave them anxious glances. *Transmitted by blood and other bodily fluids.*

Duke Upton's door opened, and a student emerged. "Victor Beck," Duke read from the sign-up sheet hanging on his door. "Glad to meet you," he said, shaking Victor's hand. "I'm sorry you've got me today. Your regular counselor is on maternity leave, and I fill in part-time when a need like that arises."

There was little time for any further talk before the break between classes would be over. The two of them quickly sorted out Victor's scheduling problem. "That was easy," Duke said. "Drop by again, if you have any other trouble."

As Victor turned to go, he saw Tiffany talking to a man in army fatigues next to the Uncle Sam poster. He hadn't seen her since the mission trip. She looked different. Her hair had changed or something. "Hi, Victor," she called. "This is Sergeant Dimon who recruited my sister into the army. Oh, hi," she added as she recognized Duke. "You always had pie in the morning at Nell's Diner last summer."

Duke grimaced, while Sergeant Dimon chuckled and shook hands with both Victor and Duke. "We haven't met yet either. Rusty Dimon. I handle the military recruiting for this area."

"Duke Upton. Temporary fill-in, substitute, and catchall person."

Tiffany continued chattering as the warning bell for fourth period rang. She and Victor hustled out into the hallway with a quick goodbye. "When

Sergeant Dimon came by our house to talk with Lydia, we all got to know him. I had forgotten about him until my boyfriend mentioned him."

"Your boyfriend?" Victor was surprised.

"Uh-huh. His name is Mike, and he's in ROTC and is thinking about joining up when he graduates. He's a junior," she bubbled happily.

Victor was surprised. Tiffany had always been a flirt. But he couldn't imagine that she would have an older boyfriend. When had she met him? It was only the second week of school. She was just a freshman like him.

"Wow," he said and then felt dumb.

"I met him this summer, waiting tables at the diner." She giggled and sped off to her class, waving her fingers at him, her ponytail bouncing. He gazed after her, noticing the flash of the green nail polish and the lingering fragrance of her sweet perfume. She was still the silly girl he had always known, but she had added some sort of drive or determination. She knew what she wanted.

High school was changing things. He'd already noticed that the summer had changed Kyle. He was practically pre-professional about his gymnastics. He was obsessed and competitive. That gymnastics camp had lit a fire under him. He even had a calendar where he wrote out the food he ate and how many hours he slept.

And now Tiffany was suddenly all grown up, talking to the army recruiter like an old friend, and probably getting ready to go to the prom. Victor felt as if he had missed something, some signal or gate or brochure of new rules.

The second bell rang as he took his seat in Spanish class. The teacher explained that she wanted them to sit in a circle every other session so that they could feel more conversational. Bridget was across from him, her feet crossed at the ankles, looking all set to participate. He could already tell that she was good with Spanish, while he fumbled a lot. Spanish words had a lot of syllables, and you had to practice their rhythm and the accent to get them right. But, he didn't want to do that in front of the circle of kids. How did she do it? Didn't she worry about what people were thinking about her?

It made him tired. It was exhausting to worry all the time about what everyone else was noticing. He had expected high school to be a bigger place, with more people, so he could be anonymous. But that wasn't quite the way it was working out. With many more kids around, everyone tried to stand out more. Kids dressed distinctively. You could tell from t-shirts if someone were on a sports team or in the band. Or they had stickers all over their backpacks. You could spot the people in the theater group, too, because they wore unusual clothes with scarves or bright shoes, that sort of thing. If you didn't belong to a group or show school spirit or something, you were weird. Victor felt out of step, and he really really really did not want to be considered weird.

His big thing had always been photography. So should he hang his camera equipment around his neck all the time, or tape his photographs all over his locker? He didn't think so. And photography didn't fit any group except for the yearbook club. He'd gone to the organizing meeting, but there were juniors and seniors who seemed to know about everything and ran the show. He could do random shots of school life, but that wouldn't add up to much. Maybe he would have to wear his summer soccer t-shirt. As if his mother would let him!

Victor slid down a bit in his seat. It was all a little lonely. Looking across the circle at Bridget, he thought again about his idea that maybe he could – or should -- hook up with her somehow.

The teacher handed a ball to a student. "Ask a question, and throw the ball to someone. *Gently!* That person should answer the question, and then toss it to someone to come up with the next question." Victor almost ducked as the ball came in his direction.

*** *** ***

After school a week later, Kyle and Victor walked out of Nell's Diner with their ice cream cones and picked a spot on the curb. They could hear the drums in the distance as the high school band came around the corner leading off the homecoming parade. The shopkeepers and customers who were crowding the sidewalk started to clap and cheer. The boys recognized Brent Sykes, who rode with the principal in a convertible right behind decorated cars with the Homecoming Court.

They hadn't noticed that Tiffany had slipped in beside them. Suddenly she was jumping up and down with excitement. "I think the ROTC is after the class floats," she said.

The boys looked at each other, wondering why it mattered.

"There they are!" Tiffany shrieked and blew a wolf whistle.

"When did she learn to do that?" Kyle asked Victor. "And what is the big deal?" he asked Tiffany.

"Mike's marching."

"I think that's her new boyfriend," said Victor to Kyle.

"He's right there in the middle of the third row. He's easy to see." She waved as the unit, looking very serious and carrying flags and rifles, marched three abreast down the street.

Kyle pointed him out. "I think I've seen him around."

Victor gulped inside. Mike was one of those thunderous upperclassmen, very big and all muscle. Victor recognized him because his locker was outside history class. One day as Victor was leaving class, Mike had slammed his locker shut, turned, and bumped into Victor. "Sorry," he had said and then wrapped his arms around two guys and headed down the hall talking loudly about getting them onto the wrestling team.

Wrestling. Victor had never entertained it as a sports option. It scared him to think about how people would associate him physically tangled up with another boy. All he wanted to do in sports was run and run. If people were going to watch him, he wanted to be free and on the move.

Nevertheless, his eyes lingered on the three, and he toyed with the idea of going to see a match. That would be so great to watch.

"So that's the man, huh?" Kyle turned to Tiffany. "You know that Victor and I need to approve."

"Don't tease me," she responded cheerfully.

"Who is teasing?" Kyle looked to Victor. "Are you?"

"Nope," said Victor.

"Seriously, Tiff. Are you really going out with this guy? He's a lot older than you. He's big."

"Yes, I am," said Tiffany as another wave of applause sounded for the football team float.

"You're sure? He is carrying a gun, or didn't you notice? You're really sure?"

"*Yes*, Mr. Kyle-my-big-brother-that-I-didn't-know-I-had."

"Well, okay. I guess it's your life. But be careful. Uncle Kyle and Uncle Victor are worried. Don't be going off drinking beer or doing anything risky."

Tiffany snorted. "Don't be stupid. My sister's already told me a million times to be careful. And. It's. Not. Like. That. At. All."

"I believe you," said Kyle seriously. "I think. But they teach us all that stuff about drunk driving and MADD and No Drugs and AIDs for a reason."

What was Kyle talking about, thought Victor. Tiffany was silly, but she wasn't dumb. And she was only a freshman girl. She wasn't going to be doing anything. Unless that guy, Mike, wasn't respectful.

The noise of the crowd around him continued. The antique cars, some of which were the old styled wheezing types, were driving by and honking their horns.

Victor looked at Tiffany as she smiled, pointed, laughed, and waived her lacquered nails. He could imagine a guy finding it easy to encourage her. He wondered if he would be easy to encourage. What if some older guy decided to make moves on him? Victor's insides flip-flopped. That would be so amazing, scary, and out of bounds. There was no way it would happen. It would shock people, he was sure. And then there were all those things like AIDs that made it a dangerous idea. People died from AIDs.

He had finished his ice cream cone, and he was thirsty. "I'm going to find a drink," he said. "Does anyone want anything?" No one responded, so he slipped away from the crush of people to be by himself.

*** *** ***

It had threatened rain all day, but it was still dry outside. Bridget's bus had pulled up in the third slot. Kids were pushing their way along the crowded sidewalk, as everyone rushed to get in the right line. Tiffany was already on board and waved at Bridget through the window. The two girls shared a bus route, guaranteeing them time at the beginning and end of every day to talk and catch up.

As she walked down the aisle and slid into the seat, Bridget could tell something was wrong. Tiffany's eyes were red. "You okay?" she asked.

"Yeah." Tiffany pulled out a little makeup mirror from a pocket in her backpack. She stared into it. "Well, I guess you can tell. I'm not good at hiding some things."

Bridget nodded. Tiffany wore her emotions on her sleeve.

"Well, what is it?"

"Oh, it's hard to explain."

Bridget waited.

"It was in English class. We were talking about *Red Badge of Courage*-- it's about the Civil War."

"Yeah. I started reading it last night."

"I guess it's about how the guy is a coward and runs away and then comes back to his unit. It makes me think about my sister and whether she'll ever be in any fighting."

"I don't think women are allowed to fight, are they?"

"Oh yeah, they are. Well, maybe not fighting, but things are changing, and women are doing just about everything except shooting the guns. My mom is getting nervous about what's happening in the Middle East. You know, the President called up some Reservists last month." Tiffany watched TV news every night.

"She'll be fine," said Bridget automatically. She would have to ask her mother what she knew about all that.

"Yeah, I know. I keep telling that to myself. I mean, Ft. Riley is in Kansas, and that can't be dangerous. But I can't help it. It makes me so scared." Tears started to roll down her cheeks.

"She's always been bossy and stuff like that. But, that doesn't mean I don't really miss her now. And when my mom gets worried, I really feel it." She hiccupped a sob. The kid in the seat in front of them turned around to look.

Bridget was swift. "Mind your own business!" she hissed at him.

"Sorry," he said. "Just looking."

"Well, don't."

Bridget put her arm around Tiffany and rummaged in her own pockets for a tissue. "It's good to cry," she whispered. "You can't hold that kind of thing inside."

"I know. But it's important to be brave and not to let soldiers know how worried you are. My mom tells me that Lydia and I never acted like we cared that much about each other when she was home." Tiffany gave a weak smile. "But it's also about Mike. He's already talking about the army, too. If you join up, there are some good benefits. Even college tuition. But people can get hurt really bad or even killed." She wiped at her tears. "Lydia never thought there could ever be a war when she joined up. She just wanted to get ahead, that's all."

Bridget was well aware that Tiffany's family didn't have much money. Their house was small, and all three sisters had shared a bedroom. Now it was just the two sisters, but it was crowded. Her mom worked an extra job on weekends.

"There's not going to be a war!" Bridget couldn't imagine the country going to war. There hadn't been any real war since, like, Vietnam, and that was sometime in the 60's when her parents were kids.

Tiffany's makeup was streaking down her cheeks. "I must be a mess," she gulped. "I just fixed my mascara in the bathroom after crying in class. The teacher let me take a break."

Bridget didn't wear make-up except for lip gloss, which was just as well.

"Shall I get off at your stop with you?" she asked. "Or do you want to come to my house? Maybe we could bake cookies or something to pack and send to your sister?"

"No, I'll be okay. My mom's expecting me home to babysit 'cause she's got a night shift schedule this week."

They rode together in silence. A girl across the aisle caught Bridget's eye and held out a full packet of tissues. Bridget mouthed, "It's okay," and smiled weakly. The girl nodded.

When Tiffany got off at her stop, Bridget waved and sat back. There were all kinds of people in the world with troubles. But that didn't mean they had to be alone with their troubles. When her dad was sick and dying, her mom made it a point that they all be together. "You don't have to cry alone," she had said.

And it was important not to hide your troubles. If you did, they would get bigger and bigger. You had to let them out.

She wished she had said that to Tiffany. She would make a point of it later. It was stupid to say things like *Don't worry. It won't happen.* Because things did happen. She knew that. And besides, what did she know about the world? If her father could die of cancer, no telling what other awful things could happen. War, for sure.

No, don't hide it. That's what best friends are for.

Bridget got off at her stop and walked to the house. Alexandra was in the front yard with a measuring tape, walking off distances.

"What are you doing?" asked Bridget.

"Oh, hi. You know how Mom says that maybe we could get a dog? We've got to keep reminding her about that. Well, I'm trying to figure out how much fence we would have to put up so it could run around outside."

"It could run around in the back yard."

"Yeah, but if it runs around in the front, people will see it, and robbers won't choose our house to break into."

"Robbers aren't going to break into our house."

"Better to be safe than sorry." Alexandra was firm.

Bridget knew better than to argue. Alexandra loved fantasy literature and tried to insert adventure into their lives all the time. Wasn't it enough that their father had died, they had moved, and Mom was working her tail off? Bridget wondered at times what planet Alexandra lived on. But, then, she was still a kid. And she could still live in make-believe.

Bridget went into the house and put down her backpack. It was okay to have a little make-believe, like about hoping that Victor would take her to the movies or something. The newspaper was sitting on the coffee table. She picked it up. Yeah, some make-believe in your life was fine, but she should be smarter about things in the news. Those stories weren't make-believe stories, and she shouldn't be so stupid about stuff that could affect her best friend. She made a piece of toast and curled up in a chair to read the headlines.

CHAPTER 11

Grace Evanston replaced the bone china cup on its saucer. They scraped together with a slightly brittle kiss. She pushed back on her chair, grateful for its rollers, but wary about staying within reach of the table. She braced herself as she stood. Erect, she cleared her breakfast dishes, happy to be back in her own home and her own kitchen. The yellow background and gilt edge of the plates were additional sunshine for this bright September day. It was her best china. When she had turned 80, she had decided to use it every day. No time like the present, and its translucent fragility gave her comfort and pleasure.

It was quiet in the house. No aides or nurses erupted in laughter down the hall or knocked on the door to check in. Grace turned on the radio to the university's classical station. The announcer's silky voice slid into the room without disturbing the calm.

Grace returned to the table and opened her book of daily devotional readings. She had been home for a few weeks, but she still gave thanks for her return to her beloved home. "Dear God, how long will You allow me to take care of myself?" She hesitated with the question, not wanting to draw down the wonderful bank account of spirit that had returned her to her china and Wash's artistic touches. The surgery and recovery had been hard, the toll one paid to live a long life. Could she face whatever came next? She hoped so. "Be with me."

But there was work to do. She read the day's Bible verses, carefully repositioned the ribbon bookmark, and drew out the list of names from Cord McDaniel. With a pen and a sheet from her box of creamy linen stationery, she started the first letter.

Dear Evan and Doris,
At the All Saints' Day service we remember those whom we have lost this year. The

children make banners in their memories and process with them in the service.

Could you share some details about Colleen, her life, and her interests, which the children can portray on the banner? Send us a note, or call the church office.

We all miss Colleen tremendously and trust that this service will celebrate her memory and remind us all of her faith and spirit.

Yours in Christ,

Grace Evanston

She addressed the letter and moved to the next name.

Grace had helped create the All Saints' Day service in the year after Vaughn's death. It had been her way of expressing her own loss. The service's simple juxtaposition of children's creativity and parishioners' mourning was beautiful and moving, and had become a fixture on the church calendar.

The last name on the list was unfamiliar to her. Sam Wallace, husband to June, father to Bridget and Alexandra. Cord had explained they were a new family joining the church. Grace hadn't met them yet. What a tragedy to lose a father and husband!

Sealing that envelope, she was grateful to be able to prepare again for All Saints' Day. She stamped the letters and slowly walked out to her mailbox. The oak tree had loosened its hold on a few leaves, which blew across the path. The sun was steady and immediate. She took each step carefully, exhilarated to be outside on her own.

"Thank you," Grace whispered to herself and to her God. "Thank you for granting me another season."

*** *** ***

Cord was still at the kitchen table working through a second cup of coffee and silently cursing himself. He had tried to change his daily routine by bicycling to work. The plan worked sporadically.

On days like today, when he mechanically filled his cup a second time, he knew that the splash of black water signaled that he was lost. A second cup was a little luxury, and simultaneously, the hole in the dike. If he let up on his iron discipline for just one indulgence, it was over. For the rest of the day he would argue with himself to avoid the donuts, cut the mayonnaise, and be brisk in his movements. And it wouldn't work. Yes, it was one day at a time for dieters as well as alcoholics.

His wife walked in with the folder of bills. "Honey, I'm ordering wrapping paper for the school fundraiser, and the checkbook looks low."

"Don't worry. I wrote the checks for the car insurance and credit card. I did it last night in some crazed fit of efficiency," he smiled at her, "which has since evaporated."

She looked at him and through him. "You know, dieting and exercising are about health and not about punishing yourself. Hang the Presbyterianism occasionally!"

He knew she was both right and had the right attitude. Why couldn't he turn off the nagging machine in his head?

She bent over the counter, filling out forms and writing a check. "I didn't get this done before the kids left, so they'll have to take it in tomorrow." She frowned. "But the balance looks low even for us." She flipped back a few pages of the register.

"It's been creeping downwards for a couple of months," he said. "It's a bunch of things: more fuel costs last winter, the computer, the piano lessons, The Splurge…." They had taken a weekend escape to Chicago for their 20th wedding anniversary.

She swept up the papers and sat down next to him. "I know you want to go to work. But should we talk about all this?"

"Yes, I want to go to work," he lied, "and, yes, we should talk about all this."

"Should I worry about money more? Should we start thinking about me working full time?"

"I think we are okay. With the 175th anniversary, I'm hoping for a boost in financial pledges. It would allow the Session to recommend a salary increase. They've been hoping to do that for two years."

"Well, you deserve every penny they pay you," she said loyally.

"I don't know, honey." He stared into his coffee cup.

She was long familiar with his bleak side. "You are the life of the congregation, Cord. People respond to you. The church is lively and healthy. It's great."

"I suppose so, but I feel like the maintenance guy. It is so predictable. You know… today, it's the budget and the confirmation class enrollment and a million other details. It's the same cycle every year, over and over. I chunk out sermons and I meet with committees." He oared his head in a figure eight as if to stretch out his neck. "You're supposed to think of cycles like mantras that can give you spiritual value. But my cycles do the opposite: I lose my faith."

She reached for his hand and squeezed it.

"It's the hamster joke: the wheels are turning, but the hamster died a long time ago. I shouldn't feel this way, but I do," he tried to smile.

Personally, she thought it was his internal pain and doubts that equipped him to be a better, more authentic preacher. But it was a tough job, and you had to love it to do it.

"I didn't mean to get you depressed talking about money," she responded. "The important thing is to be healthy and hug the kids."

"I'm not worried about money. It's more about the grindstone." He drank from his mug. "Where's the purpose and the soul?"

He stared into his mug. As she stuffed the check into the envelope, a twinkle formed in her eye. "Well, it might not be a money problem, but I am thinking about going to work full time. We've always known I would sooner or later. There are only two real problems with it." She paused and looked at him sideways. "Who would drive the kids around for their afternoon activities? And when would we have sex? I know it is routine and *predictable,* but our private time is between their catching the bus and you leaving for work. That would be out the window if I had to race off to work, too."

Cord gave her a weak smile.

"So, you've upset your vows about dieting by drinking all that coffee. Let's remember some other ones." She leaned over and started to unbutton his shirt while she gave him a long, deep, and unexpected kiss.

*** *** ***

The sign in front of his office shook slightly in the mild breeze. It was beautifully carved wood with embedded metal letters: *The Office of the Mayor.* It sparkled in the sunlight. Standing on the sidewalk, Brent Sykes could see an entire block of glinting chains and similar signs in front of businesses and offices. Wash Evanston's artistry had been carefully maintained over the years all along Main Street.

Brent opened the door, said hello to the secretary who worked full time for the city, hung his jacket on the coat rack, and started to shuffle through his in-box. He didn't get far before his personal lawyer, Arnie Gulp, knocked on the door and stepped in. Arnie's office was next door, so meeting him in this office was more convenient than the mortuary office. "Windy day," he commented as he removed his hat and smoothed his elaborate waved comb-over back into place.

"Thanks for coming here," responded Brent. He had long lost his secret hilarity at both Arnie's name and his hair. Soberly, they shook hands and settled down in the conference room. It was time to read Guy's will.

Arnie pulled out the documents and systematically passed them to Brent to read. They mutually nodded through the directions about the funeral home, its incorporation details, the bank accounts, and a sizeable gift to the church for youth ministry and the Cemetery Association. The will had two codicils. Turning another page, Brent muttered steadily through the paragraphs.

"…and sell the house, the lake house, and the apartment properties. The proceeds are to be given to Grace Evanston." Brent's chest voice helped him through the moment. He lingered over the word, *proceeds*, to give himself some time. Moving his pencil down the paper, he tapped off the next lines, but everything he was reading had turned to gibberish.

Grace Evanston! What was her name doing sitting here on this page? And this was a large part of the estate. It would be a great deal of money. The apartments had been successful investment properties. What claim did Grace have on that money? What claim did she have on his father? Brent's mind was in a whirl.

He stopped and got up to fill their coffee cups. Adding the sugar, he over-stirred with the spoon and splashed on the sideboard. He needed to take a minute to calm down. Grace was a sweet elderly widow, a bit saucy and wise. She had a creative husband. She lived a couple of streets over. What else? They went to the same church. What gave her a right to a chunk of the estate? What was going on?

Arnie accepted the coffee refill. "Yes, I was curious, but when we discussed it, Guy didn't offer an explanation. He indicated he had thought about this for a long time, and it was something he wanted to do."

The room wouldn't settle down. Dad! He wanted something to grab on to. What were you thinking?

"Oh, yeah," Brent lied quickly. "Dad had his reasons." He felt Arnie's eye on him. His own questions bumped into each other. Were they having an affair? That was appalling. How old was she? She had to be in her mid 80's. She was old enough to be Guy's mother! She actually was a mother to Dad's childhood friend. Was his name something like Val or Vern or Vaughn? That was it. He had died and, as a result, Grace had treated Guy a bit like a son. How did this compute?

His eyes darted to the top of the page. "Out of curiosity, what's the date on this?"

Arnie pointed to the signature and date. "This will has been in force since 1978. He drew up a new one when he had paid off the debts for," he checked some notes, "upgrading the mortuary and work on the lake house."

"That's about 12 years ago," Brent ran though dates in his mind. He had been living at home. Something had happened right under his nose.

"Sorry, Arnie. I was caught off guard. I thought Guy was giving it all to the church."

His second lie in as many minutes.

Arnie looked puzzled, "Well, you just read about the bequest to the church." He reached over to turn back to previous pages.

Brent scrambled. "I know. To youth ministry. I thought he had an idea about the endowment. I'm just a little confused." He would admit to that. His brain clicked into gear. "Wait, this is a codicil." He turned over the sheet.

"Yes," replied Arnie. "As I said, Guy had me draw it up to make one minor change. The original will handed the house and apartment proceeds to Grace and her husband, Washington. But he subsequently died. Guy made the adjustment in a codicil. He wasn't willing to pencil in the change and initial it. He wanted to spell it out. He was very careful about his paperwork."

Brent's eyes blinked. Grace and her husband. That made even less sense. A secret that three people had, not just two. Raw pride kept him going tightly through the rest of the session.

*** *** ***

Cord was bicycling to work after all, and it was a gorgeous day at that! It was a blue sky that only September can deliver. He had risen from his bed a second time today, and his heart had been walloping, thanks to the double dose of caffeine and his very gracious wife. Might as well keep his heartbeat up.

The traffic was picking up, so he signaled energetically. The stretch between their cul-de-sac and Main Street was a mix of commercial and residential. The auto shop had added neon signs: Tune-Up, Exhaust, Alignment, Brakes, Detailing. The garage bays each had a car, many up on the hydraulic lifts. It was a body shop. Hmmm. Could he use that in a sermon? People needed tune-ups just like cars.

He rounded the corner onto Main Street and spied Brent leaving his mayoral office across the street, going to get his morning coffee, he guessed. He waved and was surprised that Brent didn't catch his eye.

Cord's sheepish cheerfulness held up as he entered his office. Once inside he realized Spencer and Loretta Beck were waiting to see him. "I'm sorry," he said. "Have I kept you waiting?" Victor wasn't with them.

"Not a problem." Spencer was nervous. "We thought we would take a chance. We didn't have an appointment."

"Well, come in. By all means. Isn't it a gorgeous day? Here, take a seat on the couch." Cord knew he was being effusive. Their evident anxiety was sparking that in him.

They sat down on the couch and looked at each other before speaking. Spencer took the plunge. "Actually, we are here about Victor."

"Really? Is he all right?"

"With the Confirmation Class starting soon, we wanted to talk with you about choosing a sponsor for him." Loretta had found her voice. "We feel he's growing obstinate about church, and we'd like to find someone who will provide a powerful example and influence him."

"Ah," said Cord carefully.

Spencer tried to justify the concern. "He's growing distant, always buried in his hobby – you know, photography - or at a friend's house. He's pushing us away. Of course, I guess that's normal, but we want him to feel he can embrace the church as a second home, so to speak."

"We've tried so hard to be good examples," added Loretta.

"Let me interrupt you there," Cord said. "You have been terrific parents. You have given Victor great witness about your belief and faith." They were catching themselves in a web.

"But, when I was his age, my church was the center of my life. The youth group was everything to me. I don't see him having that kind of passion for his church." Loretta's voice was rising.

"Loretta," Cord said gently, "on the mission trip he was fully engaged. He worked hard, took on responsibilities, and was a very important part of the team. If that isn't passion for his church, I don't know what is."

"We couldn't get a word out of him about that trip."

Cord laughed. "Now, that's typical of any kid that age."

"So, as his minister, you think he's doing okay?" Spencer was sincerely asking.

Cord felt obliged to nod. "He's absolutely fine. A real delight. You should hear him defending his friends in some of the discussions we had about obligations to one's church."

"You see, Honey," Spencer turned to his wife, "Cord is confident in Victor. I don't think we need to worry so much." Cord often found Spencer a bit too quick to tie up the bows, but he couldn't blame him in this case.

Loretta sighed. "I'm not sure."

"We have to trust," said Cord. "We do what we can, and then God has to take over. Can you trust God?"

Loretta looked surprised. "This is a test of my faith?"

"Well," answered Cord, "I don't usually frame parenting advice that way, but yes, I guess I could. Children are crucibles. They are both gifts, and they are tests, given to us by God."

This seemed to unlock Loretta. "I never thought of Victor as a test of my faith. It has always been easy for me to be in love with Christ, and that rarely comes into question for me." She paused. "A crucible? That's the word you used? So the question is whether I love Christ enough that I can trust him with Victor?"

Heavens, thought Cord. She reveals her piety as easily as if she is cooking dinner or gassing up the car.

"Yes," Cord tried again. "And you are already powerful examples for Victor. He has the building blocks. He also has an entire lifetime to be a witness in his own right. That starts formally with confirmation. Let that process unfold."

Loretta was nonplussed, but after a little more conversation she and

Spencer allowed themselves to be ushered out and sent on their way.

I hope I gave them a new bone to gnaw, thought Cord a bit uncharitably. It irked him that they were taking something as uncomplicated and straightforward as their terrific son and creating a crisis. Why would they do that? Cord sensed that Loretta simply didn't want her son to grow up. Most parents felt that way at one time or another. Get a life.

On the other hand, Spencer was being his cautious, structured self, which Cord found easy to understand. He had responsibilities and the security of the family to think about. He wouldn't rock boats on a whim. Being careful could be appropriate, unless it was to placate fear about what life *could* be like. Cord understood that himself.

He stopped short. Yes, that's right. He understood that himself.

So, was this about the Becks or about himself? He whistled and took a turn around his office. Maybe he was hiding behind responsibilities, himself. His dreams about being a spiritual force for people did mean breaking out and taking risks.

Parishioners were their own miracle! They were *his* crucible. He was counseling the Becks, and they were a mirror right back at him. He sat down on the couch, clasped his elbows, and sat quietly for a spell.

*** *** ***

The house felt muted and dull. After mailing all her All Saints' Day notes, Grace Evanston had been sitting on the porch, enjoying the sounds of the birds, a wind chime, and the radio from a passing car. It was good to be back in the neighborhood. Returning inside, she opened a window. It slid easily. She leaned on the sill for another moment of savoring the outside energy. Straightening, she reached to turn up the volume on the radio. Perhaps they would play something with a lilt, like a waltz. Before she had twisted the knob, the phone rang.

"Hello." Her voice croaked, since she hadn't used it yet that morning. She cleared her throat and tried again. "Hello."

A businesslike voice introduced himself as Arnie Gulp, the lawyer for the Guy Sykes estate. Could he come by? There was a matter, not anything to worry about, but a matter that he needed to discuss with her in person. They could meet at his office, but he would be happy to come to her home. Brent Sykes had suggested that he do so.

A half hour later, he rang the doorbell. "Could we sit at a table?" he said after introducing himself formally. "We have some documents to look at."

She was quietly curious.

He pulled a plain file from his briefcase and set it squarely in front of him on the dining room table. "Guy Sykes included you in his will." He looked for an expression on her face, but she was simply listening carefully.

"You didn't know that? Well, then this will come as a surprise. If you wish, I can first give you a summary and then show you the relevant parts to read. It's not a complicated will, but you need to understand it."

Grace folded her hands in front of her on the table. "I don't know what to say. My goodness! Well, then, I have my glasses, but tell me the main points first."

Arnie proceeded to explain that Guy had directed him to handle the matter of selling the house and apartments before giving the proceeds to her.

Grace's eyes widened. Arnie nodded. "Yes, you heard me correctly."

She looked at her hands. Mercy! What in the world?

Arnie continued to explain the process--the way the sales would take place, and how the taxes would work. She interrupted him. "What about Brent? Isn't this Brent's inheritance?"

"He left Brent the rest of the estate--the business, and his other assets. That's a substantial amount. But he clearly indicated you were to receive a significant bequest as well. He didn't want to bother you with the business matters of the sale. He wrote it this way for you to receive the proceeds."

She broke in. "You see, I don't need the money, and I didn't ask for it. I have no idea what this is about." Her natural dignity kept her from tilting farther. She paused for a moment. "Well, Mr. Gulp, what is your advice for me?"

"Ma'am, you should probably talk to your lawyer and then a financial advisor. I can suggest some names if you don't have one, but you can, perhaps, ask your own lawyer. I can tell you that the sale will probably take a few months. They are solid properties and will move in good time."

She absorbed that for another long moment. "Maybe now is a good time to read me the exact language."

Arnie turned the pages and read it carefully to her. She had him read it twice. Arnie was enjoying himself. It was certainly a break from the routine to dispense a windfall to a little old lady. It was like banging on the front door with balloons and the lottery cameras running.

She looked out the window thoughtfully. The morning sunshine was pure and bright. She looked at her hands folded in her lap. "Would you care for some more coffee?" She asked the question as if he had dropped by for a chat. She poured carefully, bracing the lid of the coffee pot so that it wouldn't fall into the cup.

"I think I know what's to be done," she said, as she stirred her own coffee. "I propose that you sell this property to Brent Sykes for a dollar. It's his, and I have no right taking the proceeds."

Arnie hadn't anticipated this one. "A decision like that shouldn't be made too quickly. You would be forfeiting a great deal."

"As perhaps would you." She suddenly giggled at him. "Or maybe we should set the price at $500, so you can get a little commission." Arnie took a minute to realize she was teasing. He grinned at her in his surprise.

"No, Ma'am! I would not be entitled to anything, anyway. But, we should think about this carefully. Mr. Sykes's intention was that you have the monetary benefits of the sale of some of his property. Take some time to think about it before making any other decisions. There are tax consequences and inheritance issues, which you should understand. I advise you to learn about them and consider this," he was lost for a moment searching for the right word, "situation, a bit more."

"Well, I can't think about it for too long."

"You can take all the time you need, Mrs. Evanston."

She giggled again. "But I might die, you know." She abruptly lifted her coffee cup to sip. She was giggling like a girl. What silly tic was running this conversation?

He looked agape at her.

"I'm sorry, Mr. Gulp. That was a joke. I'm a very old woman. This is all a bit overwhelming and puzzling. I don't know what to say." She paused. "Thank you for explaining it to me. It is quite a surprise, and it is a solemn matter. I wasn't particularly close to Guy. He was a member of the church I go to. He was also a friend of my son's." She stopped, suddenly fearful that there was more here than she understood.

"I am at your service, Ma'am," said Arnie. "My job is to follow the instructions Mr. Sykes laid out for you."

"The long and the short of it is that I need to think about it and pray on it before I can give you direction about what I want done."

This was a new one for Arnie. Who needed guidance when receiving a windfall? Pray for thanks, maybe. But this old gal didn't mean that. He took his leave, touched by her response in the face of surprise. Money did funny things to people, and he had seen its darker sides in his day. Mrs. Evanston would figure it out.

Grace did pray as the autumn days unfolded. She didn't get down on her knees, of course. She had never prayed like that! She prayed in the midst of her daily life, as she took her walks or washed her china each morning in warm sudsy water. The sun shone, the leaves began to change color and fall. It didn't take long for God to help her form an idea.

CHAPTER 12

As soon as they slid into the pew, Alexandra popped the stick of gum into her mouth. Mr. George had slipped it to her when she shook his hand. He and Mr. Porter were like a comedy team. Their joking around was silly, but pretty good for old guys. "All hail, Alexandra the Great!" Alexandra was gathering jokes herself. Telling jokes was a way to get someone to be your friend.

Bridget was not thinking about comedy teams, but about the jokes that life played on you... like the fact that her Mom had chosen the pew right behind Victor and his parents. At least Bridget wasn't sitting exactly behind him. Her mom was. Bridget was behind Victor's mother, who was wearing a silky sailor dress and a string of pearls that matched her extremely white hair.

Bridget looked at Victor's profile. She hoped he didn't think she was chasing him. But, he was really cute. Since school had started, there had been weekly youth meetings at church, and aside from Spanish class, that's where she saw him. There was still a bit of the quartet feel from the mission trip with Tiffany, Kyle, Victor, and herself. But, mostly, Victor and Kyle stuck together with some of the other boys, and she, of course, hung with Tiffany.

A terrible squalling erupted from the back of the congregation. Both Alexandra and Bridget spun their heads around in surprise. A bagpipe skree-ee-eetch mounted above a drone as six pipers started down the aisle leading the choir. The piping was so loud that Alexandra tried saying, "Sit, Fido," in a firm voice and couldn't hear her own voice.

And it got only louder. The organ came to life, and the congregation joined in as the entire sanctuary blasted out the hymn.

When it was over, the pipes let out sad wails as they deflated. Moving to the pulpit, Cord announced, "175 years ago, 17 people, mostly of Scottish heritage, came together and held a worship service in a private home here in

Stanton. The music we will sing today represents the sweep of our history and of our hearts since then."

Three trumpet players rose while Mavis Hofmeister announced, "The next hymn is to be sung by the men and boys."

Self-consciously, the men and boys stood up. The women and girls remained seated around them; from that vantage point they could see front paunches and splitting suit coat vents. Mavis signaled a downbeat, releasing a flourish from the trumpets and launching the first verse:

God of our Father, whose almighty hand

The men's voices rumbled in contrast to the pealing trumpets.

Leads forth in beauty all the starry band.

Finding confidence, a few grins started to stretch the wide-mouthed vowels. In earnest the men powered on.

Of shining worlds...

The organ crashed in with a chord.

...In splendor through the skies...

Victor was standing with his father, sensing Bridget's eyes on his back. The dissonance of the chord distracted him. He felt a physical push on his chest from the low maw of the organ. A thrill took hold. All these men! Some were tall and in suits. A little boy was standing on the pew seat, pretending to sing from his father's hymnbook. The elderly men who shook slightly or leaned on canes were singing, too.

Victor rarely paid attention to hymns. They all sounded the same to him and he thought the verses were stupid. Ever since his voice had dropped, he wasn't confident about singing and often mouthed the hymns. Today, in the swirl of men's voices, his voice didn't matter. The deep empty part of his chest filled with air that powered out with the huge roar of the men.

...Our grateful song before thy throne arise.

As the trumpets announced the second verse, Victor breathed even deeper. His body felt pressurized as air ripped in and out of his lungs. He began to sing hard and harder, right next to his father, whose reedy voice kept strict tempo. The lowest, longest, fullest organ pipes roared around them.

By the end of the fourth verse the men were red-faced. With the last long note, the congregation burst into applause.

As the men sat down and the trumpeters drained their horns, Victor's mother glanced at him. He looked so handsome and healthy with his high coloring. It startled her to see a young man's face overtaking the boyish sweetness. His legs had caught up with his big feet, and his shoulders were filling in a suit coat nicely. She scared herself thinking how much she loved her son.

Victor's throat muscles felt as if he'd been shouting at a basketball game. All around him had been the sound of men. Just men. He felt hugely happy.

It was a great feeling--simple, big, and right.

He caught himself. Stop. It wasn't right. It wasn't right at all. People shouldn't see him all pumped up over singing with a bunch of men. These were all normal people. They were dads and grandpas and kids. There weren't any weird people here *in church*. He had to quit with all this.

For a moment he had felt so connected to all the men in the room, but he was sure it was a feeling that was unique to him. No one else had his problem, no one else in this room, in this town, probably in this whole county. It was like a sickness, a lonely sickness.

And even if there *were* people like him somewhere in the whole state of Indiana, they were seen as bad. There had been that story in the news about the congressman who had a relationship with a man. Being a *congressman* hadn't helped him. They had punished him with a reprimand. He had looked up the word, *reprimand*, when he heard it. It was a kind of punishment, but having your private life on national news had to be a punishment of its own. Even a congressman couldn't protect himself.

So what would happen if anyone suspected him of liking other boys? It would, for sure, be a lot worse than a reprimand. He couldn't *ever* let anyone read his mind. Composing his face as best he could, he tried to recreate his bored expression. Suddenly he yawned. Well, good. That made him look bored.

As Cord led them in prayer, Victor chanted to himself, be careful, be careful, be careful.

Mavis was standing at the lectern again, giving more instructions. She directed the women to form a circle around the sanctuary. When everyone was in place, she signaled the organ to offer the gentlest of flute pipes:

My Lord, what a morning.
My Lord, what a morning.

June stood under the Loaves and Fishes window, a band of colored sun warming the pews in front of her. Bridget was on her left, and Alexandra shared her hymnal from the right. The women's voices gathered around the tune, moving gently together so that stragglers didn't distance themselves. The women in the choir added a cluster of harmony. Their song rose, trailing long notes in its wake.

What a morning! June soaked up the dreaminess and beauty. Would Bridget and Alexandra gain anything from this circle of song? She hoped so. Church was a friendly constancy, a comfort in itself. Worship shored up the narrow rim around the echoing hole in her life. Perhaps this beautiful music would spill into the hole and displace some of the emptiness. She sang with an open throat and her prayer.

My Lord, what a morning,
When the stars begin to fall.

The song floated around the room. The hyperventilating men relaxed.

79

The beat dissipated into a light swaying. Voices drifted in from all corners.

Brent was sitting nearby. The men's hymn had gotten his blood moving. There was force and power in the air. It had the feel of a lion roaring, which fit his mood these days. He could have shaken his father until his teeth rattled, if he were still alive, of course. Brent was seething with frustration at not understanding what had happened.

The women's song wrapped around him and stretched out in front of him. What were they saying? My Lord, what a morning! Or was it mourning? It could be either, actually. Take your pick.

Take your pick! What choices did he have, really? Morning or mourning? Glass half full or half empty?

Hands down, it was half empty. Mourning. He was alone now. His father had died. Sharon had pushed him away. He had new obligations. And now there were directions issued to him *from the grave!*

Why the drama and surprise, Dad? Why not tell me if it was so significant? You had all kinds of time, since 1978. You knew you were dying. You knew I would learn about it when I read the will. Why not just tell me?

The only answer he could come up with was that his father hadn't trusted him, which was magnificently unfair. What had he done not to be trusted? What had he *not* done not to be trusted? How exactly had he fallen down around the vaunted trust code?

Maybe he didn't deserve the full inheritance. Maybe he was entitled to only a part of it.

His mind locked down on the thought. Maybe it wasn't entirely his inheritance. Were there were other children? Maybe he was adopted. Maybe his mother and Grace had been related. Maybe there was something unknown or bizarre like that.

A shush from nearby surprised Brent. He froze, realizing he had been slapping his rolled up bulletin against his hand. Alexandra was signaling him as she took her seat. The song had ended. Pulling himself to order, he automatically winked at her, and was surprised when she winked back.

June caught some of the exchange. She smiled a little apology. Brent shook his head to say all was well. Jeesh. She was gorgeous with that long neck and dangling earrings. It was a welcome distraction to look at her.

Meanwhile, Rev. McDaniel was calling for the offering. The choir stood for an anthem while the ushers started down the aisle. Men leaned into their wives as they pried their wallets out of back pockets.

Spencer Beck placed his envelope in the plate and passed it down to Victor. He had felt Victor's enthusiasm during the hymn. Yes, Cord had been right. Victor had a passion for church. He simply was hiding it behind the usual boyish sheepishness. Spencer was gratified. Loretta had always had the prerogative in raising Victor and delivering the observations and conclusions about his wellbeing. But the tables were turning. Victor was growing up, and Spencer could trust his own opinions about his son now.

It was amazing to think Victor was old enough to be useful. He had apparently held his own on the mission trip with the tools and work to be done. Over the years Spencer had done some house projects with Victor to show him some skills. It was great to know he was putting that to good use.

And soon it would be girls. Wasn't 14 about the age when that began? Spencer tried to remember being 14. And now he was 44. Three decades of difference. It felt like a century. And today was the 175th celebration. The church was about four times older than he was. And over 13 times older than Victor. He ran the numbers in his head as percentages.

The Doxology drew them to their feet. Victor swiveled slightly and caught Bridget's eye. They had sung the Doxology for grace at work camp meals, and it had sounded absolutely awful. She knew exactly what he was thinking and grinned. Spencer caught the shared expression. Sure thing. 14 years old and Victor was right on schedule.

CHAPTER 13

Brown County State Park spreads across the dense hills between Bloomington and Interstate 65. The park entrance is immediately beyond a small tourist enclave that celebrates the good old days of banjoes and country cooking. Tourists can dress up in long dresses, boots, and string ties and pose for portraits.

The locals appreciate the tourist trade. The park ranger, though, prefers church groups. This weekend's group comes every year and are model campers, except for their bad habit of moving the furniture. They always drag the picnic tables together for their potluck meals.

At least a dozen church families had checked in by late Friday afternoon, and he was scanning the list for Wallace. "There it is," he said, looking up at the willowy woman across the counter. "You're all set. Elm Leaf Loop, Campsite Number 27. Your group has taken over the whole Loop."

"That many?"

"Not all have showed up yet, but usually that's the case."

June Wallace paid her $10, accepted the packet of maps and fire regulations, and headed back to the car. The girls were waiting with the windows down.

"Do they have bathrooms?" asked Bridget.

"I didn't ask, but look on the map."

Hanging the campsite tag from the mirror, she backed out of the parking spot.

"This is like a real vacation," chirped Alexandra. "Look! There's a bunch of trailers down that road. People look like they live here. See, Mom, we didn't bring too much stuff. Look over there. Those kids have skateboards!"

June looked in the rear-view mirror at her daughter and smiled. Why hadn't they gone camping before as a family? "Whoops. Is that Elm Tree?

No, Elm *Leaf.*" They made the turn.

The tree canopy was high. It allowed only mottled light, which softened the primary colors of the tents. Cars and mini-vans with gaping hatchbacks spilled out their treasures. In a bushy alcove, a cluster of children played cards at a table.

June steered into #27, and immediately people descended on them. The Wallaces' car trunk was opened, and Porter Hofmeister was loping up the path with a hammer to drive in the tent stakes. The girls put on their shoes and disentangled themselves out of the back seat of the car.

Mavis bustled up and gave Alexandra a big hug. "You must be hungry. Come over soon to fix your foil dinners."

The communal dining area had taken shape. Lawn chairs surrounded a fire pit. Coolers lined an outer perimeter, and swimming towels that were slung over clotheslines created a theatrical backdrop. Four tables were grouped together; their individual tablecloths created a collective patchwork quilt.

The communal fire pit was well tended. George Morrow had arrived early, organized the bags of charcoal in a lumpy lineup, and scrubbed the grill to a shine, ignoring his aching elbow. He loved to camp, yet Duke's allergies made it impossible for the two of them to camp together. Church camping had been a mainstay for him for decades. He positioned his chair so as to oversee the dozen foil-wrapped dinner packets that were already scattered on the red-hot coals. Each packet was folded into a unique shape, a primitive form of origami.

Brent, the other fire marshal, was also there in his chair. For years, his father, Guy, had sat side by side with George at the fire, keeping children from falling in and monitoring the marshmallow frenzy later in the evening. Brent had stepped into the role the year before, and here he was again. Christ! Have I ever done anything else but follow my father around like a puppy? He didn't like feeling grumpy under the rustling trees as the smell of smoke wafted nearby. He had hoped camping would cheer him up a bit.

With her daughters exploring the campground, June prepared the foil dinners and carried them to the fire. She perched on a stump next to the hearth.

"Here, would you like a chair?" Brent offered, glad for the distraction.

"No, thank you. This stump is fine." She reached for a stick and probed the charcoal a bit. "And playing with fire is fun."

"Well, then, I won't take responsibility if you fall in."

She smiled, but in the direction of the fire pit. The charcoal undulated with heat and color. The chunks of foil darkened the coals that they touched, filling the red and orange hearth with sunspots. The heat didn't quite reach her face, but it warmed her arms and legs.

A child with a big beach towel crawled into George's lap, chilly from swimming. Settling in, she coiled herself into a ball and fell asleep. The whorl of fine hair at the top of her head was matted from her sun hat. George pulled in the smell of chlorine and childhood. She must have been swimming in a pool.

June had turned to watch the child and in the process caught Brent's eye. "I understand from Bridget that your dad was a youth advisor. I'm sorry she didn't get the chance to know him. It sounds as if he was particularly special for the kids." June had been confused by the rapid stories from Bridget about Mr. Sykes, until she had learned there were two of them, father and son.

"Thank you," said Brent. "He always loved kids. I think in another life he would have had a dozen of his own."

George looked up at him. It hadn't sounded like an entirely casual comment.

"I am sorry for your loss." She said it simply.

"And I understand your husband died recently. My condolences to you as well. Such a loss for you and the girls! You have two, right?"

"Yes. Thank you. Bridget is the older, and the other is Alexandra. The move has helped them a lot, I believe. But it has been a long process. It certainly doesn't stop with the funeral, what with the paperwork and insurance and sorting clothes and all that."

You bet, thought Brent. And then there are the upsetting surprises like a will!

June thought back to all the work generated by Sam's death. It had been just plain exhausting. Stirring the coals, she remembered she had wished she could simply burn everything. He'd been cremated, so why not? Lighting up the sky with a bonfire would have been cathartic.

She realized that Brent had said something to her. "I'm sorry," she said. "I missed what you said."

Brent repeated himself, "I was just saying that I never understood the extent of the work, although you would think it would be obvious to me, being a mortician and all."

"Oh, I didn't know that was your profession. Aren't you the mayor?"

"That's not a full-time job. The funeral home is the family business, and we've been in this town for generations. The town has been important for us, and it's good to give back." Was that what he really thought? Or was that what his father had made him think? Brent was bumping into that question all too often these days.

George, grounded with his three-year-old bundle of dreaming, lapsed into his own thoughts. He could sympathize with both Brent and June because he had cared for his own parents. In his case, it was their long decline and not their deaths that had rocked his world.

He had been their primary caretaker for nearly two years, beginning with long drives back and forth to Stanton from West Lafayette, where he and Duke had their home together. He'd made that trip two or three times a week. Finally, he had asked the bank for a transfer and moved in with his parents. There was plenty of room; a neighbor came in during the day, and he was there all night. They had managed.

His sister had made it all possible. Every Friday she drove over to relieve him for the weekend so that he could climb into his car and head home. The long miles to West Lafayette would be a countdown. Each mileage marker released a bit more of the week's stress. Often, on that drive, the sun would be setting, and the colors would light up the barns and buildings on the right side of the highway. It was a time of weekly illumination and transition.

He remembered looking forward to a deep sleep in his own bed, without nightlights and ominous calls for help. Duke would have dinner ready along with a bottle of wine and stories of the week. George's internal rhythms would switch from the sadness of aging to the exuberance of youth, as he heard the university update. The contrasts in his life were finely balanced. The young, the old. The banker, the caretaker. Vigor and fragility.

The child in his lap murmured in her sleep and abruptly flung out an arm. June looked over at George, who took the opportunity to shift his posture. "Out cold."

"Almost took one in the jaw." Brent smiled. "Your arms must be getting cramped. Can I get you anything, like a pillow or a cup of coffee?"

"No, thanks, I'm fine." George was never comfortable with small favors extended his way. Don't notice me, please. That would be the best gesture of all.

Alexandra peeked between two of the towel curtains. Her face was shadowy against the neon colors. "Can we eat soon, Mom? They start playing flashlight tag when it gets dark." She skirted around the fire to reach her mother. "Oh, hello, Mr. George." She was wearing a flower necklace.

"I think your dinners should be ready about now," George replied. "But they will be steaming hot, so don't try to gulp your food."

"I'll talk to you while it cools," Alexandra suggested. "It's boring to sit around holding sleeping kids. When I get old enough to baby-sit, I will never let anyone fall asleep in my lap."

"You're probably right. But I have to watch the fire, so it's okay to hold her and give her parents a break."

Brent listened in while watching June maneuver the foil dinner onto a plate. Her hands were slender with long fingers and no polish. There were no rings. He could see one on a chain around her neck.

Alexandra opened the foil gingerly and released the steam. "Mr. George," she asked, "why do you sit outside on Sundays and only come in for the offering?"

"You think I'm skipping church?" He grinned. "You might be right, but someone needs to be available if there are any problems. It doesn't work if I'm hopping up and down from a pew. So we stay in the back or outside."

"Could I help you sometimes? It's boring going to church all the time."

Brent smiled to himself. This kid was impertinent in a very engaging way. At that age he would never have said to his father that church was boring. But she wasn't being disrespectful. He could tell George was enjoying her as well.

George and June telegraphed messages with a glance and a nod.

"I think that would be grand, on occasion," George said to Alexandra. "Maybe we could try it and see. We don't want too many people crowding around the door. That would defeat the purpose."

"Goody!"

Brent continued studying Alexandra as she ate her food, blowing to cool it first. When she finished, she smashed the aluminum into a dripping ball.

A hoot went up from the prep tables. Everyone turned to see what was happening. "Look at the camp stove!" Porter had turned off the stove, but the flame was burning, without the benefit of gas, or so it seemed.

Kids crowded in to see. Alexandra tossed her aluminum into the fire, and it sizzled as she rushed over, bumping into her sister in the process. Bridget's eyes were red with tears from cutting onions to help Mavis. "Be careful, Alexandra," said Bridget annoyed. "Can't you see I've got a knife in my hand?"

"Well, you don't have to cry over it. I just bumped you."

"I'm not crying."

The blue flame was unmistakably visible. Porter checked the knobs for a third time. Victor wandered over to take a look. "It's a holy burner," someone said. "Yeah, a modern burning bush."

Bridget and Victor exchanged looks. Church people could be so lame. Both rolled their eyes. And then Bridget felt she had to explain: "I've been cutting onions, and it makes my eyes water."

"Oh."

She grimaced and gently waved the knife in the air as evidence.

"Have you ever played flashlight tag?"

"No," she answered. "I've never been camping before."

"Yeah? Well, we always play when it gets dark. We'll need captains for the teams. Do you want to co-captain with me?"

He had loved the game as a boy, and it still held magic. The point was to creep around in the dark, sneak up on people, and shine your flashlight on them before they saw you. The prize was to get them to scream with surprise when you tagged them. Anyone could play.

As the evening darkened, the pack began to form. Bridget sent her sister to the tent to put on a dark sweatshirt. Alexandra would be a great secret weapon on their team. She could be so sneaky.

Victor and Bridget chose their team carefully. Victor insisted that everyone choose a buddy, and Bridget told them all to *be quiet*. One boy had a ski mask and really did disappear in the dark. Someone else had a flasher flashlight for roadside emergencies. Victor confiscated it, seeing the benefits of having a siren. It wouldn't just surprise people--it would freak them out! "I'll use it to call the whole team back together," he explained, as he gave up his flashlight in exchange.

Victor and Bridget called the team to council. They whispered instructions and practiced hand signals. Mr. Hofmeister was on the other team, and everyone knew that he was clunky and noisy. They could win if their team could keep quiet and have patience to wait until the right moments to surprise their opponents. The kids all nodded seriously. The biggest problem was remembering who was on their team and who was on the other team.

With the whistle to start, the teams dispersed. Nervous giggles and whispers trailed back from the younger ones.

Victor and Bridget led the way pointing out places for kids to veer off. The brush was dense, which made it hard to walk quietly. Luckily, the whole forest rustled with light noise and provided cover.

"Stand next to that tree," Victor whispered, and he slipped over to another, fading into its silhouette. Bridget watched hard; when the tree trunk seemed to move, she knew it was Victor and followed.

Sudden shrieks erupted in the distance, followed by extended laughter and hooting. A radio played close by. Bridget and Victor split up for a circular reconnaissance around the camp bathrooms. They regrouped behind a large boulder, using a dense hedge as additional cover. Bridget rubbed her cheek where a branch had grazed it. Things had quieted down again, but then there were crunches in the leaves nearby. Flashlight beams careened off the rock as two young kids giggled and whispered right past them. Bridget and Victor held themselves completely still for almost five minutes.

"Mr. Hofmeister," Victor whispered directly into her ear as they both crouched down even more. He pointed through the hedge. She nodded, suddenly caught up in the complete glee of stalking an oblivious adult.

Turning her head to whisper back she scraped her nose across Victor's cheek. "If we can't catch him, we're really dumb."

They crept around the hedge. Very slowly. They stopped for a full two minutes, absolutely still, waiting. Bridget's stomach quivered with the fun, and she gave a little hiccup. Victor grabbed her arm to signal her to be careful. She tried to control the giggles. Victor pointed with his flashlight. She aimed hers, and with his hand pulse of one.... two...

"Gotcha," screamed Alexandra as loud and shrill as possible. Her flashlight was right in their eyes blazing from the other side of Mr. Hofmeister.

"Alexandra," Bridget shouted, "you're on *our* team! Why are you shining lights on us?"

"I was shining them on Mr. Hofmeister!"

"You're shining them into our eyes!"

"Well, move over."

"Quit shouting," rasped Victor in a loud whisper as he let go of Bridget's arm.

"Yeah," retorted Alexandra, pulling her voice down to a whispered screech. "If you hadn't been hanging on to each other, you wouldn't have been surprised."

"We were signaling each other, stupid."

Mr. Hofmeister barked a laugh.

"It's okay. We'll call it a draw. Any more hollering, and everyone will know where we are."

Victor switched off his light. The girls harrumphed to a silence.

Another hoot went up nearer the campsite. Alexandra took off, still chasing the challenge of getting someone to scream in surprise.

Victor searched his pockets for gum and offered some to Bridget. She rubbed her cheek, feeling sheepish.

"I'd say that was a legitimate tag," he said.

She laughed in relief. The game had been a lot of fun. She decided not worry that Victor might read too much into Alexandra's comments. Victor had asked her to co-captain, and he seemed to like being with her. He didn't act bothered about Alexandra.

"Everyone knows where we are. We'd better go sit by the fire and wait for kids to check in."

"Sure," said Victor easily. They started along the loop road back to the site.

At the fire, the marshmallows had been unpacked and were set out next to boxes of graham crackers and chocolate bars. Bridget punched marshmallows onto a long fork. She nicked her finger in the process and bled on the food.

"I'll get you a bandage," Victor volunteered.

Mavis, while stacking songbooks at the table, gave him the medical kit. He pried open the lid and dug out a tube of antiseptic cream and a bandage. Handing both to Bridget, he took the marshmallow fork and went to work.

Together they snagged a spot close to the coals and watched the marshmallows change color over the heat. Victor was pleased. It was easy to hang with Bridget. His face blazed and then stiffened in the heat. Had people noticed them?

Bridget smiled to herself. Victor might not be outgoing, but he was being very nice to her. She squished the cracker and chocolate together around a hot marshmallow. It was sweet and messy. She licked her fingers and idly watched other kids waving sticks and forks over the coals. Above their chatter, she became aware of her mother's laughter. Bridget looked around and spotted her sitting in a camp chair next to Mr. Sykes. They were laughing together about something – just the two of them. It surprised her, and she laughed, too, just because she felt like it.

CHAPTER 14

The bright, warm supermarket was overflowing with Halloween spirit. Candy was piled high next to pumpkins, decorative corn stalks, and apples. There were even tubs for old-fashioned apple bobbing. Brent hadn't seen one of those since he was a kid. He pulled out a grocery cart and started choosing candy for the trick-or-treaters.

"Do you know the difference between raisins and currants?" Porter Hofmeister was at his elbow, waving a grocery list.

"They're spelled differently," joked Brent.

Porter grinned.

"I would bet they're in the baking aisle with things like chocolate chips."

"I don't know where anything is," Porter said. "I'm not usually allowed to do the shopping."

"Then you'd better get it right." Brent threw some potatoes into a bag as Porter trailed along. Bending over the meat display, he chose some nicely marbled steaks.

"My kind of dinner."

"Yep. It's easy to stick 'em under the broiler." He was going for all his favorite food. It was a small reward for beginning to clean out his dad's house. Arnie Gulp had been in regular touch, and the wheels of the will were turning. The house would be put on the market after the holidays. To get himself going, Brent had engaged an estate-cleaning service. Now he absolutely had to do his part, which involved casing the joint and taking an inventory of the valuables and the like.

He left Porter stewing over the spice shelves and turned down the frozen foods aisle. June was tossing packages of frozen vegetables into the cart. "Hello, there."

As she pushed her cart in his direction, it rattled loudly. "I seem to have picked out one with a mind of its own," she said, laughing sheepishly.

"How are you?"

"Doing pretty good," he said automatically and caught himself. "Actually, I'm treating myself to a hyper-cholesterol dinner so I'll have the fuel to start clearing out Dad's house." He pointed to his steaks.

"And now you are in the ice cream aisle."

"You betcha!" He rubbed his hands in a parody of glee.

"I'm still catching up from the camping trip. Losing a weekend means the evenings get loaded with the errands."

"I would imagine you run pretty hard. The girls plus the *Gazette*. I know that's a more hoppin' place to work than people realize. It must be the major paper for – what – five or six counties?"

"Well, yes. You can't cover the news with a bunch of taxicab vouchers. I hadn't appreciated the driving involved. But I doubt if I can compete with your schedule of two jobs."

"So, then, let's not try to give prizes."

"Agreed." She looked into her cart and sighed. "But the driving around during the summer meant I could hit the farmers' markets. Now, those are closing for the season, and we're back to frozen veggies. How many ways can you cook pumpkin?"

"You don't seem to go for convenience food."

"No, I can't do it, somehow. I cook a lot from scratch. It also guarantees that I spend time with the girls doing something constructive every day." She looked tired as she said it. Maybe he should cook her dinner sometime. The girls could help him.

The idea surprised him. His usual move with women was to whisk them off to some other venue outside of Stanton. Theater in Louisville or something at IU in Bloomington.

But it would be a kick to bustle around in a kitchen. He would enjoy chatting with Alexandra, to boot. She'd have something original to say even about the carrot sticks. Of that he was sure.

But, first things first. He had to get that house cleaned out, starting tonight.

"I shouldn't keep you from getting on home to them," he said with a slightly chivalrous tone.

June smiled and agreed. "Good luck with your dad's house. It's a bear of a job."

"Now that's a cheerful send-off," he said. "I'll grab that ice cream first."

They said their goodbyes, and June rumbled off down the aisle. She waved as she turned the corner and laughed as he waved back with his favorite high-end ice cream brand in his hand. He always rationalized the richer ice cream by the fact that the packaging was only pint-sized.

He wheeled off to join the checkout line. "Hello, Mr. Sykes," the cashier said, as she moved quickly through his purchase.

Brent smiled in return. She wore a tag that said *Laura* on it, but he couldn't remember her last name. "I'll help bag," he offered. It was a good thing to do, and people appreciated it. During his campaign he had occasionally bagged groceries as a way of meeting people casually and showing industry. It always went over well.

Unlocking his car, he turned on the news and set off for his dad's house. Kids were out in one yard jumping in a pile of leaves. He noticed a streetlight was out on the intersection for his dad's street. He made a note on his trusty pad. Downshifting, he turned into the driveway of his dad's house and yanked hard on the hand break. Why was the flag up on the mailbox? The mail was supposed to be forwarded to his address.

Loaded with the bags of groceries, he pulled the mailbox open with a free finger. Six or seven catalogs slithered out. He would never get his dad's name off these crazy mailing lists!

He dumped the bags and catalogs on the kitchen counter. *Youth at Worship and Play.* Even church suppliers had gone high gloss. Popping off the cap of a bottle of beer, he started putting the food away.

With a steak under the broiler and a potato in the microwave, he flipped through a catalog for outfitting hikers. Wouldn't that be wonderful? Why not leave town and go hiking in the Rockies? He imagined settings with cold streams, efficient tents, and outdoor cooking. He thought about camping, and the thought of June brushed across the back of his mind. He pulled it to the front for a moment. Yes, she was attractive. Yes, he had imagined cooking her dinner. And, yes, she was a complicated package – kids, job, and widow. He'd shelve that for now. Too messy.

He returned deliberately to the Rocky Mountains fantasy as he worked on his steak and potato. One picture raised a location question, so he decided he needed to consult a map. Guy had remodeled the family room into an elegant den with dark paneling and leather chairs. Brent couldn't find an atlas along the shelves.

Turning, he pulled open a file drawer. The hanging files and labels were color-coded. Green for financial files – makes sense! He tried another drawer. Red for medical files – ha ha. Okay. Blue for newspaper clippings and obituaries.

And black. Who has black files?

He pulled one out. It was marked *Birth Certificates.* In a black file? The contents were only copies. The originals should be in the safety deposit box. He stopped to read his own birth certificate. Well, so much for the adoption worry. He was certainly his father's son. He had never really entertained that theory, but now there was no question about that. It said so in black and white, with a nice seal in the corner.

"Hell, what's this?" he pulled out a black file labeled *Upon Death.* Inside was a single sealed envelope labeled *For Brent Sykes.* It was in his father's writing on a plain envelope, not the embossed Sykes Mortuary envelopes. Brent felt the beer slosh in his stomach.

It wasn't a thick envelope. Legal-size. Brent disciplined himself not to rip it open on the spot. He walked himself back to the kitchen table, where he told himself to sit down and be orderly about this.

He considered the possibilities: perhaps it was a copy of an insurance policy. His father constantly harped about families missing important financial information when someone died. Maybe it was the complete list of family records. It wasn't unlike his father to be overly meticulous.

Or, maybe it was instructions about his funeral. That stopped Brent for a minute. If so, he had already blown that one.

Okay, enough. He slit open the envelope and pulled out its contents. It was a letter, six full pages long on heavy paper. No date. The handwriting was wobbly. His father must have written it recently.

Dear Brent,

I don't write easily, and I've put off this conversation a long time. It's becoming clear to me that I will die from this cancer. The way the doctors are talking, there's no other way to see it. Therefore, it is time to assess my life, because I believe people should pay up all their debts and make amends before the end. Unfortunately, I have lived most of my life under the cloud of one debt, and it's not over. I am not proud that I haven't dealt with it, but now I must, and I have to ask for your help with that.

It's about the money, Brent thought. I knew there had to be an explanation. I couldn't believe Dad would pull a fast one on me. He got up, opened another bottle of beer, and took a swallow.

First, there is a story to tell you. When I got out of high school, I went directly to work for Pop because his health was failing. The Korean War was on, but I wasn't called up for medical reasons that included my flat feet and the old hearing problems in my left ear, and, of course, I was married already. However, my best friend, Vaughn Evanston, was called up and sent over.

It was a big deal in town when someone came home from war. One kid from our high school was killed there, and his funeral was a huge affair with a flag-draped casket and all that. I think the whole town came to pay respects.

When Vaughn came home, we had a party for him. It started with a large group of people, but by later in the evening it was mostly those of us that had been together in high school with him. It was summertime and muggy hot. We were in someone's back yard, and we drank and danced and had fun. After that was over, I took your mother home. She was pregnant with you and tired, but she told me I could go on out with Vaughn to celebrate some more. He and I drove out to the lake. It was different out there in those days, not built up with houses. It was quiet--a place to go with a girl, or to go skinny-

dipping late at night.

We each had a bottle of whiskey, and we sat on the pier and sweated while we talked and drank. I got pretty drunk, and I know Vaughn was drinking hard, too. He started talking about Korea, telling me the real stories and not the dressed up stuff he had told others.

He had been lucky to get a communications job at the base, and that meant he was part of a signal division or group. He learned Morse code. Since he could already type, he also did some reporting for the base newsletter or something. Newspapers were always his thing. To me it sounded like he had drawn some pretty light duty.

Time passed. I was only half following his stories and drifting off into my own thoughts. I was a little annoyed, because he wasn't asking about what had happened back at home. He just wanted to tell me about his big wartime experience, which didn't sound particularly stressful or dangerous to me. My head was swimming around, and I was kicking the water to see if I could get my legs moving. They were like rubber. I remember that feeling as if it were yesterday.

Vaughn was wound up a lot about his stories and talking a blue streak. I kept kicking, kind of building up this upset feeling that he had come home as a big war hero, when all he had done was put on a uniform and done some fancy desk work. Meanwhile, I'd been stuck in this town. Looking back on it, I can see that I was pretty jealous. But at the time, I was getting hot under the collar. I started to get in his face a bit so I could burst his bubble. He'd been quite a stiff in high school, so I started in about girls. Maybe his uniform had helped him on that front, meaning sex. I got on a kind of jag about those Korean girls.

At one point, he leaned over in that unbalanced way that happens when you've been drinking a lot, and he gave me a punch. I remember it was sort of playful, so it didn't stop me from talking. I think I said something crude like, "Could you finally get it up?" And he shoved me again, only this time it was not playful. The whole thing bothered me even more. I said some more angry things. We tussled, shoving each other around on the pier. At one point, I came back at him with, "Or maybe it isn't girls you like." When I said that, it seemed to flip a switch.

He answered me by saying something real close into my face like, "And what if I don't?" The way he said it was obviously defiant-- I had no doubt what he was telling me, and he was practically spitting on me, we were so close. The two of us were into something ugly. I hit him hard, and he fell into the water. Maybe his head hit the pier on the way down. Dad later said he had a bruise on his scalp. But at the time, everything I remember is dark, blurry, and very fast. I have gone over it a million times since then.

Brent stopped reading. His mind was buzzing. Small wonder that he'd never heard this story! It was ugly, and the gay subtext made it uglier. He could see why his dad had never told anyone. He had been ducking responsibility, for sure.

He never came up, but I didn't get that right away. The punch had also sent me off balance so I nearly fell of the pier myself, but I don't remember much after that. Maybe I hit my head, too. I might have passed out or faded out a couple of times. I was confused, and thought at one point he'd hidden under the pier or was doing some trick, but it was too dark to see. I yelled a bit, and I vomited at one point. I remember stumbling back to the car to turn the car lights on, but that just made the water darker. I don't know how long all this went on. It could have been ten minutes or over an hour. Eventually, I got it together to drive to town to get help, but there was no way to help. They started a search and found the body early the next morning.

Everyone thought it was a horrible accident, and I wasn't about to make it seem to be anything else. We had been best friends, so Dad didn't let me near the body or the preparations for the funeral. God knows how he pulled it off. It was the last funeral he handled by himself.

I was in shock, I guess. It was awful. I'd taunted him into a fight, and I must have killed him. I have never told anyone the truth. No one. No one. I was afraid and horrified, and I've lived with this all my life.

There, I've said it at last.

Your mom knew I was terribly upset, and so was she. So was everyone. The whole thing was a tragedy. Vaughn had been my best friend. When I relived it in my head, I couldn't shake the memory of his owning up to being a homosexual. I was shocked by that, and it still turns my stomach. But, I didn't mean for him to die.

Then things started changing fast. Dad was getting more confused and frail; he and Mom were soon dependent on me. The business was in my hands. You were born. My whole life felt like a train wreck, but I had to get up every day. So I kept on going with the routines of bills, the business, the house, mowing the lawn, raising you, and all that. We lived with Mom and Pop, and I had their affairs to deal with. Your mother's death was devastating, putting everything about Vaughn into the farthest back corner of my mind. Eventually we had to put Pop in a home, and then he and Mom died. It was just the two of us left.

Sometimes, when I gassed up the car, I would look down the road to the edge of town and want nothing more than to drive away, as far as I could drive, and never come back. In so many ways, I felt my life was ruined. But I had you, and that kept me from doing anything rash. Those thoughts faded a bit over time, but they have never gone away. I carried my grief about your mother and the secret about Vaughn like some dark, very high, blood pressure inside me.

This letter isn't about excuses or how I led my life. I had to have someone know the truth. After I die, there will be only one person left who was affected, and that's Vaughn's mother, Grace. It's too late to tell her the truth, and I have never imagined bringing that heartache to her. I can't take back what I did. The one thing I am doing, however, is naming her in my will. It's the only way I can begin to repay her and make any amends. There's plenty of money, so it won't set you back, but I had to tell you so you would understand. I am asking you to see that the will is executed properly and not contested. I owe that much to her for the pain I've caused. She isn't aware of the bequest, and if I told her now, I would have to lie about why I was doing it, and she would see through it and wonder. Grace is smart like that.

You are my only son--by telling you this, I am putting a lot on you, Brent. I am asking you to keep a secret and accept my decisions and directions. I'm not asking forgiveness, just for you to handle the bequest discretely. I debated whether to do this, but I couldn't walk away from the idea once it came to me. Brent, I am not a brave man, but I can make this payment towards my obligation.

I have always kept you close and have been proud of you. I know you understand what it is to have obligations and will help me with this one. You have been loyal and faithful, and I love you very much.

Your father,

Guy Sykes

Brent sat staring at the page. It was lying on the table next to the glossy catalog pictures of mountains and hikers. The contrast was stark. He curled his hand around the neck of the beer bottle. The glass fit hard into his palm.

His father's request left him breathless. He'd devoted his life to doing what his father wanted him to do. And now there was more. Always more. Guy had caught him in a mesh of obligations: don't hurt Grace Evanston; don't contest the will; suck it up that you don't get all the estate; I did it all for you and your mother; redeem my suffering; pay it off. He had been set up.

What made his father think that Brent could lie effectively to Grace? How did he think that *money* would make up for what had happened?

Was this what a father did? Was it right for a father to leave his son, his sole inheritor, both a diminished estate and a tale of uncontrolled anger? His legacy to Brent was a grubby secret of death. Where was the honor?

Brent slammed the bottle on the table. His wrist yelped with pain but the bottle didn't break. He stood up, flipped it in his palm so it became an extension of his arm, and brought it down again full force on the edge of the table. Glass and beer went everywhere.

He jumped back and felt the sting of cuts on his arm. Yes, Dad, slice at me, shower me with little stabs. What am I but your gullible son? I believed in you and imitated you. I *worshipped* you. Wasn't I the good son, running a perfect funeral or shaking every hand in Stanton? You told me never to blink. I didn't need to, because I did it right. You insisted. Shit. Now you tell me to carry a secret, handle the arrangements, pick up the pieces, and stand tall as the blood money flows through my fingers. Christ!

He had a strong sensation of being smothered. His lungs wouldn't take in enough breath, and his head felt light. Guy had held him close and tight. But now he saw it was not simply to impart a legacy, but to hide behind him. I am now the front guy for an obligation. The bagman. He's asked me to pay his debt.

Dropping the jagged remains of the bottle's neck, Brent could see his father standing next to him, watching, as if at a memorial service or a wake. He used to dress for them in the expected sober black suit, conducting himself with great respect for the family and the deceased. He was never disturbed by a mourner's grief or hysteria. He taught Brent to tend to quiet things at a time like that, to give people a sense of order and calmness. He would adjust flowers or straighten bunting.

"Don't treat me like that," Brent panted at the image. "Don't treat me as if this is something that can be managed by smoothing the linens or combing the hair." He swiveled, skidded on the beer and broken glass, and banged hard into the counter. The cupboards loomed over him, walls on walls.

Brent lunged for the back door. Outside, he yanked open the car trunk and fished out his gym bag. Pulling out his sweats and shoes, he changed his clothes right there in the driveway under the cold light of the kitchen window. The bleeding on his arms continued to trickle down his skin. He welcomed the minor pain.

Slamming the trunk shut, he set off running. He didn't pace himself, just tore down the street. He pumped his legs, stamping his feet down as if trying to compress the earth further. But he couldn't beat back his thoughts.

He had been sucked in by his father's varying persona. He could be the affable mayor or the hearty friend to kids or the appropriate undertaker. Brent had long watched him shift to fit the situation. He thought it was a skill, and Brent had tried hard to imitate it. But it had been a deception.

Brent had never suspected anything and had… He stumbled, not able to see the sidewalk clearly. Front porch lights cut into the engulfing darkness of the evening, but only partially. Off balance for a moment, he careened out to the smoother street surface. He kept his legs moving, and in a couple blocks he turned onto the county highway.

Even as his brain churned, his strides settled down to a rhythm. He passed the last gas station on the edge of town. He ran and ran. Without any streetlights, the sky loomed huge and black. The cornfields leveled the landscape. The vastness of it all began to slow him down. A car screamed, going by at least at 60 miles per hour. He was of no consequence next to such speed. His chest was shooting fire at his brain. Panting hard, he slowed to a jog and then a walk.

Hopping a fence, he picked his way through the stubble of a cornfield. The rows marked a disciplined rigidity, and the stalks were sharp, so he stayed on a careful track, turning occasionally at right angles and stepping across rows. It was a child's game. Stay straight, turn left, and go straight again.

He had done just that--marched in exactly the direction dictated to him. He had blended his life into his father's expectations so much that he couldn't begin to separate himself out.

But it was the betrayal. His father's endgame was hiding this story until his death, until *after* his death. That was particularly galling. He was expecting Brent to be compliant. He had boxed him in. He had treated him like a little boy, lying first to spare him and then – what – to protect him? Or to protect himself? In the end, it came full circle. Brent was left with the backpack. He had to support the will. He couldn't explain the truth to Grace. He couldn't even show his true feelings. He had been made complicit.

The lights from the town were far away and feeble. The distance to the light seemed nothing to the distance he had lived from the truth.

He did some squats to keep his leg muscles from quivering. His face was cooling in dark air. He couldn't stay in a cornfield all night. He turned around with a dramatic gesture to himself, twisting his upper body and sawing at the air with outstretched arms. With heavy steps, he crunched his way out of the maze.

Back onto the black top, he started a slower jog home. He passed the gas station and the town's incorporation sign. He turned the corner, and the streetlights lit the neighborhood. Again, he noticed the streetlight that was out on his father's corner. He slowed to a walk near the driveway. He stopped at the mailbox and repositioned the flag so that it was all the way down.

The hiking gear catalog was still on the kitchen table. The remains of the steak were cold, its streaking fat congealed and glazed with glass shards. The kitchen clock surprised him. It wasn't much past 9:00. It should have been about 2 AM. He looked at his watch to confirm.

He peeled off his jacket and used the broom at the doorway to clear a splinter- free path into the dining room. Drinking a small glass of water, he stood still at the sink for a moment. He could feel his legs twitch. He reached his elbows over his head to stretch out his shoulders. Slowly, he started to rebalance. And slowly, he surveyed the kitchen, the chairs, the curtains, the knick-knacks, the pictures, the pots, the key rack, and the mixer on the counter. He had a full house to clear out. A fuller house than he had bargained for.

CHAPTER 15

It was a Saturday morning. Teenagers were sprawled on the pews, barely awake. Rev. McDaniel surveyed the scene. "Listen up! I want the confirmation class members to stay put. The rest of you are going to help set up downstairs." Porter and Mavis were celebrating their 40th wedding anniversary with a big reception after church the next day. For once the church was cooking for Mavis, rather than the other way around.

A huge arrangement of chrysanthemums came through the door. A man announced from behind the jungle, "Delivery. Flowers for a reception."

"We only need the chancel flowers up here. The reception flowers go to Fellowship Hall downstairs." Cord turned. "Would the 7th and 8th graders please show him where to go? And remember that the youth are getting paid for helping out. The Hofmeisters are making a donation to support the next mission trip. So keep the goofing around to a minimum."

It was the first session of the confirmation class. Shortly the 9th graders would join their faith partners in a classroom.

Victor didn't want to show it, but he was pleased that Mr. Sykes had agreed to be his faith partner. He had decided to ask him on the day of the funeral. Mr. Sykes had been pretty cool. He had even invited them to ride in the limo to the cemetery, as if they really mattered to him.

His parents had been happy about it, too. "Brent Sykes is one of the most dedicated people you could choose. He holds two demanding jobs and still is always at church."

Victor was pretty sure that if you were mayor, you would always show up at church to be seen and to see people. That was part of the mayor deal, wasn't it?

Bridget's faith partner was Mavis. The choir director had become a surrogate grandmother and made her feel so comfortable. Faith partners were a tradition at First Pres, and when she had heard about it, June thought it was a fabulous idea. She was pleased with Bridget's choice. Her girls could use as many adults in their lives as possible. It would add insulation to the still drafty shed of their family.

The adults were gulping coffee together when the kids entered the room. Cord pinned the names of famous people on everyone's backs for an icebreaker game of 20 Questions. "Is he in the news?" "Is it a man?" "Is he American?" Gorbachev was guessed the fastest. Then Mandela.

The room broke into pairs of teens and faith partners. They shared their earliest personal memories of church. Neither Victor nor Brent could remember his baptism, but both had been expected to attend Sunday school without fail.

Victor hadn't thought about how a mortician had to be part of so many services, either at church or at the funeral home. "I've heard a lot of organ music in my time," said Brent sardonically.

For his part, Brent could see from Victor's descriptions that he was more than jammed under his parents' thumb. Well, aren't we all? he thought with an inward sourness. To avoid that for now, he changed the subject to ask about Victor's hobbies, and then asked what he liked to photograph.

Victor started by explaining about his equipment. Brent could see that he had a natural enthusiasm right there under the surface, available for the asking. Did people ask very often? If his memory and experience served him, adults talked at a kid like Victor, rather than with him.

Cord interrupted the chatter to invite everyone to choose confirmation projects. Tiffany and some other girls were recruiting people to paint the nursery. Victor shuddered. The last thing he wanted to do was to paint things baby blue!

Another adult waved the room to be quiet and suggested people think about ways of celebrating the church's 175th anniversary. That gave Brent an idea. How about Victor photographing the church's memorials in honor of the anniversary? It could be a great way to capture some of the history of the congregation. Mavis overheard and said she could help point out the music memorials and the carillon history. Maybe Bridget could help with the research?

The kids hemmed and hawed. Kyle wasn't interested in joining in. He wanted to work on recycling. Using Styrofoam cups at coffee hour was pretty stupid. Bridget was shy of the memorials idea, not knowing much about the church. But the chance to do something with Victor was exciting. Could they handle it themselves? "We'll be here to help," said Brent.

Finally, all was settled, and Victor and Bridget were a team. Kyle elbowed Victor. "What!" said Victor, knowing happily that Kyle was teasing him about doing something with a girl.

"Nothing at all," said Kyle with mock innocence.

"This can be the start of your professional portfolio," said Brent, slapping Victor on the back. Victor was a good kid--he did not need to be the pushover that Brent had been growing up. Go for it, he thought. And don't ignore this cute girl either.

*** *** ***

At home, Victor couldn't think of anything to do. He had to get out of the house. He checked his pocket for his wallet and headed for the garage. His bike was trapped by the car bumper. You'd think his dad could park with less of an angle. Victor lifted the bike up over the corner of the car and pedaled down the driveway.

Saturday afternoon was a busy shopping time at the mall. Victor scooted through the crowded parking lot and locked his bike to the bike stand. "Hey, Victor! What's up?" It was Kyle coming out of the wall of glass that was the entrance to the mall.

Victor affected boredom. "Nothing much."

"Are you coming or going?"

"Coming," but he wished he could say he was going. He didn't want Kyle trailing around with him.

"My mom's in the car. She's got me running errands." Kyle held up some tickets. "She's all worried that she won't get seats for a movie tonight. She's going out with Dad." He rolled his eyes.

A car horn beeped.

"Jeez!" He waved. "Okay! Okay!"

"See ya."

Victor slid past a mom negotiating a stroller through the doors. The back-to- school sales were over. Fake cobwebs trailed the entrance to the costume store.

The bookstore was a couple of stores down from the main department store. Inside, Victor headed for the photography section. The clerk at the register had dreadlocks. Victor vaguely recognized him and tried not to catch his eye. He pulled down a couple of books from the shelves in the adjacent travel section and leafed through them. Would anyone really think he was interested in Nepal? He gave up and moved on to photography, past the Ansel Adams shelf, where he spotted the book he was after. I'm a photographer, he reassured himself. It's perfectly okay to research various styles and techniques.

He opened the glossy pages and studied the men in the pictures. The camera had it just right. They were dancers, and the picture was in black and white. In some pictures they wore masks. No scenery. Just fantastic leaps caught in mid air. One was a cluster of men in a choreographed pyramid. Muscles rippled. The power of the men supporting the others gave Victor a huge feeling of safety. They didn't bow or flinch. It looked as easy as holding air. They were so strong.

Victor loved that picture. Four men, three men. Two men. One man. Some were African Americans. Mostly, they were white. All of them were calm and steady in an arrangement that had no reason to exist. Why pile men on top of each other except to show their trust and strength?

Victor looked at the credits for the picture. He had memorized them already, but he was hungry for anything he could learn about the picture. For the hundredth time he thought about buying the book. Where could he hide it at home?

Reluctantly, he closed the book and put it back on the shelf. He held on to the picture's magic as he slipped out of the store and then left the mall. Climbing on his bike, the wind gusted, and leaves whirled around him. A school bus carrying the wrestling team passed him on the road. Wrestling season had started recently. They were leaving for a match, he assumed. Now why wasn't that pyramid of men in the picture okay like a wrestling team? Victor thought about that as he pedaled. What was the difference? He knew that a picture of the wrestling team on his wall would be unnoticed, but he sensed the book with the photo of the pyramid of men would send off alarms and things he didn't want to imagine.

CHAPTER 16

All Saints' Day was another windy day. Bare branches whipped in the trees above. The raked piles of leaves undulated like the sand of a shoreline during a hurricane. Grace dressed with care. She put on a tailored suit, along with a small flag pin. It was a day to be in careful form, despite the breezes whipping at hems.

She arrived at church early and took a seat next to the aisle. The children were getting in their robes for the banner ceremony. An older girl whom Grace didn't recognize was lecturing one child about holding her banner straight.

Alexandra had taken an interest when Grace's creamy stationery letter had arrived in the mail in September. "They didn't do this in Chicago, did they? What kind of banner will they make for Dad?"

"I don't know for sure, but do you want to help them make it?" June asked her.

"If it's about Dad, I want it to be just right."

June had called the church and asked if Alexandra could help with her dad's banner. Mavis had promptly called back and invited Alexandra to be her apprentice. "The younger children will listen more to a fifth grader than to an old lady like me. And, besides, you weren't here in Stanton as a little child to make a banner yourself. So, you can catch up this way."

Alexandra liked Mrs. Hofmeister. She was Bridget's faith partner. And they had made good foil dinners on the camping trip. An apprentice title seemed pretty good. She thought about adding that to her business cards.

"I hear your dad was a photographer," continued Mavis. "His banner needs to show he had an artistic eye. The Jordan twins are working on it. You can help them. I'll call their mother, Norma – Mrs. -- Jordan."

A few more phone calls and it was settled. Norma was delighted to have Alexandra join them. She and June agreed that Alexandra would go home after church with the Jordan's and June would drop by later to pick her up.

Alexandra thought about the banner, discussed some ideas with June, and prepared some patterns to cut out in felt. She carried her folder of patterns in the car with the Jordans and explained her ideas to the twins. After lunch, Kyle helped them clear the kitchen table so they could spread out the banner.

"Keep the twin-a-bin-a-lins in line," he said to Alexandra. "And, you two, no glue on the floor or chairs or counters or refrigerator or stove or door." He disappeared down the hall with Jumpy scurrying along beside him.

Alexandra proved to be a real asset. The twins stuck to their tasks, eager to impress her and Norma was delighted. They had enough material and scissors for everyone to keep busy. Even with a leisurely break for a snack, they finished up the banner in good time, right down to a yarn nest for the bird. Sam had been an avid birdwatcher. The layout worked, and the colors stood out. Even Kyle approved.

Norma greeted June at the door when she came to take Alexandra home. "She's been a huge help. You can't imagine how much glue two children can spread around a kitchen!"

Alexandra was in a whirl to show off the banner. "Oh, Mom! See? They did a good job drawing the windows for the skyscraper. That's supposed to be Chicago. And don't you just love the nest? It looks so-o-o cozy! If I were a bird, I would want to sleep in it."

"They were on their best behavior for Alexandra." Norma spoke from her heart. "It made it special to know this was about her father. I'm so sorry for your loss."

"Thank you." June smiled. "I'm glad Alexandra wanted to do this. I think it's good for her." She looked fondly at her daughter, and Norma wished she could do more.

"Well, the twins are a handful, but if she ever wants to come by and do another project with them, they would be thrilled. I'm afraid they've adopted her as their very own big sister." She stopped at that. It was enough to tell June it had been a success. She wasn't sure she could sufficiently describe the rest of the story.

As they had been spreading out the large blue piece of felt to begin their artwork, the twins had started with a bull's eye question: "Were you sad when your Daddy died?"

Alexandra thought for a minute. She slowly pulled out the S-A-M letter templates she had brought. "His full name was Samuel, but he always went by Sam. These look a little bit like a newspaper headline, don't you think?" Without taking a breath she continued, "Yeah, I was sad, but I had been sad for a long time while he was dying."

"Were you there when he died?"

"Yeah, he had come home from the hospital, but we knew he was dying. They let him come home so he could be with us. That part was called Hospice. We spent a lot of time sitting in some big chairs in his bedroom."

"Was it smelly?"

Norma clamped her mouth shut to avoid shushing her daughter. The question had come so easily.

"You get used to it. Mostly it's medicine smells. And that's not much." Alexandra started to outline the letters for his name on white felt.

"Did they burn him or bury him? Your daddy. When our hamster died, we buried him. He didn't look any different when he was dead. He was just still. I thought the eyes disappeared when you die. But they didn't."

"Why did you think that?" Norma couldn't help interrupting.

Alexandra answered instead. "I used to think that, too. You know how in the movies people always close dead people's eyes? I thought they did that because they were covering up the empty holes."

Actually, they *are* covering up empty holes, Norma said to herself.

"But I've figured it out. I thought the eyes disappeared because when you die you see God and it burns up your eyes." Alexandra explained. The twins stopped gluing the bird cutouts to consider the comment. "But that's not what happens. I think what really happens is that they close dead people's eyes because the person is kind of sleeping with God. And I don't think that works so well with your eyes open."

Norma looked at the top of Alexandra's head. Her hair was crisply parted and pulled back in a braid. She was bent over her work, talking as she steered her pencil around the felt. The twins resumed their gluing. No one noticed as Norma retreated into the dining room, unable to control the tears channeling down her cheeks.

When she returned, the discussion had moved to a debate over a lacey border around the banner's edge. Alexandra didn't want it to look too dressed up. Her dad hadn't been a fancy guy, and she didn't want to make it seem like a Valentine or something.

The banner, in due course, met with Alexandra's full approval. It was backed in dark blue that looked like Lake Michigan. The gray skyscraper doubled as a border up the left side. The birds and nest filled the opposite corner.

Now it was hanging from its dowel in the back of the sanctuary next to eight other banners. The twins were in their choir robes and were bursting to show Alexandra their one addition. "See, we added a picture of you and your sister on it. Your mom gave it to us secretly so it could be a surprise. It's stapled on. Mom helped us. We thought glue would ruin it." Alexandra looked it over carefully and was pleased.

Grace overheard the exchange. This must be one of the daughters of the new family. Well, two blessings for the church: a new family and someone to help corral the twin girls. They had been a handful since they first arrived in the nursery.

Taking her seat for the service, Alexandra insisted upon sitting next to the aisle so she could see everything. As the processional hymn started, she clutched the arm of the pew and peered to the back as the children began to process. "Hold it up straighter," she said out loud as they passed her. June overheard and smiled deeply within herself, even as her throat contracted.

After the sermon, the prayers were extended as Cord called out the individual saint's name. Once the name was intoned, an older child took up a mallet and hit a large brass gong. *Samuel Wallace.* Each banner was solemnly paraded down the aisle to the center of the chancel. The time stretched a bit, as the deep note of the gong floated in the air.

June's thoughts floated, too. She had lived Sam's death a dozen times while he was hospitalized. Walking down the grocery aisle or stepping out of the shower, the thought would arrest her and reverberate through her. Some day he will be gone. He will be no more. No more. She would be left alone among boxes of macaroni and ground coffee, or naked in the shower, clutching a towel to herself, alone with nothing but shaking sadness.

But he wasn't dead, she would scold herself. Stop it! Why live out a nightmare that is in the future? You can't give up on him! Are you crazy? She had never heard of anyone practicing death this way.

Too soon, though, he did die, slipping away in the quiet of the early morning. Truly gone. Those odd times when she had practiced mourning did her no good. She was unprepared and couldn't recognize what was happening. Grief, the way she thought it was supposed to be, simply didn't happen. She couldn't cry. There were no reverberations through her body. She walked through the hours, a container with nothing in it to spill.

Instead of a wave of trauma, she found the funeral to be a series of more oddities. The schedule was abnormal. There were special colors to avoid wearing. She had to talk to funeral ushers and cemetery representatives. People said things like *condolences,* a word she could never say herself, so hard to pronounce and officious.

The girls had anchored her. Or maybe she should say that they had grounded her. Was it sea or land that she was crossing? She couldn't tell. But she had to get them through the passage or the pass. There was that, and the drive to get Sam through it as well. He couldn't walk or sit or turn over at the end. How could he leave? How could he rise up and pass through the Opening?

It wasn't until the funeral was over, and people were gone, and the girls back in school, and the paper work started, and the dry cleaning picked up, that she discovered the hidden container of grief. She looked out of the window over her kitchen sink at the brick wall of the next apartment building. It was blank. And she knew Sam was gone. She had turned and groped her way into the small bathroom, also blank, purged of all the paraphernalia of sickness. She had closed the door, turned on the bathroom faucets, and without further ceremony cried and sobbed and talked to the walls, underneath the sound of the pouring water.

"Where are you? Where did you go? How did you get there?"

Now, months later, hearing Sam's name, feeling the alert of the gong and then hearing the sound fade, she gave him over to God. "Sam, can you hear the gong? Go with it. Let it carry you through the air." Alexandra crowded next to her. June took a breath, and her chest quivered while her eyes seeped tears.

The parade of banners continued. *"Guy Sykes,"* intoned Cord. The gong reverberated as a bright orange banner advanced down the aisle, swaying slightly to the left. Brent was sitting bolt straight as if the pew back had been freshly varnished, and he shouldn't touch it. June fixed a look on him, hoping to clear her eyes. Everything about Brent radiated rigidity. Her own flummoxed heart went out to him. She hadn't picked up any of this obvious pain and sadness that evening around the campfire. He was alone and deeply lonely, she thought, despite his public persona. Complicated man.

The ritual of the banners had not been something Brent was looking forward to. Hadn't one funeral been enough? His question was ironic. He realized he was gaining irreplaceable insight into the feelings of families after a death.

Arriving at the church, he avoided his usual seat down front for a seat in the middle of the congregation. It was enough that he was there, *for God's sake.* He knew he could contain his martyrdom to himself, but invectives continued to snake across his mind.

He reviewed the order of the hymns and then caught Grace's eye across the aisle. He lifted his hand in a salute, and she nodded with a light smile. His note had arrived a week earlier.

Grace,

We are moving ahead with Guy's wishes. The house has been put on the market, and the apartments have received some bids already. A sale should be in the near future. I know that Arnie Gulp has been informing you of our progress.

Let me say that Guy lived his life regretting the death of your son and his dear friend. I am pleased he could put that to rest by arranging his affairs the way he did. I hope his gesture brings you joy and happiness.

Best regards,

Brent

It had taken him two hours of pacing, drafting, and talking to himself to get that written. But it had to be done. He refused to let his tussle with his father spill over onto an elderly friend.

Grace had been quite relieved upon receiving the note. She was even more relieved by his expression across the aisle. He had looked directly at her--no false humor, no raised eyebrows, and no other drama that she could detect.

The service began, and Brent took himself in hand. Internal swearing really was inappropriate at church. But the stained glass windows, the music, and the pacing of the service bore down on him. The familiar geometry of the pews hemmed him in. The entire setting fanned the questions that were now sitting in the middle of his life. Why had his father set him up? Did his father really think he could buy peace? Maybe he had bought his own peace of mind, but it seemed to Brent that he had created more hurt than he had soothed.

He watched as the banner for his father floated down the aisle. Its fluorescent orange background was studded with red hearts that framed pictures of children. He was reminded of the campfire coals and thought about the outdoors, the Rockies, the fantasy of leaving, and the encircling web of his responsibilities. He forced himself to sit still, but he could not find it in himself to lean back in the pew.

After the last banner passed by, the full collection bobbed in a mass down front. The choir started singing; the children twisted and bumped banners so as to look at all of them. Their exuberance washed over June. Her tears came naturally and easily now. Alexandra and Bridget exchanged looks, and Bridget carefully pulled a tissue out of her pocket.

And then the service was over. People stepped into the aisles, greeting and hugging each other. More tissues emerged. Grace stayed in her seat watching the scene. It had worked out well as usual. She should be satisfied.

But she wasn't. She had caught a glimpse of Brent's face and posture; despite her first impression, she could see that he was not happy. That lawyer, Mr. Gulp, had not told her the truth. Things were very wrong with Brent. She felt guilty and confused and, frankly, angry as well. She hadn't asked for this situation. But obviously people didn't take it in stride when an inheritance was cut up. Drat. What should she do? Should she talk to him? "Hello, Brent. Your father gave a truckload of his money to me and not to you. I didn't ask for it, but I've got it now. Have a nice day." She should write to an advice columnist for suggestions on the phrasing.

Brent had snapped his hymnal shut at the end of the service and took a moment to straighten his tie and fold his bulletin so he could slip it into his jacket pocket. He turned to see Alexandra standing in the aisle. She was banging her straight arms against her sides. She looked at Brent and then took a bead on him. "My dad died. Your dad died, too, didn't he?"

"Yes," he said. "He died in the summer."

She continued without taking a breath. "When mine died, lots of people kept hugging me. People I didn't even know. I didn't like that, and I'll bet all kinds of strangers didn't hug you. You're lucky that you're a grownup."

"People did hug me, but mostly they patted me on the arm. They were trying to make me feel better."

"Well, did it? Because nothing made me feel better. It all sucked."

Her mother turned briefly from another conversation. "Alexandra, that's for the movie script, not church."

Alexandra's gaze stayed on Brent's face. "I'm not supposed to swear." She grimaced.

Brent finished tucking the bulletin into his inner jacket pocket and considered her. Then, he bent and whispered in Alexandra's ear. "Same for me. It sucked big time."

Her face relaxed to its young smoothness. He stuck out his hand, and she shook it. Neither said anything else.

Mavis came by. "Victor is down front, ready to take your pictures with your banner and banner carrier."

"Yep," Brent said. His game face was well intact as June extracted herself from a conversation. "I'm Victor's confirmation faith partner, and I know he's quite a photographer."

"He's got a tripod and a flash," Bridget said, as she started leading them all through the crush of people.

She twirled suddenly to face June. "Mom, is my hair okay for a picture?" If Victor was going to photograph her, she wanted to look great.

June smiled at her daughter. "You look beautiful!"

"You always say that."

The Jordan twins were jumping up and down trying to spot them through the crowd. Alexandra joined them and directed everyone to stand in a line. Victor told them to crowd together more and look as if they were surrounding the banner.

Kyle was with him. "Look sharp now, and leave Alexandra alone," he scolded his little sisters.

"I don't mind," Alexandra said to him. "Just be sure the banner is straight."

"Okay then," Kyle continued. "One on each side of her."

Victor apologized for the flash when it went off too soon. They tried again. As they smiled for the camera, June wrapped herself in the spirit of all the girls arrayed around her. The snapshot would catch the tumble of energy of the children and Bridget's eagerness to smile for Victor.

"Your turn, Mr. Sykes." Victor shifted his tripod a few feet.

They found the young boy with Guy's orange banner, and he stood tall next to Brent. The resulting picture caught the brightest of the banner that seemed to illuminate the big smiles on both faces. It did not catch the churning behind Brent's eyes.

CHAPTER 17

J.J. Travers pulled the letter from the little cubby that was his mailbox in the village store that served also as a post office. It was the first Christmas card of the year. He turned over the heavy luxurious envelope. Of course, it was from Grace Evanston, and, judging from the postmarks, it had taken over ten days to get to him here in Central America. Not too bad. Mail from the States was unreliable.

It was hard for him to think about Christmas in this nearly equatorial climate. But Grace was the right person to inaugurate the season. She had been a faithful holiday correspondent for decades now, maintaining their slender mutual tie.

Before opening the letter, he picked his way across the rutted road and sat down on a low concrete wall beneath the village's announcement board. Flour paste glue and the odd nail held up the small posters and sheets of newspaper. Various notices in Spanish announced well baby examinations and the name of the mayor. The noonday sun was warm but not hot. J.J.'s hat shaded his eyes and kept the top of his balding head from reddening. He took a moment to appreciate the contrast with the winter at home.

A young boy on an oversized bicycle was coming up the street. Alternately he stood on one pedal and then the other, while struggling to keep the front wheel from wobbling too far. The basket of potatoes leaned dangerously left and right. The market had been over by 8:00 in the morning and, as with some children, he had apparently been allowed to stay for morning classes. But now, he had a load to deliver. JJ waved.

Digging into his pocket he pulled out his penknife, ready to read his mail. Catching himself, he unwrapped his lunch before slitting the envelope and pulling out the note. He did not need to hurry back to the clinic. Things slacked off for the extended noon hour, so he could read and eat at his leisure. But the habits of a lifetime were hard to break.

Most of his holiday correspondence would be disrupted this year. It would prove how many people actually read his cards last year and noted the news that he planned to take an assignment in Guatemala on a medical mission. Even those who had updated their address books and knew where he was wouldn't send their cards early enough. He would be getting notes into February. Not a bad thought, actually.

He opened Grace's card, appreciating that she had taken a moment to write. She must be quite elderly now. He himself was 64, so she could be closing in on 90. He thought about that for a minute: 86? 87? Maybe she had been a teenager when Vaughn was born. He didn't think so, but what did he really know? He had only spent a handful of hours with the Evanston family, and that was nearly 40 years ago.

It had been another age, another world. Or had it? He remembered the chaos, the insidious creep of war. The little international news he got these days seemed perhaps a terrible parallel. He wondered if the US would find itself at war again soon. It worried him deeply.

But back to Grace Evanston. What in the world did she have to say to him that would fill two sheets? He turned the page and could see that she had filled both sides. Three pages in all. This was a record. The old gal was suddenly prolific, or maybe lonelier than ever. He took a bite of food, settled in, and started to read. Her handwriting took careful reading. She formed her letters in an old style proper way, but the shakiness of age gave them a filigree look. They were a challenge to decipher.

Dear J.J.,

Merry Christmas from here in Indiana! You are far away, I believe, and I hope I have addressed this correctly so it will reach you.

We are having a mild winter here in Stanton. Nevertheless, I have to bundle up just to get the mail. What cold we have can get into the bones…

It was a bit surreal, reading a letter from her. The only time he had seen her was at Vaughn's funeral. Yes, here he was, on the downside of middle age, in a dusty corner of the world, a long way from Indiana. The tenuous contact he had with this elderly woman was from another life long ago, and that history touched a part of him that had lived in yet another life on a third continent. He idly paused to watch a jeep bounce along the road kicking up a trail of the dust. Funny, the only thing that connected all these continents and stories was the dust. It was timeless and everywhere. And, of course, it was a symbol of death, wasn't it?

He could never forget the dust of Korea. The gray dust silted in corners and coated surfaces. The snow was darkened, and food was gritty. The path to Building #4A next to the airstrip had been crunchy gravel that morning in 1951. The dirt and pebbles had frozen overnight, but shook apart as he stomped on them. His boots were already coated with dust. As he walked and gulped at his coffee, some sloshed out and splashed on the toe. The dust streaked.

The US Army command occupied significant territory around the airstrip. Barbed wire edged the perimeter, but the phalanx of sheds and low buildings created a wall of protection, too. Along one side, larger buildings provided places for maintenance equipment and spare parts storage. The sterility of the architecture was lost, however, in the hive of activity between the buildings and the planes.

The coffee had begun to kick in, but the headache was hanging on. That's why they called them hangovers. In those days J.J. had been a fair-sized man, and he could drink a lot. The night before he had put a fair amount away, more than he could accurately remember. He pulled up his shoulders and tried to adjust his vision down the long runway. Yep, he could still see hangers through the hangover, which was a common and very stupid joke around the place.

J.J. felt particularly stiff and plodding. Normally, a Fred Astaire fluidity loosened his joints and prevented him from being an unmovable bulk. In high school, coaches had commented on the natural spring to his feet, loose and light. He could bend over, hug his knees, and smile between his calves. In the mirror, when he practiced, it looked hilarious to see his face poking between the army boots and GI camouflage pants.

He had been entertaining the guys and girls last night in the bar. That's where he had been drinking. He used the physical gyrations and balancing as a monitor, rather than counting drinks. He never completely lost his balance. He never lost that reserved place deep inside.

Now it was the cold grit of the morning. The day was starting out with the predictability of a soldier's day -- the usual swearing and grumbling, the usual bad food. The coffee, though, was strong and scorching hot. It had just about busted the mist across his eyes.

At 0710 hours the first of the day's planes was due with a load of new soldiers. J.J. needed his boys to get these new boys checked in fast: the shots, the kits, the files, and the orders. He pulled open the door of the corrugated building where the set-up was underway. It took rigorous logistics to process a planeload of people, and another one would land before they would finish with the first. He hated to keep guys waiting in line after their long flight. They had a war to fight, not lines to stand in.

Radios crackled and clip boards snapped on forms. When the bus rolled up with the first wave, the hive of activity roared up a notch, as if the queen bee had flown in.

J.J. didn't mind his job. Better than the front lines. The boys coming off the planes were usually scrambled by the changes in time, as well as the dawning reality that they were a long way from home. J.J.'s internal radar could track the anxiety, even if it were only traces on an otherwise determined face. Going to war was serious stuff. He tried to be neither officious nor mechanical.

He saw Vaughn for the first time around 0900. J.J. was at his desk; all around him were the rustling of carbons and the cha-chunk of date stamps. Looking up, he saw the man standing at his desk at attention. His eyes were as black as a hawk's, and he was missing nothing, clearly reading the papers and orders upside down.

J.J. flipped a few pages, confirming the numbers on the file with the orders. "You're from Indiana," he said. "Big skies out there."

The recruit was alert. "Yes, sir!"

"Good apple pie, too, I imagine." He squished the stamp into the inkpad. The pad was drying out, so he had to pound it very hard.

"Yes, sir!"

"We have great apple pie here, too, if you like the pie part and don't expect apples." He slammed the stamp hard again on the cover sheet. It made a pale mark, almost too pale to read. He filled in a couple of numbers to make it clear.

"Yes, sir!"

"Your papers are in order. Line up for shots over there by the file cabinet."

If they had opened enough of the boxes with the serum, the line wouldn't have built. And if the line hadn't built, he would have stayed where he was and refreshed the inkpad from the filler bottle kept in the drawer and stamped in the next arrival.

But the main medic called for him to help with the lengthening line of men. So he left the filler bottle next to the bone-dry ink stamp and swung over to help. Heading around the file cabinets, he started preparing shots and checking sheets. He plugged one man, and then Indiana was up next. "Right arm, soldier," he said, indicating for him to roll up his sleeve. He wiped down the arm with alcohol, checked the flow of the serum through the needle, and started the injection. The two men locked eyes over the needle for a silken thread moment. J.J. pulled out the needle, re-swabbed the area, and put on the bandage.

"It might swell a bit over the next 18 hours," he added automatically.

Indiana rolled down his sleeve, stood up from the chair, and moved to Station 5. That was all. There was no more to remember, except that there was all to remember.

J.J. moved on to the next man in line, and after giving about six more shots, he returned to his desk post, refreshed the dry ink stamp, and resumed checking files and orders. The line of men had grown so that he had no chance to think for himself as he fought down the back-up for the next two hours.

That evening, as he took off his boots, he wondered briefly if there had been anything in Indiana's glance. He couldn't tell. He wanted there to be, but like much of his personal life, he took nothing for granted and knew his only possible option was to wait and watch.

It was a week later when another line of men allowed them to cross paths again. Holding out his tray in the mess line, he watched the server with ladles in both hands pour out gravy two trays at a time. Moving his tray up quickly to accommodate the double action, it clanged against his gravy partner. J.J. looked up at the tray's owner to see Indiana. The flashing look lasted only as long as the clang hung in the air, but it was long enough. Their eyes had locked. They moved on, neither indicating with a smile or nod that they recognized each other. Just the look.

And a third time the very next day. A glance that held a second too long. And no other gesture. With that, J.J. didn't worry anymore whether it had happened. He could start on Part Two of the worries.

And so it went. Four, five, six encounters. Four, five, six times their eyes locked, held wide. Neither blinked. The time hung between them in the way it did between the moment a car went out of control and the moment it hit an embankment. The sixth time, J.J. raised an eyebrow. Indiana raised his chin. Still, the looks and the arching could have been ignored. Except that with each encounter J.J. felt something ever sharper hitting him in the ribcage. It was the sharpness of danger.

Apparently Indiana was not being shipped out. He was assigned to the news staff office. This was confirmed when he whizzed by one day on a motorcycle with a typewriter strapped on the back. It was so bulky it probably threw the motorcycle weight off center. But it had *News Staff* stamped on its high black back. There was no locked glance that time. He wasn't sure Indiana had seen him.

Encounter number seven lasted through a blink. Encounter eight was again in the mess. J.J. deliberately sat a table away on the opposite side. Twice their eyes bumped and carefully slid away. And then Indiana changed his posture, swinging his leg out into the aisle. The boots and pants were regulation but somehow hung on him as if tailored to him individually. He owned his strut and was saying so. J.J. impeccably stood up, bussed his tray, and left. It took a force of will.

The carefulness of it all was the ritual of J.J.'s life. He stored each bit away, a curator of the moments. He cared for them in his store of memory. He often thought about people who worked as spies. What was it like? He didn't know, but he could guess. He imagined that spies had to watch everything--reading signs, gestures, and expressions. They couldn't over-read. They had to test, check, and re-check. He supposed that patience was part of the required temperament. How else could they watch, wait, and watch some more before making a move?

He couldn't understand why anyone would choose intelligence work. On the one hand there was the routine--the cover, the patience, and the waiting. Maybe that gave a person the necessary reserves for the whiplash of emotions--the fear, desire, danger, and pulsing sweats. But why? Why divide your life like that if you didn't have to?

J.J. was deeply practical, however. He saw what he wanted and went for it. When he was about 14, he had figured out that to get what he wanted, he would have to manage one side of his life carefully. Very carefully. He didn't dwell on fairness; he dwelt on what he wanted. If there were a price, he would pay it and get on with it. He had planned to go to college and move to a major city, because he wanted the anonymity of a city. He had hoped to do something in medicine. He wasn't sure if he had the ability to be a doctor, but he wanted to try. It was his other passion.

In an odd twist, Korea had intervened and delivered a form of fairness. It had interrupted his plans, but it had interrupted a lot of people's plans. The call-up fell on everyone. It was very scary until he found himself behind a desk. And then he realized the bonanza. The Korean conflict was all about men--a world of men--men in all sizes, shapes, and colors. Men everywhere. Tall, bleached, tan, tight, athletic, hairy, funny, cocky, sweet, swarthy, everything. No touching, but lots to watch. He decided to enjoy the watching. His life was on hold like everyone's, but he could still watch.

He and Indiana had now logged ten encounters each with unmistakably direct, down into your soul, locked looks. But the stakes were too high. He figured he had to log another ten, before figuring out if there would or could be anything more. Never mind that each encounter left his heart strangling his lungs and his skin on alert. He could still fight down the raw sexual rush. He wouldn't be stupid, but he knew his blood was rising.

And then there was the break. It was a late winter day or maybe an early spring day, depending upon which way a person viewed the progress of the snowmelt. The days were getting a little longer, stretching into a later dusk. In the evening, a group had decamped to the bar district together, choosing it over a barracks card game. J.J. and his buddies headed for the Peacock Bar.

The Peacock was one block over from the main noisy bar street. The noodle stand next door had good soup. Their kimchee was strong; its smell oozed into the bar and sat on the floor, like a heavy low fog. The Peacock was one of a half-dozen favorites of the soldiers. The madam there had ropes of fake pearls and an amazing capacity for names. She dressed her girls with little in the way of clothes, as well as little tiaras of brightly colored feathers.

Of course, J.J. wasn't looking for female companionship, although he found the bargirls fascinating. His genuine interest in them made him something of a favorite. They were young, tough gals, doing what they had to do. He recognized the reality of their lives and respected it. Since he never gave them any business, he was careful to avoid monopolizing their time. His real reason for the occasional bar spree was simply to have a cover story. Who would suspect him to be a lover of men if he spent time and money in such a place?

And it gave him an audience. When his ballerina sister had taunted him for not being able to do the splits, he had worked his body into a highly flexible pretzel. His contortionist routine played well in the bars. He encouraged it, knowing that if he kept himself the center of attention, he could actually deflect eyes. The more laughs he got, the more catcalls for his stunts, the less likely anyone would notice that he never went upstairs. The guys were too busy getting ready themselves or just laughing at his stuff.

There was one person who did notice -- the madam. It was her business to notice. She was there to catalog the men and their choices and match them to girls. However, she had a soft spot for J.J., because his antics enticed boys in and kept them laughing.

That evening, he was upside down blowing cigarette smoke between his legs, which, when he could manage smoke rings, drew great hoots from the crowd. Bronx cheers and whistles competed with the thumping music coming from loud speakers.

When he stood up, Indiana was there. "I can read upside down, but that doesn't take twisting my body all to hell," he said with a grin.

"Yeah." J.J.'s blood rushed back into place and pounded into a peak pulse at the same time.

"Want a beer?" Indiana asked.

"Already have one." He indicated his bottle on the table and sank into his chair. Then he realized it was the only free one. A girl was heading towards them. Clearly the madam had dispatched her to Indiana. He was new meat.

"Hello, Joe," she said with a laugh. "Buy me a drink, will you?" J.J. watched him, alert to everything.

"Ma'am, please allow me to offer you a drink and the companionship of this whole table of fine men," he said, upending J.J. right out of his chair. He handed the girl into the chair and delivered her a drink. The guys all grinned. J.J. found himself standing at the bar next to Indiana, beer in hand. It had been a flawless deflection.

"Vaughn Evanston," Indiana said with an extended hand.

"J.J. Travers."

Their eyes met and they shook hands. J.J. was sure he could get lost in those black eyes.

Nevertheless, he stayed on course. The next hours sailed by in a freewheeling conversation over beers. Others joined in, and they took over

117

a large table. J.J. did some more acrobatics. People peeled off, and more crowded in. They told jokes. Ordered food. They swapped stories of hometowns and argued baseball. For most of the crowd it was an effort to chase away the unspoken dread and homesickness. For J.J. it was an effort to confirm the unspoken, and find here what he hadn't found at home.

The madam had her eye on them all evening. She was happy to sell them food and drinks. She wanted to sell more, which she knew she could with time. They were good boys, high blooded.

In the next few days, J.J. and Vaughn saw each other twice in the mess tent, where they ate a quick meal across from each other. On Sunday J.J. was deeply surprised to look up from his seat at services and see Vaughn stepping into his row to take the vacant seat next to him. He could have kissed the longwinded chaplain that day.

Vaughn told him he was off on an assignment for ten days. "Wish me luck. I haven't seen anything of this country yet." They shook hands, and he was gone. J.J. joined the ranks of lonely, craving hearts. Everything he was learning about Vaughn was moving him further down a road and into an intersection of his carefully mapped hopes. The man was fun and deeply alive, apparently keen to everything around him. He was strong and knew what he wanted. And J.J. knew exactly what he himself wanted. He thought of locking his arms around his chest, rubbing up against his cheek, and pumping himself to exhaustion. He tortured himself wondering if he had it right. Did Vaughn stare at everyone with those black eyes, seeming to illuminate what you usually kept far away from the light? J.J.'s own emotions surged up and down between the doubts and the fierceness of his certainty. Where was the truth?

And then the evening came when the covert changed to overt. Crammed into a corner table, J.J.'s group spotted Vaughn at the bar's doorway. Demanding that he come and play victim to a new joke, the men opened up a seat. Throughout the evening, the beer flowed, and men got up to hit the head. Vaughn was slowly shuffled over next to J.J. The two men were then slammed against each other on the bench as another wave of men and girls wedged next to them. The room was smoky and dark. Cemented together, J.J. felt the hard muscles in Vaughn's shoulders boring into his. Twisting to find some room, the guy on the other side of Vaughn hunched forward, putting his elbows on the table. With the ease of that new sliver of space, Vaughn pulled up both his arms in a touchdown gesture and then slid them across the back of the high bench. Doing so, he gently brushed the back of J.J.'s neck in a light, casual, intimate stroke of his loose fingertips.

J.J.'s heart simply stopped. His neck burned white hot. He held his gaze on a conversation happening down the table while he counted to ten. Then he turned to face Vaughn. The black eyes, the smile, the cocked head were right there, inches from his face.

"Yeah?" Vaughn said. It was an invitation like no other.

The moment hung, freighted, in the middle of the bedlam of the bar. It wasn't a matter of suspense--it was a matter of changing his life. The proposal was as clandestine as it was public. He couldn't protect himself any longer. What was public and private would be redrawn. Could he do it?

It only took a second. "Yeah," responded J.J. A second pair of eyes, hands, ears, arms, legs. He knew it would be a tangle.

Through the rest of the evening it was the beer chugging, the girls, the cards, the jokes, the loud music. It was also a hand on his knee for a moment, and then sliding up his thigh as Vaughn stood up to leave. J.J.'s body felt ready to explode.

The honking of another jeep startled J.J. back to Guatemala. He smiled to himself with the memory and pulled off his sunglasses to clean them. The noon sun was both bright and now hot, and the slight shade from the notice board wasn't helping much. The creamy notepaper was a glare for a moment, and then a beautiful tracing of his heart.

Their love affair had been a stymied one. It was romantic and silly and hungry and virile all at once. And very scary. They could find ways to talk, but privacy doesn't exist in army life. Lacking options, they had returned to the Peacock Bar one evening. As Vaughn joked, it was better than sitting at the base entrance under the flagpole. They drank and talked. J.J. stepped out to take a piss. As he passed the madam, she had caught him by the sleeve and in a low voice asked if he wanted a room. He had brushed her off, but she had persisted. "No, Joe," she had whispered. "A room. No girls. A place of private. You like that, Joe. You pay rent. Make you happy, Joe."

J.J. was astonished. What kind of radar did the woman have? He told the story to Vaughn, who was equally astonished. He slipped off to have a chat with her and got the same offer. "She says others call it the Cockpit," he reported back in a very soft voice, but with a huge grin.

Finding a safe room was winning the war. The room, a brilliant ploy, was reached by ducking through the same curtain of beads that all men had to pass to meet the girls. If one of them winked at the other boys at the table, paid the madam, and then zeroed through the curtain with the beads clashing and clamoring around him, the other would wait a piece of time and hook up his belt and repeat the exit caper. No one would think about it twice. Down the hall, the door that seemed to protect private living quarters turned out to be another passageway that connected with the building next door. It was there the Madam would send them. There, Vaughn and J.J. could close a door and close out the world--which they did.

CHAPTER 18

Choosing a Christmas tree and hauling it home was not one of June's favorite things to do. Sam had enjoyed it and had always done it. She hated the sticky pitch.

She picked up the girls right after work. The evening was chilly. If only she'd taken five minutes and changed her clothes. At least the tree lot was a grassy knoll, more inviting than the urban parking lots in Chicago. The strings of outdoor lights were like jump ropes, anxious to arc in a full circle from the stiff wind.

With help, June and the girls strapped the tree on the top of the car. On the road, she was very conscious of the branches flopping on the roof. She hoped the soft slaps of the boughs wouldn't damage the paint on the car.

They dragged the tree to the front door. If it had been shrink-wrapped in North Carolina in October, it was determined to spread widely now. "It was nice of the guy to cut off the bottom. I haven't a clue whether we have a saw or not," she said with all the cheerfulness she could command.

Bridget had retrieved the tree stand from the basement the day before. Still in their boots, they were able to prop up the tree. Alexandra crawled underneath and twisted in the screws. The needles jabbed at June as she steadied the trunk. Carefully they spread the red quilted skirt around the base of the tree. The beautifully proportioned white spruce reached a foot short of the ceiling. The star ornament would fit comfortably. June stepped back to admire it. Thank God that's done.

She needed to wash her hands and change clothes. Something hot to drink would be good before fussing with the lights. Heading for the kitchen, she heard Alexandra counting the light bulbs that were dead. Great. One more detail she had missed.

After fruitlessly scrubbing the pitch into her skin rather than off it, she made cocoa and popcorn. Forget about dinner. The oil sizzled, the corn crackled, and a homey aroma filled the air. Popcorn was about good times, cozy times. It was about family. She felt her throat clench, and without warning her eyes filled with tears. She tightened her face, but just as suddenly a sob escaped. Coming through the basement door with boxes of decorations, Bridget scurried into the living room and whispered to Alexandra. Together they converged on June.

"Sorry, bunnies," June said, covering her eyes with one hand.

"Oh, Mom, we can have a family cry," said Bridget. "We haven't had one in a little while."

The girls stood straight, waiting for June to sob or breathe or talk.

When the hospital released Sam for at home Hospice care, they had made a pact about crying. Alexandra had wanted to be brave for him and not cry in his presence. June had told her that it was important to cry, or she would feel sick inside. So the girls had suggested they cry together, but out of his hearing. Since it was a matter of health, Alexandra reasoned, they needed to log enough cries to wash out their insides.

Sam knew, of course. Those were his girls, all right. Alexandra was always working on a scheme. And Bridget was ever loyal.

His photographer sharp eyes caught their expressions and radar communications. They also caught the light on their faces, the color of their eyes, and the wisp of hair escaping a barrette. During the day he kept his vision sharp, soaking up every chance to watch them.

His turn to cry came late at night, when blurred vision didn't matter. June would hear him and stir from her deep chair by the bed. She would bend over him and cup his head in her hands as he reached up to her elbows to hang on. She would breathe in his smell as her hair fell forward into her eyes. Her breasts swung underneath the nightgown and grazed his fingers. Hugging him close was difficult with his bones protruding and the pain ever ready to stab. But her whispers were close to his ear.

In the kitchen she blew out a sob, scattering the top bits of popcorn in the bowl. "It's the Christmas tree lights. Sam always did them, and then last year he watched us do them, remember? He was able to sit up that evening." The girls both sniffed and leaned against her. She took a deep breath and struggled with the lingering pain. She gulped.

"It's okay, Mom," said Alexandra. "If you didn't cry, I would worry that you were forgetting him."

"But I remember later that night he was in such pain. I had to give him extra morphine. I think God could see that and answered. We only had the tree up maybe three days when he died."

The girls were quiet. They couldn't remember for sure how long he had lived after the tree was decorated. Alexandra reached for a piece of popcorn that had landed on the counter. Her head swiveled suddenly as the doorbell rang. June sniffed hard and blew her nose. "Who could that be?"

Mavis and Porter stood at the door bundled against the cold. "We hope we aren't interrupting, but we are only dropping off a basket, especially for my faith partner here. Merry Christmas, Bridget."

In the flutter of inviting them in, June almost sobbed again. What generous people! The basket was heavy, almost hard to balance with all the jars, tins, and cheeses. "I know young people don't always go for the real cheeses, but maybe your mother will eat those. The cookies are for you."

They toted it into the living room and chatted about starting the decorating. Alexandra found a box of fudge with her name on it. "Mom!" she called. "This is for me! I should eat it right now before the ants find it under the tree."

Porter chuckled. "Of course you should. I've had many presents ruined because we left them under the tree. You could even get mice if you aren't careful."

"We should be going, dear," said Mavis. "June hasn't even had a chance to get out of her work clothes."

"Oh, Mom, could they stay and have hot chocolate? Please, please?"

June and Mavis exchanged an adult look. "Can you spare the time? It would be special to have you with us while we work on the tree."

Porter was shedding his coat in a flash. "All right, young lady. But no chocolate until we get these lights up."

"Maybe you could excuse me while I get changed. This suit's had a bit of a beating today." She smoothed her skirt and felt the sticky pitch on her fingers. "Bridg, maybe you and Mrs. Hofmeister could put on some music." Impulsively, she gave Mavis a hug as she left the room.

*** *** ***

Later that evening, June retrieved a few bags from her closet. The tree needed a present or two underneath it. Untangling ribbons from the box of wrapping paper and laying them out on the kitchen table, she chided herself. What had possessed her to pack and move recycled ribbons from Chicago? Of course, the huge silver bow was traditionally on the first present to be opened. But why bring the rest of them? They had gotten badly tangled. Carefully, she pulled out the silver one, not yet sure which gift it would grace.

What to start new? What to hold and keep?

She stopped for a minute and wandered into the living room. The tree's fragrance took her back to summer camp as a child. She remembered steep mountains and pine trees with their funny-looking bark, like overlapping mottled pancakes. One pine grove had been next to a suspension footbridge at the edge of the camp, where she had crunched across soft beds of needles to get to it. She had adored that bridge, hanging on to its sides as she had crouch-walked from one side to the other. The bridge would sway, and her heart would jump. She never looked down, imagining a river rushing below instead of the dry creek bed.

When was the last time she had walked that bridge? Was it really nearly 30 years ago? Was that possible? She could still remember small details, such as the splinters in the wood and the warmth of the footstones where she stepped off the last slats. There was also the burn of the rope as she hung on tightly and inched across. But she couldn't remember the trail that led away from the bridge. Maybe she hadn't ventured beyond the bridge. She couldn't remember hiking in that direction. Where did the trail go? Why was the bridge swinging so high over a dry ravine? Who had built it?

At the time she hadn't thought too hard about its purpose or mechanics. The bridge was simply a scary, exciting, and unusual place. Her heart would thump hard inside her chest, no matter how often she crossed the bridge. Her whole body would start quivering when she reached the middle of the bridge and tested to see how a small shift could set it in motion.

Where had that curious and daring girl gone? June looked down at her hands, at the bits of pitch still spotting her palms. Now she was a mother and a widow, and the pitch on her hands was an annoyance rather than a badge of adventure. She had car payments and a closet full of suits. What had happened? One minute she had been Alexandra, jiggling the ropes to test a swinging bridge. The next minute she was standing in a living room sniffing hard at the fragrance of a Christmas tree. Her life was like a vacuum tube. She was one place unable to comprehend anything but the thrill of danger and - whoosh - she was someplace else, grown up and loaded with demands and responsibilities, unable to swing freely.

Her eyes closed around fresh tears. She'd lost her innocence. She'd lost Sam. She was lost and alone. She could hardly bring herself to think it. She had her girls. How could she say she was alone? But, she was, and Christmas brought it all up. No one was there to say, "Sweetheart, you are terrific!" No one shared the parenting. And no one was there to buy the Christmas tree and set it up. She took in a shuddering breath.

"Mom, are you all right?"

Her eyes shot open to see Bridget in her nightgown at the door, backlit by the hall light. Her hair was in a braid. She could have stepped out of a chapter of *Little Women*.

"Sweetie! You're still up? I'm having a sentimental moment. Here, come over here." The two folded themselves up on the couch together, and June blew her nose. "Can you smell the tree?"

"Yeah. It's cool to have a big tree that almost reaches the ceiling. The star seems to be really shining over us from way up there."

"One of the benefits of moving out of the city."

They both were quiet for a moment. June fixed her eyes on a Christmas ornament that had come from her mother. There was another from Sam's mother, and others of yarn, Popsicle sticks, and sparkles made by the girls. The tree was loaded with memories. They added up to a lot of family life and a considerable lifetime. That was what the whoosh had been about. There were plenty of memories of those years. Her world started filling itself in again.

"I was wondering if we should drive up to Chicago over vacation for a visit. Would you like to do that?"

Bridget surprised her. "Alexandra might like that. But I want to be here in case there are things to do with people."

"You mean parties?"

"Yeah, there's a caroling party. And there's a group who might go to the movies or even bowling. They think it's funny that I've never been bowling. They do it in the winter 'cause it's something to do inside when it's cold."

It was still working. June had not tried to grab at early signs of victory. But the pieces seemed to be fitting into place: school, church, work, and the new house. She liked Bridget's friend Tiffany very much. She was such a practical, sturdy, and determined girl. Maybe Victor Beck figured in the picture as well. She knew better than to ask directly.

"But, Mom, we can go visit Chicago if you want. I know we're trying to be busy and not think too much about Dad." Bridget shifted the pillows. "But we have to think about him sometimes."

"Of course, honey. Dad is always close by. We'll keep putting his silly bird ornaments on the tree for the rest of our lives." She crushed her daughter in a deeper hug. Her heart swelled. Sam would always be with them, both his life and his death.

They nestled together in quiet.

"Mom," Bridget started carefully. "Mom, we know you will always love Dad. But wouldn't he want us to start making new friends and finding new people to love?"

June thought for a moment. "Oh course," she said. "He wouldn't want us to be lonely. It isn't about jealousy or forgetting about him. He would understand that." She was happy to think that Bridget was valuing her new interests and affections so much that she was weighing her father's possible opinion. Yes, Victor was certainly a part of this.

"Well, Alexandra and I have talked about it. We think it would be okay if you started dating."

June was startled. She was more than startled. "And what in the world got you two talking about something like that?"

"Well, you were talking to Mr. Sykes on the camping trip. It made me happy to see you laughing and happy. He's nice. And he's single!"

June burst out laughing. "You two scamps!" And as she said it, she knew Christmas didn't dish up old memories as much as it continued to give her the most wonderful Christmas gifts. She was magnificently grateful for her daughters.

Brent Sykes. Hmmm... She drew out that thought as she turned off the tree lights and went upstairs to bed.

CHAPTER 19

The annual holiday party had been in the works since Thanksgiving. The group was planning to carol at the assisted living center before going to Victor Beck's house for food. Loretta always imagined her house full of Victor's friends. "It would be easy, honey. Invite some friends over, and you can play pool or watch movies." She was stockpiling food and cider.

When she called Cord to confirm the announcement in the church bulletin, Loretta apologized. "I want everyone to feel a warm welcome. Victor can be a bit standoffish, you know."

Cord wasn't going to engage Loretta in further anxious discussion about Victor. Loretta and Spencer had given him enough insight into unnecessary hand wringing for now. His wife was repeatedly telling him to stop hand wringing about his hand wringing. Heading Loretta off at the pass, Cord told her Victor was just fine and, furthermore, had a great little partner in Bridget to work on his confirmation project. "And it's not a make-work project. The Session is quite delighted. It will be of genuine value to the church to have a pictorial record of our memorials, especially this anniversary year."

Loretta sighed inwardly. They hadn't heard boo about Bridget since the camping trip. Victor hadn't even mentioned a confirmation project.

At the dinner table that evening, she asked about the project. Victor mumbled in return, "Yeah, Mr. Sykes suggested it. I'm going to do the photography, and Bridget wants to organize it and write the captions and stuff."

Loretta raised an eyebrow in Spencer's direction. "You'll need space to lay it out. There's not enough room in the basement. We could put leaves in the dining room table, and you could work here."

Victor shrugged.

"She's such a nice girl."

Spencer sensed the pressure on Victor but knew his wife meant well. The girl was a beauty, all that dark hair.

"Sure, Mom, whatever. But why'd you have to invite everyone for the caroling party?" Kyle was okay and a couple others. But he didn't want *all of them* coming over. The younger boys would act dumb, and the girls were snoopy. They would want to see his room, and his mom would want to show off his photography.

And why couldn't she order pizza like a normal person? No, she was cooking lasagna and salad and a bunch of garlic bread and stuff. And serving it on plates with silverware! It was like a dinner party or something. Sighing inwardly, Victor was glad when his dad changed the subject.

*** *** ***

They drove together in vans over to the Golden Fields Assisted Living Community. "You have to park in the visitor's parking area," announced Tiffany, whose grandmother lived there. "Some people are in wheelchairs, but at this place they don't just run the TV's all day. They play music and have classes and lots of stuff."

Comfortable with her superior knowledge, she said hi to the people at the reception desk and told them what the group was up to.

An elderly man with watery eyes greeted them and introduced himself by saying he had been a member of the church for over half a century, if they could imagine that. He seemed pleased to be their host and led them to the dining room. After passing out song sheets, the advisor gave them the first pitch. The youth croaked through a couple of carols. The old people might be sad, but having the youth sing carols was really sad. Some of the younger boys were only pretending to sing.

Bridget had observed their host with interest. "He must know a whole lot about the church," she said to Victor as they were settling back into the vans. "Maybe we should interview him about the memorials."

"You can if you want. I think the memorials folder has all the information you could need. It's the photography that will make the real difference."

Was Victor teasing her? Or being snippy? It would be nice to know. They had felt like friends after the mission trip and on the camping trip. And now they had the confirmation project. But each time is was like starting over, as if he hadn't met her before. It didn't add up.

"Yeah?" she decided to tease him. "A big old dark picture of a bell? That'll make a huge difference."

"Are you kidding? My photography is world class," he teased back. "People look at the pictures first. They don't read the captions first. The pictures are what it's all about. Right, Jordan?"

Kyle shrugged his shoulders, "Yeah, well I hope you're better at taking pictures than at singing. That was pretty horribilific back there, Beck."

Victor snatched at Kyle's hat.

Kyle stretched as far as his seatbelt allowed, grabbing Victor's hat.

"Cut it out back there!" shouted the dad at the wheel. "You're making the whole car shake."

"Sorry!" they both said in unison as they put on each other's hat.

"Hey, I like it," said Kyle.

They burst into the door at Victor's home, shedding coats and scarves. "You can take off your boots and leave them here at the door," said Victor's mom. She pointed them towards the dining room. "The food's in there."

Bridget couldn't miss the framed photographs in the entrance area. She suddenly felt very much at home. Their house was filled with her father's photography. Her mom had hung many of them even before they had unpacked all the boxes. "Did Victor take all of these?" she asked Mrs. Beck.

"Oh, yes. He's quite a shutterbug. He's also learning to mat and frame."

Bridget looked at the pictures. She didn't have a keen eye, but she had learned some things to look for. There weren't any people in his pictures, just objects. He took things from odd angles. One was taken lying on the ground at a gas station looking up at the gas hose pumping gas into the car. Victor must have gotten really dirty doing that. The picture had a mate. The other was also from under the car looking at the tail pipe. The straight pipe and the limp hose were both in a silhouette.

There was another pair of car part pictures. The bumper was in one; the dashboard was in the other.

A third pair framed an open car truck and an open glove compartment, caught through the glass of the window.

An adult called from the dining room, "Listen up, everyone. Into the dining room so we can say grace."

The room quieted down for the briefest of minutes and then resumed its buzz. Bridget joined the jostling line for food. Kyle was next to her still wearing Victor's hat. "Real dishes. Not pa-per and plas-tic. En-vi-ron-men-tal-ly Smart!" He punched each syllable.

"Yes, and Loretta, this is wonderful food," one of the advisors chimed in. The worst thing about working with kids was eating their food. Tonight the salad had feta cheese!

As Victor stood at the end of the line, some girls passed him to sit on chairs in the corner. They had been arguing. "But that's so gay," said one with obvious disdain.

"Yeah, isn't it," confirmed the other.

Victor's ears went on alert.

It was times like these that made him sweat inside. Would he ever stop feeling this way? It never varied. He felt parts of himself, including his brain, tighten. He knew what he had to do. What was he waiting for? Get on with it.

Looking around the room, he saw Bridget. She was holding a plate and nibbling on her food, but she was looking at the one large photograph that this mother had hung in the dining room. He went over to her.

"Hi." He hadn't planned much beyond that. Now what should he say?

"Hi. I didn't mean to sound mean in the car about your photography," she said. "I hadn't seen it before."

"Yeah, well, you can see a lot of it here. My mom kind of goes wild hanging it all over the place."

"I'm supposed to say something about your style, I guess," she continued.

He was a bit surprised. "Well, I like cropping the pictures and getting them cut down to the main thing. Landscapes and stuff are too big and busy and sort of wide." He stopped, not knowing if she had meant for him to talk like that.

When he took pictures, he wanted to get something fixed in a frame. Just one thing. He didn't want all the complication of peripheral vision. He wanted to nail one thing.

It was hard to do. You took the picture, and then when you looked at it, you saw all kinds of other stuff in it, like the background and surfaces. If you took a picture of a car, you began to see bumper stickers, tissue boxes in the back window, or stuff hanging from the mirror. Or there was a piece of trash on the road underneath it. He wanted to airbrush out half the picture.

He actually liked the idea of photographing the memorials. It was about taking single shots of single items.

"So you must plan your shots pretty carefully?" she asked.

"Yeah, you could say that. Like the car pictures. I wanted to find pairs of things that are alike but not quite. It's mostly about getting the right exposure and light."

Victor hadn't met a girl who cared about the artistic side of photography. "Do you like photography?" Even before he was done with the question, he knew the answer and felt stupid. Her father had been a photographer, and she would be loyal to him. He should think before asking her something that would bring up her father.

To his relief, Bridget responded easily. "I like it because of my dad. But he mostly did pictures for his job, so they were of people, weather, car accidents, or just about anything. He couldn't do much to set those up, of course. But he did more artistic pictures of the family. We have a billion pictures of me and my sister growing up."

"Same with me because I'm an only child." Good. He hadn't said something dumb.

"We don't remember to take pictures now. My mom doesn't know much about cameras and Dad's equipment is pretty technical and complicated. Maybe you would know about figuring them out." Whoops. She had said too much.

"Yeah, I could probably figure them out. I'll bet it's expensive stuff if it's professional. You ought to know what you have."

He always forgot how easy it was to talk to her.

Would it be okay for Victor to look at her dad's camera stuff? She would ask her mom.

"Come play some pool, you guys." Their conversation was interrupted and ended naturally.

Bridget kept quiet most of the rest of the evening. Tiffany drew her into a circle of girls cutting out snowflakes. They sat next to each other, and Bridget listened as Tiffany chattered. They had established a pattern of adjusting to and complementing each other.

Tiffany had gotten to know Mike's little sister pretty well. The two girls had been on the phone that afternoon because of a recent drama that required Tiffany's comfort and advice. The little sister was in middle school and had a crush on a boy in her class. But her best friend had gone and told the boy. This had been horribly embarrassing, and the sister had called Tiffany in tears. "Girls shouldn't be so mean to each other," observed Tiffany. "It's such an immature thing to do. You have to support each other. My sister tells me that all the time. She sends me letters about how army women look out for each other. She's got a couple of specific friends who do that, but it isn't just friends. Other girls, too."

Tiffany talked about her sister all the time now, and Bridget could see why. Kuwait and Iraq were big in the news, and it was confusing and scary.

Bridget felt her problems weren't so important in comparison. Take her non-existent love life, for example. Bridget remembered the time when she had a crush on a boy in seventh grade. They had held hands a couple of times and sat next to each other at lunch. It was kid stuff. The next year her dad was sick. She had been sad and often lonely at school even with her friends around, because no one really understood what was happening. And there certainly weren't any boys who were sympathetic, or even knew.

But now there was Victor, and tonight he had been so nice.

Being in his home made her feel closer to him. He was complicated and kind of serious. And then he had a mom who seemed a little over the top. She didn't seem to understand kids. The dinner had been too fancy--more like a grownup party.

Maybe he was a little moody at times because of all that. And he seemed cuter all the time. She could tell he was taller than last summer because he looked down at her more now. She flushed thinking about that.

Parents were knocking on the door to pick up kids and take them home. Everyone started fishing around for shoes and scarves. When the door closed for the final time, there was one remaining coat on a chair, two bags of cookies, and plates and cups all over the kitchen. "You see, I was right," Loretta said happily. "So many nice young people! All you need to do is invite them over, and they have a good time. I saw you talking a lot to Bridget. She's got such gorgeous hair."

Victor shrugged. He hadn't thought about Bridget's hair. "I talked to all kinds of people tonight," he retorted. Wasn't she always telling him to *include* people in conversation?

"Yes, well, all the same. She's beautiful and has lovely manners."

He was glad the evening was over. He helped clean up and then went to take a shower and watch television. As he undressed, he realized his mom had changed all the towels in his bathroom and had put out stacks of little embroidered hand towels. He had seen them in the downstairs bathroom, too. He climbed in the shower and started to scrub himself with his faithful sea sponge, but the soap smelled very sweet and flowery. This wasn't his deodorant soap. Why did his mom need to change the soap in his bathroom? Did she think kids were going to take showers? He was going to be walking around smelling like a garden. He turned the hot water up and stood under the stinging hard spray.

The room filled with steam, misted with perfume. He felt his shoulders scalding. He turned off the water and rubbed himself down with a towel.

The mirror was steamed up. He stood straight and looked at the blurred image. He was hot pink from the heat, and it made his hair look darker brown. The white towel around his neck made his shoulders look broad. Lifting weights was working. He strained to see if his torso looked more muscular, but the image was fogged. All he could tell was that he was pink.

Pink. His body had leaked pink. How scary! It looked raw and blistered. He sat down on the toilet, and the cold lid felt good. Raw, blistered, pink, and gay. He dropped his head down between his knees. Stop it! He almost said it aloud. Everyone turns pink in the shower.

But what if people made even a small connection between him and something gay? He wasn't a limp wrist kind of person, but there were lots of ways that people could get ideas. He might say something, or they might see him looking at the photography book at the bookstore, or they might notice how he watched other boys. Then they would find other clues fast enough.

He had to guard against all that, keep things very tight and locked down. He couldn't smell like flowers! And he had to keep his mind from going there. Stop thinking about it. He had to think straight. No more wishful thinking. If it ever came out, his mother would just die. His father would be shocked and disappointed. Other kids would freak out. People would laugh at him and tease him. They could also attack him. He was sure of it. He didn't want to imagine the kind of violence that might happen.

He absolutely had to file it all away. No more looking at pictures. No more thinking about boys or fake wrestling with Kyle or any of that stuff. No more. None. He had to be nice to Bridget. And that really wasn't that hard. He had to give himself a more complete cover. He couldn't risk a crack. He had to keep people from even forming the thought--stop it at the source.

The fan was pulling the moisture out of the room and clearing the mirror. In it he saw a guy flushed from the shower. He scrubbed his hair with the towel, brushed his teeth for two full minutes, marched himself with his pure mind to his room.

CHAPTER 20

The low sun made the day feel old before it had started. It was fiercely cold outside; earlier slush on the streets had hardened into a washboard pavement.

Inside, needles covered the carpet under the heavily decorated tree, and the bright red poinsettias drooped. The congregation was similarly exhausted from Christmas. Men had set their belts on a looser notch after all the heavy eating. Women plucked at their blouses, hoping the buttons weren't straining too badly at their buttonholes.

Brent stuffed his dark glasses into his pocket as he stepped into the pew behind the Beck family. The service began, and as the choir proceeded down the aisle, Brent tried to sing, holding the hymnal high and with both hands to open his chest. The tempo made it a chore. Down front he spied Alexandra enduring the hymn as well. She was raising her shoulders dramatically with each line, showing the effort it took to breathe and sing.

His gaze shifted to June. The back of her head formed a lovely curve off her neck. She was sharing her hymnbook with Bridget, one long arm resting lightly on her older daughter's shoulders. It seemed to be an effortless embrace. What a lovely circle of a family!

Mercifully, the hymn ended, and he took his seat with everyone else. June's daughters settled in, one on each side of her. Was her lovely circle of a family truly lovely? Or did it just appear to be so?

The world had sharpened for Brent in the time since he had found his father's letter and mustered through the arrangements and instructions of the will. For one thing, he was slightly suspicious of things that looked idyllic.

He was on the downhill side of disposing, selling, storing, and organizing, thank God. His basement had new industrial style shelving filled with boxes of family memorabilia and papers. Each load, each signature, and each decision had both met an obligation and shed it. And each step fashioned itself as a revelation: is this for real, or is there another story to it? The Christmas season for him had been about untying the knots and snipping the tape that had wrapped up his previous life in a ribbon. To prove how much he was questioning the old, he treated Christmas Day like any other and went to the movies.

But now it was the New Year, and here he was in church again. Was he ultimately just a creature of habit? Or did he have a new tablet on which he could write?

He continued to look at June and her girls as questions ticked through his mind. What did he want, really? What was he trying to do? What was he trying to be?

June's effortless little circle of love took on a larger meaning. What did it mean to love? To trust? To be honest about it, he had some rough spots there.

Cord had moved into the pulpit, and Brent realized that he had missed a chunk of the service. He glanced at the couple next to him. They were listening attentively; the husband was cradling his wife's hand in both of his. How can they be sure? he wondered. At that very moment Spencer, sitting in front of him, whispered something to Loretta and extended his arm across the back of the pew and around her shoulders.

Brent almost groaned. Okay, love is everywhere. What about him?

The service droned on. As Cord spoke the benediction, Brent had made some tentative deals with himself.

He tapped Victor on the shoulder with his bulletin. "Come by my office sometime. We need to catch up." Victor nodded, and Loretta flashed Brent a grateful smile.

"Sure," said Victor.

Brent shook some other hands and deliberately moved up the aisle against the flow of people. "June," he said. "How was your Christmas?"

June smiled at Brent as she put her hand on Alexandra's shoulder. "We had a pretty special time, didn't we, girls? It was a first for us in many ways, and we did a passable job of it."

"Good," said Brent. "I'm glad to hear that. I finished clearing out my father's house. Then I went to the movies."

It was already a conversation he knew he could trust.

"The movies!" said Alexandra.

"Yes, the movies."

"Didn't you get any presents?" she asked.

"Nope. I didn't want any presents. Believe me, Dad's house was full of too much already, in case I needed a duplicate of anything. You know-- televisions, ladders, couches. Do you need anything? A mop? A microwave?"

June laughed. "No, we're already crowded in our little house. But I'm glad you've got that behind you now."

Together the four of them chatted down the aisle to the door. Brent shook Cord's hand, passing on the gunslinger gag. His grip was firm and he meant it, when he said simply, "Good to see you, Cord."

"Ah, Brent." Cord responded to his relaxed face, noticing that they had both dropped the honorifics. "And it is good to see you, too." He slapped him lightly on the shoulder.

"Alexandra, Bridget, and June. I hope the New Year is starting well for you."

*** *** ***

When Victor dropped by his office, Brent filled the candy bowl and told him to sit down. "You haven't been here before, have you?" he asked.

Victor hadn't been entirely sure about visiting someone at a mortuary. The other Mr. Sykes had brought them over for a tour once. But he'd never been in the office. There was a desk, but there was also plenty of room for a couch and some living room type chairs. The coffee table had a big catalog on it, apparently with options for flower arrangements and coffins.

He shrugged as he looked around. Maybe he should have worn some nicer clothes. "We came on a tour with your dad," he said. "But I've never been to a funeral here."

"Yeah, that's right. Dad would show kids around the place. I hope it was interesting. It's a special business. It was the family business, and so I've been around it all my life. Your dad is an engineer, right?"

"Yeah. I don't think he expects me to do the same thing that he does."

"Family businesses are a little different that way. It's an asset that the family owns, so it's about figuring out what profession you want to follow, but it's also about dealing with owning something that has a lot of value. It could be sold. But it's not like an advertising agency. It has community roots and carries a family name, so it was strongly associated with who I am and my family and our place here. That's hard to give up."

Victor hadn't thought about any of that. His dad worked at a company, but it didn't mean much to him. Once a year there was a company picnic.

They munched on some candy.

"How's the memorials project going?" Brent asked.

Victor shrugged again. It hadn't really started, and he needed to do something about that. It involved calling Bridget and thinking about things like their friendship. He felt guilty about letting things slide. And it made him tired. "We haven't really started."

He doesn't want to do it, thought Brent. Was Bridget the problem? How could that be? Or was it teenage lethargy? Brent wanted to tell Victor to get

135

on with it, but Victor practically resonated with tension about what he was supposed to do. Better not to be pompous by saying something like, "Oh, it'll be a lot of fun."

"You will when you want to." Brent was gratified when Victor smiled back. Jeesh. It wasn't that hard to give kids a little room to figure things out themselves.

He switched gears. "Listen, I have two tickets for the IU basketball game. Saturday. How about coming with me?"

"Really?" Victor was startled into a full grin. "Okay."

*** *** ***

A snowstorm the next day blocked roads, but by Saturday things had cleared. Nevertheless, Brent picked Victor up early, and they headed out on the state highway to Indiana University, over the hills and past Brown County State Park. They talked about camping trips, Victor's classes in school, the IU team and its record the past few seasons. Victor had never actually attended a game, and he was excited.

"I thought you played basketball," Brent said, puzzled.

"I only did for one year in middle school. It's mostly been soccer since then. My dad follows sports in the paper, but he likes to be around the house when he's not working. He helps me a lot with my photography."

"I would think that would be the fun part of having a teenager, taking them to games."

"Huh? I don't know that they think being parents is fun. More like a responsibility."

Well, thought Brent, gusto wasn't the word he would use when describing Loretta and Spencer. "I guess I wouldn't know, since I don't have kids." He hadn't meant to criticize Loretta and Spencer, even indirectly. He chided himself. No need to poke at someone else's parents.

"Do you want kids?" Victor wasn't sure it was good to ask the question, but Mr. Sykes had brought it up.

"Actually, I have always thought that I didn't. I don't know why. It seemed to me to be more fuss and responsibility than I wanted, since I already have a lot on my platter. But I'm not sure that people should ever say never, if you know what I mean."

They both stared out of the window for a moment without talking. They could hear whistles as police directed traffic at the lights near the stadium. Before turning into the parking lot, they could see huge piles of snow banked along the perimeter. "I hope we can find a good parking spot," Brent commented. They searched up and down a couple of rows and found one not too far from the entrance. "It'll make it easier to scoot out at the end."

Picking their way across black ice on the pavement, they could hear drums pounding from the sports arena. The stands were filling quickly, and the room pulsed with sound.

The game started fast, and the fans were pumped. As the teams ran off court at half time, Brent shouted over the noise that he would get some drinks. "You hold the seats." He left his jacket draped over the bench.

Victor watched idly as a line of college guys pranced onto the court in hula skirts. They were making a show of themselves, with long blonde wigs and heavy lipstick. Their hairy legs looked ridiculous. They had painted their torsos with Greek letters and fake bras. After line dancing around the edge of the court, they formed a high kick line.

Brent returned with food and drinks. He laughed and pointed, "Bunch of guys acting gay."

Victor felt everything go black for an instant. What did Mr. Sykes think about gay people? Did he think they were guys being women? He managed a shrug with his shoulders. These guys weren't gay at all – just a bunch of dumb fraternity jocks.

There was nothing he could say or do. He attacked his hot dog and chugged his drink. Brent laughed again as the line broke up and the guys started flirting with each other, pinching each other through the skirts as they minced off the court.

A guy sitting behind them slapped Brent on the shoulder and leaned forward to say, "Whaddya think? Are we going to get a butch drill team now?" Brent turned slightly to respond, but the man was already talking to someone else. Victor wondered what he would have said.

On their drive home they talked about the game and the coach. Television cameras had been there. "It's big pressure on these players, being in the spotlight."

"Do you feel like you're in the spotlight as the mayor?"

"Not like that, obviously. But you can't be a public official and stay out of sight. People notice what you do. People find you whether you like it or not. They have complaints and ideas. They want to talk with you or at least to you." He chuckled.

"Do you think about it much? That people are watching you?" Victor wasn't sure he'd said that right. "I mean, does it bother you? Do you feel as if you are always on stage or something?"

"No. Not any more than the usual being in a small city like Stanton. People like to talk about each other, not just about me. And, then, I don't have anything to hide either." He had said it easily. But, it was entirely untrue on so many levels. His whole life was about putting on a game face, lining up behind others' expectations. It wasn't a spotlight, perhaps, but it was a candle that never burned down.

It had seemed the way to live for so long. Amazing how you could live one way for 38 years, and then it stopped being the right thing. Sort of. There was that constant dilemma of moving forward with his own life, but, no matter what, he still had his father's secret, and it folded in on him at times, like right now, in this conversation with Victor.

Victor was quiet. What if you did have something to hide, he wanted to ask. Would you be the mayor if you had a secret? Could you hide your secret from everyone for your whole life?

The moon was shining cold above, reflecting off the snow. He could easily make out the line between the mountains and the sky. The trees were harder to distinguish.

Mr. Sykes seemed to be thinking about something. Victor tried to look at him out of the corner of his eyes. He talked to him as if Victor were an adult. He wasn't used to talking to kids, so he talked liked they were adults. That was cool, like explaining how he felt about having children. Adults wouldn't normally say that to a teenage boy. Victor thought about that for a minute. Mr. Sykes didn't have kids because he wasn't married. Was he divorced? He didn't think so. Why wasn't he married? Was he gay?

Wow. Could Mr. Sykes be gay? No, not a chance! He wouldn't have said those things about gays back at the game. He wouldn't have called any attention to it. But, in some ways, if he were gay, his comments worked. By calling someone else gay he had tricked Victor into thinking about himself and the frat boys, not about whether Mr. Sykes was gay. It had the opposite result. Double wow. That's a pretty complicated game to play.

The car hummed along the country road, up and down the Brown County hills. Both Brent and Victor were silent, each lost in thought.

CHAPTER 21

Bridget was experimenting with her hair. It was long enough for a good braid, and she could twist it up as well. She'd gotten great hair sticks in her Christmas stocking. The chopstick thing had been cool but had gotten old. She had always envied the sleek and smooth buns of ballerinas. But pulling her hair back tightly like that only half-worked. Her bangs were still growing out, and her hair was chronically frizzy.

She was impatient. It had taken too many weeks to get organized with Victor to start their confirmation project. They'd talked about it a few times at church and once at school in the halls. He seemed okay about it but never did anything. Finally, today they were going to meet Rev. McDaniel at the church and start taking pictures of the memorials. Victor should be by soon. He was going to check out her father's photography stuff first.

She heard the doorbell ring and her mother answer it. She decided on a ponytail held back with a broad red elastic band.

Victor was sitting in the kitchen drinking coffee when she appeared. June had called it café au lait, dumped in a lot of milk, and reheated it all in the microwave.

"Bring that with you, and we can go look at Dad's stuff," Bridget suggested. June bit her tongue to keep from warning about spills. They were getting to be young adults, drinking coffee and all.

She checked in on them a few minutes later. Victor was looking over light meters, clearly appreciating the additional toys. She suggested he try using some of them at the church. "Let's get in the car."

When they arrived, they found the church door locked. Victor tested it again, pulling hard to be sure. "I guess Rev. McDaniel isn't here yet."

"We'll wait in the car where it's warm."

"I wonder if it's heated up in the tower. I guess it can't be, since the bells ring outside." Bridget shivered a bit. Rev. McDaniel had promised to let them into the church and open up the carillon tower for them.

"Here he comes." Cord was pulling up behind their car.

"I think he works a seven-day week," said June. "Be sure to say thank you to him." She watched Bridget and Victor greet Cord. She could feel her daughter's increasing tension. Bridget was eager to do the project, anxious to see Victor, and finding ways to connect with him like offering the camera equipment. Young love was hard.

Cord waved from the doorway as he unlocked it. They disappeared into the building, and June shifted the car out of neutral. As she pulled away from the curb, the carillon rang the full hour. She had never been around a carillon before. How could metal clapping be so gorgeous? The sounds followed her down the street and around the corner.

Inside the church, Cord steered them towards the Deacon's closet. Victor knew it well from years of finding hiding places when they played Capture-the-Flag at youth fellowship. The miniature room was new to Bridget. She breathed in the smell of silver polish and cedar.

Together they reviewed the Session's list of memorials and figured out which items were stored here. Cord gave them hints for locating the furniture items. "Look for the plaques. There should be one on each." He showed them keys, cupboards, and locked boxes. "Have at it, you two," he said, as he left to work in his office.

Without much ceremony, Bridget began opening the velveteen bundles, spreading the host, the communion pitcher, and the plates across the table. Victor fretted about the lighting. They decided to take the silver into the sanctuary to photograph.

"I don't get it," Bridget said, holding up the very heavy, cold, silver chalice. "I know you're not supposed to say this, but communion doesn't seem so special to me. It's just eating. If we were Catholics and thought we were eating the body and blood of Jesus, maybe it would mean more. It's just bread and grape juice. No big deal."

Victor was trying various angles. "My dad told a story of a man who was an alcoholic and totally worried about drinking communion wine, real wine. Not grape juice. You know, alcoholics can't drink *anything* if they want to stay clean. But communion shows Jesus was winning – winning over death, I guess. So when this guy finally drank the communion wine, he could stay in control and not fall down into drinking alcohol again."

Why did he forget how talking with Bridget was like this? He always had something to say. Things just showed up in his mind. He could even talk and look through the camera lens at the same time.

"Well, I've been taking communion for as long as I can remember, and it never does a thing for me. It doesn't make me feel better or worse."

Victor didn't respond immediately. He was worried about the flashes reflecting off the silver. He shifted his position and framed the shot. The battery flash hummed back to life.

Bridget was looking for something to do. "Is there anything we can do to make this silver look more alive? I feel like we should toss the plates like Frisbees or something. They all look the same. I know it's expensive, but so what?"

"It's okay," said Victor. "This is just a picture for the record. It's not meant to be fancy. It's not the one picture that counts. It's the group of them."

He angled around taking shots. For a while it was very quiet except for the clicking of the camera.

Both of them wrapped everything back up and started checking for plaques in the sanctuary. "I've got a ton of homework this weekend, and my sister never seems to have anything. I remember having homework when I was her age."

"The work's not too hard here until you get to high school. That's why I learned so much about photography. I had time for extra stuff."

"I don't have any serious hobbies," Bridget said. "Maybe I should try something. In Chicago we would go to museums and ice skate in the winter. Family stuff."

"Ummm. Well, I do stuff so I can get away from my family. Being an only child means I'm the center of attention already. And they never miss a beat. My parents are big into church, so I have to do that. We come every single week. Perfect attendance."

"That's dedication."

"Yeah, they're kind of obsessed." He would never have said that to anyone else. "When we're camping, even though half the church is at the park, we always come back early on Sunday to go to church."

"Don't you get sick of going to church all the time?"

"Yep," Victor sighed. "But it's easier to go than listen to my mom when I try to stay home."

"Sometimes my mom lets us off the hook," said Bridget. "She's more pushy about it here because she wants us to meet people."

"Yeah, I wish I had your mom." He sighed again.

Bridget thought this over while they searched the pulpit for its plaque. "They sure didn't want anyone to find this," she said, as she discovered it on the underside of the podium itself. She had to move the vestment to see it clearly.

"I never knew there were so many plaques around this place."

Luckily they were getting through the list, although the last big item was the carillon. "Do you still want to go up?" asked Victor.

"Sure," said Bridget. "That's going to be the best part."

Victor distributed the camera equipment between them, and they headed to the back of the sanctuary. Victor had been to the top of the tower many times, but Bridget had never seen the bells. Cord had unlocked the door in the vestibule. The first half-flight of stairs was a staircase which then turned into a metal switchback unit like a fire escape. A small room at the top had a little window on the door to peek in. The console inside didn't look like the keyboard she expected. Instead, it was a length of small pedals at waist level.

They opened the console room. Victor took pictures, squeezing against the wall so that he could get the widest angle. It was tight, so Bridget stood in the doorway out of the frame.

"Back in Junior High Fellowship, one of the big things was getting to play the bells." The carillonneur had showed them how to hit the pedals with a fist. Only a few were activated electronically for ringing the bells on the quarter hour.

The clock over the console said 11:14. They waited, and when the bells started, they covered their ears. It was only four notes, but the sound was deafening.

The last short flight of six stairs above the console deck was nothing more than a broad, very steep stepladder. Bridget went first and Victor followed, worried as his camera swung and hit the bar. Reaching the top, Bridget stepped forward and edged along the catwalk that encircled the bells. It was a tight path, giving way at times to little platforms. So many bells!

"Are we going to take individual pictures of every single one?" she asked.

"Naw, that would take forever, and it would make a boring layout."

"So what do we do?" She zipped up her jacket. It was cold.

"We'll take pictures of the biggest ones and some examples of the smaller ones. You okay with that?"

He began to set up his tripod. There were long shadows around the bells, and he wasn't sure whether to use the flash or long exposure. Bridget kept up a stream of conversation as he frowned and shifted equipment. He twisted around to shoot from various angles, at one point lying on the uncomfortable catwalk to capture the inscription on the biggest bell. Twice the bells rang the quarter hour, and they covered their ears. Bridget could feel the sound against her rib cage, like fingers tickling.

Finally, they were done. Adjusting the straps on their shoulders, they started down the ladder. Bridget was following Victor, but as she reached for the banister, the equipment swung away from her shoulder. She tried to correct her balance a split second too late. She stumbled forward onto Victor, who extended an arm to brace her, but managed mostly to jab her with the tripod that he was carrying. She rebalanced, rubbed her elbow, and grinned with some embarrassment. "Are you okay?" he asked.

"Yeah, it's just that the stuff swings so much."

"Do you want me to take those cameras? I can carry them."

"Oh, no, I can do it." Bridget caught herself. "Thanks."

Victor suddenly smiled directly at her. "You're welcome."

Bridget felt the force of the smile and enjoyed it. She smiled back. They were standing very close on the landing outside the console door. They held each other's gaze, and then, surprising himself as much as her, he leaned over their moats of camera equipment and kissed her on the mouth. She saw it coming and met him half way.

The kiss lingered for a moment. Its experimental pause was a gentle and sweet message for her. For him it was a full count to five. He closed his eyes.

Everything was suddenly very wrong! And it was his fault. It was bad to mislead Bridget like this. He couldn't face her, but he couldn't hurt her by yanking back. He kept his eyes closed. *Three... four... five* and he broke it off.

He had answered one question, for sure. Kissing a girl wasn't hard. It also wasn't much of anything. Her lips felt very soft and thin. Flimsy. He wanted something more scratchy, full, and firm.

And, he didn't want to do it again. Ever. He had that figured out. However, he had to set it right. He didn't want to trick her. She was special, a real friend. He couldn't lie to her. She was smart about people. Maybe she would understand.

He took a breath. He had to say it, but suddenly the bells started a whirring wind-up. The full boom of the Big Ben call began, followed by the eleven strikes for the hour.

He couldn't be heard, but the words came out in a rush. "I'm sorry. I think I'm gay."

Unable to understand him, Bridget shook her head again and then laughed. The bells continued to ring *seven... eight...* Her laugh was lost in the din, but her look of pleasure was clear. Victor knew she hadn't heard, and he knew he couldn't say it again. He froze in confusion. She saw his blank look and put her hands over her ears.

Nine... ten... eleven... The bells came to a stop. "It's awful loud," she shouted. They both turned to walk down the last stairs. The ringing in her ears slowly disappeared. The ringing in his head only got louder.

CHAPTER 22

"Hey, Victor!" Tiffany called. "Sit up here with us."

Victor had argued with himself for weeks about attending a wrestling match. He didn't know anyone on the team. Would it be obvious why he was there? He told himself it was school spirit. The tournament was at their high school this year, and there were matches scheduled over three days. He finally decided to attend the finalist matches. The crowd would be bigger, and he might not be noticed.

Hearing his name, he looked up and saw Tiffany sitting with her boyfriend. He waved and started up the steps on the risers. Mike had his arm around Tiffany; she patted the empty seat next to her.

"I didn't know you liked wrestling," she said. "Mike's cousin is in the heavy weight class and is going to wrestle soon."

Victor tried to sound completely natural. "Actually, I don't come much, but I thought I'd show some school spirit."

Tiffany grinned at him. "That's nice."

"You play any sports?" asked Mike.

"Yeah, soccer. I'm not real good, but I've played it since I was a little kid, and I like the game."

"Cool."

Tiffany leaned against Mike, snuggling further into his arm. "I don't know much about wrestling, so Mike has to explain a lot. Things can happen really fast, like when someone gets flipped over. But most of it is watching them strain and push against each other."

They all turned to watch. Victor marveled at the way the wrestlers' muscles bulged, and how they scrambled to grip each other. He could feel his own body tensing and responding. His face started to flush. Oh, God, he thought. I can't let anyone see me.

He realized he was caught, sitting next to Tiffany. He was glad she was giggling into Mike's ear. He couldn't stand up and leave so soon. And he couldn't trust his body. He started to stare at the basketball nets and at the people in the stands across the court--anything neutral and boring. Oh, God, he repeated to himself. He felt like crying. It was terrifying. He was losing it right there in the gym with hundreds of people around him.

The buzzer ended the match, and people jumped up to applaud. Tiffany and Mike were already on their feet, so Victor pulled himself up. He pulled at his sweatshirt and stamped his feet self-consciously. He had to move. He had to. His heart was pounding. He couldn't stay here. He couldn't.

"Gotta go," he said. Tiffany's face looked puzzled as she kept applauding. But he barreled down the row and ran down the steps. As he burst out of the front doors of the high school, he gulped at the air. He started to walk home. It was a long way to go, but he needed to move his legs hard and fast. He stepped things up to a trot and then a run. Finally, his heart was pounding for a different reason. Oh God, oh God, he panted to himself.

CHAPTER 23

"What do you think is the deal with Victor?" Tiffany asked.

They were sitting on Bridget's bed, and she was teaching Bridget to knit. Growing up in a big city hadn't helped Bridget learn basic things, she had observed. She didn't know about knitting, sewing, or washing a car. At least she knew about cooking.

However, that wasn't entirely fair. Bridget also knew a lot about taking care of sick people. She had learned that when her father was sick. Tiffany really respected that. It was easy to teach her the other things, she figured.

"I don't know, actually. It makes me a little mad. He kisses me in the bell tower, and then he does nothing. He doesn't call. We haven't done anything with the memorials project since then. Maybe I did something wrong."

Tiffany was ready for that. "No, you did *not* do anything wrong. I think there's something going on with Victor. He's acting sort of odd these days, even for him. I mean, he's always been a little shy and quiet."

"Anyone looks shy and quiet next to Kyle and you."

"Yeah," Tiffany giggled. "But he barely talked when we saw him at the wrestling match, and then he ran out all of a sudden."

"Really. Well, maybe he'd forgotten something. His mom fusses over him too much. He is sort of on a short leash."

"I think that freshman boys might be in high school, but their maturity is about in the sixth grade." Tiffany was very sure of this. "Take Kyle. It's pretty cool that he's into his gymnastics and is starting to go to bigger competitions. But does that mean he should walk out on his friends? I never see him with Victor anymore. They weren't together at the wrestling match, and they used to go everywhere together. Kyle doesn't even come to youth group most of the time." Tiffany equated maturity with loyalty and taking responsibility. "So, maybe Victor is also off buried in his photography and forgetting about anyone else."

Bridget had no theory about boys. She liked Victor a lot. She always felt easy and comfortable with him, but that was when they were together. When they weren't together, it seemed to get complicated. She wasn't sure this was an adolescent boy problem as Tiffany had labeled it. Victor was quiet and seemed to live a lot in his head. She thought she understood. Her mom had told her that she was a little introverted herself.

But her feelings were hurt. "Well, I hope he is developing all those bell pictures that we took. It would be nice if he would let me know."

"You guys have a good project. But it's a big one. We got our painting project done in one morning. So, whether he likes it or not, you'll have to spend time together."

Bridget glumly worked on her knitting. She was pulling the yarn too tight, and when she tried to correct herself, the next row turned out too loose and stretchy. She couldn't get it right.

Tiffany took Bridget's needles and inspected the scarf. "We can fix that. Let's take out those two rows. That's the good thing about knitting. You can unravel it whenever you want." She showed Bridget again how to loop the yarn around her fingers to meter out the tension properly. They worked together quietly for a moment.

"I think you should do two things." Tiffany had a plan. "You should call him up and make him come over with the pictures so you can start working. Just give him orders like that. And, we should also think about other guys. It's not like Victor is the only guy around. Maybe you would get interested in someone else. Maybe he'd notice you if you were less available."

"Well, he was the one I met early on when I moved here."

"Yeah, I know. But the high school is big, and there are other nice guys. Mike has a bunch of friends, and you should meet them."

"I don't know if my mom would like me getting involved with someone older."

"You're kidding." Tiffany was surprised. "They aren't older as in gone-off-to-college or anything. Everyone's in high school."

Bridget didn't say anything. Her mom was just an excuse. Mike was really nice and polite, worked after school, and was buying his own car. But she hadn't really had a boyfriend before and didn't want someone who was really experienced. She would worry all the time that she wasn't doing things right. She rolled back on the bed and looked out the window. "Oh, all right," she said. "I'll bug Victor. And we'll see what happens."

Tiffany smiled. "Good. That project gives you a lot of chances to get him out of his head."

*** *** ***

147

June was standing by her desk when her phone rang.

"June? This is Brent Sykes. I'm wondering if I could drop by and see you for ten minutes."

"Of course. I'm free until our first deadline meeting at 11:00."

"I promise I'll walk right over, and it won't take long."

He was true to his promises. She offered him the free chair in her cubby and raised her coffee cup. "Can I get you some?"

"No thanks. I'm fine. I'm already over-caffeinated this morning. I just wanted to make a quick suggestion." Brent was there for a reason, but he was also looking for ways of bumping into June that weren't always in the aisle at church. The freezer aisle at the grocery store couldn't be counted on either.

"We've got three people from Stanton who are being posted to the Middle East." Noting June's raised eyebrow, he added, "I know, because Jack Hardinger gave me a call about it." Jack was the local Congressman. "I'm not sure how he learns about these things. Maybe they are briefed, or maybe families call his office.

"Two men are career military. They have families of their own, but their parents are here in town. The third is Lydia Cantor. You might not know her, because I think she went into the army before you moved here. But she's from a family at church."

He noticed that June was nodding. "Oh, of course. Her sister, Tiffany, knows Bridget, I expect."

"Yes, we heard the news last night. Mrs. Cantor is very proud of her daughter but also very anxious, as you can imagine."

"I'm not sure if I can imagine something like that, to be honest."

"We'll be following her," said June. "It's a new kind of story to be tracking military women in combat."

"I'm trying to brainstorm ways in which Stanton can show its support. So I thought I'd check with you folks and pass things your way."

June nodded. This was, of course, the good thing about being a local paper.

Brent had some ideas. If nothing else, he would encourage the town council to pass some votes of appreciation at the next meeting, and they would make it a routine agenda item to share updates on the three and any others that were overseas.

They chatted some more, and he thanked her for her time.

June continued to sip her coffee and then placed a call to Cord McDaniel. Yes, he had heard the news and had visited with the Cantors the night before. Next she called the library and asked for help with references for the history of women in the military. It was getting close to the 11:00 meeting, so she used the few remaining minutes to study the enlarged map of the Middle East that had been posted on the conference wall. Other staff began to take their seats. "Operation Desert Storm has arrived in Stanton," the executive editor said, opening the meeting.

*** *** ***

Alexandra raced from the car to the church doors. George Morrow was just pulling one of them open.

"Well, you made it!" he exclaimed.

"Yes, I was sure I'd be late," she replied breathlessly.

"Not at all. We can set things up together. Do you remember what we need to do?"

"Of course!"

"First, I need to take care of some dog poop on the walk there. Why don't you get the folding chairs and the bulletins so we can fold them?" George set off for the janitor's closet.

Alexandra peeked into the empty sanctuary and didn't see the bulletins in the last pew. She wasn't sure where else to look. She clomped into the coatroom. Although there was no snow, she was wearing her high boots, because she thought they made her legs look really long. She dragged the two folding chairs out the front door which George had propped open.

Returning to the coatroom, she pulled out the short stepladder, set it up in the middle of the room, and climbed up until she was standing on the top.

"Oh, honey!" George cried, suddenly entering the room. "Be careful. You should never climb to the top step. It's not safe at all."

"I was trying to see the box of bulletins. It isn't up here." She started down the four steps of the ladder.

"Oh, they aren't on that shelf. Weren't they in the last pew? Let's take another look. The secretary always leaves them in the sanctuary."

Alexandra jumped off the last step and thumped out. George returned the stepladder to the corner. She could have fallen. What a reckless streak kids had.

They found the bulletins, and set up their folding operation. Alexandra always chose to use George's American Express card to sharpen the fold. He told her she had expensive tastes. "I do?" She didn't realize he was teasing.

"Well, you could have chosen the gas card."

"Oh, I will when I learn to drive. Then it will be valuable. I've already decided that when I drive, I'm going to have a car that has a cover for the steering wheel that is polka dots. I haven't decided the color. And they will match the big dice things that people hang from their mirrors. Won't that be cool? Then, if I ever lose my car in a big parking lot, I can tell by looking inside. Cars look the same on the outside."

He laughed out loud. What a pleasure to have her helping out.

Porter arrived, and the three took their places. George's smile continued as he heard her parroting the phrases he and Porter used. "Glad to see you brought your mom and dad today."

At the end of the service they reviewed their contract. "We've done this three different times now. I would be greatly pleased if you want to continue, Alexandra," he said seriously. "But I think we need to check in with your mother."

June was agreeable. Alexandra could continue, but they would set a schedule. Half the time she could help Mr. George. Half the time she would sit with her family. If she wanted to change anything, she was to call Mr. George. "My number is in the church directory, but here is my card just in case."

"Oh, I have a card, too. Mom, are you carrying any of my business cards? I want to give one to Mr. George."

With the card exchange, there was a formal shaking of hands and a great deal of grinning.

*** *** ***

It had worked! Bridget had seen Victor at church and wagged her finger at him. "We have to get this project done."

To her surprise, he had said, "Okay. Shall I come over this afternoon?" Maybe she should act more like Tiffany.

Victor had arrived before they were finished with lunch. He brought a pile of pictures that he had printed, and they spread them out on the dining room table. "First, we should figure out what order we will put them in. Should we do them from the oldest to now? Or should we do them by where they are in the church?"

They agreed on a process, and Bridget started to make labels.

Together they cropped, moved, piled, rearranged, and discarded. By the end of the afternoon, they had done a lot and realized that they had a lot to do.

Victor came over twice after school that week, riding the bus home with her. They talked about classes, teachers, and upperclassmen. The more they worked on the project, the more they had to talk about.

On Saturday Loretta drove them to the mall and helped them choose a large photograph album.

On Sunday afternoon, they asked June to put the leaves in the table. Systematically, they laid out all the pages and stood back to survey the full effect. "How about something to eat to celebrate?" suggested June.

Alexandra was standing with one leg pulled up behind, practicing holding her balance. She watched Victor and Bridget sip cider and walk around the table making little adjustments. "It must be cool to go up in the carillon tower. Was it dusty and full of rats?"

"Oh, yeah," said Victor. "It's very dark, and the bells pound in your ears when they ring. I think there are bats up there, too. We heard some of them swoop by."

"I don't believe you."

He ignored that. "I'm glad we took enough pictures of the individual bells. I think the collage worked. Lining up pictures of the bells would have been boring to look at.

"I think the tower all by itself on this page is the best," added Bridget. She didn't want to talk with Alexandra about being up in the tower.

"So, are you done? And you won't take any more pictures?" Alexandra had more questions.

"We took pictures of everything on the list that Rev. McDaniel gave us. We checked them all off."

Alexandra walked around the table very slowly, looking at every page. Victor and Bridget adjourned to the kitchen for pizza.

"Come and get a piece," June called Alexandra.

She came in the kitchen and started picking off a piece of pepperoni.

"Take a whole piece, sweetie."

Alexandra ignored her. "You're missing one," she declared.

"Missing one what?" asked Bridget.

"A memorial."

"How would you know?"

"Well, I happen to know that you are missing one."

"Yeah?" said Victor.

"Go see for yourself. There's a plaque-thing in the coat closet near the front door of the church, and you don't have a picture of it."

"There's no plaque-thing in the coat closet," Victor and Bridget said simultaneously.

"Yes, there is!"

"Yeah, well where is it in the coat closet?" asked Victor.

"You have to get up on a ladder to see it, because it's above the shelf above the coats."

Bridget and Victor looked at each other. "That's weird. You mean it's kind of hidden."

"Yeah, I guess so. I saw it when I was looking for the bulletins up on the shelf."

"Why would you put a plaque where no one could see it?"

"How should I know? Some of the others were hard to find, too. Remember?"

June was pulling on her coat. "Alexandra, it's time for us to go pick up the puppy." She had finally relented to Alexandra's pleas. "Let's leave

Victor and Bridget to finish and clean up."

Alexandra twirled in place. "Oh, *yes!* What should we take? Do you have the leash?"

June handed Alexandra the new leash and hustled her out of the room.

The door slammed. Victor and Bridget were left to resume their pizza eating. "That's weird about the plaque. She's probably just making it up."

"Well, she makes up a lot of stuff, but not about real things in real places. It's probably there, and someone made a mistake and missed putting it in on the list."

They agreed to ask Rev. McDaniel about it at the first chance they had.

"Victor," Bridget said. "Do you want to go to a movie sometime?" She had been working up to that. This week of working on the project had been great.

Victor had known it was coming and had dreaded it. The photography project was a reason to be together. That seemed to cover the bases for now. It had been okay, especially because they had work to do. He asked himself for the hundredth time, why couldn't they just be friends?

But he knew she felt differently, and it was his fault for kissing her and making her think something else. What a stupid thing to have done! Since then she had laughed more around him, occasionally touched him on the arm, and even once, on the chest. It was like electricity when she did — a jolt of pain, not a burst of stars. He didn't want to hurt her, and he didn't want to lie. He hated thinking about it.

Well, could they go to the movies? It was just the movies. "Yeah," he said, hoping his voice sounded right. Maybe they could get some other people to go with them. "And I wouldn't even mind if we had to take Alexandra along. She's a pretty cool kid."

Bridget stared hard at him. "Are you kidding me? Alexandra? She's a pain."

"Yeah, probably, but I don't have any little sisters or brothers, so I think she's pretty funny."

"You're bizarre."

"No, I'm not!" Woops. He had said that way too fast. But he had to wipe ideas like that right out of people's heads, even though he knew it was teasing. "You're just hard on her. She's okay."

"Whatever." But Bridget was dismayed.

The doorbell rang. "It's probably my mom."

Bridget answered the door.

"Hello, my dear. That hot pink is a great color for you." Loretta was carrying a big fashionable purse, and her hair was clipped back with a huge barrette.

"Thank you. Victor is getting his stuff together. We're in the dining room." She led the way. Victor was carefully stacking the pages in order.

"Your mother will be glad to get her table back, I'm sure."

"Oh, she's okay about it. 'Specially when we're working on something for church."

"Well, what are you two going to do when this project is over? Maybe you could come over for dinner some night, Bridget."

Bridget wasn't sure what to say. Victor should be inviting her, not his mother. "Thank you. That would be fun." She didn't think she could say anything else and be polite. She would have liked to say, "I think you are embarrassing your son!"

"We shall have to do that sometime. I gather your mother isn't home?"

"No, you just missed her. She had to go with Alexandra to get our new dog."

Victor couldn't leave fast enough. He hustled off to the car with all the papers and folders, barely saying goodbye. His mother waved and continued chattering as she walked to the car.

Bridget stared after the car. She felt sorry again that Victor had a mom who butted in on his life so much. Maybe he didn't ask Bridget to do anything because his mom would drive him crazy with questions. Bridget could almost imagine that to be true.

But it was about Victor himself. She knew that. He was nervous around her. He was comfortable when they were doing something, but that was it. But hadn't the kiss been really nice and romantic up in the tower? She had played the scene over and over in her head.

Bridget knew fairy tales weren't real. But sometimes they came close. She still played a story in her head about her dad and a day long ago when they had walked on the beach along Lake Michigan eating ice cream. She had been a little kid and was wearing a Cinderella costume with a long full skirt that stood out when she twirled. Her dad had a camera and took her picture as she was spinning on the sand, feeling her feet boring a hole down into cooler sand. It had just been the two of them, and later he had put the picture of her into a fancy frame. She still kept it on her bureau.

Maybe Victor was a photographer first, kind of like her Dad. His pictures signaled a serious side to him. She would have to pay attention to Victor's pictures more.

*** *** ***

Victor was furious. Inviting Bridget over for dinner was such a bad move. Why was his mother pushing him so hard toward her? Well, he knew why. But she was so aggressive! It made everything ten times worse. She watched every little move he made around girls. He would never get it right under normal terms, even if he wanted to. And he didn't want to. He didn't want to be with girls like that. But his mother was determined to be right next to him--watching, pushing, commenting, and breathing down his neck. She cared so much about this.

He refused to talk in the car, although he wasn't sure his mother even noticed. She was going on and on about Bridget and her sister and mother and the shopping she had just done. Victor was close to blowing up by the time they got home. He stomped upstairs and turned on his stereo seriously loud. Deafening. Could he shake his mother's voice out of his head?

When she called him for dinner, he didn't hear. His dad pounded on his bedroom door. "Hey, Victor! Dinnertime. Is it necessary to play that music full blast?"

"Yes, Dad," Victor answered in a flat, sarcastic voice. He heaved himself up from his bed where he had been staring at the ceiling.

"Victor." Spencer looked around the room. "Is something wrong?"

"No, nothing."

"You sure?"

"*Yes, I am sure!*" Victor pushed air through his teeth. Was there anything, anywhere, anytime when he could have any room to live?

"You are acting like a five-year-old. Where is this temper coming from?"

You don't have a clue, thought Victor. You and Mom are all eyes and ears and watching and pushing me into a corner, and you wonder where my temper is coming from? He had to hit something. He was quivering.

"Leave me alone!" he shouted.

His dad stared at him for a moment, then turned and left the room. Victor slammed the door with all the force he could find.

Downstairs, Loretta looked shocked. "What is happening?" she started to press.

Spencer cocked his head. "I don't really know. Something is bugging him. Let's just leave him alone. That's about all he said. If he's hungry enough, he'll come down."

"You think that's best?"

"Trust me. I was a teenage boy once."

They pulled up their chairs and shook out their napkins. As they bent their heads to say grace, the music upstairs started pounding again.

CHAPTER 24

As people entered Fellowship Hall, Mavis Hofmeister handed them each a shiny necklace of plastic beads. "It's a wild night." Jazz played in the background, but not too loud. The elderly crowd was the fan base for Shrove Tuesday pancakes.

Victor had seen a movie recently, a murder story set in New Orleans. It had included scenes of the flamboyant and costumed Mardi Gras. He compared that to the room with long tables filled with families eating pancakes, and it was a lame effort. He was dead sure no one at church had ever *been* to Mardi Gras. No one from Stanton would ever imagine, much less participate, in a parade like that.

Tiffany had arrived earlier with her sister and mother. The line into the kitchen for pancakes hadn't been long, and she had already gone back for seconds. Her mother wasn't getting much eaten, however, as people kept sitting down at their table and asking about. She wished they could stop thinking about the Gulf War for 30 minutes. But that was impossible. She bit into her sausage and wondered what her sister was getting to eat. Or, maybe she was sleeping right now. The time difference confused her.

Victor could see that the Cantors were the center of attention. He had talked to Tiffany a couple times and had heard about Lydia's letters home. Bridget had told him about the embedded journalist that was with Lydia's unit, and he'd watched the jerky video coverage that was on television. It was all pretty scary. He hoped it really would be over fast. It was only 3 years and 2 months from his own 18th birthday.

He settled in with his plate of pancakes and had almost finished when Bridget showed up. "Should we find Rev. McDaniel and ask him about the hidden plaque?" she asked.

"Sure. But eat first."

Cord was also polishing off a stack of pancakes. The syrup on his plate pooled deep enough to wade in. Yes, he would cut out sweets for Lent. This was his last gorging for 40 days.

"Rev. McDaniel?" Bridget sat down across from him. Victor was behind her. "We finished taking all the pictures from your list for the confirmation project, but my sister says we've missed one. She says she saw something above the shelves in the coat room near the front door. Could you go with us to look?"

Cord frowned briefly. "A memorial in the coat room? I don't think so."

"Yeah, she says it is kind of hidden. Maybe it's been forgotten because it is hard to see."

"Well, I certainly need to stand up and move with all the syrup that is now clogging my arteries. How about if we go now?"

The three headed down the hallway. Cord unlocked the door to the large and quiet sanctuary. The carpet muffled their footsteps as they passed under the stained glass windows, the colors lost in the dusk.

Entering the dark coatroom, Cord fumbled to find and push in the ancient button switch. The center ceiling light created more opportunity for shadows than illumination. "Where do you think she saw it?" Cord asked.

"I don't know. Just stand on a chair and look. My sister said she was on the step ladder, but she's short."

Cord pulled out the folding chairs and frowned again. This was exactly the wrong chair to stand on. He carefully placed his feet in the center. Any unbalanced move, and the chair would collapse, folding around his legs. He made a radar sweep of the shelf. "A-ha!" he said. "She's right. There's a plaque here. Let's see, it says, '*My son, my son.*'"

"Nope, I don't know anything about this. I don't see any names on it. Maybe there's something on the back. It looks like the ones that Wash Evanston made. He was Grace Evanston's husband and died about ten years ago. Very fancy."

"Some of the other plaques are fancy like the one on the organ. Did he do that?" Bridget asked.

Cord peered down at the attentive duo. "Yes, that's one of Wash's plaques. Tell you what. We'll take this one down, and you can take a picture of it. Then we should take it over to Grace and ask her if she knows about it."

Victor wasn't one for visiting old ladies. "All I need to do is take a picture of it. Bridget is the one who's doing the research."

Bridget wished he had been interested in coming with her. Just once!

"Sure," Cord agreed. He knew Grace would enjoy visiting with Bridget. "We'll do that." He hopped down and clapped them on their backs. "Good detective work, you two. The Session will be grateful to have a more complete inventory."

Bridget recovered her good humor. It did feel a bit like detective work, finding clues and chasing them down. It was just too bad that Victor couldn't see that. His loss.

Cord folded up the chair. "Now, it seems to me the dinner includes dessert, if you can believe it, after all that syrup." They headed back to the Fellowship Hall, which, with all the sugar consumption, was louder than ever.

CHAPTER 25

Loretta had decided a buffet lunch would be the perfect thing. Victor and Bridget wanted to show their confirmation partners the progress on the memorials booklet, and Loretta thought food was in order. She sent out an invitation to come to the Becks' home after church.

There would be nine people altogether. Loretta planned a buffet with a simple centerpiece of dried flowers. It took next to no effort to lay out plates, silver, colorful napkins, and glasses ahead of time.

"It's a progress brunch; not a progressive dinner," she said to her husband cheerfully.

The guests arrived, waiting first in their cars to be sure the hosts had returned from church ahead of them. Alexandra presented Loretta with a tin of cookies they had baked the day before. Brent came with flowers. Porter carried in a ham. "Little ham sandwiches belong on a buffet table," Mavis said, as she opened a mustard jar. Loretta moved items around on the table to make room. They had more than enough food now!

"What's your cat's name?" Alexandra asked Spencer.

"Toodles."

"Where did that name come from?"

"It's made-up, I guess. Just an affectionate name. I think it's a cross between noodles and toots."

"We named our dog Doc. You know, after the scientist in *Back to the Future*. Sometimes, it sounds like you're calling him Dog. So it's like a double meaning. Get it?"

Spencer nodded in return.

"I was the one who figured that out."

June had been listening in. "Yes, we had a family conference, and Alexandra has signed up to be the main caretaker of Doc, so she got to choose the name."

"Good idea," said Spencer. Alexandra had loaded her plate with five ham sandwiches and was looking around the room. "You can sit anywhere you want," he added. The room had a circle of chairs plus two footstools. She chose one to perch on.

Brent waved his fork at her. "I heard you talking about a new dog," he said.

Alexandra carefully sipped her drink before putting it on a side table. She had filled it to the brim. "That was something Mom promised us when we moved. She didn't really remember the promise, and it took a long time to remind her."

June was approaching. "Yes, my mind is getting feeble in my old age."

"Mom, don't say that. I figured it out, and you are exactly four times older than I am, and I know kids whose parents are five times older than they are. That's old age."

Spencer's face lit up.

"My dad plays with numbers like that all the time in his head," Victor said in a low voice to Bridget. "See how he loves that? Watch."

"Do you follow any sports, Alexandra?" Spencer asked.

She half nodded, but her mouth was full.

"It's a great way to figure out percentages and play with numbers."

"Yeah," she said. "I've just started to understand that."

"Well, let me show you. Honey, where's the newspaper?"

"I'm sure it's in the living room," Loretta said.

"Come with me," said Spencer. "We'll use the coffee table in there, and we can spread out our plates, too."

The two decamped to the living room. "Under ten seconds," said Victor to Bridget.

"Alexandra loves attention," she responded.

For a moment the room was quiet as everyone settled in and worked on their plates. Loretta asked Mavis for a recipe. You could hear the murmur of Spencer's voice from the other room.

Brent turned to Bridget and asked about Tiffany and if they were hearing regularly from Lydia.

"Tiffany is doing much better," Bridget started. "She was much more crazy worried before everything started to happen, and Lydia was still in Kansas. At least that's how it seemed to me. I think now that Lydia is in Iraq, she's decided she needs to be calm for her little sister and her mom."

"They are wearing a game face," said June. "I know they appreciate the attention they are getting from the community. Estelle was telling me she doesn't sleep well but made a joke about that not being a huge problem because she works the night shift. I don't know that I could be even fake-cheerful in such a situation."

"Sure you could, Mom. I've seen you do it," said Bridget easily.

"It's surprising what you can do when others depend on you," commented Brent.

"Well, she's as much a hero as anyone. I mean the families left at home. At least the war is going to be short." Estelle had told June that was all she prayed for these days. *Get it over, God.*

"Tiffany watches television all the time. It's always on, even when they are doing homework and stuff. They want any news they can get."

Loretta was hoping to change the conversation, but Mavis saved her by asking about the large sideboard. Was it a family antique? Brent was also knowledgeable about furniture, and soon there were two or three conversations underway. When Spencer and Alexandra reappeared from their statistics orgy, Loretta happily announced dessert.

As they returned to their seats with pie, Porter commented to June, "Confirmation is a big step." He sounded officious, but she knew he was genuine. "I'm glad our tradition doesn't rope children into these questions when they are only seven or eight. Church membership should be for people when they are old enough to make the decision themselves."

"We haven't directly asked Victor if he will choose to be confirmed," Spencer said.

Victor looked up in confusion. "Huh?"

"I'm pretty sure I'll be joining," said Bridget. She had already talked about it with her mom and Mrs. Hofmeister.

Loretta was alarmed. "Why, I'm sure that Victor is planning to be confirmed. Aren't you, dear?" It wasn't a question.

"Well, it's his decision," said Spencer.

"Yep," said Porter. "It's up to you."

"We've done our bit," Spence continued. "Now it's in your hands. Besides, it won't stick if you don't decide yourself. Unless, of course, you grow up and marry someone who has twice your faith and sees you stay with it." He raised a palm in his wife's direction, as if to introduce her.

Loretta ignored him and looked at Victor. "But, sweetheart, how could church be so meaningless to you that you wouldn't join? It's been part of your life since you were born."

Victor was nonplussed. What did his father mean about him getting married, especially with Bridget right here all eager to be his girlfriend? How could he calm his mother down? He didn't need her suddenly whacked out about his lack of faith. And who said he wasn't joining the church?

"What makes you think I'm not joining the church?" he said to his mother. "Of course I am." That was hardly the problem on his mind. Joining church was an easy one. Sure! It was nothing compared to his other worries.

"I don't see the big deal," piped in Alexandra. "They pass that sheet of paper every Sunday, and I always check the box that says I'm a member. I'm already a member of the church, aren't I, Mom?"

"Yes, you are, honey. Confirmation is about becoming an adult member, so you take responsibilities like voting and committee work and things like that."

"You mean like those long meetings with the potluck dinners?

"Yes."

"Well, who cares about that? You have to take a whole class all year and do this big project just to vote in the meeting?"

They all laughed. Mavis gave her a little hug. "No, it's more than that."

"Let's move to the basement and see the project before we have coffee," suggested Loretta.

Brent hadn't missed Alexandra's stiffness in response to Mavis's hug. He snagged her as the others started to move out of the room. "Your logic is good, Alexandra," he said very seriously.

She stared at him.

"If membership is just about voting occasionally, it does seem overdone. But it's the same when you are a citizen. You can just vote in elections and stop there, or you can get involved. That's why I'm mayor, because I think voting is only a small piece of the responsibilities we all have."

Alexandra was skeptical. Why was he saying this to her?

"You think I'm pulling your leg?"

"Not sure."

"Well, I'm not. When I was a kid, adults either lectured me or teased me. I'm not trying to do either. I just want to tell you something about myself."

"Why?"

"Well, first, I'm a politician, and that's what politicians do. But mostly it's because you're making a real point, and I like to talk about real things with people, not about make-nice things."

"Oh, okay. Then I'll think about it."

"Good." Brent was sure as shootin' that he had been nothing like Alexandra when he was a kid. He stepped aside so that she could go down the stairs ahead of him.

People were clustered around the table, studying the laid-out pages. Some read the captions aloud.

"It would look more professional if it were printed," Bridget hedged. All this work, and it still looked like a scrapbook.

"See this memorial?" Victor pointed to a page. "We didn't even know about it, and Alexandra found it."

"Yeah, in that room where everyone hangs their coats. No one knew it was there until I saw it," said Alexandra proudly.

"*My son, my son.* Do you know what that is about?" Mavis was curious.

"Apparently the only thing that can be figured out is that it was probably made by Grace Evanston's husband," explained June.

"It certainly is in his style." Porter was also interested. "I never knew about a memorial plaque in the coat room."

"I saw it when I climbed on the step ladder. It was up high, behind the shelf."

"Really!"

"Cord is going to take the kids to see Grace and find out what she might know about it," Spencer explained.

"It's a strange place to hang a plaque. No one will see it there," commented Mavis. "I wonder which 'one son' this is about. Grace and Wash had only one son. He died young, back during the Korean War."

"Maybe that's the connection," said her husband. "But why was it hidden away?"

"There are other plaques that you don't see easily, like the one on the pulpit. It's underneath it. Victor practically had to stand upside down to take a picture of it."

Brent was looking at the carillon pictures and turned to June. "Those bells make Stanton famous," he said.

"They are so unusual and beautiful to hear," she agreed.

"People are always asking me about them. It's such a great love story, especially because it's about a banker, who was probably just a quiet guy in a suit most of the time."

June laughed. "There is something about it being a tower, too. It makes you think of Rapunzel letting her hair down from the top of a tower."

Victor had been watching Mr. Sykes more closely since their Indiana basketball game together. No doubt about it. Mr. Sykes was not gay! He was doing a pretty careful number flirting with Bridget's mom. It wasn't really obvious, but you could tell he watched her at times. And mentioning a love story! Jeesh!

Which just proved the point again that there weren't any other gay people in Stanton. Of course not. And, if he could easily see around Mr. Sykes, for sure someone would see around him. It wasn't if, it was when. He swallowed hard.

And then there was Bridget over there. She had been listening hard to the talk about the bells and the tower and the love story. She's remembering that kiss, he was dead sure. How was he ever going to keep that fairy tale going for her? That's what it was. A fairy tale. Ha ha!

They could have a nice thing going. They just clicked when they were together. But if they got any closer, she would see through him. She was no idiot. And to think that he had actually told her in the tower! He had just blurted it out! What had he been thinking? And the wrestling match had freaked him out. God, it was hard to keep under control.

Loretta steered everyone back upstairs and served second helpings of the lemon meringue pie. Its sticky sour-sweetness made Victor feel ill. He went to the kitchen, drank a glass of water, and returned to the group to clear plates. Once that was done, he went up to his room. He knew his mother would be furious, but he couldn't face anyone anymore.

*** *** ***

Later in the afternoon, buried in the Sunday crossword puzzle, Spencer could hear Loretta stowing the silver and starting the dishwasher. She had done a beautiful job with the brunch.

It was too bad that Victor had disappeared up to his room. Loretta had been undone, standing in his bedroom doorway and lecturing him afterward. He had mumbled something about a stomachache.

"You could have politely excused yourself. Instead, you disappeared. It was unbelievably rude. And, think of Bridget. It was like a slap in her face." Loretta was beside herself.

"Yeah, well you aren't Bridget." He knew he had no excuse that she would accept.

"I should make you write an apology."

"Jeesh, Mom. You sound like she's my girlfriend or something. *She isn't*. And it was a stomachache! A bad one!"

Loretta turned abruptly and left.

Hearing all this from downstairs, Spencer thought about Victor's prickly side. It was more and more evident these days. He hadn't seemed very happy showing off the project.

But Loretta needed to look at the larger picture. Parents need to have patience. There were plenty of signs that he was growing up well. It was clear he was going to join the church, for one.

And, it was clear he liked Bridget, precisely because he didn't want to admit it to his mother. Spencer thought it was great that Bridget was figuring in the picture a bit. Nice kid. Her sister was a busy bee, for sure, and very smart. And her mother seemed unflappable. There were times he wished Loretta could be unflappable, but her silky elegance still turned his heart upside down.

Spencer admired women deeply. Their intuition, spirituality, and feminine third eye all awed him. He hoped Victor would grow up to understand those dimensions. Had he done enough to explain that sort of thing to him? They'd given him regular habits and taught him good manners. Those things built character. He was looking less like a boy, filling out and getting his height. And he was responsible. This photography project was not a make-work thing. They were doing a terrific job of it. Perhaps his photography was a source of artistry, more than a hobby. He could get terrific satisfaction out of that over the coming years, find an outlet for expressing himself, and develop some good technical skills. Spencer looked at his crossword puzzle with satisfaction. The more words you could fill in, the more words somehow fell into place.

CHAPTER 26

June waved to Cord from the front door as Bridget slipped by her and dodged drips to the waiting car. The hard rain of the afternoon had stalled out at a drizzle, but the trees were still shaking off the beating. Cord's windshield wipers scraped loudly as they drove off to visit Grace Evanston.

"Most of the children in our church grew up making banners with Mrs. Evanston for All Saints Sunday. So it's time you knew her better." "Mom says she was the one who wrote a letter to us about Dad's banner last fall."

"Yes, that's right. She doesn't do much more than that these days, but it is her way of staying involved."

They headed towards Stanton's oldest residential neighborhood full of small cottages. Cord parked, and Bridget noticed the ornate mailbox and elaborate railings on the porch.

Cord smiled. "Hard to miss the artistry. You can see why she wants to stay in her home as long as possible. Wait until you see the fireplace mantel."

Grace met them at the door, and as they seated themselves on the couch, she nudged a tray on the coffee table in their direction. "Please help yourselves," she said. "I'm a little shaky, and might spill if I try to serve you."

"I'm happy to pour," said Cord, sitting forward on the couch with his knees bumping the coffee table.

They settled in with a sip or two. Cord asked about her health. She was 100% fine. The surgery last year had been a miracle. She was able to walk better than she could have imagined.

Bridget looked around the room. There was something odd, and she couldn't put her finger on it. Things seemed to be normal for an old lady's house: a crocheted afghan on the couch and a candy dish. The side tables, however, were crammed with pictures. Bridget realized there were no pictures on the walls. Well, actually, where were the walls?

Grace noticed her gaze. "The room is almost all doors, isn't it? People built these old houses in phases when they needed space and grew more prosperous. So now we have a humble-jumble. This room was probably a central hallway at one point. It might have been the first room that they built and lived in. Then they fanned out to add the kitchen and bedrooms. Wash, my husband, made the mantel to emphasize the one thing in the room that isn't a door."

"Which leads us to the reason we are here," said Cord. "Even though I never knew Wash, I feel I know him from his art work."

He picked up the brown paper bag with the plaque in it. "Bridget and Victor Beck have been doing a confirmation project. Well, Bridget, why don't you tell about it?"

"Well, um. Victor Beck and I decided to photograph the memorials in the church for a scrapbook for the 175th anniversary. Victor's good with cameras, so he's taking the pictures. And my mom is a journalist, so I figured she could help me with the layouts and writing the captions for the pictures."

Grace smiled at the girl. Well, she was hardly a girl. Young people grew sophisticated and confident quickly these days.

Bridget explained about their project and then about her sister. "She's sort of snoopy and is always into things that aren't her business. Anyway, she was helping Mr. George…"

"George Morrow," Cord explained to Grace.

"…with the bulletins one Sunday, and she climbed up a little ladder in the coat room to see where they were on the shelf, and she saw this plaque."

Cord interrupted. "They must have built that shelf sometime after they mounted the plaque, because it was completely hidden from view. I don't think anyone has seen it in decades."

Grace set down her cup carefully. She knew exactly what was coming. It had been nearly 40 years, but it would be Wash's plaque for Vaughn. Oh my goodness.

"Excuse me," she said. "Could you explain that again, about where you found this plaque?"

The question had been her companion for decades. It was time now for a lively young woman to sit in her living room and tell her the answer. Wash had put it in the coatroom above a shelf. That was a safe place to sequester it. Imagine! She had walked by it every week for all these years. Everyone had been passing by it all along.

"On which wall?" she asked. Cord explained that it was the one opposite the window. He drew the plaque from its wrappings.

"Yes, I know this plaque," she said softly, touching the honey wood again. "I remember when Wash made it. He did it in a frenzy of activity during a very hot summer."

"Can you tell us the story behind it?" asked Cord.

Grace paused. "Yes, but let me think about what parts to tell," she said.

Cord and Bridget looked at each other.

"Oh, no." She protested, catching their glance. "I am happy to tell it. I was thinking about the time and the place. It has many overtones, you see." They waited quietly.

"Perhaps I should start by saying 'Once upon a time, a long time ago,' but it isn't a make-believe story, and I am afraid it doesn't have a happy ending.

"Wash and I had a son named Vaughn. He was a lovely boy, our only child. He grew up here in Stanton; he went to school at the old elementary school and then to high school. He was baptized in the church and confirmed there, too, as you will be this year, Bridget.

"When the Korean War got underway, he was drafted. It seemed that we had just finished a war, and suddenly our country was in another one. I can't tell you how much the news these days disturbs me! We keep walking into senseless wars. I am so worried about our young people, especially little Lydia Cantor." Grace stopped for a moment. Lydia had made many a banner as a little child. She had made one for Wash the year he had died. Oh, dear. Now she was all grown up and facing danger herself. How utterly horrific!

"I remember how deeply frightened Wash and I were for our son. It was such a terrible time." Her voice, however, spoke the words as matters of fact, born from years of bleaching out the emotion. She didn't need to build anxiety for this lovely young Bridget.

Cord saw it coming. He knew her son had died, and he had already pieced together the meaning of the plaque. This was the story Guy Sykes had told him in the hospital. He was curious, though, about how Grace would describe the death of her son.

"We were so relieved when he returned from Korea. He had told us in letters that he wasn't in harm's way, but it was hard not to be afraid. War is war, and the Korean War had some very bad spots.

"But, after all that worry, he came home. And, it was odd, but he seemed to have thrived from the experience. He looked tremendous, all muscles and tan and strength. And he had so much confidence!

It had made a man out of him in the best sense. I couldn't believe I had a son like that." Her voice softened further.

"One of the first nights he was home, he went out to celebrate with a friend. It was Guy Sykes. He died last summer, so you probably never met him, Bridget. He was the father of Mayor Brent Sykes.

"At the time, we didn't worry about their safety. How can you worry about a grown son going out for the evening after he has survived a war? We went to bed early, and I remember that night as a terribly hot one. We opened all the windows, but no air moved anywhere. We slept lightly, and I remember hearing a car drive up and park at the house very late, maybe even close to morning. But, instead of Vaughn coming in, the doorbell rang. It was the police, who had come to tell us that Vaughn had gone missing after an accident at the lake. They found him early the next morning."

"Oh, I'm so sorry," said Bridget. Cord was surprised at her immediate sympathy. But, then, she had lost her own father.

"Yes," continued Grace. "I can't tell you how terrible it all was, the irony of losing him in the safety of his own hometown. It was a random horrible accident. Wash nearly lost his faith as a result. Mine was shaken, too.

"But that's not the story you came to hear. That was our tragedy, but it isn't the real story of the plaque."

Cord was lost. Wasn't this enough reason to mourn and create a plaque?

"When I was cleaning Vaughn's room weeks later, I found letters that led me to understand that our son was what you call these days 'gay'." She stopped for a minute. "My goodness! I've never actually said that out loud in all these years. In those days, I didn't even know what word to use. Being gay meant being cheerful and joyous. I didn't have any understanding of the other meaning of the word, homosexual. That was something no one ever talked about.

"But the letters were clear. He loved another soldier, another man. In fact, that man came to his funeral, but we didn't understand any of this at the time. It was a deep shock for me to learn the truth, but also a strange relief. I had always felt a distance from my son. There was some sort of shadow between us. When I learned about him being gay," she stopped. "There, I said it again."

"Words are different when they are finally spoken," commented Cord quietly.

Grace resumed, "When I learned about him being gay, the shadow disappeared. It lightened my mind, believe it or not." She smiled at the memory. It sounded incongruous to say that out loud, too.

"But, it was close to disaster for Wash to hear this information. I had to tell him. To me it was part of what Vaughn was. But to Wash, in those days, it was a terrible thing. He made that plaque, I think, to express his deep pain. He worked on it for days, down in the basement. When he was finished, he took it and mounted it in the church. I didn't know where he had put it, and he never told me." She paused for a moment, thinking of how long it had been.

"But now you have told me," she continued. "And, Cord, that shelf has always been there, and I am sure he put it up there purposely so no one would see it and yet, it would be there in the midst of everything." Her face softened. "It was Wash's cry to his God. I never asked where he put it. He died without telling me."

Bridget was listening so hard her mouth had fallen loosely open.

Grace finished up. "So that is what I can tell you. And, since Wash has died, it is my story. I don't believe it needs to be hidden any longer." She smiled at Bridget. "Your little sister was sent along so that we could tell it now."

Bridget was suddenly on the edge of her seat. What a story! This had been a secret for years, longer than she had been alive. Wouldn't her mom and dad both be amazed! She corrected herself: her mom.

Cord knew a pastoral comment would be in order. "Grace, I can't tell you how much I appreciate hearing the story. It is tragic. I am sorry for the pain of it and the pain involved in recalling it now."

Grace reassured him that for an old lady, there was not a little value in speaking truth to one's minister. The story had been left for a long time. And in this day and age, these things weren't the shameful things they were then. She had loved Vaughn. "Sharing his story now when people are more aware and understanding of these things is a good thing," she explained.

"Then, can we ask your permission to include a picture of the plaque in the memorials book? We'd also like to hang the plaque in the church where everyone could see it."

Grace agreed that including a picture was a good idea. "Perhaps you and Victor could make some suggestions about where it might hang now in the church," she said to Bridget.

The three of them talked longer, but finally it was time to go. "Shall we share a prayer before we leave?" Cord asked Grace.

Grace agreed, and Cord suggested they take hands. Holding Mrs. Evanston's cool and very thin hand, Bridget was embarrassed that her hands felt sweaty.

"Dear Lord," Cord began. "We are grateful to spend time together speaking with each other from the heart. We ask blessings for Grace's son, Vaughn, and her husband, Wash, who filled her life with love and now memory. We ask you to remember all who have departed. Be with us all, in our going out and our coming in. Be with us through the night and into the day that will follow. We ask this in the name of your son, our lord, Jesus Christ, Amen."

"Amen," said Grace firmly. She looked sharply at Bridget. "And let me say one more thing before you go, Bridget, my dear. The story I told you tonight was not about death, but about life. It takes a great deal of maturity to understand that, but it was." She stopped with that pronouncement, knowing she sounded like an old lady. Perhaps her words would echo for

Bridget in time.

Bridget nodded, not sure what to say. "Thank you for letting us come and visit." It was a lame way to end their conversation. "I know about losing a family member, so I hope I understand your story the way you mean it to be told."

Grace reached out for a little hug from her, and with that send-off, the visit concluded.

*** *** ***

As promised, Cord dropped Bridget off at youth fellowship. It was movie night, and Porter was unloading pizza from the trunk of his car. The usual advisors were out of town, so the Hofmeisters had volunteered to step in. For once, the menu stymied Mavis. Pizza could not be baked at home. She had put her energies into planning dessert, instead.

Bridget was dancing inside with excitement. Where was Victor? She had to tell him first. Impatiently, she helped set out the pizza boxes, paper plates, and napkins. When Victor finally arrived, she almost jumped on him. *"I've got to talk with you."*

What could be such a big deal? Victor didn't like her taking him to a corner table so the two of them could talk privately. It looked like she was ordering him around.

But Bridget didn't notice his edge. She barely touched her food while she poured out the story. Mrs. Evanston... her son... army... Korea... died right after he came home... drowned... was *gay*... Mr. Evanston made the plaque... went to hang the plaque by himself... it was a secret... Mrs. Evanston didn't know.

"Isn't this unbelievable? Really amazing? I mean, he really meant for this to be hidden for a long time. Like a time capsule. And we found it out."

Victor couldn't swallow the pizza. He tried his drink. The bite finally went down like a rough stone. He coughed hard.

Bridget's face was flushed. "Mrs. Evanston never knew where her husband had put the plaque. And he was so upset about their son being gay that he didn't tell her."

"Are you sure it's okay to tell people about it?" he managed to say.

"She said so, since everyone who was part of the story has now died except herself. And she thinks it is now a story that people would understand. It's okay with her."

Victor felt a window close inside him. People *had to die* before they could be honest about this stuff. He couldn't tell Bridget why this frightened him so much. He couldn't be a part of this. He couldn't talk about it naturally. He couldn't be excited about finding out this secret.

Porter and a couple of the kids joined them. "Okay with whom?"

Everyone could tell Bridget was wound up

As she talked, Victor felt his throat tighten and tighten further. His stomach started to hurt as if he had been hit hard. He started to sweat.

Porter was listening hard, and the other kids were silent, absorbed in her story. Porter saw some younger kids heading for their table, but he waved them off. "Ask Mrs. Hofmeister about dessert." He needed to handle this immediately.

Bridget came to the end of her narrative.

"I'm surprised at Wash Evanston," Porter started. "I knew him to be a fine, dedicated member of this church. And Grace Evanston is a good Christian."

Unsure about his tone, the table of kids looked at him. "But, let me be clear with all of you. Just because Mr. Evanston wanted to hang a plaque for his son doesn't mean that he condoned the sin of homosexuality. I'm sure he was grieved that his son died. It was a tragic accident at the time."

He continued, "However, I don't want any of you to think that homosexuality is anything but despicable and trashy and sinful behavior by people who are very very sick. They are sick morally, and they are sick socially."

Victor felt the room swim. Sweat was running down his ribs. A nasty taste formed in his mouth.

Porter's voice was rising. "It's a disgusting, perverted, animal thing, and I am sure that Wash hid the plaque because he knew that his son was damned. It sounds like Wash was praying for his son's soul, because he knew he was going to be lost in hell."

The kids sat in uncertain silence. No adult had ever spoken like that at church. They looked down at their plates and greasy napkins.

Shocked, Bridget couldn't think of a thing to say. The Hofmeisters were nice and special people. How could he be saying such things? She knew gay people in Chicago, and they weren't sinners or perverted. Mr. Hofmeister was wrong, but she didn't know how to say that to him.

The other table of kids suddenly let out a big "Booooooo." Everyone jerked around to look. A parent smiled over at them. "All I asked was how the movie was rated. Sure got their dander up!"

"Dessert," called Mrs. Hofmeister, emerging from the kitchen with a tray of sauces and nuts for the sundaes. Kids jumped up, eager to get away from the tension. "Me first!"

"Oh, yeah, sure," said Porter. The interruption had been enough to break his breath. These were good kids. He didn't need to lecture them further. "Don't forget what I said, and let's get the movie going soon."

In seconds, Bridget and Victor were the only two left at the table. Bridget was still in shock. "It was like he was mad at us," she said.

Victor couldn't respond. He stood up to clear his place. The floor was spongy as he walked away from her. Or was it his knees? He was sinking. His legs were about to give out on him. He forced himself to the trashcan, threw away his plate and napkin, and then slumped into a chair on the perimeter around the screen. He pulled his cap over his eyes. Another kid threw himself into the next chair and dug into his mountain of bananas and ice cream. "Let's get going!" he yelled.

Victor's t-shirt had turned into a soggy rag underneath his sweater. His brain pounded with a fearful logic. Mrs. Evanston's son had been gay. She was like a saint in this church--old, kind, nice, and respected. But she had hidden this story for decades. Until after everyone had *died!*

And look at how Mr. Hofmeister reacted! It was almost half a century later, and he got all angry about it and said being gay was perverted, horrible, and dangerous.

People hated gays. People would hate him. He hated himself. He didn't want to be gay, and he'd tried to stop it but it wouldn't stop. It would come out.

He was terribly frightened. There was no way out of this. His entire body was scared. And, he couldn't stop himself. People would know.

When it came out, they would all hate him. Look how fast Mr. Hofmeister had changed from being a nice guy to being really angry, really ugly. And this guy had been dead for forty years! If people hated gays who had been dead for forty years, he didn't have a chance. *Forty years!*

The movie started, and everyone shouted about turning the lights down.

If you wanted to be gay, you had to be a movie star. Everyone expected them to act crazy, do drugs, and be over the top. They weren't normal people with normal families. But he was supposed to be normal. He lived in a normal town with normal parents, school, and church. When they found out, they would all turn against him. They would attack him. God would attack him.

Everyone was watching the movie. Victor looked at the screen, and it didn't make any sense. He couldn't sit here and pretend to watch. He didn't belong anymore. He couldn't stay. He slowly slid his chair back until he was behind the others. He wanted to get up and run, but he held himself down. Slowly he edged away, and no one paid any attention. Quietly, he got up and left the room. If they noticed, maybe they would think he was going to the bathroom.

He pushed out the church door, doubled up over the curb, and gagged. Nothing came out, but his stomach pulsed. He started down the street. He gagged again, and his body broke out in another sweat. At the next corner he finally vomited, but it only made him feel dizzy and weak. He wiped his mouth and spat, but the taste of bile remained. Slowly he straightened up and started to walk. He splashed into a puddle. His feet and ankles were soaked. His whole body was wet now. It didn't matter. He couldn't stop shaking. He had to concentrate to move his feet properly.

At his back the carillon bells started to ring the hour. He turned for a moment. The tower was a huge black blot in the sky growing higher and higher. He swung around and started to run.

*** *** ***

Arriving home, Victor went around to the back door, hoping to slip up to his room. Loretta called out from the living room. "Hello, honey. How'd you get home?"

"I got a ride. The movie was really dumb." He knew he didn't sound normal.

"Are you okay, dear?"

"Yeah, I'm fine." It took everything he had to hold back the panic. "I'm going upstairs to read." She never questioned him when he said he was going to read.

"That's great."

He closed his door quietly and fell on the bed. His lungs were heaving. He rolled on his back to breathe. The ceiling was moving down on him. The ceiling light was a big eye watching him.

There were only two choices: he would try to hide his secret forever but give it away at some point because he couldn't control everything – not with his mother watching or Bridget watching or anything. Or, they would figure it out on their own at some point. Either way, he would never know when it was all going to hit.

He couldn't read in his room forever. What if his dad or mom walked in and looked down on him like the eye in the ceiling light? They would see he was hideous, perverted, deformed, and deranged. They would call him those names, or whisper them when they walked past. There were so many of those names: pervert, freak, fag, sinner, homo, fruitcake, reject. They would stare at him, pointing.

He curled up in a ball and held tight. His body shook in convulsive, automatic jerks, beyond his control. He tried to bite hard, holding his jaw tight. His wet clothes weighted him down but didn't dampen the spasms one bit. Clutching himself harder, he knew his body wouldn't change. His head might say something, but the rest of him couldn't listen.

He would never be what they wanted. His parents. The people at church. The kids at school. Shit! Angrily, his leg kicked out at the sheets. His wet shoes got knotted up in the quilt. He kicked and kicked, scraping against the mattress. He started to sob. But no tears came with the deep, painful heaves against his ribs.

*** *** ***

The next morning, Loretta was returning from the store. The garden looked dirty with soggy leaves and muddy run-off. It had been a long and, at times, pounding rain. The sound of the wind had woken her a couple times in the night. A large branch had blown down onto the sidewalk. She would have to get Spencer or Victor to haul it away.

The front door was locked. Shifting the grocery bag to her other arm, she fished around for her house key. Where was Spencer? Had he said something about running errands? And where had Victor disappeared? His bedroom door had still been closed when she had left.

Entering the house, she deposited the bag on the counter. The house was intensely still. Usually they left the radio on, a homemade trick to ward off intruders. It never failed her. When she opened the door and heard it, she felt as if someone was home. If she didn't, she immediately felt its emptiness. How odd. It had been years since Victor had forgotten to turn on the radio when he left.

Then she saw a photograph on the kitchen floor, and a few more leading into the dining room. A window must have been left open, and wind must have blown them off the table. But, why would a window be open? It was cold outside.

She picked up the picture and went into the dining room. All the windows were shut. Papers littered the floor, apparently swept off the table with a single, broad, curving swipe. A glass had been knocked off the sideboard.

The broken glass crunched under her foot, and fear flooded her. What had happened? Who had done this? A complete quiet crowded the house. She wasn't alone. She made herself go into the living room. Everything was in its place.

Mounting the stairs she called, "Victor, Spencer, are you here?" Her voice startled her, and she started to run up the stairs. "Spencer! Victor!"

At the top she could see the closed bathroom door. She pounded the door with the flat of her hand. "Victor, Spencer, are you in there?" The responding silence was a blank answer.

She pushed on the door. She expected it to be locked, but it swung open, and there was Victor in the bathtub. "Why do you have your clothes on? Where did you get pink bath oil? And you've got blood on your shirt!" But, before these thoughts had made it through her mind, she started to scream.

CHAPTER 27

The reception area of the church office was empty and dead quiet. Brent tried to make the door click loudly to announce himself. The carpet muffled his footsteps. Poking his head into Cord's office, he said, "Saw your car outside and took a chance I could interrupt you.

"Come on in," Cord said cheerfully. "Great to see you."

"I agreed to be one of the readers at the Thursday evening service and thought I would pick up the instructions. I might not make it to church tomorrow."

"Absolutely. I'm just here finishing my sermon, trying to carve out a free evening to go out to dinner with my wife. It's her birthday."

"Well, then, she deserves a wild date."

"Yes, she does." He grinned at Brent.

"Too bad it's a work night."

"Yes, and Palm Sunday is one of those challenging Sundays. The story is the same every year. How many ways can you skin a cat?"

"Never thought of it that way. When I give speeches, the whole point is to repeat myself."

"Wouldn't that be nice? Here, sit down. I've got the instructions somewhere in a folder." He rummaged around on his desk.

"What is this?" asked Brent, looking at the Evanston plaque on the coffee table. "Oh, wait a minute. The kids were telling the story the other day. They found this in the coatroom."

"Actually, Alexandra Wallace found it. It's a great story." Cord unearthed a bright green folder from a pile on his desk. "Ah ha! Here it is." He handed Brent a sheet of paper.

"Of course. She's quite a kid!" Brent grinned.

"Grace says Wash made it in memory of their son who died in a freak accident back in the 1950's. It's interesting because, by her account and she's quite up front about this, he was gay. They only learned that after he died, from letters they found. Her husband was doubly distraught and made the plaque to vent his grief. Apparently he then hid it in the church and never told her where." Cord stopped abruptly. Brent had thrown up a hand and looked as if he was seeing a ghost.

"Brent, is something wrong?"

"You're talking about Vaughn Evanston, right? Who drowned out at the lake?"

Cord nodded, "And your father was there. Of course, you know about this."

"Well, not directly. But, yes, Dad was with him that night. He left a letter to me about it. I found it in his things at the house, last Christmas. Vaughn Evanston was his best friend, just back from Korea."

Cord spoke carefully. "Yes, your father talked about this during one of my last visits to him in the hospital."

"He did?" Brent said slowly. "I knew nothing until I found the letter."

"It was in confidence, of course."

Brent considered this. "I understand." He paused. "He claimed responsibility for the accident. It seems that Dad provoked him, and they fought."

"And Vaughn died."

"Yes. And this haunted Dad his whole life. He left special instructions in his will, that the proceeds of the sale of the house and some other property go to Grace."

It was Cord's turn to look surprised. "Really! That's quite a bequest."

"It was a complete surprise to me." Brent felt the flush in his face crawl down his neck. "I knew nothing about any of this until I read the letter. Well, to be accurate, I learned what was in the will and was surprised by Dad's directions. Then I found the letter."

"That's a hard way to hear the story." Cord was taking in the twists and turns in Brent's expression.

The door to the anteroom suddenly flew open, and Cord's wife interrupted them. "Honey, can I talk to you for a minute?"

"What's wrong?"

"I'm sorry. I need you in the other room. Sorry, Brent." She waved hastily.

Cord signaled to Brent to stay seated, and he stepped out, closing the door. Brent leaned forward and picked up the plaque, weighing it between his two hands. Up until now the story had revealed itself on papers with carefully chosen words. The will. The codicil. A letter.

The plaque, however, was heavy and dark. It had dimension and craftsmanship. *My son, my son.* Brent could feel the weight of the grief.

Vaughn had been their only son, their only child. Two parents had produced only one precious offspring, reducing the number from one generation to the next. The son was a concentration of everything they had.

And I am a concentration of everything Dad had, he thought. It's like reducing the sun through a mirror so that it burns the target. Yes, he, too, was an only child. He alone received the legacy.

The voices through the door penetrated his brain. "...kept getting a busy signal on the phone... drove over... hospital called. Victor Beck is in the emergency room ... an attempted suicide. Spencer and Loretta are asking you to come immediately."

"Oh, my dear Lord. Oh, my God."

The door swung open, and Cord almost ran into Brent, who was on his feet. "Suicide! I overheard. Victor Beck? That can't be possible!"

Cord's wife nodded, stricken.

"Yes. I don't have any more information. But I need to go right now."

"Of course. Of course. Go."

"Can I call you later? I'm terribly sorry to interrupt our other conversation. It's very important, too."

Brent held up his hand. "It can wait. It's waited nearly 40 years." His heart was pumping. "But I'm Victor's covenant partner. I've spent time with him this spring. He seemed fine. There were no signs of trouble like this!" Victor was a child of the church, and he had some responsibility for him. What had he missed? He was clueless! What terrible secret was Victor carrying?

Cord was pushing his arms into the sleeves of his jacket.

Brent couldn't contain himself. He knew he was delaying Cord. He knew his questions needed to wait. But he found himself imploring. "What is going on? He's just a boy! What can I do to help?"

"I will give you a call later and let you know what's happening." They shook hands quickly, glad for the physical touch.

"Yes, go."

"Could you lock up?"

"Oh, sure."

"Thanks. And turn on the answering machine."

Brent stood at the reception desk, suddenly alone. The glass top held down typed instructions about the copier and endless lists of committee members. He stared down at them.

His reflection in the glass hovered in the midst of the notices. For an instant he was displaced, and it was Victor standing at the table in his basement peering down at the photographs. They were parallel people. Each was an only son. Each carried weights and legacies from parents. He felt tears coming on.

But, Victor was just a boy, finding his way. What could have called up suicide? What secret terror was crowding him? What had Brent missed? What had they all missed? Brent rubbed his fingertips along the image in the hard, shiny glass as his vision blurred.

*** *** ***

The emergency room seating area was relatively empty. For once, the receptionist recognized Cord and sent him along to a room. Spencer and Loretta were seated by the bed. Victor lay asleep with bandages on his wrists and IV tubes in his arm.

Spencer's face was rigid; his arms circled Loretta, who was sobbing into his neck. "Cord," he said, "thank you for coming."

"My wife brought me the message. Spencer, Loretta, I'm so very sorry."

Loretta roused herself. "Oh, Cord, I found him and got him here. He was in the tub with blood everywhere. I just went through the motions. It's all so horrible, so awful!" The tears were pouring down her face.

"It's finally hitting her," Spencer said, reaching for a chance to explain at least something. "We're waiting until his blood pressure is better, and then he can move to a regular room. The doctor says he is out of immediate danger. It was terribly close. A little longer, or if he had cut deeper..." He stopped for a moment. "He was unconscious--we don't know for how long, but now he's sleeping."

Cord stepped to the side of the bed and stood there looking at Victor. His pale skin contrasted with his hair, which looked artificially dark. The blankets swaddled his body right up to his throat. "Warm this child!" Cord ordered God. Catching himself, he closed his eyes for a moment and said a brief prayer of thanks for a young life spared.

Loretta sobbed a long, gasping breath. Cord stroked Victor's shoulder lightly, hoping to give the parents another minute to recover. Finally he turned and said simply, "He's a beautiful boy." Loretta's face crumpled further, almost collapsing. Spencer's eyes were sockets of starkness. He reached into his jacket pocket, pulled out an envelope and handed it to Cord.

I'm sorry, Mom. I'm sorry, Dad. I'm sorry, Bridget. The words were written clearly on the front. Inside was a photograph. The picture was of the Vaughn Evanston memorial plaque. It was one of the shots Victor must have taken. He had used a black, felt tipped pen to obliterate the border with the words: *Being gay means hiding. Hiding. Hiding. I can't see. I can't photograph. I can't hide anymore.*

Cord looked directly at Spencer whose eyes were now filling with tears. "He's gay?"

"We had no idea."

The phone rang and Alexandra answered. "Hello, Rev. McDaniel… I'm fine… Yeah, she's here." She handed the phone to her mother.

"June," Cord began. "I have some troublesome news to share, and I need your help." He explained why he was calling.

When she hung up, June looked sharply at Alexandra as she called, "Bridget!" She decided Alexandra needed to understand the situation as well.

"Let's sit at the table, because we need to talk." The girls looked at each other, their eyes widening. "That was Rev. McDaniel."

"I know, Mom. I answered the phone." Alexandra's sarcastic tone was triggered by her mom's visible anxiety.

"Of course. I'm sorry." She started over. "Rev. McDaniel was calling from the hospital. He's there with Victor who is okay but…" she took a breath, "…he's in the hospital because he cut himself on the wrists. It seems that he was trying to kill himself."

Bridget stared at her. "He wha-a-a-t?"

June repeated herself slowly and gently.

"Why would he do that?"

"It's not simple, I am sure. He must be very unhappy or depressed or angry. When people do these things, they are trying to take themselves out of their pain."

"But what pain was he in? He wasn't in any pain like that!" Her bewilderment made her voice higher.

"Maybe trying to hurt himself was a way of calling for help."

Alexandra was stone silent. This was definitely something for older people to deal with.

Bridget wasn't on firm footing. "What kind of help? He's quiet at school. He can be goofy at church. He's kind of shy, maybe. But, he's my friend – not my *boyfriend*." She looked pointedly at her sister. Then she began to unravel. "He tried to kill himself?"

"Sweetie, come here." She gathered her daughter in her lap. "It's very hard to understand. There's another thing that Rev. McDaniel told me. It might help you understand. He said that Victor left a note, addressed to his parents and to you, telling them that he is gay. He's a homosexual."

"I know what that means," said Alexandra.

Bridget's eyes took on a different color. June continued, "You are clearly a special friend to him, honey. It's important for you to hold that knowledge with you. And, Mr. and Mrs. Beck have asked me if you could come to the hospital."

Bridget sat like a stone for a minute. "Yeah, okay." She was quiet for another moment. "Sure. Yeah, sure. I can go." She rubbed her face hard and then looked at her mother. "Would you come with me?"

"Yes. Of course. I am happy to take you and stay. Whatever makes the best sense and is helpful. But," she turned to Alexandra, "I don't think we can take you. I'm sorry to leave you, sweetie, but I don't think this is a time for a crowd of people to visit. When there's a crisis, it's important to pay attention to what people really need."

Alexandra was pretty sure she could be helpful, too, but she knew very well about hospitals and crises, and that the adults made the big decisions. "Do I stay here by myself?"

June regarded her carefully. "What do you think? Do you want to, or would you rather go somewhere? I would rather not have you here by yourself. I could call the Hofmeisters. They always say you can come by anytime."

Alexandra liked the idea. "Yeah. That would be okay. Can I take some videos?"

"Bring one along. I'm sure they have a VCR. I'll call and ask them."

Twenty minutes later she was dropping Alexandra off with Mavis and Porter. June repeated the generic story she had told them on the phone. Victor had been hospitalized because of an accident. He was asking for Bridget to visit. They weren't sure of the timing.

"We can keep her as long as you wish. It's wonderful to have someone visiting. We didn't have any plans, so don't worry a minute about us."

Alexandra became the center of attention as soon as the door closed. Mavis had been cleaning the kitchen. She offered Alexandra some cookies from her stash in colorful tins on the counter. A choir sang softly from her tape deck.

After drinking her milk, Alexandra wandered into the living room and stared blankly at the TV for a minute. "Can I call Mr. George?" she asked Porter.

"Sure, honey. His number is on the refrigerator door, and you can use the phone right over there by the couch."

Alexandra punched in the numbers. "It's ringing. I wonder if he's home. He might have gone out to the movies or something. Do you think he likes movies?"

Porter had resumed watching the game.

"Mr. George," Alexandra said into the phone. "This is Alexandra Wallace. Surprise! I wasn't sure if – like - calling you was a good idea, but Mr. Porter said it was okay."

"Well, certainly, child." George had picked up the phone in his own living room. "It's always a good thing to get a phone call from a friend. Are you getting ready to help me tomorrow?"

"That's kind of why I'm calling. I'm at Mr. Porter's house because my mom and Bridget are at the hospital."

"Is something wrong with your sister? What happened?"

"Oh, she's fine. They went over because Victor tried to commit suicide, which is really bad. And he had to be taken to the hospital. He's - uhm – gay, and he said so in his note. And he had Bridget's name on it so his parents wanted her to come over to the hospital for when he woke up."

George had been enjoying the excitement in her voice and the pleasure of a little comrade's call. The actual meaning of her words came on slowly. "Alexandra, say that again. It sounds very serious, and I want to be sure I understand you."

"Oh, huh, Victor tried to kill himself, and they took him to the hospital." Alexandra didn't notice that Porter had turned to stare at her. "His parents are really upset. He's gay, and I think maybe my sister knew or sort of guessed it. I don't know. But he was really unhappy. You must be really unhappy to want to kill yourself.

"So Rev. McDaniel called and asked if Bridget could come over to the hospital. He wanted to know if she would be okay with that. Uh, so, that's why I'm staying here so that Mr. Porter and Ms. Mavis can take care of me, and that's why I called you because I am sure I'll be there in the morning at church, but maybe I'll be coming with the Hofmeisters. I don't know yet."

"Well, thank you, my dear, for telling me. That was very considerate of you. How about if I talk to Mr. or Mrs. Hofmeister for a minute?"

"Sure," and she handed off the phone.

"Good God, Porter! What's going on? Alexandra just told me that Victor Beck – I assume she's talking about him – is in the hospital."

"I'm as surprised as you. I just overheard her. The mother didn't tell me any details. I can sure understand why. They just said they wanted to visit him and couldn't take the little one."

"What a disaster! The family must be in shock." George couldn't come up with what to say out loud. Porter was the last person he should be talking with right now.

"It's horrendous!" Porter was in a form of shock himself. "He thinks he's gay? How could he possibly imagine that he's a homosexual? He's barely in high school. He's still a child." Porter stopped himself, aware that Alexandra was at his elbow. Children! They shouldn't even know about such disgusting things. No wonder Victor wanted to commit suicide if someone had put in his mind that he was gay. What kind of twisted world was this!

After a little more pruned conversation, the two gave up and said goodbye. Porter turned his attention to Alexandra. Together they dug the video out of her backpack and set it up to play. He explained about the remote, which was no challenge to her. He then went into the kitchen. Turning up the choir on the radio, he started to whisper hoarsely to Mavis.

*** *** ***

Having hung up the phone, George stared at the pillow on his couch. The pillow, a lovely spot of color, looked back at him. He wanted to hide his face in it. Victor was only a boy, barely a young man. How could he be old enough to feel such horror?

"Duke!" he called, unable to focus on standing up and moving to find him. "Are you there?"

Duke appeared in the doorway to the kitchen rubbing salve on his forearms. "I'm covered with scratches." He had been cutting back the pyracantha bush in the backyard. "What's up?"

"Terrible news. One of the kids at the church has attempted suicide." All the misery and grief of his own younger years washed through him. "They say he's gay and it was tied to that. He's in the hospital."

Duke was silent, rubbing his skin. "Do I know this one?"

"I don't know. His name is Victor Beck. He's probably at the high school. I think he's old enough for that. I don't think I would have ever particularly mentioned him."

Duke was thoughtful. "The name sounds familiar. Maybe I've met him."

"Dark hair, a little tall for his age, maybe. Quiet. A little awkward."

"Sounds like dozens of kids at the high school."

George rubbed his face. "Did you ever think about suicide?"

"Not seriously, but as a sort of test to myself. You know: was I that miserable?" He started to unlace his work shoes. "And I wasn't. It was always clear to me that I needed to live in a different place. I had to get out of that town."

"I never had a plan like that. I was just depressed." George remembered that tight, anxious feeling. It had come back to him in the split second he heard about Victor. His own teenage years were confused, grim, and full of self-lectures about trying to be a good person. He had been completely in the closet, of course, and not sure at all about what demon was in him. But he had never heard the call of death! He had never wanted to end himself – just end the poisonous thoughts in his head and what they did to his body. No young person should be so self-hating as to try suicide!

"I should have known," George continued. He punched the pillow as he spoke. "I see things. I look for things, especially at church, where people need the odd friend or a bit of attention. But I missed this. Completely missed this." He felt an ancient fear rising in him. He couldn't miss things. He had to be on guard. A sense of self-protection took a grip on him.

Duke was not as obsessive about their life and privacy as he was. Stanton was George's town, and Duke didn't have generations of relationships in the vicinity. Duke was also not a banker with a reputation of trust to maintain. His career had been in college towns where there was a broader social code.

George had always worried enough for the two of them together. In some ways it fit his personality. Money management was a risk-averse job. Carrying a shield of caution had always been in his makeup. As a teenager, his confusion about his sexuality never worked itself out in risky behaviors. Later, even in the joy of loving Duke, he had nevertheless devised a way to reshape the Victorian house into two apartments. They built a kitchenette upstairs and added a separate entrance. They could maintain separate addresses and two visible mailboxes on the porch. And it wasn't all that bad to have two dens, since Duke had smoked like a chimney for years.

"What would you have done if you had noticed?" asked Duke, quietly.

George did not yet want to hear that question, but he knew it had to be asked. He was retired now, and times were changing. Couldn't they come out a bit to the world? They had enjoyed a more open society in West Lafayette. Now that they had settled in Stanton for good, Duke had notched up the argument.

"Okay, so what does one do? Would coming out have kept Victor safe?" George gave into some defensiveness.

"Well, with all your celebrated *people watching,* what else have you learned?" Duke always cut through George's equivocating.

George thought about the Beck family--kind people, steady church members. Loretta was annoyingly pious and equally annoying in her parading of it. Spencer seemed to be like George himself, a belt and suspenders kind of person.

George hauled himself up from the couch and pulled the church directory off the bookshelf. Flipping through the pictures, he found the Beck family picture. Unremarkable, the three portrayed a normal middle class church family. The photographer had arrayed them with the son standing and Spencer and Loretta seated. The boy was clearly more comfortable behind the lens than in front of a camera. He looked as if he were under his mother's thumb, with his hair carefully combed and his regimental khakis and blue blazer.

"This is Victor." He showed the picture to Duke and then flipped on through the directory. Each family had the starched, formaldehyde-filled look created by commercial photographers on the church circuit. The backgrounds were mottled. The various pyramids of people spoke of forced arrangements for the camera. How many of these were also forced arrangements for the church and for society? How many family men were living under false pretenses, struggling to do the right thing? How many women and mothers were hiding their true selves while dedicating their lives to loyalties and duties? His own picture brought him up short. Of course, the picture was of him alone. No Duke.

And wasn't that a shame? Duke had turned his whole life around. After years of cowering, he was engulfed in affection, teasing, bluntness, and honesty. He couldn't imagine an intimate life under other terms. And, it was as certain as the sunrise that some of the pictured couples were creating pretense well beyond two mailboxes on the front porch. He knew stories of dutiful love and terrible pain. He looked at his church family again, wondering where the stories were. Absently he fanned the pages. So many people! Duke was looking over his shoulder.

"Do you think I should go and see him?" George was asking himself as much as Duke. He closed the book and took his car keys from the silver dish on the side table.

"You mean the kid in the hospital?"

The two men looked at each other. "Yes."

"Well, you know what I would say, but it is your decision," responded Duke.

George tossed the keys up and down, weighing them each time they landed in his palm. They were lighter each time. He threw them a bit higher and then a bit higher. Each time he caught them. Once more, up they went, and this time they fell to the floor.

Duke stooped to get them. Wordlessly, he reached out to hand them to George.

It was a split second pause, but then George took them. The two men embraced, and with a deep breath, George let himself out his house, closing the beautiful Victorian smoked-glass front door behind him.

*** *** ***

Cord and June came out of Victor's room together. George was sitting in the waiting area. He had a deck of cards and was playing a game of solitaire along the coffee table. "George," said Cord.

"Hello, Reverend."

Smiling awkwardly, he said to June. "Your daughter called me to talk about tomorrow and greeting people at church. She spilled the beans about Victor."

June grimaced.

He turned to Cord, "I don't want to intrude, but I was terribly concerned."

"Victor will be fine. He lost blood and was unconscious for a time, but he's stabilized and conscious. He's asleep right now. We're very lucky. A fraction closer, and the story would have a different ending. It's a very dangerous kind of wound."

"Thank the Lord."

"We are very grateful that God was watching him. Now he needs time and rest and understanding. His parents are with him. So is Bridget."

"Is there anything I can do? Perhaps I could wait and bring Bridget home for you," George turned to June. "That way you can go claim Alexandra now."

June seemed to appreciate the idea. Depend on Alexandra to be a town crier! She should have talked about confidentiality, but it was too late now.

As if reading her thoughts, George added, "Alexandra is a terrific girl and one of a kind. She didn't overstep. She wanted to explain that it was a serious matter that might keep her from joining me tomorrow." He let it go at that.

After June departed, Cord sat down next to George.

"Thank you for coming. I didn't realize you had a special connection to the Becks."

"I didn't either." George felt the veins in his neck pulsing. He looked at his cards for a minute and then swept up his game and started to shuffle the deck. "This is hard for me to say, Reverend, but the truth of the matter is that I'm gay." He cut the cards in front of him a few times. "I have lived a great deal of my life here in Stanton without very many people knowing. I've never introduced my partner, Duke, at church. We have lived a very careful life."

George was gay? George Morrow? Cord said the first thing that came into his head. "But I've been to your home."

"Duke lives in the apartment upstairs that connects to mine downstairs. I'm sure there are people who see through the deception, but we keep it up. The world has come some distance, but I am not sure how much of that tolerance extends to Stanton."

Cord didn't know what else to say. He certainly hadn't seen through the ruse; he hadn't even thought to look.

"But, when I heard about Victor this evening, well, the bottom dropped out of my heart. I've watched him grow up. He's a child of the church, and whatever our differences, we all agree about loving and nurturing our children. We're not a church if we let him slip through our fingers."

Cord grasped the evident sentiments: guilt, grief, and remorse. "I believe we all share this reaction." He thought of Brent.

"But, I've particularly let him down. And maybe not just him. There are probably others, too. I've been quiet and careful all my life. Bankers do that, you know. The old-fashioned kind, at least." He paused to collect himself. Then he shrugged. "Then a kid like Victor comes along and sees no one around him who understands him or recognizes him for who he really is. He might be loved, but he isn't known. So I've protected myself and left him vulnerable and alone."

His jaw was locking up. He couldn't continue.

Cord broke their silence. "George, none of us has been there for him. This isn't only your cross to bear."

George tapped the deck on the table as if taking a sounding.

Cord continued, "You can't tear at yourself for what you did or didn't do for Victor. Lord knows, if there is anyone who has had his head in the sand, I guess it has been me. I haven't been a pastor to Victor, and I haven't been a pastor to you, either." The words were out. This wasn't a time to equivocate. The more he thought of his professional and personal shortsightedness, the more devastating it was.

George was chagrined. "Oh, I didn't mean to accuse you or for you to take any offense. I'm angry with myself. The real problem is silence and ignorance, and I am the first one to know about that. I was the one who didn't use what I know." It was pouring out of him now. "I know in my heart that we have to be a community. God wants us to be His family. All of us are His children. And I, me," he pointed a finger at his chest, "George Morrow, turned myself into a secret and took that out of the community. I was pretending to be in the church, but," he shook his head hard, "I wasn't really there. I specifically wasn't there for Victor."

The tables were turning. George's voice was that of a witness, born of wilderness, loneliness, and fear, yet instinctively full of grace. His face, his posture, and his words conveyed it all.

Cord stared at him hard, holding the moment. Sitting on plastic furniture in a waiting room full of faded plants and discarded magazines, George was standing witness for his soul.

And me? Cord thought. As the presumed pastor of the moment, I must name this, acknowledge it, and help him bring it out of the shadows.

"May I ask a favor?" Cord said. "I want to step back into Victor's room and tell Spencer and Loretta that you are here. I'll tell Bridget that you'll take her home when she's ready. But, may I offer you as a Deacon to be here with the family for support and help?"

George nodded. "That would be fine with me."

Cord continued, "We'll get them through this, and when Victor is released and is home, we will figure out the next steps."

"Sounds like a plan. If you could smooth things over that way, I'll take it from there."

And so it was. Loretta was instantly grateful. She didn't know George well, but better a man to play this role than a woman. She flinched at the thought of sympathetic cooing and casseroles and pies. George's calm was striking; he didn't seem the least bit shocked or appalled. And right now she could not bear any judgment from others.

"I am only here to be useful," George had said. They were speaking in the hallway. "Run errands, take messages. You should go and eat, perhaps. I can sit with him."

"Will you pray for us? I don't know if I can right now." Loretta wondered if he would be an intercessor. Would he pick up for her where she had failed in all her prayer and discipline?

Spencer's eyes filled, and he put his arm around her shoulders.

"Yes, I will." George nodded towards Victor's door. "Loretta and Spencer, I want to be here without any pretense. My partner, Duke, and I both weathered difficult years when we were young. I sincerely want to help. This isn't because I'm on a church visitation committee."

They both stared at him for a moment, rearranging their universe for a second time that day.

"You're gay?" Spencer's voice was muddy.

"Yes."

They continued to absorb the information.

"But you're a banker!"

George had to grin. "Yep. And a very risk averse and conservative one."

Spencer's smile was lopsided.

Loretta turned to her husband. "He's an usher at church!"

Spencer's smile normalized. "Yes, honey. I think the point is that he's actually very conventional."

"We don't need to talk about me anymore for now." George was steering them back towards Victor's door. "I'll be here in the waiting room."

*** *** ***

Victor stirred, foggy and weak, but he opened his eyes. He looked at them all, and they looked back. His parents were both there. And so was Bridget, with hair like a firestorm of black around her face. She looked straight at him and said, "You're okay. We're all here."

His mother bent over him and kissed him. He could barely hear her say, "You're okay, honey. We love you. You're fine and we're all here for you. Go back to sleep."

And he did just that, immediately, on command. He had never slept with someone watching him before. Now he could.

Later Spencer walked Bridget out to the waiting room. "I'll run you home," George said to her. And then to Spencer, "I'll come right back. And then, if you want to take a break, go get something to eat, I'll be here."

And so it was. Much later in the evening, when Spencer and Loretta emerged from Victor's room, George was long back at his post in the waiting room with his deck of cards and books. They looked wrung out. Spencer had convinced Loretta to let him take her home. "You need to sleep so we can be with him tomorrow. He's going to be all right now."

"He'll need you both to be rested tomorrow," encouraged George. "Go home. I'll be right here." After they left, he settled down in the armchair next to Victor's bed. He watched the darkness and contemplated the frame of light around the door from the hallway.

Sometime later, Spencer stepped back in. "I got her to bed, and gave her some sleeping pills from the doctor. And I cleaned up the bathroom." He couldn't say anything more.

The two men sat near Victor's bed until dawn. Neither spoke. The night nurse's footsteps went by regularly. Victor slept. The outline of his body was visible through the light thermal blanket. His breathing was easy. His arms lay on his side, one swaddled with gauze.

Each man watched. Spencer counted Victor's breaths. And George prayed. "Please, God, no more. Give us light."

CHAPTER 28

Brent woke as dawn broke across the lake. His arms, draped across the steering wheel, had acted as his pillow. They were prickly and numb, and he slowly bent them into his lap. He was cold.

He had fallen asleep to the quiet lapping of the water on the pier, his drowsiness enhanced by the whiskey from the bottle at his side. He fully acknowledged the irony of drinking whiskey at the lake. Shivering, he closed the car window and turned on the ignition. His face in the mirror was not pretty. He could feel the stubble on his chin that needed shaving. Thank goodness no one policed after dark except in the summer. He would have been in the papers. But, to hell with that. He'd survive.

It had been a lonely night preceded by a lonely afternoon. He had left the church and driven around aimlessly. Going home made no sense. He wasn't hungry, and whatever errands he had planned to run were forgotten. At one point he had driven by his father's house and then out on the state highway. He stopped and walked around in the cornfield where he had wandered in straight lines last November. The field was muddy, and his shoes were completely soggy by the time he returned to the car.

He drove home, changed his shoes, and looked up June's address. Her blue bungalow looked inviting with its comfortable yard and bright yellow front door. There was no car in the driveway, and no one answered when he knocked. Probably they were shopping or doing something else enormously typical for a family on a Saturday afternoon. He imagined a picnic despite the remaining wet from the storm, or a game, or the movies. Each sounded like a slice of sheer happiness, just being together.

He sat on the front steps for a few minutes until he thought that might appear odd to any neighbors. So he set out again, wandering and unfocused.

He had dinner at the diner at some point and tried a movie, but being alone was utterly oppressive, and he left. Eventually he set out for the lake, via the liquor store. Maybe the pier and the water could answer some of his questions. Revisiting events, recreating a setting--he simply wanted to lay it all out. He had arrived with the moon bright in the sky, so bright it had outshone the stars. Where did he fit in this vast universe?

Brent wasn't sure any answers had appeared. However, he could honestly say that he had a better understanding of the sequence of events that had raised the questions. The narrative was interconnected: Wash, the artist, and his son, Vaughn; Vaughn, the soldier, and his friend, Guy; Brent, the boy, and his father, Guy; Brent, the man, and his church protégé, Victor. There were connections of place and relationships. It was a geometric drawing of points and lines. But what did this tell him about how boys turned into men? What did it mean to be a son and also a man? Most importantly, what did men mean for each other?

The lake sparkled in the path of the early sun. The rest of the world was gaining color, coming out of its palette of black and white.

Brent decided he had opened the can enough for now. If he hadn't figured out the contents, he had certainly punched through the container, and the internal pressure had been released. He needed something to eat. He got out of the car and did some stretches in the brilliant light. Taking a final deep breath, he returned to the car, put it into reverse, did a three-point turn, and headed home.

*** *** ***

As people stepped outside, the carillon was ringing overhead. The bells changed the nature of the air. People looked up to the sky, not down at their feet. The tower stood tall as the ringing poured out.

Brent paused at the sidewalk, nodded to a few people and then turned back to scan the crowd. June and Bridget were emerging through the doors.

"Where's Alexandra?" he asked.

"She's helping Porter today. We thought we would wait outside for her." She noticed his hollow eyes and casual clothes. "You weren't in church?"

"No, I've been out at the lake, taking in the view and trying to figure things out. You know what's happened to Victor?"

June nodded. "We visited yesterday at the hospital."

"Oh, of course. I stopped by your house yesterday after I learned the news."

"Did you? I'm sorry we weren't home." She meant what she said.

"Bridget!" Tiffany was calling from the door.

"Go ahead," said June. "We've got time."

190

The girls ran towards each other, colliding into a hug. June and Brent couldn't hear what they were saying, but they didn't need to. Their animation was evident; they hung onto each other as they moved to a quieter place on the lawn.

"It's a lot for them to absorb," said June.

"It's a lot for all of us to absorb. I'm Victor's faith partner, and I'm sick that I didn't see that anything was wrong. I am going to drop by the hospital today," said Brent.

"I think it would mean a lot. This is obviously about Victor, but his parents could use the support, too. They are completely undone."

"I understand. It's about Victor, it's about his parents, but it is also about all of us. This is a wonderful community, and we watch out for each other. But we missed this one. I don't know how, but we missed it."

All evening, Brent had considered the possibility of having a child, losing a child, and being vulnerable to such heartache. He had gone over various funerals he had managed. The ones for children had always been fraught with emotion and a sense of injustice at a young life cut down. But Victor was different for him. After a few short encounters, he could picture himself with his arm on the boy's shoulders, as he had seen June do with Bridget. It wasn't for support, and it wasn't for control. It was simply affection. The circle of affection.

Victor had punctured the professional cellophane he had always wrapped around himself. Had he been callous, dismissive with grieving families? Had he supported parents as they needed and deserved? He hoped so, but he didn't know. He would know better now. From now on he would be honoring the risk that parents took, to engage in each other, to have each other, to form a family, to love each other deeply, and to live lives so connected.

He looked around at the other families heading for their cars in the parking lot. So many people did this foolish thing of loving until it hurt. And now he would, too.

June touched him on the arm. He had stood so still for a long few minutes. "Brent," she said. "What is it?"

He smiled at her, marveling at her sturdiness. Her long willowy form defied her rootedness. "Perhaps we can have dinner and talk when this settles a bit."

"That would be good."

Alexandra appeared at their elbows. "I heard that," she said. "Is that like a real date?"

Brent laughed. "Oh, yes. And you are not invited. Please accept my apologies. I hope that doesn't hurt your feelings."

"Naw. You don't have to complicate for me."

"I think you mean *compensate*, and I'll take your word for it."

June asked Alexandra, "Do you think we can get Bridget to break away and come home now?"

Alexandra left them at a run to career into the two girls. For once, they simply opened their arms, and the three shared a group hug.

*** *** ***

George looked up from his solitaire game to see Brent coming down the hall, looking at room numbers. "Yes, you're in the right place. His folks are with him."

"I'm Victor's confirmation partner," Brent explained. "I was with Cord yesterday when he got the message. I had to come by." Brent wasn't sure what George's relationship to the family was.

George replied, "I understand. I had a similar reaction, and Cord asked me to stay and offer any Deacon support I could. It's the least I can do. Thank God and the stars and the moon that he's alive!" He rubbed his hands together. "It breaks my heart that it had to happen."

"It's a terrible thing." Brent was saying the obvious. Time to dive in. "What's happening now? I assume he was medicated, sleeping, and all. But what are the protocols when this happens?"

"Well, first, they wanted him to sleep. And he sure has. All evening, all night, and most of the morning."

"Is he having visitors?"

"He's probably a bit groggy. Let me check with Loretta and Spencer. I'll let them know you're here."

George tapped on the door, spoke quietly, and waved Brent in.

Brent stepped into the room. "I thought I'd come by and say hello."

Spencer had stood up. "Thank you for coming."

Victor gave him a weak smile. "Hey, Mr. Sykes."

Brent touched Loretta lightly on the shoulder. "I don't know if visitors can be helpful right now, but I want to offer any support I can."

Loretta's expression spoke of vulnerability and pain. And yet, Victor seemed collected and relaxed.

Brent turned to Victor. He didn't want to sound formulaic. "I know you have friends and teachers who will be there for you. But I guess I take this confirmation partner responsibility pretty seriously. I wanted to come by. I hope I'm not intruding."

Victor gave him another weak smile and raised his un-bandaged arm. Brent leaned forward and shook his hand. Victor returned the squeeze.

Spencer clinked the change in his pocket. He couldn't imagine how to engage with people. Bridget, George, and Cord had slipped in with great intimacy. But now the public world was knocking. How were they to do this? What did a person say at a time like this?

Brent smoothly took a chair. "If you don't mind," he said, and started in. "When Victor and I went to the IU game, we talked about being in the public eye. Remember, Victor?"

Victor nodded.

"I told you that it wasn't too hard. In a town like Stanton, being mayor is not like being on network TV all the time." He smiled ruefully. "But, I wasn't totally truthful. I've lived all my life in Stanton doing what was expected of me. I followed in my father's footsteps, lockstep, and I didn't think much about what people thought, because it wasn't about me, but about the row of corn that my father had planted. I hid behind him, to be honest, and marched in a straight line.

"So, I have to say, Victor, that I've been wrong. I began to learn that when my dad died. A person has to first be true to himself, and not everyone else around him. I didn't say that to you in the car, and I'm sorry. I should have been more honest with you then."

Loretta's head seemed frozen in its angle, staring at him.

Victor nodded, his eyes clear and focused. A little color had returned to his cheeks.

"I'm sorry," said Brent again. Turning to Loretta and Spencer. "I don't mean to be giving a speech. But I want to make it crystal clear how much it means to me to be connected to Victor and stand with him now."

Spencer couldn't get his head around it. This wasn't a time for everyone to go into personal therapy. Victor had nearly died!

But Brent had said enough for Loretta. She would grab at any lifeline being thrown to her son, whatever the terms. If it meant turning over some of her son to others, she would do it in a heartbeat. "Brent, I am not sure I understand, but if it means you are here for Victor, I am so grateful." She paused and looked at her son. "I am so eternally grateful."

Victor didn't flinch. His mother might be over the top sometimes, but she was in his court. It was good to feel safe.

*** *** ***

After Brent's visit, George shooed Spencer and Loretta off to the cafeteria. "Are you up for company, or do you want to nap?"

Victor shook his head. He had gotten out of bed and was wrapped in bathrobe, sitting in a chair. "No, I'm pretty sure I don't need to sleep anymore."

"Good," said George. He pulled out a scrapbook from his bag. "You're a photographer, so I thought I would show you some pictures. They're mostly sentimental, but I think it's better than watching TV or reading magazines."

With that, George began to tell his stories about growing up, his family, and his hobbies. He talked about being lonely and depressed, about drinking a lot in college. And then there were pictures of Duke, and he told about meeting him. The pictures showed both of them with long sideburns and dark hair. "I know," George said. "It's hard to believe I used to look like that." He flipped a few more pages.

"I've met him," said Victor suddenly, looking harder at a more recent picture of Duke. "He's one of the high school counselors."

"I thought you might have seen him at the school."

Wow! Two gay men right there, one at church and one at school. Victor was more than surprised. He'd never guessed.

*** *** ***

Spencer and Loretta found the hospital's cafeteria and carried their trays over to a booth in a quiet corner. Neither was hungry, but each wanted to put on a good show for the other. Sitting at the faux butcher-block table, they picked up their plastic knives and forks and began the unadorned meal.

"This business with George Morrow is such a surprise." Spencer had always liked George.

"Yes, he feels like family already."

"He's someone you can trust. He's very loyal. That's what stands out."

"What if we had lost him?" Loretta blurted out. The trauma was so close. The icy cascade of feelings poured over her.

"But we didn't lose him. He's alive and safe upstairs. You were a complete tiger, getting him to the hospital."

"I was on automatic overdrive. I didn't have a single thought except to get help."

"Thank God you came home when you did."

They relived the events of the previous day with the comfort of a safe outcome: the bathtub, the blood, the ambulance, the medics, the ER, the warm blankets, the sedatives. It was a story they would repeat in their minds for months and years to come.

Slowly they edged toward the hard discussion. "But why? I can't understand why he did it," Spencer could find nothing that made sense.

"I don't know, honey." Loretta covered her face with her hands. Tears seeped between her fingers.

Spencer was silent. He was as lost as she was.

"I don't know." She choked out her words. "I keep saying to myself that I might have planted the seeds. I could see something in his photography. A starkness. He resisted girls, like Bridget, and I thought he was just being an impolite, immature boy. He didn't want to embrace his faith. Somehow I didn't understand, I didn't see, I have failed him…"

"Sweetheart, that is wrong!" This had little to do with whether they had

194

taught Victor to believe in a personal Jesus. She couldn't blame herself for that. Christ!

Her voice was rising. "Don't you see? He's my son. I pray and I try, and I pray and I try, and I pray and I try, and look what happens."

Spencer had never directly contradicted her before. "Stop it. This isn't about how you are as a mother or your faithfulness."

Her hysteria was rising. She started clapping her hands together. "See, I put my hands together like this and pray and pray and pray and pray..."

"Loretta, listen to me. If you have to think that way, you must see that God saved our son. He saw him through his hour of need." Spencer took a deep breath, slid out of his bench seat, and moved over next to her. He locked her hands into stillness between his as she sobbed into his sweater.

CHAPTER 29

The next morning Cord McDaniel took himself to the hospital for a round of calls and some quiet time with Victor. They said little, reported a bit on the day before. Victor seemed positive and relaxed, happy to have company.

In contrast, Cord thrashed internally. *When two or three are gathered together in the sight of God.* The phrase had been running through his mind. It was a statement of community. He concentrated on the phrase, *in the sight of God.* The community didn't need to gather physically, but was still pleasing to God.

We have exactly that sort of community in our midst, he thought. How large is it? How much is it acknowledged? The questions unsettled him. He had wished for a connected flock, with great spiritual fire. He had been so cocky about knowing his congregation and finding it pedestrian. He'd been so ignorant!

A counselor arrived to meet first with Victor and then with his parents. Cord took his leave, punching the automatic button that operated the hall door next to the elevator. It heaved open, creating enough width for a hospital gurney.

Cord had never had any real connection to a gay person or a gay community. Sure, there were a few radical types back at graduate school, but no one he particularly knew. And on one level he didn't care. Even thinking about gay sex seemed to be an indecent sort of voyeurism. Why would anyone care about another person's sex life? The idea of gay sex never particularly bothered him. It just didn't, so there.

Yes, he heard the church debate about ordaining gays into ministry. It seemed to him to be a very small problem. He had no sense there were very many gay people interested in the ministry. He thought it was a fringe issue, not a central, weighty problem. Anti-gay people were animated by a phobia and simply found homosexuals useful scapegoats. That's what he thought.

He had been so... so... oblivious!

Cord had paused so long that the automatic hall door whooshed shut. He punched the button again, and the door whooshed back open, stirring a swell of breeze on his face. He'd never noticed that breeze before. Well, he had never stood around watching doors flapping open and shut before either. Or discovered that there were gay people close to him and in his congregation. Or realized that he had been a blind man leading the blind.

He had always liked George. How could you not? He was a nice older fellow in the church, helpful and thoughtful. Steady and dependable. And Victor was a child of the church, a member of the congregation since birth, now going through his teenage years, polite and healthy looking. What's not to like? Obviously he hadn't known Grace's son, but if he were anything like Grace, he must have been a wonderful spirit.

How could someone imagine directing anger or viciousness towards any of those three?

He found his car and drove out of the parking garage. Stopping at a light, he watched two preschool boys holding hands, leaning forward watching the traffic, and clearly bursting to scoot across the street. Their mothers, one with a stroller, were cautioning, "Wait for the green light. That means we can walk. Okay, now."

The pair was off, and the mothers followed behind. Cord watched the little parade cross in front of him. The boys continued to hold hands as they trooped on down the sidewalk. The driver behind Cord tapped the horn, and he realized he was ignoring the green light. The boys had caught his imagination--the two of them joyously holding hands and marching forward.

Of course, at fourteen, the world didn't work that way. Victor might have held hands with a boy when he was three, but at fourteen it was taboo.

Taboo. That's a deep rejection. If something is taboo, it's not just impolite or weird. It's deep down and woven into the social fabric and moral values.

Cord frowned. Victor wasn't confused about himself, nor did he seem to be a teenager without friends and family. His note stated a truth. But he had slashed his wrists because his truth was a deep taboo. Cord couldn't imagine self-destruction without some compelling force. Victor knew his homosexuality was challenging, and perhaps violating, something very deep in the community for which he would be shunned.

Shunned. The thought was primal and tribal. It meant being cut off by family, community, and church. Cord's hands gripped the steering wheel. Shunned. The threat was so palpable to Victor that he had — when you got down to it – shunned himself. He did it first. He subscribed to the code.

What a horror! His flock of birds, his congregation that should swoop and soar with the Holy Spirit, had flown tightly together. They had formed such a swarm, listening to some unspoken radar, that they had completely abandoned the child who wasn't on their channel. They had forced him against all his humanity to attempt to destroy himself.

Cord pulled to the curb. He looked down at his hands locked on the steering wheel. He bent forward, his head on the steering wheel. Should he pray? Should he steer? Should he cry? Should he lament? He didn't know what to do. And he was as guilty as the rest.

There was a tap on his window. Startled, he jerked up. He had stopped a block short of the church, and his car was still running. "Are you all right?" the jogger asked. "I saw you pull over and slump over the wheel."

Cord lifted a hand. "I'm fine. Just checking something. Thanks very much for asking."

The jogger, running in place, gave him a salute and continued on down the block.

Cord's heart was pumping as if he were the one jogging. He started to pray. "Dear God, help me understand. What have we done? What have I fostered? Have I encouraged the mob? He is a child of this church, a son to all of us. We didn't love him. Well, of course we loved him. No, we loved him for us, rather than loving him for who he is." He stopped, unable to be sensible. He was washed with grief, extravagant in his self-condemnation. How could he have been so oblivious and simplistic and stupid and nearsighted and fumbling and dense and unaware and superficial and ignorant and... he ran out of words.

*** *** ***

It was Wednesday, and George knocked on the Becks' front door. He was carrying a 1000-piece jigsaw puzzle. Loretta opened the door and waved him in. He passed the card table in the living room, which already displayed a completed 500-piece puzzle of overlapping shots of baseball diamonds.

He and Victor upended the new puzzle on the basement table that Victor used for framing photographs. They moved two floor lamps to stand guard at opposite corners, and set to work turning every piece up and moving obvious colored pieces together. Both were quiet except for exclamations when pieces fit together.

Loretta came down an hour later and asked if they wanted anything to drink. "Sure," they answered in unison. George looked up for a moment and smiled. Loretta smiled back and affectionately rubbed Victor's shoulder for a moment.

The afternoon meandered along as the edge pieces found their places, and a number of garish fish began to take shape. Their colors were the easiest to spot. Bit by bit, an aquarium emerged, with a murky corner and a miniature castle creating a jungle gym in the center.

By dinnertime, they were well on their way. Spencer carried a beer down to George and pulled a chair over to one of the lamps so he could read a magazine that had come in the mail. Loretta called them for dinner, and with great reluctance all three stretched and came upstairs. They grinned foolishly when she asked them how it was going. "We're addicted," said George.

The quartet had a peaceful dinner, and by 9:50 the puzzle was completed. "What say you?" asked George as they stretched. "I know you've got a vacation this week, but do we have one more in us?"

Victor grinned. "Sure. But we're going to run out of tables soon."

"There's always the floor, but I'm getting a little old for that," replied George.

"Tomorrow's Thursday. I have a counseling session in the morning that's in Indianapolis."

They settled on the afternoon. Spencer walked George to his car. "I can't tell you how much peace you have brought us," he said. "Time seems suspended when you two are working on those puzzles. It was a great idea. It's given us time to catch our breath."

George shook his hand. "It's odd to say, but I've had a wonderful time."

*** *** ***

Kyle didn't get it. Gay guys were supposed to be interested in fashion and feminine stuff. Victor wasn't like that at all. He had always been just like any of them. They'd been together forever. He was totally normal when they went on sleepovers and mission trips. He slept like the rest of them. He used the same brand of toothpaste. He wore the same clothes. Was the photography stuff a kind of artsy thing? Kyle thought maybe so, but weren't most newspaper photographers men? They couldn't all be gay...

"It's all fuckedupilus." Why would Victor try to kill himself? He just couldn't believe it. He'd known this guy all his life. Victor had never seemed very interested in girls, but a lot of guys weren't. Kyle himself was picky and didn't care for very many girls. They weren't interesting and spent their time gossiping.

Wow! Maybe there were a whole bunch of people who were gay and Kyle hadn't known it.

*** *** ***

For the first time in her life, Loretta chose not to go to church on Maundy Thursday. The Christian world was revisiting the stalk towards death: the last supper, the last meeting, the last blessings, and the last hour for prayer.

She couldn't bear the thought. On Good Friday the crowd would start to jeer, "Crucify him!" The image terrified her this year. Imagine Victor chased by a mob, another ugly thought she had to wipe from her mind.

Her house was a necessary cocoon right now. She had to restore its safety and intimacy. It would take a long time before she would nonchalantly enter her front door. Now her ears jumped at sounds, either the radio or an answer to her strong "Hello!" Her skin prickled walking up the stairs. She noticed closed doors. Even the photographs on the walls had become glass-encased messages. She wanted to take them down. No, she wanted to leave them up.

She would never forget the shock of finding him and struggling to pull him from the tub. Red water had splashed everywhere. His skin had looked bleached and almost translucent. It still did. When he asked her help with the bandages, she managed to peel off the adhesive and apply salve where the skin was raw. The stitches were dark, a series of hieroglyphics on the papyrus skin that barely covered blue channels underneath. Afterwards, she shuddered for ten minutes in her bedroom, hugging a pillow from the bed.

What a twist of horror! And yet, he had opened his eyes to her again. He had come home. She clung to the miracle, repeating her new mantra of thanks, "He lives, he lives."

A new frenzy took over – to warm him up. She threw the bloodstained towels away and bought him new clothes: new pajamas, a new bathrobe, slippers, and oversized soft sweatshirts. Everything hung loosely on his frame, but the warm dark colors gave him a cushioned look.

She spent hours in the kitchen cooking snacks, fun food, good dinners, and desserts for him. He would wander in, and she would give him something to nibble. They didn't speak much, but he bent into her hugs. "Thank you, Lord."

*** *** ***

For Victor, Good Friday broke the pattern of visits from George. Coming home from the hospital, Victor had felt enormously peaceful, and the puzzle projects had extended his calm. In the concentration and quiet he had begun to adjust to his new self.

When he had cut himself, he was only focused on stopping the noise and the pain. Watching the blood mix with the water was like watching his noisy insides flow into the outside world. Whoever and however and whatever he was had emerged for the world to see and know. And with that, the noise and pain had stopped. His wrists still ached, but that could barely be called pain.

In many ways he hadn't changed, just quieted. The people around him, however, acted and spoke in new ways. His parents hugged him all the time, telling him over and over how much they loved him. Bridget had looked at him directly, "We can be better friends if we don't have secrets like that." He had never imagined that people like Rev. McCord would be so concerned. And George was an unexpected pal, a gentle uncle. Who would have ever guessed that! Yes, his mind was calm, and he could enjoy those around him.

The week had been full with sleeping, puzzles, and drives to Indianapolis for visits with the counselor. He was learning a lot. Being gay was not very unusual. He wasn't so rare. The counselor, a lesbian, had sessions with him one-on-one. They also met as a foursome with his parents. His mom and dad had a lot more to say than he did, and he listened. He could understand. They were afraid he might get depressed and cut himself again. He knew he wouldn't. But he could tell that they would worry for a long time. He was sorry about that, but couldn't explain that it had been necessary to kill that other Victor, the person they thought was Victor, so that he could emerge. He hadn't understood about the two Victors until he saw his blood mix with the water.

*** *** ***

Spencer was early for the noon Good Friday service. He sat in the pew quietly, holding his hands palm down and heavy on his knees. People slipped in around him, coming in quickly because they had stepped out of work for the short hour. As the service opened, Spencer found himself focused on the stained glass window of Christ reaching to the frightened disciples tossing in their boat.

A soloist stood to sing. The piano introduction was familiar, plaintive.

> *O sacred Head, now wounded, with grief and shame weighed down,*
> *now scornfully surrounded with thorns, thine only crown:*
> *how pale thou art with anguish, with sore abuse and scorn!*
> *How does that visage languish which once was bright as morn!*

As Bach's great chorale took over, Spencer began to weep.

> *What thou, my Lord, has suffered was all for sinners' gain;*
> *mine, mine was the transgression, but thine the deadly pain.*
> *Lo, here I fall, my Savior! 'Tis I deserve thy place;*
> *look on me with thy favor, vouchsafe to me thy grace.*

The soloist clasped her hands in front of her. Her voice was pure and clear, without a hint of a quiver. This indeed was The Passion.

> *What language shall I borrow to thank thee, dearest friend,*
> *for this thy dying sorrow, thy pity without end?*
> *O make me thine forever; and should I fainting be,*
> *Lord, let me never, never outlive my love for thee.*

Tears were sheeting down Spencer's face. Nothing would ever be the same. Victor had been snatched from death. The grace of God and the gift of life were being offered to him. His beloved son had borne his ignorance, his disconnection, his distractions, and his transgressions. He had no plan, no response, and no understanding. It was all he could do simply to lean forward in the pew, his head on his arms.

"Thank you, thank you, Lord God! Thank you for saving my son."

CHAPTER 30

June had planned a formal Easter dinner with all the trimmings. It was the only time of year she served lamb, and Bridget and Alexandra agreed that the green mint jelly had Easter egg dye in it. It was so green!

Late in the afternoon, all three were in their kitchen doing the dishes. June always insisted on washing the good china by hand. It didn't seem right to leave it to the mechanical spray of the dishwasher.

Porter and Mavis had just left, having filled the house with the spirit of grandparents. Mavis had brought a knitting project for Alexandra, who wanted to keep up with Bridget. Porter had carved the meat. Bridget had been quiet throughout the afternoon, just as she had been all week. The new puppy, Doc, was the center of attention.

June rinsed another soapy plate and handed it to Bridget to dry. Alexandra was returning the silver forks to their slot in the special velvet-lined box. Out of the corner of her eye June watched Bridget polish the plate and polish it some more.

"What is it, honey?" she finally asked quietly.

She was greeted with silence.

"Just think, we've been here in Stanton for almost a year now. It was soon after Easter last year that we were packing up and getting ready to move."

Bridget carefully – too carefully – placed the plate on the counter. June handed her a second one. "They're so nice, Mom."

"Who?"

"Mr. and Mrs. Hofmeister. I mean, she is my faith partner, and they bring us cookies and Christmas presents, and they pay attention to Alexandra, too." She was reciting something she had been listing in her head.

"But Mr. Hofmeister was so creepy that night, and I think that was the reason Victor cut himself." She burst into tears.

June froze. "Can you tell me what you mean, sweetie?"

Bridget was convulsed with sobs. June pried off her soapy plastic gloves and pulled Bridget to her.

"At movie night," she sobbed into her mother's sweater, "Mr. Hofmeister told us that gay people were sinners." She could hardly get out her words. "He said they were perverts and scum and all this ugly stuff. I didn't know what to do. He seemed so angry, and I'm sure that's why Victor left early, and that's the last I saw of him before the hospital. Oh, Mom!" They clung to each other for a long moment, June stroking her daughter's hair.

Alexandra was quiet, watching. She picked up Doc for something to hug.

June could feel her heart pounding. "Here, let's go sit down on the couch." She signaled to Alexandra to come. They sat close together as Bridget continued to cry. No one said anything for a long time. Doc finally yelped for freedom, and Alexandra let him go.

"The first thing to remember," June said firmly, "is that Victor is okay. He had a crisis, but he survived. He and his family are together, and they love him."

Bridget nodded. Alexandra got up and handed her the tissue box. "You're going to need more than one," she said.

"The second thing to know is that you aren't to blame for any of this."

Bridget's word tumbled out. "But I was his friend, and he didn't tell me, and I didn't figure it out on my own, and I didn't say anything back to Mr. Hofmeister, and… and… and then it was too late."

"You did absolutely nothing wrong, Bridget. Nothing. You are still Victor's friend, and you clearly mean a lot to him. Don't ever forget that he wrote his note not just to his parents, but he also included you."

"But how could Mr. Hofmeister be so nasty and mean about gay people?"

Ah, there is the problem, thought June. Now what do I say? How do I know what makes people judgmental and hateful?

"Oh, honey. I don't know if I can explain that. I can't excuse it. But people have so many sides. We saw his sweet and good side today, and we see that most of the time. You have to remember that part of him. I guess sometimes people carry a dark side for some unknown reason. It comes out as a surprise. I had no idea he carried those ideas and feelings." She didn't know how to make it simple or what was underneath it all.

"I can't explain or excuse it," she tried again. "And it is a terrible thing when people can be wonderful in some settings and suddenly turn into different people in other ways." She realized that she was seething inside. How could he have poured out his vitriol to *kids at a church movie night?*

She tried some more. "I'm very very very sorry that this has happened. No one should say those things to anybody. That was wrong. Adults shouldn't do that. People shouldn't do that."

"I just keep thinking that was why Victor did it." Bridget started to wail again.

And again June patiently held her daughter tightly and waited until the tears had slowed. They talked and cried, until Alexandra turned on the lamps at the end of the couch.

June carried these things in her heart into the evening. After the girls were in bed, she checked on them to be sure they were sleeping, and then she called Brent.

"I'm so sorry to call so late," she began.

"Not at all." Brent often received late night calls, but he had popped off the couch when he heard her voice. "Has something happened?"

June told him the story, explaining that she would call Cord in the morning, but that she needed some perspective now.

Brent listened. Yes, he could well imagine that Porter had gone off on a tirade. He had diffused similar invective himself.

"We saw no clue of that sort of thing from him," said June. "He's been a surrogate grandfather to the girls, and that has been so special this year."

"You find all kinds in a community," responded Brent. "Not that it excuses anything, but can we ever really know what goes on with other people? And we have no idea what we set in motion with our words. Who would have guessed this would unfold with Victor this way?"

They were both silent for a moment. "I'm so sorry," June started again. "We barely know each other, and I didn't mean to break into your evening. But we have this connection through the kids, and I wanted to share what I had learned."

Brent felt oddly joyful. They were partners in this matter. She had just said as much. This crisis was stirring up all sorts of things. "Wait a minute. Tell me again what Bridget said about that movie night."

She repeated what she had gleaned.

"I think I have another twist to this story, June, but I don't think I should share it over the phone."

"You could come over. The girls are asleep, and I'm hardly going to be going to bed soon. I'm way too wound up about all this."

"Are you sure you would feel comfortable?"

"I suggested it, didn't I?"

He acquiesced, and within 15 minutes he was at the bright yellow door for the second time in a week. He barely tapped, and she answered. "We can sit in the kitchen."

She had made coffee. "It's decaf, and I have leftover lemon pie from Easter dinner, too. Would you like some?"

They pulled up their chairs, leaned elbows on the table, and started to talk. "It's a difficult story. It's about my father."

June's eyes widened as she listened. Brent talked and talked.

The next morning at breakfast, Bridget said, as she wound her hair in a twist away from her face, "I think I had a dream last night that you were downstairs talking with Dad. It made me feel really good."

June turned at the stove to look at her. "Yes, well, it wasn't Dad. I was talking to Brent Sykes, who came over after you went to bed."

Alexandra frowned. "He did? Didn't Doc bark or anything?"

"I invited him because we were talking on the phone about our conversation on the couch yesterday."

"You told him?"

"Yes, I did. It's a serious matter, and I wanted his advice. I will also call Rev. McDaniel this morning."

Bridget tilted her head to pull her elastic through her ponytail.

"I wish you would do your hair somewhere other than at the table, Bridg."

"Oh, sorry." She picked up her toast. "Is something bad going to happen?"

"I think something bad already happened. It's more about what pieces we can pick up and how we can learn some lessons. Where can we go from here?"

After the girls had left for school, June did call Cord. "I'm sure you can imagine how upset Bridget is. I am just so extremely grateful that Victor didn't succeed in killing himself."

Cord listened and sighed deeply. How terrible! How immensely terrible! His congregation had fault lines he never dreamed of. His ministry was going to be the biggest challenge of his life from now on.

CHAPTER 31

The special Session meeting convened slowly. People straggled in, bearing tales of schedules on steroids. Anyone who thought December was a crowded month should try springtime. One Elder was still recuperating from chaperone duties at the all-night prom party.

The agenda offered little zip to the evening. Who cared if non-members wanted to use the church for weddings?

Cord had primarily called the meeting for the purpose of examining the Confirmation Class and voting on accepting them into full membership. The names of those 9th graders were read, and Cord was about to comment about the class and their remarkable talent, as indicated in their confirmation projects.

"I need to ask," Porter's voice was tense, "what are the guidelines as we prepare for the examination and the vote?"

The Book of Order was named. The questions were reviewed. Cord explained, "These are the usual questions, although Session members can ask further questions."

"We talk about voting our conscience," Porter said. "That's how I should approach this vote?" It wasn't a question.

Cord responded as if he'd been queued for a lesson in Presbytery polity. "Absolutely. We Presbyterians are very faithful to the idea of free will and conscience."

Porter followed on: "Can you remind me what our policy is about admitting homosexuals into membership?"

Cord felt the jolt. But the clerk got there first, crisp, and officious, his eyebrows choking each other in a rough single line across his forehead. "There is no policy. People who come freely, and upon examination through these questions show no hesitancy, are welcomed."

"Well, I see we don't ask them directly about being homosexual. But if a person is choosing a lifestyle of sin, how can we vote to accept him as a member?"

Only one person looked mystified. Everyone else had a bead on the situation.

"This isn't the Inquisition, Porter."

"Hold it," Porter said. "I don't appreciate that comment. That was personal."

"I apologize," the Elder said immediately. "But a gay lifestyle is not sinful."

"It is condemned in the Bible."

"My God!" said another. "I mean, what kind of gay lifestyle could a fourteen-year-old have, anyway? That's the age when everyone wishes that they *had* a lifestyle." Another Elder giggled nervously.

"I think Porter's got a point, though. If we ask a person whether they are seeking to be free of sin, how can we reconcile this sin in our conscience?"

"But it isn't a sin!"

An hour later the room was grim. One Elder had stepped out for a frustrated cry in the bathroom.

"Folks," said Cord, "Presbyterians vote their conscience. Presbyterians also believe in the Word. We speak and hear first of love and grace. We also speak and hear of freedom and choice. Our children are our greatest gift. There will be a vote, but not tonight. For now, I'm going to take the prerogative of the chair and draw this meeting to a close."

His closing prayer begged for help with all the spontaneous eloquence he could muster. He was learning fast what true preaching and witnessing were now required of him.

*** *** ***

Mavis was still in her bathrobe, and Porter hadn't shaved yet. Sitting at the kitchen table, neither noticed nor cared that the coffee cups, butter, and jam hadn't been cleared. No music emanated from the tape deck on the counter.

"We can't leave the church! We've been members for years--for decades!" Mavis was stunned that he would suggest it. "You can't just pick up and leave a church because you are mad at the minister. I love my choir, and you're on the Session. It's part of our lives."

"And how am I supposed to feel faithful and religious when I know that congregation is condoning and... and *sanctioning* homosexual behavior? It is promoting sin! I know it's been doing this for a long time, and it finally came to a head. Last night's meeting was a joke. I can't respect or belong to a church like that. They're asking me to confess my sins, when the church won't confess its own!"

"They aren't in favor of sin!"

"They're about to confirm Victor Beck knowing full well that he says he's a faggot."

"Porter, listen to yourself. He's a boy--a fourteen-year-old boy! We've known him all his life! We've known his parents for longer than that. He's going through a teenage thing, and no church should push away a child just because he's a teenager trying on some wild ideas." Mavis had never been so furious. The children of the church were the only children they had.

"All the more reason to take a stand and get that boy back on track. That McDaniel was gutless last night."

"Porter, don't attack the minister."

"Well, he was! He let people talk on and on and on, and then he said some namby pamby thing about how we have the Word of God, and we each have a conscience. Where was his conscience?"

"Stop it! I cannot have you attacking the minister. It's wrong. If you start, it will turn things into a fight. Everything will unravel. People will start to attack the staff and the Session. Then, they'll start attacking the music and me." Mavis had her back up.

"So, what you're saying is that we should stick to being sops. You keep on baking your cookies, and I'll hand out bulletins, and we'll pat the kids on the head, and we'll live this lie so that we don't stand for anything!"

"Porter, how can you say that?"

"You can't take communion and ask for forgiveness of sins if you don't stand up when you see a sin – an awful, ugly, putrid sin. Mavis, it's unnatural. You know that. Men with men! I can't even think about it. We can't condone that when it is going on right here in our church."

"Porter, stop!" Mavis slammed her hand on the table. "You sound hateful! I don't know what I think about homosexuality--I don't think about it. Why should I? It is *none of my business!* You can think about it if you want. But I won't have you attacking our church – my church! It takes all I have to bake all those cookies and lead all that music, and I do it so our church will be a strong group of people together. It is about caring for each other, and not destroying things."

"I am not trying to destroy our church!" Porter shouted. "I'm trying to put some honesty back into it--some honesty about sin."

Porter and Mavis had never screamed at each other before. The sudden silence between them was awful. They stared at each other for a long moment.

Slowly Mavis stood up and started to clear the table. As she put the dishes in the sink, she opened the tap full force. Over the sound of the running water she said, "I'm going to clean up and then start my baking."

She waited a moment. "I need some things from the store, and the list is on the board. If you don't go get them, I will go shopping this afternoon."

Porter left the room without saying anything in response.

*** *** ***

The white scrawl on the locker couldn't be ignored. *Victor is a faggot.*

Bridget saw it from the other end of the hallway. Kids pointed at it as they passed. She moved quickly.

At that moment, Victor was climbing out of the car, his first day back at school. Loretta had driven him, a last gesture on her part as she sent him back into the world. "I can take the bus home," he said, as he closed the car door.

Shadows of suddenly leafing trees mottled the brick exterior of the school. Kids walked up the sidewalk bent at the waist, leaning as if into gale wind, in order to balance their enormous backpacks. Victor's bag hung off one shoulder. His stitches were healing well, but he didn't want his sleeves dragged up by the backpack harness.

Everything was the same, but everything was different. He saw kids he knew, and noticed, as usual, the cracks in the concrete steps. Posters urged *Just Say No to Drugs* and trophies crowded the shelves behind locked glass cases.

Coming around the corner in the hallway, he saw a group of kids in the area of his locker. Kyle stepped away from the crowd and grabbed Victor's arm. "Hey, Victor, you going to Geometry? I'll walk with you."

"Okay. I've gotta put some stuff in my locker first."

"No, hey, just carry it. I'm kind of in a rush."

Victor decided to store his books after second period. "Well, I guess so."

Kyle thumped him on the back. "You doing okay? Come on. We can take the stairs."

"I know the way," said Victor. The last thing he had expected was that someone like Kyle would fuss over him. The counselor had talked about people being awkward and even distant, but not fussing, exactly.

Kyle chattered loudly about a movie he'd seen over the weekend. "You have to see it!" But his voice didn't cover the commotion behind them. Victor looked back to see the principal, his Spanish teacher, and Bridget approaching the group around his locker. They all looked grim. The kids were stepping away from the wall of lockers.

Victor paused. His locker had the poster on it.

He turned to Kyle who had stopped mid-sentence. "Wait, Kyle, I've gotta go check this out."

He started back.

"No," Kyle's voice followed him.

"We wanted to surprise you," said one kid, as he joined the group. The others looked sheepish, but some grinned. The poster said "Welcome Back" in pretty bad writing, and there were signatures around it.

He studied it a bit, grinned at one *Mickey Mouse* signature. "Thanks," he said in a generalized way. "Beautiful graphics." The whole group burst into a loud laugh.

Then no one knew what to say. Kyle pulled on his arm. "Now we *really* will be late. Come on!"

They disappeared into the stairwell. Meanwhile, the principal, teacher, and Bridget looked at the group. The silence extended. Finally the principal spoke, "You all did a very special thing just now. Thank you. It took some fast thinking. We'll figure out what steps to take next. If you could just go to your classes and carry on, I think that would be the best thing to do."

The kids all smiled weakly. "We almost blew it. He was coming around the corner just as we were trying to tape it up."

"It was Bridget who told us to make it happen while she went to get you."

"Yeah, but we didn't have anything. We stole the paper right off the bulletin board in that classroom." Someone pointed across the hall. "And we had to fold it cause it was way too wide. We didn't have any markers or anything."

The Spanish teacher smiled. "I'll let Mr. Coffer know who looted his classroom."

It was hard to head off to class. The principal added, "How about if you would each write your name on a paper and give it to me before you go? I would like to know who helped out here."

Other students were pushing by as the warning bell sounded. The kids wrote out their names and left one by one. The principal held Bridget back. "And the boy who took him off to class is Kyle Jordan, right?"

"Yeah, that's right. The two of us go to church with Victor."

"Which church?"

"First Presbyterian. The one with the bells."

"Right. Well, Bridget, you've done a tremendous thing here. You need to go to class now, and we'll take it from here. Thank you for your quick thinking!"

The teacher gave Bridget a squeeze on the shoulders.

*** *** ***

Duke stood at his office window, cranking it open. He had to push on the glass in order to help the fixture, which stubbornly ground its teeth at him. The air flowed in like a cool storm front, challenging the heavy heat from the tenacious radiators. It might be spring, but winter was still in the heating system pipes.

Turning he ground his pencil into the gray industrial-strength pencil sharpener, and was gratified to hear it chew the wood.

Spencer and Loretta knocked on the door. That hadn't been part of the plan, and it would surprise Victor to see them there. But he had called them immediately after the principal had dropped in.

When Victor showed up during his lunch period, his eyes widened as he saw his parents sitting on two folding chairs crowded into the office. Before he could say anything, Duke greeted him, "Hello, Victor. Have a seat." He drew him in and closed the door. "Well, son, you have got yourself about ten of the best friends a guy could want."

Sitting knee to knee, the Beck family heard the full story together. Spencer couldn't shake a sense that he no longer understood the world. There was no sense-making to be done. Loretta stroked her son's arm, crunching the thick softness of the sweatshirt. How ever could they pad him with enough protection?

Victor, however, said with complete calm, "Hey, he's right. That's ten more friends - real friends - than I was sure of a month ago."

*** *** ***

About the same time, the principal was placing a call to the First Presbyterian Church. After introducing himself to the church secretary who answered the phone, he asked for the name of the minister. "Cord McDaniel. Would you like to speak with him?"

"Yes, thank you." It was a clipped voice.

"Cord," she called. "It's from the high school. He sounds urgent."

"Rev. McDaniel? This is Chet Ballows. I'm the principal at the high school. I'm not sure we have met."

"I'm not sure, either. My kids haven't made it through middle school yet. Of course, I know who you are. What can I do for you?"

"I'm calling because we've had an incident here at the school, and I thought you should know about it. I understand that Victor Beck belongs to your church."

An alarm bell went off for Cord. Now what?

The principal continued, "This morning we discovered an anti-gay slur on Victor Beck's locker. I apologize for repeating the language. It said, *Victor is a faggot*. Again, I apologize for the language, but I want you to have the information."

Cord's heart dropped. Oh, Victor! "This is unhappy news to hear. I appreciate the call. I will need to check in with the family."

"They have already been informed, and Victor and his parents met with a counselor at noon."

"I assume you have no idea who did this?"

"We're working on that, although I doubt we'll nail it down. But what I wanted to tell you is that there is also some good news as well. Two of the kids who apparently attend your church along with Victor were fast-thinking ringleaders in responding." He continued to explain Bridget and Kyle's role.

Cord's heart lifted and expanded. "I'm glad to hear that. I am so glad to hear that! Thank you so much for calling and letting me know."

"I thought you could build on that. Victor and his family need explicit support, and those kids were instinctive and fast when they saw the graffiti. We will do everything we can, but the school can't perform miracles. That's more your department."

"Yes, well, we shall see. We have at least one gay man in the congregation who has already stepped forward and been enormously helpful already. I suspect we are only in chapter one of this book."

"There are other gay kids at the high school. There have to be. But to my knowledge, none of them is out of the closet, as they say. Our counseling staff is meeting to figure out what we can do as well. Shall we stay in touch?"

"By all means. Let me know if I can be of any help."

Cord put down the phone and promptly picked it up again. He rummaged through his church directory and dialed George.

At the sound of George's voice, he blurted out, "George, this is Cord. I need your expertise."

"What expertise is that? Banking?"

"No." Cord barked a laugh. "No, I need to know about the gay world. What books are out there? What organizations? I need a crash course."

George laughed. "I'm not sure how much one learns in books about this, but there are certainly resources, if that's what you are looking for." He put Cord on hold and went to get a folder. Cord yanked a fresh notebook off his supply shelf and was ready with his pen when George returned.

*** *** ***

After leaving the school, Loretta dropped Spencer off at work and drove to the mall. She hurried quickly to the bookstore. There, without pausing, she headed towards the sign, "Women's Health, Gay and Lesbian, Alternative Medicines."

She studied the dust jackets. A month ago she would have looked at the other patrons and wondered what kind of a person would shop in this aisle. Now she knew. It would be a person like herself.

Starting down the length of the colorful shelf, she loaded books in her arm. Her forearm stuck to the glossy cover of the bottom book. Steadying her stack with her chin, she shifted her purse strap and headed for the checkout counter. "This is a great book," the clerk said, tapping on the third in the stack. Clueless about a response, Loretta reached for her credit card.

*** *** ***

A card arrived for Victor in the mail. The envelope was hot pink. The handwriting had extra loops and circles. Little hearts took the place of the dots over the "i's."

Dear Victor,

I hope you are feeling well!!! I am really sorry things have been so bad!!! I've known you for I guess my whole life. All those years of vacation Bible school and flashlight tag have to count for something!!!!! So, I just wanted to say that it doesn't matter to me if you are gay or straight because we're still friends and I want you to know that. Don't let the jerks at school get you down!!! ☺

Your friend,

Tiffany

P.S. Actually it does matter if you are gay or straight because if you are gay you can't be in the army. Maybe someday they will figure out that gay people are as brave as anyone. I think you are incredibly honest and brave.

CHAPTER 32

"And who are you?" asked the elderly woman dressed completely in red, as she stepped into the church's vestibule and extended her hand.

"You know Alexandra Wallace. She's my helper today," exclaimed George, who was looking particularly natty in his red jacket.

"I see that Porter Hofmeister isn't with you today."

"No, he's backed off the greeter duties for now. Alexandra is helping me." George smiled fondly at the girl.

"Well, it's high time we had a woman at the door," she said to Alexandra as she accepted a bulletin. They looked at each other eye to eye, and Alexandra realized she was as tall as a grown-up person, even if the grown-up person was old and maybe a little stooped.

"I like your red outfit," she said, companionably.

"Why, thank you. You are never too old for color, young lady. Remember that."

Grace Evanston was coming up the walk carefully on the arm of a middle-aged man with a deep suntan.

"Welcome, Grace!" George said, stepping out of the doorway to take her other arm.

"Good morning, George. Hello, Alexandra. I want you to meet J.J. Travers, the man who should have been my son-in-law," said Grace.

"Then double welcome!" George added with a wide grin. "We heard you were coming to visit."

"It's good to be back."

It had been nearly 40 years since J.J. had been in the First Presbyterian Church sanctuary. During the funeral all those years ago, he had sat in the pew directly behind the family. They had been grateful to him, a war buddy, who had come so far for the service. It was the most intimate seat they could offer such a friend.

J.J. remembered liking Vaughn's parents immediately. They had been gracious, doing their best to welcome a guest despite their grief and the tragic circumstances. For the entire visit, he had barely been able to present himself normally, nearly crying at every turn. He was also angry, resenting, as he did, that there were so many strangers involved in the grieving and the funeral services. They held a claim over Vaughn that he did not know and could not share. Their grief mixed with memories of his birth, school, camping, neighborhood, and family.

He had wanted to knife through all that. His own memories were impossible to share, intimate only to him. He was the one who had counted the freckles on Vaughn's back, gripped his strong thighs, and enjoyed lightly stroking his stubbly beard. Who else knew his secrets, his fears, his acrobatics, and his hopes? Who else had lost a future? J.J. was to be left solitary and alone.

Holding himself like a soldier, he had blocked out as much of the funeral as he could. If he had listened, he would have broken down. His eyes had bored visual holes into the carved leaves and vines on the pews. His mouth had been dry, as if he could taste the life of a termite eating through the dark wood.

The funeral had been on a hot day, as hot as only a summer day in the 1950's could be when men wore ties, suit coats, and hats. The women had flushed cheeks under molded hats with the tiny veils over their eyes. Paper fans swished in ever repeating half-circles. A flag had covered the coffin, and J.J. remembered growing irrationally anxious that Vaughn must be horribly hot inside, wrapped up and trapped by such heat.

Today, those memories were alive, but no longer filled with scorching pain. Now there was no coffin and no heat, and his clothing was looser and kinder. And, there were no secrets. J.J. sat comfortably next to his elderly friend, enjoying the hints of his former lover in the shape of her nose and the set of her eyes.

His life had taken many twists and turns since that day long ago. It had served up sadness, acceptance, and, eventually, new love. All in all, he had enjoyed a good life so far. And now it had served up a new surprise, which looked to move his plans in an unexpected direction. Grace's letter at Christmas had been an enormous surprise and created exciting and new opportunities. The money for the clinic was both a miracle and a reason to stay in Guatemala and commit to a longer contract.

Her later letter about finding the plaque and the opening of the love story to the enterprising young people had brought an unexpected coda to that first song of love. In the salutation of that second letter, Grace had greeted him as a son. Were the funeral today, he would be part of the family in the front pew, she had written. She should have said so earlier. Now she was called to talk about it more readily. She was learning the danger and sorrow of silence.

Deeply touched, J.J. planned at once to add Stanton to his itinerary during his short trip back to the States. He had to thank her for her enormous graciousness.

The congregation sizzled with energy. The members of the Confirmation Class, sitting down front, sported what was clearly the first corsage or boutonniere for many of them. Mothers wished that a hairbrush had been applied better. Fathers observed how tall the boys had grown. Grace looked them over and sent up a prayer for their peace and safety.

The service unfolded. After the little children were excused and scampered off to their class, Grace nodded to J.J. He rose and slowly escorted her from the pew to the lectern. With him at her side, Grace leaned into the microphone. "Today is the great day of Pentecost. Before the Scripture is read, I want to welcome J.J. Travers. J.J. stands for Jonathan Justice Travers. His middle name comes from his mother's side of the family. I wish I could say that he carried the name Evanston as well, because in many ways J.J. is my second son. I am thrilled for you to meet him."

She smiled at him. "He is visiting," she continued, "during his brief trip back in the United States away from his home in Guatemala, where he works with children in a church-sponsored health clinic. Today, his worship community there will be reading the same Pentecost story we are about to hear. His presence and our reading will remind us that this is a day when all languages and all people are united by the grace of God." She turned, and from her mounted step, it was easy to kiss him on the cheek.

After the sermon, Cord stepped in front of the altar and invited the confirmands and their faith partners to come forward. Mavis gave Bridget a little hug. Tiffany was pale and nervous. Brent shook Victor's hand and then took his place behind him. Victor in his jacket and tie stood erect, almost exactly eye to eye with Brent.

Cord addressed each confirmand, and then asked each faith partner to speak. In their various pews, the parents listened with great intensity and pride. Eyes glistened.

"Bridget Wallace," Cord announced. "Examined by the Session, Bridget comes to this congregation seeking full membership--its rights, responsibilities, and privileges. I invite her faith partner, Mavis Hofmeister, to introduce Bridget."

Mavis put her arm around Bridget's waist. "This young lady came to us only a year ago and has already shown herself to be a smart, persistent, and caring person. We are so sorry her father isn't with us to share in this day, but she is joined by her sister and mother, who love her very much. I am privileged to vouch for her."

June was calm and deeply grateful. Sam would have had plenty of commentary about Stanton, but he would have appreciated the support and friends they had found here. Whatever life served up for Bridget, she had earned her own way into people's hearts and would continue to do so.

As Cord continued through the list, Alexandra leaned over to her mother and whispered in her ear, "Mom, I already know that I'll join the church when I'm in 9ᵗʰ grade. So maybe I don't need to go to those classes." No time like the present to arrange your life, June agreed. Just get on with it. And they surely would.

"Victor Beck," Cord announced. "Examined by the Session, Victor comes to this congregation seeking full membership--its rights, responsibilities, and privileges. I invite his faith partner, Brent Sykes, to introduce Victor."

Brent smiled at the congregation, and particularly at June and Alexandra. "Victor and I have worked together this year as he has contemplated church membership. He is a talented young man, a photographer who has enriched our church's life with his images. He is a seeker, someone who demands a life filled with honesty, integrity, and openness." Brent's well-practiced, public voice suddenly cracked. The congregation was electric in its silence. Victor looked down at his hands and then up again. "Together this year, he and I have struggled with the questions and challenges of our faith. He has enriched my life enormously, and I am committed to supporting him in his. I congratulate him on his confirmation."

The confirmands knelt along the front, and Cord, with the respective faith partners, laid hands on each head for the blessing. Bridget could feel a slight tremor in Mavis's hand on her head. She hoped Mrs. Hofmeister wasn't getting old. She never wanted to lose her.

Brent felt Victor's hair and skull under his hand. It was a physical act, a touch of love from Elder to youth; man to boy; son to son; man to man. The blessing was for health and love, a world where children can interrupt the inherited cycles of fear and hate, a world in which doors are pulled open.

THE POSTLUDE

All the cars had pulled out of the parking lot. Cord stored away his robe and turned off the cooling system. Church services were over, and he could head home for lunch.

The carillon tower loomed in the warm afternoon sun. The lilacs bobbed slightly in the breezes, casting off fragrance like incense carriers. A bright blue sheet from the morning's worship bulletin was enjoying its half-life as a paper airplane, blowing along the step in front of the church. Another wisp of breeze guided it up until it caught on a low branch of the holly bush, creating a blue, deep-throated blossom. The announcement was visible among the folds:

Gay and Lesbian Teens Support Group

Beginning Sunday evening, July 6, at 7:30 a monthly support group for gay and lesbian teens will meet in the downstairs lounge. Open to teens of all faiths, this is an opportunity for talking, listening, and sharing information. Refreshments will be served.

Adult Advisor: George Morrow. Teen Advisor: Victor Beck. Made possible by the Guy Sykes Memorial Fund.

Later in the afternoon, a small whirlwind loosened the blue flyer from the holly prickle and sent it swirling up and up the side of the stalwart tower, while the bells of the carillon signaled the quarter hour.

THE END

219

ABOUT THE AUTHOR

Martha Johnson is an executive with a more than 30 year career in public and private organizations. She has served in both the Clinton and Obama Administrations and was appointed to two commissions with the British Government. Her career has also spanned the IT, architecture, strategic consulting, and auto industry. Johnson has delivered over 50 public speeches on topics including sustainability, leadership, and government effectiveness. She has been featured repeatedly in the press and has testified before the US Congress.

Outside of her professional life, she has been the Clerk of Session at the First Presbyterian Church of Annapolis, MD. She is an Honorary Life Member of Presbyterian Women and has published a book on youth worship, *Awesome Youth Sundays*.

Johnson was graduated with a BA from Oberlin College and an MBA from the Yale University School of Management.

She is married and has two adult children.

In Our Midst is her first novel.

Learn more about the book and the author at:

www.InOurMidstTheNovel.com

Made in the USA
Charleston, SC
20 January 2013